Praise for the novels of Rick Mofina

"Taut pacing, rough action and jagged dialogue feed a relentless pace. *The Panic Zone* is written with sizzling intent."
—*Hamilton Spectator* on *The Panic Zone*

"*The Panic Zone* is a headlong rush toward Armageddon. Its brisk pace and tight focus remind me of early Michael Crichton."
—Dean Koontz, *New York Times* bestselling author

"Mofina's on top of his game, pulling together a wickedly complicated plot with great skill and assurance. Genuinely chilling."
—*RT Book Reviews* on *The Panic Zone*

"*Vengeance Road* is a thriller with no speed limit! It's a great read!"
—Michael Connelly, *New York Times* bestselling author

"A gripping no-holds-barred mystery...lightning paced... with enough twists to keep you turning pages well into the wee hours. *Vengeance Road* is masterful suspense."
—Allison Brennan, *New York Times* bestselling author

"[A] well-crafted and timely thriller."
—*Publishers Weekly*, starred review, on *Six Seconds*

"*Six Seconds* should be Rick Mofina's breakout thriller. It moves like a tornado."
—James Patterson, *New York Times* bestselling author

"*Six Seconds*...grabs your gut—and your heart— in the opening scenes and never lets go."
—Jeffery Deaver, *New York Times* bestselling author

"A great thriller."
—Lee Child, *New York Times* bestselling author, on *Six Seconds*

"One of the leading thriller writers of the day."
—*Penthouse* magazine

"A lightning-paced thriller with lean, tense writing... Mofina really knows how to make the story fly."
—Tess Gerritsen, *New York Times* bestselling author, on *A Perfect Grave*

RICK MOFINA

IN DESPERATION

MIRA®

MIRA

Recycling programs for this product may not exist in your area.

ISBN-13: 978-0-7783-2948-0

IN DESPERATION

For questions and comments about the quality of this book please contact us at Customer_eCare@Harlequin.ca.

www.MIRABooks.com

Printed in U.S.A.

This book is for
Lou Clancy,
who gave me my first job as a reporter.

DAY 1

1

Phoenix, Arizona, Mesa Mirage

Cora Martin was propped against two pillows in her bed when she heard a faint noise and put her book down.

Was that Tilly?

Her daughter was asleep down the hall.

No, that sounded like it came from outside.

Cora listened for half a minute. Everything was quiet. She dismissed the noise as a bird or the Bannermans' darned cat. The clock on Cora's night table showed the time: 12:23 a.m. She returned to her book. After reading two pages she began drifting off when she heard another strange sound.

Like a soft murmur. This time it came from a far side of the house.

What the heck is that?

Cora got up to investigate, groaning. She had to go to work in a few hours. She needed to get some sleep.

Wearing only a cotton nightshirt, she padded down the hall to Tilly's door. It was partially open, as usual. Her eleven-year-old daughter was asleep on her stomach. One foot had escaped from the sheets. Cora moved to her bedside, adjusted it then took in the room: Tilly's stuffed toys, posters of Justin Bieber and Cora's favorite—the drawing of two happy stick figures holding hands, titled *Mommy & Me*.

Cora smiled.

Soft light painted Tilly's face. She was more than a beautiful child to Cora; she was her lifeline, her hope and her dream.

I love you more than you'll ever know, kiddo.

She stroked Tilly's hair, then went to check the rest of the house. Cora had rented the small, ranch-style bungalow at an amazing rate from a widowed Realtor who didn't hide her maternal fondness for single working moms and their daughters.

Cora checked the front and back doors then the windows in each room. Nothing was amiss. She reconsidered what she'd heard. It had kind of sounded like someone walking around the house.

She thought of calling the police but pushed it aside for now.

Should I go outside?

It would be better to check the alarm system. She went to the console on the wall to inspect the indicator lights. Cora wasn't afraid to check the yard. This was Mesa Mirage, almost hidden among the larger east valley suburbs of metropolitan Phoenix. Mesa Mirage was a tranquil community of retirement villages and golf courses. It didn't have its own police department, but it was served by the County Sheriff's Office, supported by volunteer posses and was safe.

Almost crime-free.

Everything was in order, according to the light sequence of the alarm system. Good. Cora was thirsty. She'd get a drink in the kitchen then crawl back into bed and sleep.

Finishing her water at the sink, she touched her fingers to her lips. She had forged a good life here and she would do anything to protect Tilly.

Especially from the monsters she'd buried long ago.

Cora's attention shifted to the knock on her front door. Who could it be at this hour? Moving through the living

room, she looked at the window and glimpsed two uniformed officers at the door.

Police?

She opened the door.

In the instant Cora absorbed their grave faces, half
in shadow under the porch light, she was pricked by a
twinge of unease.

Something was wrong.

Not the kind of wrong that accompanies a late-night
visit by the police, but something darker. She had no time
to ponder it.

"Sorry to trouble you, ma'am," one of the officers said.
"We're checking on the welfare of residents here. Is everything all right?"

"Yes. Why?"

"Can you tell us how many people are in your home
tonight?"

"Just me and my daughter. Why?"

As one of the officers took notes, a thousand points of
concern flashed across Cora's mind. She glanced to the
street for a patrol car, finding a late-model sedan. She
didn't think the two men were with the county or the volunteer posse. She scanned their uniforms for a shoulder
patch and found one. But since she really never encoun-
tered police, she was not sure if the officers were from
Mesa, Tempe, Chandler or Gilbert.

"I'm sorry," Cora said. "Who are you with?"

"We're with the task force," the first officer said.
"Ma'am, are there any firearms in your residence?"

"No. I hate guns. What task force? What's this
about?"

"Earlier tonight, an inmate escaped custody, a
convicted murderer. He was sighted in this area of the
community."

"Oh my God."

"I'm afraid there's a bit more to this. May we
come in?"

"Yes, of course."

Cora let the two men enter her home. Inside, the officers looked around Cora's living room.

"Where's your daughter located at this time?" the first officer asked.

"Down the hall, in her bedroom. She's asleep."

The officer nodded to his partner.

"We'll check on her welfare."

"But she's fine." Cora watched the second officer quietly enter Tilly's room, while the first officer spoke to her.

"It's routine," he said, indicating the kitchen. "Let's go there and I'll explain."

The first officer went directly to the sink over the kitchen window that looked out to Cora's backyard. He pulled a pocket telescope from his utility belt, clenched one eye and gazed through it.

"The suspect is in the house directly behind yours, one row back."

"I don't understand."

The officer turned to her and she noticed a scar running along his jaw.

"We're here to help set up a perimeter for the SWAT Team," he said.

At that point the second officer emerged, nodded to his partner and approached them at the sink.

"Ma'am?" The first officer offered Cora his scope. "Take a look. It's the house with the pool lights."

She was apprehensive.

"Go ahead."

Her kitchen seemed to be closing in on her as the two officers now stood near. *Was this a dream?* She took the telescope, raised it to her eye, not sure what she was looking for when pain shot through her skull. Her hair strained her scalp, pulled by some force. Duct tape peeled, Cora's mouth was sealed before she could cry out. The invaders moved her swiftly and silently to a kitchen chair, taping her ankles, her wrists and her chest to it.

Terrified, Cora looked down the hall.

The first man drew his face to Cora's.

"Your daughter is fine. Look at me!"

Cora tried to talk.

"Are you going to cooperate so we can get through this quickly?"

Cora nodded.

"We do not want to hurt you, or your daughter. Understand?"

Cora nodded.

"If you resist, we will kill your daughter in front of you."

Cora sobbed against the tape.

"Do you understand? If you cooperate, you survive."

Cora understood.

"We know you work for Lyle Galviera at Quick Draw Courier."

Cora nodded.

"I'm going to remove the tape and we'll talk. If you scream, if you refuse to cooperate or if you lie, you and your daughter will die. Do you understand?"

Cora nodded and the second man yanked the tape from Cora's mouth.

She gasped, swallowed and listened to the first man. "Lyle uses his company to distribute our product and move cash to be cleaned. Where is the money?"

"I don't know what you're talking about!"

"He stole five million dollars from us."

"No! This is a mistake! Are you looking for drug money? Lyle's not involved with drugs. I've got nothing to do with drugs. This is all wrong—it's a mistake. Please leave us alone! I don't know what you're talking about!"

"We can't find him. Where's the money?"

For the next thirty minutes the invaders ransacked the

house. *What did they do with Tilly? They must've tied her down.*

Or worse!

"Where is our money?"

"Did you hurt my daughter?"

"She's not hurt. Where is it?"

"I told you this is wrong. This is a mistake!"

"Listen to me. You will find Galviera and tell him to return our money."

Sobbing, Cora shook her head.

"This is a mistake. I don't know anything about this."

"You know. You do the books for his company."

"No. No. I'm the office manager, the secretary. I know he left a few days ago for business in San Diego, then in Los Angeles."

"He is not in California."

"But I made the travel arrangements. Please, I don't know what you're talking about. Please leave us alone. Please. This is a mistake."

"No mistake."

The first man turned to his partner. After speaking in rapid Spanish to him, the man left the house and returned with a large suitcase they placed before Cora.

"Remember," the first man said. "Do not scream."

The second man went down the hall to Tilly's room. Seconds later Tilly emerged, her mouth covered with duct tape, eyes popping with fear as they met Cora's.

Tilly was in her pajamas with the unicorn pattern; her wrists were taped in front of her in a praying position as she hugged a hastily balled collection of items. Cora could see jeans, a pink shirt and white sneakers. *Was that her toothbrush sticking from the heap?* It was as if she were rushing off to a sleepover.

Fear twisted Cora's stomach.

"It's going to be okay, honey." Cora tried to comfort her as the second man opened the large suitcase and positioned Tilly inside, bending her knees to her chest, then zipping her closed as if he were a magician preparing a trick.

"What are you doing?" Cora raised her voice. "Wait! No."

The first man drew his weapon and pointed it at the bag where Tilly's head would be, moved his finger to the trigger and turned to Cora.

"Have you forgotten your need to shut up and listen?"

"Yes, please, please don't hurt her. I'm begging you."

"If you do as we say, she will not be harmed. Understand?"

Cora nodded.

"We are taking your daughter with us."

"No. Please!"

"Listen carefully. Lyle must return our money, or your daughter will die. And if you go to the police, your daughter will die."

"Tilly, sweetie, everything will be okay. Do what they say. Tilly, I love—" Tape was replaced on Cora's mouth.

"Your binding is not that tight. You should be able to free yourself in a few hours," the first man said. "We will return your daughter unharmed after Lyle Galviera returns the money he's stolen from us. He has five days."

The men left with the suitcase holding Tilly, leaving Cora alone, bound to a chair, sobbing in her kitchen.

2

An anguished cry rose from the morgue's viewing room.

"Mi hijo! Mi hijo!"

Paula Chavez bent over the corpse of a young man in his late teens, her son, Ramon. Her face creased with pain. She stared into his open eyes then at the bullet holes in his tattooed chest. Helpless against the horror, she caressed his face and pressed one of his cold hands to her cheek.

It was evocative of Michelangelo's *Pietà,* Jack Gannon thought, watching from across the room.

He turned to Isabel Luna, who had raised her camera to shoot several frames of Paula Chavez. At times, the priest and morgue workers had to steady the grieving mother, who was now childless.

Ramon was sixteen. He'd been Paula Chavez's last living son.

She'd already lost two others to the violence this year.

The sorrow in the air was as biting as the smell of chlorine and the reek of death.

For much of the day, Gannon and Luna had been riding along with forensic experts and coroner's staff, pinballing from homicide to homicide, when they had come to the fringe of a squatters' village. Paula Chavez was in a ditch on her knees weeping at the crime scene tape near her son. A priest prayed alongside her while windswept garbage and desert dust enshrouded them.

The priest brought Paula to the morgue. A coroner's van brought her son. Gannon and Luna had followed them here, where workers had set Ramon's corpse on a table next to the bodies of six other people murdered across the city so far that day.

Now, after taking half a dozen pictures, Luna lowered her camera and indicated to the pathologist who'd granted access that they were finished.

Gannon and Luna stepped outside into baking heat as another coroner's van delivered two more white body bags strapped to gurneys.

Another corpse, another coffin, another grave. Another day in Juarez, a battlefield in Mexico's drug wars.

Welcome to Murder City.

Gannon slid on his dark glasses, and as he and Luna walked to his rented Ford he reflected on Paula Chavez. She lived in a shack and earned less than ten dollars a day running a tiny hamburger stand. She'd lost her husband and sons to the violence. Gannon thought of the pain carved into her weatherworn face, the agony of her cries, how she embodied the toll exacted by the carnage. These images burned into his memory. *The impact of random cruelty.* Throughout his years on the crime beat he hammered the heartache he bore for people like Paula Chavez into a quiet rage that he used to fuel his work.

Gannon was a journalist with the World Press Alliance, the global wire service headquartered in New York City. He'd been dispatched to Mexico to file features in the WPA's ongoing series on the drug wars. Correspondents from the WPA's Mexican, Central and South American bureaus had provided exceptional coverage, but his editor, Melody Lyon, wanted more for a new series.

"The cartel wars have been spilling into U.S., Canadian and European cities with increasing violence. We need to understand why this is happening," Lyon had told him. "We need you to take WPA readers beyond the statistics, the corruption and the bloodbaths. Take us deeper. Find the human faces on all sides. Take us into the inferno."

As part of his research before leaving Manhattan, Gannon had contacted Isabel Luna, a crime reporter with *El Heraldo,* a small family-run newspaper in Juarez known for its courageous reporting.

Few knew more about crime in the region than Luna.

Her father, the paper's editor, had been murdered several months ago for exposing cartel ties to corrupt officials. His death left Isabel defiant and forged her determination to continue his crusade. She did not hesitate to respond when Gannon called in advance of his arrival.

"I propose we work exclusively together while I'm in Juarez," he said. "Your English is better than my Spanish and I admit I'll need help. In exchange, I'll share the resources of the WPA. We could buy your photos or pay for joint work on exclusives."

"Call me when you arrive," she said.

During their first meeting in *El Heraldo*'s hectic and cluttered newsroom, which had reminded Gannon of his campus paper in Buffalo, he told Luna of the stories he had in mind.

"I'd like to profile you."

She blushed and a crooked smile nearly blossomed on her face. It waned when he told her of the other story he wanted to do.

"I want to write about cartel assassins, the young ones they train to be killers. I'd like to interview one. Do you think that's possible?"

A somber look flitted across Luna's eyes as she scanned the newsroom, focusing on nothing before inhaling slowly.

"It's possible," she said.

"Will you help me?"

She looked at him for a long moment before she said, "Yes."

In the back of his mind Gannon suspected Luna had her own reasons for pursuing a story on cartel assassins. As with most murders in Juarez, her father's killer had not been found.

Now, as they left the morgue, Gannon glanced at Luna, in the passenger seat studying her camera, reviewing the crime scene photos she'd taken that day.

"You got some nice stuff there," he said. "You see anything that looks like an organized cartel hit?"

"No. Just everyday murders, low-level barrio gang members and Juarez drug dealers. It's terrible to say, but it's true."

Luna called her paper to ensure her desk alerted her to any breaking stories as she and Gannon continued roaming the city.

He took in the sprawling metropolis. Juarez was a factory town with a population over one and a half million. It stood on the Rio Grande, across the U.S. border from El Paso, Texas, where close to eight hundred thousand people lived in relative safety and peace.

Gannon figured he had seen most of Juarez since he'd arrived three days ago. *Or was it four?* He'd filed news features but had yet to go beyond what had already been reported on the tragedy of the region.

Juarez's despair had first greeted him with the panhandlers dotting the Santa Fe Street Bridge from El Paso. The city's beauty was lost in a cloak of desperation and in the dust from sandstorms that laced the low-rise stores and office buildings along the streets.

The downtown bled into bars, cantinas, neon and the never-ending come-on from the hookers in the red-light district. Beyond were endless strip malls, roadside taco stands, pizza shops and neighborhoods of concrete houses and apartment complexes.

Farther out was the bullring.

Then there were the hundreds of huge factories, the *maquiladoras,* where the women of Juarez earned a few dollars a day working in shifts assembling appliances, electronics and a range of exported goods.

At the city's edge, beyond the simple wooden crosses of the cemeteries, along a jumble of paved and unpaved sandy roads, among the cacti, tumbleweed and scrubland, were the clusters of shantytowns. Here, Gannon thought, amid the shacks, lived the enduring human virtue: hope.

No matter the odds, one must never abandon hope.

As Juarez rolled by, Gannon, a thirty-five-year-old loner, who grew up in blue-collar Buffalo, was visited by a cold hard fact: he had no one in his life. All he had was his job.

Stop, he chided himself, and turned to Luna.

"If you'd like to knock off, I'll take you home. Or we can eat first."

"There's a good restaurant near my paper," she said.

It was after sunset when they'd finished dinner. Their conversation was centered on recent history of the drug wars.

Luna said that Juarez was a marshaling point for those yearning to escape poverty by fleeing to the U.S. It was also a major transit point for drugs, and cartels battled for control of the smuggling networks that gave them access to the U.S. market. This was how Juarez came to be one of the world's most violent cities—with a homicide rate greater than any other city on earth. To battle the violence the Mexican government had deployed thousands of troops and federal police across Mexico.

But the cartels had infiltrated all levels of police.

"Imagine," Luna said. "You're a Mexican police officer and the cartel offers to triple your monthly pay for your cooperation. You've seen the conditions most people live under."

Gannon agreed.

"And," Luna added, "if you refuse to cooperate, the cartels threaten your family. This is how they've grown, and they operate with military precision and firepower. The cartels have unimaginable reach and domination everywhere."

Luna caught herself. Embarrassed, she cupped her hands to her face. She'd never spoken so much to Gannon.

"I apologize for boring you."

"Don't," Gannon said. "It must mean you're comfortable with me. I still want to profile you, but you've been so quiet. I know very little about you."

Luna told him about her life.

She was thirty-one. Her mother died from cancer when Luna was young. Her father remarried. She had a stepbrother, Esteban. She'd lived in Los Angeles when she attended UCLA. After graduating she'd returned to help with the paper. She was married to a human rights lawyer and they had a four-year-old son. They were guarded about their lives.

"Because of the cartels and what happened to your father?"

Several long moments passed before Luna answered. "You must never tell anyone this, but I was there when my father was murdered. I saw his killer."

"Did you tell police?"

"No. We told them there were no witnesses. My husband and stepbrother urged me to trust no police. My father's death was an orchestrated cartel hit because of his editorials about the cartels corrupting police. The killer came to my father's house as a courier, very nonthreatening. He didn't see me, but I was there and I saw him. One day we will find him."

Luna stopped.

"I'm sorry," she said. "I don't like to talk about it. My father was a respected man. I don't have the influence he had. No one among the Juarez press does. He was incorruptible. Please, Jack, you must never reveal what I told you. If the cartel knew that I was a witness, they'd kill me. Swear you will not tell anyone, please."

Gannon gave Luna his word, then drove her home to her family.

That night he stepped out onto his hotel balcony.

He gazed upon the twinkling lights of the city. He could hear sirens and see a helicopter's searchlight sweep over the latest killing, and a creeping sense of looming failure came over him.

How would he make sense out of this chaos?

He was tired and his thoughts shifted back to himself, the price of being alone. Unlike the teen gangster in the morgue, Ramon Chavez, no one would mourn Gannon. His parents were dead. He'd been estranged from his older sister since she'd run away from home some twenty years ago.

Shut up, he told himself. *Quit wallowing.*

He got into bed.

But before sleep came, Gannon fell into his usual pattern of wondering what had happened to his sister.

Is she still alive?

3

Fear pulsed through Cora Martin.

This can't be happening! It's a nightmare! Wake up! Come on, wake up!

Cora's cries for Tilly were muffled by the duct tape sealing her mouth. She tried to move but was fused to the kitchen chair.

Please, God. Protect her. Please.

Questions blazed through Cora's mind.

How could this be happening? How could these fuckers just come into her home and take Tilly? Could it be connected to her own trouble years ago in California?

No.

It's impossible. No one knows about that. No one must ever know. No, they said this was about Lyle. But Lyle couldn't be involved with drug cartels. She trusted him. My God, they'd talked about living together. About marriage! This was a horrible mistake. It had to be!

Cora forced herself to concentrate.

Calm down. Think.

Her arms were tingling. Her blood circulation had been squeezed by her bindings. Cora's kitchen chairs were Windsor-style, armless with a fan backrest. The invaders had duct-taped her wrists behind the narrow back and they were starting to hurt. She kept making fists so she wouldn't lose the feeling in her hands.

Tape bound her chest to the chair's back and her ankles to the legs.

Time was slipping away.

She rocked the chair, got up on her feet, only to lose her balance and fall back, sitting in the chair. It wasn't easy to move. She had trouble directing her weight. She could try smashing the chair but it was metal and heavy. She couldn't risk hurting herself.

She had to find a way out of this.

You have to do something now!

Again, Cora rocked until she got to her feet. She bent forward, tensed her muscles and, using the weight of the chair, kept herself upright. By carefully shuffling her feet with the heavy chair affixed to her back and legs she painfully inched her way across the kitchen like a grotesque snail.

When Cora reached the drawer where she kept utensils, her heart sank.

The splayed legs and angle of the chair kept her from reaching the handle with her hands.

Cora growled into the tape.

Those motherfuckers better not hurt my baby!

Don't give up! You have to do this!

Carefully contorting her body with strategic leaning, her fingers blindly brushed the handle to the utensil drawer. Her arms, legs, shoulders were ablaze as she forced herself up on her toes and with one great heave got the drawer open. She rattled it until the plastic tray erupted with utensils. Finally the weight against her position demanded she sit.

She fought the pressure.

Come on! Come on!

She shook as her fingers clawed at the disgorged spoons, forks, knives. *There!* Battling the weight brought waves of pain before she seized as many knives as she could in one solid grab. Her nostrils flared and her breathing roared as she sat, clenching the knives behind her.

Eyes on the ceiling, fingers sweating, Cora sorted the knives and ran her thumb along each blade, one by one. The first was a butter knife. So was the second. *Damn. Wait!* The third had sharp serrated edges.

A steak knife.

She dropped the others. Working her fingers down the blade to improve her grip, she delicately sawed at the edges of the tape. The first ripping sound encouraged her to work harder. It was followed by another, then another as she sawed without stopping until the tape gave way.

Relief flowed into her arms as she brought them forward, pulling the tape from her mouth, gulping air as she yanked the remaining strips of tape from her wrists, massaging them before cutting her chest and ankles free.

She reached for her kitchen phone, jabbed the button for 9 then 1—

If you go to the police, your daughter will die.

Recalling the kidnapper's warning stopped her cold. *She wouldn't risk Tilly's life.* Cora aborted the call. She had to find Lyle.

She called his cell phone, got his voice mail and left a message.

"It's me! Something bad has happened to Tilly!" Cora broke down. "She's gone, Lyle! They're going to kill her! Call me!"

Then she called his home number, her heart racing as it rang. No answer. She left a message. Then she texted him and urged him to call.

Cora fumbled through her bag for her notebook, struggling with her composure as she called his hotel in San Diego.

"Blue Sapphire Regency, how may I help you?"

"I have to speak to one of your guests, Lyle Galviera."

"One moment please, I'll connect you—"

The line clicked with the transfer.

"Front desk? May I be of—"

"I need to speak to one of your guests, Lyle Galviera! It's urgent!"

"Of course, that last name again?"

"Galviera. G-A-L-V—"

Rapid typing on a keyboard.

"Lyle Galviera of Phoenix?"

"Yes, that's him!"

"I'm sorry. We had a reservation for Mr. Galviera but our records show that he never arrived."

Cora hung up, called Lyle's hotel in Los Angeles and got the same result. *What was happening? Where was he?* She stood there, her mind racing.

Do something! Go to the office. Look there!

She dressed without showering and ran to her car.

Dawn was breaking and freeway traffic was light as Cora sped west then north toward Phoenix Sky Harbor International Airport. Quick Draw Courier's depot, a squat single-story warehouse, was located amid the industrial buildings southwest of the terminals.

Cora could see the delivery trucks backed to the rear loading bays where the night crew was going full tilt processing orders. She parked out front by the landscaped entrance to the administration office. At the card lock, she swiped her employee card and punched in her security code. She entered and hurried to her desk.

No one was in at this hour.

She closed the door to her office, hit the lights and started her computer. Tilly smiled back from her screen saver before Cora navigated to the itinerary she'd prepared for Lyle's business trip.

She went to the website of the airline he was using and called. She rushed through the prompts only to be put into the queue for a living, breathing agent. While holding, she checked her cell phone for any response from Lyle.

Nothing.

She opened another file for Quick Draw Courier's credit card. Lyle used a company card for all business. While still on hold with the airline, Cora used her cell phone to call the credit card company's security department and report a lost card.

"Could you please give us details on the last transaction?" Cora asked.

The card was last used to pay for a business lunch in Phoenix. The agent provided the time. It was the day before Lyle had left for the trip.

"Would you like us to cancel the card now, ma'am?" asked the agent.

"No, thank you. We're hoping it will turn up. Thanks."

Cora finally got through to a human being at the airline. She begged the agent to help her confirm if Lyle had boarded any of the flights she'd booked for him.

"Unfortunately airline privacy policy prevents us—"

"Please! This is a family emergency! The ticket was purchased with our company credit card. I'll give you the number to verify."

A tense silence passed.

"Please!" she said. "It's extremely urgent! Please!"

"Give me the number. I'll check with my supervisor."

Cora recited it and the agent said: "One moment please."

As seconds ticked by, Cora looked at the online news pages showing sports scores; celebrity gossip; international news out of London on the Royal Navy, Hong Kong on business mergers, drug-war murders in Mexico. Then the line clicked.

"Sorry for the delay, ma'am. I can confirm that the departure ticket purchased by your company has not been used, nor has it been adjusted to a different date or flight."

Cora hung up and concentrated.

Today was Monday. Lyle was to have left Friday morning for San Diego. Tomorrow morning, he was to fly to
Los Angeles and return to Phoenix on Thursday. Cora
had expected to hear from him later today but was not
concerned that he hadn't called or emailed her over the
weekend. She was not clingy and it was no big deal if he
didn't call every day. And, as far as she knew, things were
quiet with the business.

But now Cora was desperate.

She dialed the home number for Ed Kilpatrick, the
operations manager. It was 5:15 a.m. Ed usually started
at 6:00 a.m. Maybe she'd catch him at home. He was accustomed to early calls from the guys in shipping.

"Hello."

"Ed, this is Cora."

"Hey, Cora, what's up?"

"Sorry to bother you at home."

"I was on my way in. What's going on?"

"Have you heard from Lyle since he left for California?"

"No. Is something going on?"

"Some people had been asking about him over the
weekend."

"Did you call him?"

"Yeah, but he's not answering—maybe his phone or
BlackBerry's not working."

"Could be—I don't know. I sent him an email Friday
on the new shipment deadlines for Zone Five. I need an
answer by this afternoon, so if you hear from him tell
him to call me. I gotta run. I'll see you later."

Cora drew her hands to her face and exhaled. Through
her fingers she saw Lyle's empty office across the hall and
went to it. She scoured his calendar, his notes, anything
for a clue. She searched his trash bin but the weekend
cleaning staff had already recycled everything.

Her cell phone was ringing in her office.

Cora ran back to her desk. *Please be Lyle.* The number was blocked.

"Hello?"

"Mommy!"

"Tilly!"

"Mommy, please help me!"

"I will! I love you! Are you okay? Where are you, sweetheart?"

The phone was shuffled.

"So you got free?"

"Yes. Don't you hurt her!"

"Where are you? Did you find him yet?"

Cora recognized the voice of the man who had invaded her home.

"I'm at the office going through his desk! I'm doing all I can! Let her go! Please!"

"Find Lyle Galviera or we'll release your daughter in pieces."

The line went dead.

Cora stared at the phone, sank into her chair, dropped her head to her desk and sobbed. She hadn't slept. She couldn't think. She didn't know what to do, or where to turn.

What if they killed Lyle? What if he was dead somewhere?

She fought to keep herself together.

There had to be something she could do. Someone who could help her.

She stared at her computer screen, vaguely remembering an item on drug wars in Mexico. It was a newswire story. She scrolled through the website. Here it was—from the World Press Alliance, a feature that profiled the people victimized by one day of violence in Ciudad Juarez.

She studied the byline.

Jack Gannon.

She knew him, yet she didn't.

He was from Buffalo, just like her. For years, wherever she'd lived, she'd followed his byline. She'd visited
the web editions of the *Buffalo Sentinel* before he left for
the World Press Alliance, a big wire service.

Now that he was with the WPA, Cora saw his stories
everywhere. *It was like he was always near.* Just knowing
how he was doing had been so important, she thought,
biting back her tears. Her fingers traced his name on the
screen. She considered the letter she'd written to him a
million times but never sent.

She never had the guts.

Cora thought of Tilly and shut her eyes to deflect her
agony.

If ever there was a time that Cora needed to reach out
to Jack Gannon, this was it.

His email was at the bottom of the article.

4

Ciudad Juarez, Mexico

Startled from sleep, Jack Gannon was trying to grasp why he'd awakened and where he was when the bedside phone rang again.

Hotel. Mexico. Still in Juarez.

He answered.

"*Buenos días,* Señor Gannon. As requested, this is your wake-up call. Your breakfast will be delivered shortly."

"Thank you."

Groaning, he hung up and reached for his cell phone to check for messages. Was there anything from Isabel, the other WPA bureaus or headquarters in New York?

Nope. Nada.

He shaved, showered and had just finished dressing when his breakfast arrived at the same time as his cell phone rang. Gannon set the tray on the desk, gave the server a tip and took his call.

"Jack, this is Isabel Luna. I've learned from a good source that a power struggle is going to explode within one of the major cartels and that assassins may be used."

"Do you know where or when?"

"Not for a few days at least. I'm trying to get more information. Can you meet me at *El Heraldo* at 9:00 a.m.?"

Gannon glanced at the bedside clock. He had time to do some work.

"I'll be there."

This could be the key to getting access to a cartel assassin, but he decided against alerting his editor in New York.

Better hold off until he had something nailed down.

He switched on his laptop and took a hit of coffee. As he ate his toast, sliced bananas and oranges, he reviewed the WPA's summary for the pickup of his last story. His profile of Juarez's drug war victims and the morgue was used by some two thousand English-language newspapers and websites in the U.S., Canada, the U.K., Australia, New Zealand, Hong Kong, parts of Africa, Europe, Central and South America and the Caribbean.

The *Chicago Tribune, Dallas Morning News, Vancouver Sun, Irish Times, Sydney Morning Herald* and *South China Morning Post* were among those who gave it front-page play.

Not bad, he thought, checking his email box for the address tag at the end of his story. Most reporters hated this feature because, while much of the spam was filtered, what you mostly got were emails from religious nuts, political zealots, scam artists, idiots and nutcases. A story rarely yielded a solid lead to another story, but it did happen.

You had to check.

Typically for Gannon, an article would attract about a hundred emails. He was adept at getting through them. *Like panning for gold.* He'd sorted about half, flagged three to consider later. Before continuing he reached for his coffee and locked onto the subject line of one email:

Your Sister Cora Needs Your Help Now.

He froze.

Cora? After so many years?

He set his coffee down, swallowed, then opened the email.

Dear Jack:

Reaching out to you like this is extremely hard, but above all I want you to know that in my heart for all these years I thought of you, Mom and Dad every day since I left Buffalo. Losing touch with you was one of the most painful mistakes I've made in my rocky life. You don't know how many times I came close to calling you but I couldn't find the strength.

I told myself I was stupid and as time went by I wanted more than anything to call you, to try to make things right with my family, to be sure you knew everything about me before it was too late. I had planned to do that once I started to get my life together and in the last few years I was getting things together, I really was.

Jack, I can never make up for hurting you or the lost years and I understand if you hate me and ignore my plea for help.

But I pray to God you won't.

I'm in trouble, Jack. It's an urgent matter of life and death and I believe you're the only one who can help me. This is not a hoax. I am your sister, and I've been following your reporting career for all these years. I was the one who told you to follow your dream, took you to the library and got Mom and Dad to buy you that old Tandy computer so you could write. And now you're with the World Press Alliance traveling the globe. I'm so proud of you but I need your help.

Jack, I'm begging you to contact me as soon as possible.

God bless you.

Your big sister,

Cora

Gannon felt the little hairs at the back of his neck stand up.

Cora.

It had been more than twenty years since she had walked out of their lives. Anger, love and unease swept through him as he looked at the contact information she'd left: email, cell phone, home phone, office phone and home address.

She was living in suburban Phoenix.

Well, to hell with her, he thought. *It was too late. Mom and Dad were dead. They'd died brokenhearted. The wounds were too deep. Besides, she probably wanted money, or an organ, or something.*

Call her.

Because there was a time he'd loved her with all his heart. It didn't matter that she had left his life; the truth was she'd had an effect on it. The truth was, no matter what, she was his sister.

I'm in trouble, Jack. It's an urgent matter of life and death...

Before he realized it, he was gripping his cell phone and calling. He stepped out onto his balcony and into the morning heat bathing the city as the line clicked through.

"Hello."

A woman had answered.

"Cora?" he asked.

"Yes," she said, emotion rising in her voice. "Is this Jack?"

"Yes."

"Oh God, is that really you?"

He went numb at the sound of her voice, somehow different with the passing of time, yet somehow the same as it pulled him back across two decades to Buffalo.

He is twelve and trembling in his bedroom; his heart is aching. He flinches as doors slam and screaming rages in an Armageddon between Cora, Mom and Dad.

"We know you're taking drugs, Cora!"

"You don't know anything! Stay out my life! I'm almost eighteen!"

"Please, honey, listen! We love you!"

"I'm leaving to live my own life! I'm never coming back!"

Cora left, all right. And no matter what they did, or how hard they searched, they never saw her again.

She'd become a ghost.

Now that ghost was pleading across a lifetime, over a phone line between Phoenix and Juarez, Mexico.

"Jack?"

"Yes, I got your email."

A long crackling filled the chasm that yawned between them.

"Jack, they took my daughter! Help me!"

"Your daughter? You have a daughter?"

"Yes, and two men dressed like police officers came to our house last night and took her!"

"Call the police."

"No! They said they'd kill her if I went to the police!"

"What?"

"They said the man I work for owes them a lot of money."

"Who do you work for? What the hell are you involved in?"

"Listen, I think the kidnappers are drug dealers. It's like the stuff you're writing about now in Mexico."

"Damn it, Cora, are you still screwed up with drugs after all this time?"

"No, Jack, I've put that behind me. I'm a secretary for a courier company. Jack, I don't know why they took my daughter!"

"What about your husband? What's he doing to help?"

"I'm not married." Cora released a great sob as she continued. "I don't know why they took Tilly. That's her name, Tilly. She's all I have!"

It was their grandmother's name.

"She's my little girl. She's eleven years old and they said they'll kill her if I don't help them get their money back. Help us, please! I don't know what to do, or who to turn to!"

Gannon hesitated.

"Jack, she's your niece!"

My niece.

Gannon's breathing quickened as he looked out at Juarez, trying to comprehend what was happening. In a matter of minutes, he'd gone from being alone to having two people in his life.

Two people who desperately needed him now.

It was a ninety-minute flight from El Paso to Phoenix.

He could be there in a few hours.

5

Four hours after Cora's call, Gannon's Southwest flight landed in Phoenix. Now, as his 737 taxied to the gate, he resumed questioning the wisdom of setting aside his story in Mexico to rush to Arizona.

Am I making a mistake?

He had tried to reduce his risk. Before lifting off, he'd called Isabel Luna at *El Heraldo,* telling her that he had to leave Juarez for an urgent personal matter in the U.S. Now, in the seconds before the pilot cut the engines, Gannon emailed Melody Lyon in New York, informing her that he'd temporarily left his assignment to fly to Phoenix. He knew that wouldn't go over well and by the time he stepped from the jet, Lyon had called him to confirm it.

"What the hell are you doing in Phoenix? Your assignment's in Juarez."

"Something came up."

"Who authorized this trip?"

"I'll pay for it."

"I don't care. I want you in Mexico. That's your story."

"I know, but—"

"I was under the impression that you were working on securing the assassin's profile. The WPA needs that story, Jack. The Associated Press and Reuters have been killing us. Why are you in Phoenix?"

He couldn't reveal the truth—damn it, not yet. Hard-pressed, he searched the terminal for an answer.

"I have an inside lead on a possible kidnapping."

"A kidnapping in Phoenix? I haven't seen anything on it."

"No one knows. It's just emerging."

"Did you alert our bureau there?"

"No. Not yet. Melody, don't tell anyone anything yet. Let me follow this."

"Is this connected to the drug wars?"

"Maybe. I'm not sure what this is. I have to check it out. If it falls through, I'll be back in Juarez tonight. All I'm asking for is a little time, please."

"I'll give you twenty-four hours and I want updates, Jack."

As Gannon's cab wove through the east valley suburbs, doubt continued gnawing at him. Ever since he'd broken a global exclusive out of South America and the Caribbean a few months ago, senior WPA editors had been pressuring him to deliver another big story.

So what was he doing here? Was he making a mistake by ignoring a potentially huge story out of Mexico?

And for what?

Cora.

It was tearing him apart. His sister was a stranger to him. She was messed up when she'd run away from their family. It had devastated their parents. How could he forgive her for what she'd done?

And now this.

What if she was still messed up?

But she had found him, now, after all this time. Something he'd buried deep and long ago warmed to that fact. And she had a daughter, his niece. How could he turn his back on them? They were family. That's what he told himself as his cab turned down Cora's street and came to a creaky stop in front of her address. Gannon paid the driver, approached the house with his stomach tensing and rang the bell.

Twenty-two years since he'd seen her.

The door opened to a woman in her late thirties.

Cora.

The sun lit her face, made a bit fuller by time. The way the corners of her eyes creased reminded him of their mother and father. A bittersweet smile blossomed as she spoke his name.

"Oh, Jack!"

She engulfed him on the step, nearly knocking him backward. She held him tight as she sobbed. Gannon felt something in his throat rising, his eyes stinging, for he never believed he would ever see her again.

They went to her kitchen and in the brief awkward quiet punctuated by Cora's tears, they studied each other. As her red-rimmed eyes took stock, Gannon felt as if he was twelve again, holding the attention of his hero.

"I knew you would grow up to be a tall, handsome man."

She had become a fine-looking woman, a mother, he thought.

"Help me find Tilly."

"I'll do what I can," he said, absorbing all the changes in her as each of them grappled with the time that had blurred their memories over two decades.

Cora offered a weak smile, worry lines cutting deep around her mouth, replacing the gleam that had always lifted him before the day she walked out on everything back in Buffalo. A tsunami of remembrance, outrage and regret rolled over him, and Cora saw his mood dim.

"I've been a terrible sister."

"You should have come home."

"I wanted to. So many times, but I couldn't face you, Mom and Dad."

"They died not knowing about your life, your daughter, their granddaughter."

She turned away.

"I know. I saw it in the *Sentinel* on the internet."

"Then why didn't you come to the funeral?"

"I wanted to, but I couldn't."

"Why? If only you had come home before they were killed. You could have worked things out with them. They searched everywhere for you."

"I just couldn't."

"Why? That's what I don't understand."

"It's too hard to explain. Please don't judge me."

"Judge you? Cora, I don't even know you."

She turned to the counter for a tissue box.

"I go by Cora Martin."

"Martin? Did you get married?"

"No, I changed it because of, well, because of mistakes."

"Is that why you didn't want us to find you?" He shook his head in disappointment.

"Jack, it's not easy to explain. You have every right to resent me," she said. "I'm not seeking forgiveness, but resentment can be a poison. I mourn the time we've lost. I regret choices I've made. Don't take your anger out on me now, Jack. I need your help. I have to get Tilly home safe."

"Tell me what happened."

Gannon took a long, deep breath and Cora related every detail from the night before. He listened, saying little until she'd finished.

"I don't know why this is happening to us," she said. "I don't know who to turn to, Jack. I thought you would have sources, people who know about this stuff and that you would know what to do. Help me find out who took her. Help me get her back."

"Call the police, Cora."

"No. They said they would kill her if I went to the police."

"Are you involved with drugs in any way, Cora?"

"No."

"But you were?"

"Yes. I used drugs, yes, but that's all in the past. I've changed my life."

"No one from your past would do this?"

God, I hope not. They told me I would never be free from what I did. Never. They told me I would always be looking over my shoulder. I can't tell Jack. I can't tell anyone. I have to protect Tilly.

"Cora, does this have anything to do with your past life?"

"No, I've been living a clean life, a good life, for years."

"What about Lyle? You say you're dating. What do you know about him? Is he involved in drugs?"

"If he is, he's hidden it all from me."

"Can you find him?"

"I've been trying and trying. He's disappeared."

"Who else knows about this?"

"Only you—and I called Tilly's school."

"You told her school she was kidnapped?"

"God, no, I said she wouldn't be in today. Only you know what's happened, Jack."

"From what I know about these things, they usually involve a drug debt. The cartels will kidnap someone close to get their money. That looks like the case here."

"Maybe it's all a mistake?"

"Call the police, Cora."

"But they said—"

"You have to call them, or it looks like you're involved."

Cora put her hands to her mouth, nodded, then reached for her cordless phone. Her fingers trembled as she pressed 911.

"I need the police. My daughter's been kidnapped…"

As she stayed on the line confirming her name and address, Gannon walked through the house, finding Tilly's room. Police would soon process the room but he wanted to see it, to get a sense of his niece.

Her white-and-pink bed was unmade, left the way it was when the invaders abducted her from it. On the wall nearby there was a cork bulletin board plastered with birthday cards, a drawing of two people holding hands called *Mommy & Me,* and photos of Tilly with her friends, their smiles and eyes blazing with adolescent zeal.

She sure resembled Cora.

Under the board was Tilly's desk. Math, history and science textbooks were stacked neatly on it to one side. Also on the desk he saw Tilly's homework: a handwritten essay. He began reading it:

The Swiss Family Robinson
Book Report
by Tilly Martin
    The Swiss Family Robinson by Johann David Wyss is an exciting story about a family who is shipwrecked on a deserted island and how they must work together to do all they can to survive…

"…how they must work together to do all they can to survive…"

The significance of her words jolted Gannon. He studied Tilly's neat cursive style, the forward slant, the generous looping of the *g, y* and *p*. He recognized that it was precisely the way he wrote.

A family trait.

It hit him full force that Tilly was his blood and that he was her uncle. That's when he heard something for the first time since entering the bedroom.

Ticking.

It was coming from the metal clock with a clown's

face on her dresser. It grew louder, with the exaggerated smile of the clown screaming to him that time was ticking down on his niece's life.

6

Something's not right here.

"Play the mother's call again."

Special Agent Earl Hackett concentrated as his partner, Bonnie Larson, turned on her pocket-sized recorder and replayed the 911 call Cora Martin had made twenty minutes ago.

As Hackett wheeled their unmarked sedan from the FBI's Phoenix headquarters he got a bad vibe about this case. After he and Larson had listened to the call several more times Hackett reviewed the key facts.

The mother says two men in police uniforms kidnapped her daughter. These "cops" said her employer, Lyle Galviera "distributed their product" and stole five million dollars. She says it happened at 12:30 a.m., but calls it in now, more than twelve hours later.

"This is a cartel operation," Hackett said as Larson activated the dash-mounted cherry.

The engine hummed and they cut through traffic to the expressway. While Larson worked on her cell phone gathering background from analysts at the field office, Hackett assessed matters. Cora Martin's call first went to the County Sheriff's deputies. They responded, took Cora's initial statement and were backed up by Phoenix PD, which had the Home Invasion and Kidnapping

Enforcement Task Force. The so-called HIKE unit was created when Phoenix became America's kidnapping capital, averaging a kidnapping a day, usually arising from drug and human smuggling wars. But lately, HIKE was stretched. And because this new case involved a child and potential interstate flight, it fell to the FBI. Hackett and Larson had the lead, with support from other agencies.

As they drove across Phoenix, Hackett boiled things down.

Most of these cases involved criminal-on-criminal acts. Many times people never reported them to police. They paid the ransom, cleared the drug debt and the hostage was released.

Or things ended with a corpse.

You could argue that there were no true victims in this type of crime, but this one involved an eleven-year-old girl so he kicked his biases aside. As the city blurred by, he undid his collar button and loosened his tie. His gnarled face fixed into his perpetual grimace, the flag of his life as a twice-divorced hard-ass who was raised in Yonkers.

What did he have in this world?

Two ex-wives; four grown children, none of whom would speak to him; a slight limp from a gunshot wound; and a bastard's attitude that hardened as he counted the days to his retirement.

Hackett couldn't remember the last time he smiled. Maybe when the Cardinals won a game? His outlook was shaped by the crap he'd faced from his time as the FBI's legal attaché in Bogotá, Guatemala City and Mexico City. He was intimate with the work of narcoterrorists. His limp was a daily reminder of his role in the botched rescue attempt of an American aid worker, taken hostage by cocaine traffickers in Colombia.

The narcos had been tipped that police were coming and the aid worker, a red-haired medical student from Ohio named Betsy, and three Colombian cops, died in the firefight. Later, while recovering in hospital, Hackett learned that one of the cops had been on the traffickers' payroll, a betrayal that, like his bullet wound, had scarred him.

That was ten years ago and since then Hackett had watched helplessly as the drug lords, with the increasing power of Mexican cartels, extended their reach deeper into the U.S. Corruption greased the drug trade, a fact evinced by the latest memo concerning cartel infiltration of U.S. police ranks. Intelligence showed that cartels were suspected of having "operatives" applying for and getting jobs within U.S. law enforcement. This threw a cloud of mistrust over joint-forces operations, underscoring that you never knew who was on your side. It was an affront to Hackett, who abided by the Bureau's motto: Fidelity, Bravery and Integrity. These factors weighed on him as they came to Mesa Mirage.

Larson had finished taking notes over the phone.

"No complaint history on the caller's address. The mother has no criminal history, a spotless driving record. No registered firearms. She's unmarried and no custody issues—the same for Lyle Galviera. He resides near Tempe and is president of Quick Draw Courier. No arrests, warrants or convictions. He does not possess any firearms. His company is clean."

"And we've got people moving on his company and his home?"

"Yes, based on the statements the kidnapped girl's mother gave to the sheriff's deputies we've set things in motion to expedite search warrants on Galviera. And we've got our Evidence Response Team rolling to the mother's house to process it as soon as possible."

"I'm concerned about the time that's passed since it happened. How many people have walked through that house, contaminating our scene," Hackett said.

"I figure we'll want to get the place processed quickly and get a task force set up in the house," Larson said.

"You figured right."

Hackett considered Larson a solid young agent. Three years out of Quantico, she'd grown up in Pennsylvania, the daughter of a Pittsburgh cop. She was quiet but sharp, and one of the few agents who could stand working with the walking slab of embitterment known as Earl Hackett.

They neared Cora Martin's street and recognized a number of unmarked county and Phoenix PD units. As the FBI had requested, they were keeping a low profile but positioned to immediately choke all traffic in the neighborhood.

Hackett stopped their sedan at Cora Martin's house. A man answered the door. The two agents held up ID.

"Special Agents Earl Hackett and Bonnie Larson. FBI," Hackett said.

"Jack Gannon." He swung the door open. "My sister's over here."

He indicated the woman sitting on the couch, twisting a tissue in her fists. Her hair was messed and her eyes reddened. After the agents introduced themselves, Hackett said: "Cora, a lot of people are going to work full tilt to get Tilly home safely but we're going to need your help."

"Anything."

After assessing the house and making calls for support, Hackett and Larson talked further with Cora.

"Will you volunteer your property to be processed by our Evidence Response Team, who will look for anything to aid us?"

"Yes."

"Good. While they do that, would you and your brother come to the Bureau with us now to help us with a few questions?"

"Leave? No. I don't want to leave—the kidnappers could call."

"We'll put an agent here and we can arrange to have

any calls that come to your landline go directly to a dedicated line at the Bureau where you can answer. We will
not miss a call."

Upon returning to FBI headquarters, a redbrick and
glass building at Indianola Avenue and Second, the agents
took Cora alone to a separate meeting room, leaving
Gannon to wait in a reception area.

"Would you like something to drink?" Larson asked
Cora.

She declined.

"All right, tell us what happened," Hackett said.

Cora recounted everything. Hackett grilled her, often
coming back to the same questions several times. What
did she remember about the men? Had she ever seen them
before? Height, build, scars, tattoos, accents? What did
they touch? Did she still have the duct tape they'd used
to bind her? Did she get a look at the car, a plate? The
model, make? Prior to the kidnapping had there been
any strange incidents? Did Tilly report anything odd at
school, like strangers watching her, approaching her?

What did she know about Lyle Galviera? Did the five-
million-dollar demand mean anything to Cora or the business? Was he a drug dealer, a drug user, a gambler, a big
spender? Did he have debts? What kind of businessman
was he?

"Let's go over this again." Hackett read his notes. "The
kidnappers told you that Lyle uses his company to distribute their product, launder money and that he's stolen five
million dollars from them. Do you know which group or
gang this is linked to?"

"No. I wish I did but I don't."

"More than twelve hours went by before you called
police," Hackett said. "I need you to explain the delay to
me again."

"I told you, they said that if I went to the police they
would kill Tilly. I told absolutely no one. I did all I could

to try to find Lyle. I don't know where he is. When nothing worked, the only person I told is my brother, Jack. I begged him to help me and he told me to call the police."

Hackett let a few moments pass in silence before he and Larson left Cora alone in the room.

The agents sent for Gannon, leading him to a separate room where Hackett sipped coffee from an FBI mug and flipped through his notes.

"And what's your line of work, Jack?"

"I'm a correspondent with the World Press Alliance."

"You're a reporter with the newswire service?"

"Yes."

"And you were in Mexico when she called you?"

"Yes."

"Where in Mexico?"

"Juarez."

"Really?"

"Yes."

"And what were you doing there when she contacted you?"

"I was working on the WPA's series on the drug trade."

Hackett and Larson exchanged a look of unease.

"Is that right?" Hackett asked.

"Yes."

"Who did you talk to down there? What were you doing?"

"I talked to other journalists, morgue officials. It's all in the profile that I wrote. The WPA will put out a day-of-death feature."

"A 'day-of-death' feature?"

"Yes, it'll likely run in tomorrow's *Arizona Republic,* and about two thousand other papers around the world."

"I'll have to read it," Hackett said. "Is it possible there's a link to your activities in Mexico and what's happened to your niece? Like maybe you pissed somebody off? Cartels have been known to go after journalists."

"I know, but I doubt it," Gannon said.

"Why?"

"I've only been there a few days and my sister said that the people who took my niece asked for Lyle Galviera, said he owed them five million dollars. Until today, I'd never heard of the guy."

"Would you say you and your sister are close? Keep in touch regularly?"

"No. She ran away from home when she was seventeen and I was twelve. I never saw her again, until today."

"So it's fair to say you don't really know your sister that well?"

"It's been difficult, yes."

"And here you are, directly from Juarez, Mexico?"

"That's right. Here I am."

Hackett stared at him for several long seconds before he and Larson met with other people in the Bureau and made a few calls. Then they led Gannon to the room where Cora had been waiting and questioned them together.

"Cora," Hackett started, "I need to know more about Tilly. Does she have any medical condition we should know about?"

"No."

"Does she have a boyfriend?"

"God no, she's eleven."

"Does she use drugs? Is she flirtatious? Does she spend a lot of time chatting on the internet?"

"No."

"Is she a good student?"

"Yes. She has above-average grades. She likes school."

"Describe her relationship with you."

"She's a good girl. We have a strong relationship. There's just the two of us in our family. We're as close as any mother and daughter can be."

"Where's Tilly's father?"

"I don't know. He's been out of the picture from the start. I raised her alone."

"Again, characterize your relationship with Lyle Galviera. You indicated it's more than boss-employee."

"I started working there five years ago and last year we started dating."

"Are you engaged?"

"No. A few months ago we talked about marriage but we decided to keep dating, see where things go."

"Describe Lyle's relationship with Tilly."

"He adores her and she likes him."

"Can you think of anyone who would have reason to take this kind of action against you?"

Cora was stabbed by the memory of California.

No one must know what happened. It can't be connected to Tilly's abduction. She can't be the one to pay for my mistake. I have to keep that night in California secret. No one must know. Not Jack, not the police, no one. I have to protect Tilly. This is the one thing I have to keep secret until I know who took Tilly.

The one thing.

The kidnappers said this was about Lyle, not me. Please let that be true.

"No."

"What about Lyle and his company—any enemies?"

"I can't think of one. Everyone likes Lyle."

"Is the company involved in the trafficking of narcotics?"

"I told you, no, not to my knowledge. I know we were facing some hard financial times. Lyle had to lay off a couple of people and told me to watch office costs, but drugs? No, this is all wrong."

"You said that this morning the kidnappers called you at your office?"

"Yes. When I got loose, I went there immediately to try to find some clue as to where Lyle was. They called me on my cell phone and put Tilly on."

"Did she give you any idea where she was?"

"No, it was only for a second and she sounded so scared."

"How did they get your number?"

"Tilly would have given them my cell phone number."

"Have you ever been involved with illicit drugs, Cora?"

She was struggling to hold herself together and covered her mouth with her cupped hands, feeling her brother's eyes upon her.

"Yes."

"Elaborate."

"For about ten years, starting when I was seventeen, I was addicted to drugs—pot, coke and crack. I was messed up. I drifted across the country. I hit bottom. I cut myself off from my family. Then I got pregnant with Tilly. I got clean for her, started over with her. I changed my name from Cora Gannon to Cora Martin."

"Why did you change your name?"

"To put my past behind me and start over. I moved to Phoenix, put myself through college and started a new life. I got clerical jobs. I've been clean since."

"So it's been about twelve years since you've used?" Hackett asked.

"Yes, about that."

"Did you deal?"

"I didn't deal. But I knew dealers."

"Do you associate with them now?"

"No."

"Do you think anyone from your past could be involved in this?"

"I knew bad dealers, but that was a long time ago, another life. Anything is possible, but no, I hope not."

"Can you provide us with names of those old dealers?" Hackett asked.

"I never knew their real names—they were street names. There was Deke, a white guy in Boston about fifteen years ago. Before that, Rasheed, a Middle Eastern guy in Toronto."

Larson made notes.

"When did you last have contact with people in the drug trade?"

"About twelve years ago. My old life is dead, behind me."

Hackett stared at Cora. Fine threads of doubt and apprehension webbed across his face before he said, "Are you telling us everything we need to know?"

Several moments passed before she answered.

"Agent Hackett, I've made mistakes. I have not lived a perfect life but I am a good mother and I swear to you I am not involved."

"All right."

Larson's cell phone rang. After listening for about ten seconds, she said: "They're almost finished processing the kitchen and the living room."

Hackett adjusted his sleeves.

"We'll take both of you back to the house in Mesa Mirage. The task force will set up. We'll have people from VAP, our victim specialist unit there too, to help you with anything you may need. You're going to have a lot of police keeping you company."

"Whatever it takes," Cora said. "But there's something I need from you."

"What's that?"

"Your word that you will do all you can to bring Tilly home."

Cora's request gave him pause. It was identical to the plea he'd heard from the mother of the aid worker from

Toledo, Ohio, who'd been taken hostage by Colombian
drug traffickers.

*"Give me your word you will bring my daughter
back."*

He did.

But he brought her home in a coffin.

Now, looking into Cora's face, Hackett told her the
truth.

"I give you my word I will do all I can to find your
daughter."

"Thank you."

He stared at Cora. "And to arrest the people responsible."

7

Phoenix, Arizona

A few miles north of Mesa Mirage, at the South Desert Bank & Trust, Bill Grover, the assistant manager, realigned the stapler and pen holder on his desk.

The two FBI agents sitting across from him were studying the files Grover's branch had assembled with some urgency. The action was in response to a warrant to provide the FBI with records on all of Lyle Galviera's financial dealings and those of his courier company.

The agents, Ross Sarreno and Winston Reeve, were the Phoenix Division's white-collar crime experts. They wore dark suits and somber expressions. Whatever they were chasing, it was serious, Grover thought.

First, they confirmed that there'd been no activity on any credit or bank cards held by Galviera since the day before he was to depart for his California business trip. However, on that day, there was a cash withdrawal from one of his accounts for nine thousand dollars.

This guy was planning something, Reeve thought after he and Sarreno studied the company's banking files.

"These records show the company is in trouble," Reeve said.

"Yes." Grover cleared his throat. "The big boys were securing their hold on Quick Draw's regional market. About two years ago, Lyle's outstanding debts climbed to about four million dollars. A few times he came close to not making payroll. We could no longer extend his line of credit. Things were getting dire. We were talking about Chapter Eleven."

"Then he turns things around, appears to have found a source of business and funds," Reeve said. "Ten months ago he begins knocking down his debt with significant weekly payments, fifty-, seventy-, ninety-five-thousand-dollar range."

"He said it was the result of a new business model."

"But all of the transactions were in cash," Reeve said.

"That's correct."

"This is a courier business. It does not deal primarily in cash. The transactions could be indicative of money laundering. Under the law there's an obligation to report this activity," Reeve said.

Grover reached for the file, tapped at specific pages.

"You'll see here that Currency Transaction Reports were filed with the IRS for all of his cash transactions over ten thousand dollars."

"What about SARs?"

"This bank filed three Suspicious Activity Reports with the Financial Crimes Enforcement Network at Treasury."

"What was their response?"

"Nothing to us. We did our part."

"The bottom line here, plain and simple?"

"He owes $1,950,000 by end of next month and if he does not pay that amount in full he will lose his company. Now I know Lyle built that company practically from the time he was a college kid and I don't think that he was going to let that happen under any circumstances."

The agents closed the files, thanked Grover and left. Next stop: Cora Martin's bank in Mesa Mirage to scrutinize her records. Heading to their car in the lot, Reeve turned to Sarreno.

"Our guy was in a dire financial situation, then found a sudden and significant source of cash. Someone dropped the ball. This should've raised flags," Reeve said.

"Sure raises some big ones now." Sarreno was reaching for his cell phone. "I'll alert Hackett and Larson."

At that moment, Vivian Brankowski, manager of the Tranquility Palms Condominiums near Tempe, reread the document the two FBI Agents, Douglas and Allard, had presented her.

Shocked, she watched the words leap at her from the pages: *"…United States District Court…Search Warrant…affidavits…electronic data process and storage devices, computers…"* The list went on, but offered no details as to what it concerned, other than the property listed for Lyle Galviera.

Vivian stood there in disbelief. This sort of thing never happened at Tranquility, a sedate community of urban professionals.

"Ma'am?" Agent Allard said. "We don't want to force the door. Do you have a key and a floor plan?"

"Mr. Galviera uses Tranquility's cleaning service. I have a key."

It was the Segovia model, a two-bedroom multilevel condo with a balcony overlooking the small lake. Several swans were gliding on the surface when the FBI backed a white panel van into the driveway.

Vivian felt like she was trespassing as she opened the door to Mr. Galviera's home for the agents. But the warrant gave them legal access. With mute efficiency, the agents snapped on latex gloves and began seizing and cataloging Galviera's computer, personal files and other belongings.

Vivian stood at the doorway watching in disbelief. Mr. Galviera was a first-rate resident. Always smiled and chatted. *Now the FBI was searching his home, taking things. Good Lord, what was going on?* She stared at the warrant for the umpteenth time but failed to find an answer.

"Can you gentlemen at least tell me what this is about?"

"Sorry, ma'am," Agent Douglas said. "We can't discuss it."

Ed Kilpatrick's jaw dropped when the FBI and detectives from the county arrived at the main office of Quick Draw Courier's depot. They gave him a copy of the warrant authorizing them to seize the company's computers, files and phone records, among other items.

"What the hell is this?" Kilpatrick asked.

Heads turned and conversations halted as management and administrative staff watched.

"We're not at liberty to share other information at this time," Agent Hutton said.

"But you'll shut us down. Our customers are relying on shipments."

"That's not our concern, sir," Hutton said. "Have your people step away from their units now."

Kilpatrick and his staff complied with the order, then scrambled.

"Bobby! Get Lyle on the phone—tell him what's going on. Agnes, call our lawyer, Kendall Fairfield. His number is on the firm's calendar in my office."

Kilpatrick was stunned as he watched FBI agents and county detectives shut down and disconnect computers. He tried to think.

"Gloria, can you get through to Metrofire Computer Solutions? Tell them we need emergency backup—now. Then start calling our clients. Tell them we're having a major computer issue."

Bobby Wicks shouted to Kilpatrick that he could not reach Lyle Galviera.

"Damn." Kilpatrick ran his hand over his face,

remembering Cora Martin's call from earlier. Did she actually come in today? "Has anyone seen Cora today? Maybe she knows what the hell is going on."

8

Cora's phone rang.

All activity in her home ceased.

She held her breath and looked at Gannon.

This was the first call on her landline since she and Gannon had returned to the house with Hackett and Larson a few hours earlier. During that time a stream of agents and detectives had flowed through her door. The FBI had put a trace on her home phone to identify incoming calls.

"This call's from the Phoenix area," said the agent working at a computer laptop equipped to record calls.

As the agent locked on the address, an FBI hostage negotiator put on a headset to listen in. He had a clipboard and pen, ready to give Cora instructions. She looked at the negotiator. He nodded.

Her hand trembling, she answered on the third ring.

"Hello."

"Cora, Ed at the depot. Are you coming in at all this afternoon?"

"I can't."

"Have you heard from Lyle yet?"

"No. Have you?"

"No, but—you sound upset, Cora. What's going on?"

"It's just—it's a thing with Tilly. I'm sorry, Ed."

"Well, we've got trouble. We've got the FBI in here with search warrants and nobody knows what the hell's going on. We can't reach Lyle. Have you had any luck? Do you have any idea what's happening, Cora?"

"No, I wish I could talk but it's a bad time."

"Man, tell me about it."

"Ed, I need a favor."

"What is it?"

"If you hear from Lyle, tell him I need to talk to him now."

"That makes two of us, kid."

Cora hung up and thrust her face in her hands. Hackett, Larson and the dozen other law enforcement people from the FBI, the Phoenix PD's HIKE unit, the County, the DEA and U.S. Immigration and Customs who'd joined the case, watched her for several moments before continuing their work.

When Cora regained her composure, she resumed describing the suspects to the FBI's sketch artist, a blonde woman with red fingernails.

"The one who spoke had a Hispanic accent," Cora said. "He had a scar along his left jawline. He had narrow eyes. He was in his mid-thirties, about five feet ten inches, one hundred and sixty pounds, slim build. The silent one was in his early thirties, about the same height, weight and build. Both had short black hair. The car was a light-colored Ford. I think maybe a Crown Victoria. It looked like the one my friend at church has."

As the artist worked with her on the faces of the suspects, the magnitude of her daughter's kidnapping began to sink in.

Investigators had moved fast, filling Cora's living room with tables of equipment, including extra phone lines, GPS, radios and encrypted fax machines. She had volunteered her phone, bank and computer records, everything. They examined it all. People worked on laptops, talked softly on cell phones, drank coffee, consulted files and shared notes, while uniformed officers came and went after updating detectives. Still others continued searching her home.

So far, they'd determined that the call Cora had received at her office from the kidnappers was made on a prepaid cell phone bought with cash at a corner store in Tucson. From there, the trail went cold.

After finishing with the artist, Cora joined Gannon in the hall, watching the FBI's evidence team. They'd finished with the kitchen and living room and were now processing Tilly's bedroom. It was the first time Cora had looked into her room since the abduction.

Since the moment when she'd last checked on her daughter.

Cora took a deep breath as her eyes went around the room. The room where she'd tucked Tilly in, the room where she'd listened to her dreams, chased away her fears and promised to keep her safe.

Now, seeing the evidence people in there with their protective clothing and latex gloves—people who worked in the aftermath of evil touching Tilly's most private things—felt like a violation. Yet it was eclipsed by the greater desecration committed by the monsters who'd stolen her child.

Where was Tilly? Time was slipping by.

Panic rose in Cora's stomach and was stifled by a dog's yelp.

Through the bedroom window she glimpsed the K-9 unit sniffing in her yard for evidence. Down the street she saw other detectives canvassing the neighborhood, interviewing people. Cora dreaded the fact that soon everyone would know what had happened. Her attention was pulled back to the living room, where Hackett was huddled with agents and detectives. Not far under the surface of the investigation, his suspicions toward her bubbled beneath his cold, insistent frown.

"Are you telling us everything we need to know?"

She had nothing to do with Tilly's abduction and nothing to do with drugs. Cora and Tilly lived a good life. Still, Hackett's mistrust tore at her, made her feel guilty for not knowing Lyle, for every sin of her past.

Like the secret she'd kept buried for so many years.

Did one single act, all those years back, deliver Tilly into the hands of a drug cartel now? No, it can't be. It's just not possible. It was so long ago. That was another life. No one must know about what I did. I have to protect Tilly.

"Excuse me." One of the agents had follow-up questions. "Could you tell us what she was wearing when she was taken? It's for the alert."

After Cora described Tilly's pajamas, and the sneakers, shirt and jeans Tilly had been carrying, the agent asked for a recent photo. She found one of Tilly taken at a friend's birthday party.

"This was last weekend."

There was Tilly with other eleven- and twelve-year-olds at the mall, laughing in the food court, eyes bright with innocence, on the cusp of adolescence, her whole life ahead of her.

Would she ever hold her again?

Cora then saw forensic people bagging Tilly's old toothbrush and comb. "For DNA analysis," someone said. She watched them process Tilly's computer mouse for fingerprints.

Hackett approached her.

"Cora," he said. "Were you aware of the seriousness of Quick Draw's financial trouble?"

"Like I said, we had to cut some staff and watch costs. Lyle told me we had faced rough times but that he'd taken care of it."

"Did you know where his influx of cash came from?"

"No, he did the books. He never showed me the company's finances. I ran the office. He ran the company."

Hackett took a moment to assess her answer.

"All right, in a few hours we're going to hold a press conference and make a public appeal for Tilly and for Lyle."

"What?" Cora said. "No! The kidnappers said they would kill her. God knows what they'll do to Tilly when they learn I've gone to the police."

"Your daughter's life was in danger the second they stole her," Hackett said. "We can't deal with these people. Right now secrecy is their best weapon."

"But we can't have a press conference. There has to be another way!"

"There isn't. At this time, we have no leads on your daughter's location or safety. We have no leads on Lyle's whereabouts. We have no leads on the suspects, or the gang involved. We have no choice, none."

Hackett shot a glance toward Gannon.

"It could be the only way to get Tilly home," Gannon said.

"Earl," Larson said from down the hall. "Call from EPIC."

Gannon's ears pricked up. He knew EPIC was short for the El Paso Intelligence Center, the multi-agency operation at the U.S.-Mexico border that coordinated information on Mexican cartels and human smugglers.

Gannon had an idea and took it to a quiet corner of the house. Up to now, he'd been useless in the search for his niece. Using his cell phone, he called Isabel Luna in Mexico.

"Isabel Luna, *El Heraldo*."

"It's Jack Gannon." He lowered his voice. "I'm in Arizona and I need your help but this is confidential. You can't report any of this yet."

"Of course, Jack, we are working together."

"An eleven-year-old girl has been kidnapped from her home in Phoenix, Arizona, by narcos. They claim a Phoenix businessman who runs a courier company stole five million dollars from them and vanished. He has five days to surface and return the money."

"Has any of this been reported?"

"Not a word yet, but you must keep this all confidential."

"Why the secrecy?"

"The girl is my niece."

"Your niece? Do you know who took her?"

"No, my sister works for the man the kidnappers are trying to pressure."

"What can I do to help you, Jack?"

"I need you to find out who might be responsible. Can you check with your sources in Juarez, see what you can dig up confidentially?"

"I will at once."

Gannon ended the call and exhaled just as his phone rang.

"Jack, Melody in New York. Where are you and what do you have?"

"I'm in Phoenix and we have a story."

"What is it?"

"An eleven-year-old girl has been kidnapped from her Phoenix home, likely tied to the theft of five million dollars from a cartel."

"I'll put it on the next news budget. You write us a first hit. We'll need it in about thirty minutes."

"No. We can't write anything yet."

"What?"

"Alert our Phoenix bureau to expect a news conference with the FBI late in the day."

"News conference? Isn't this our exclusive?"

"No, it's complicated."

"We need exclusives, Jack."

"I know and this could lead to one. You have to trust me."

"What's going on?"

Since he'd already told Isabel Luna, Gannon surrendered his information to the editor he trusted most.

"The girl who's been kidnapped is the daughter of my estranged sister, Cora—my niece. I'm sorry, but it's complicated. I'll explain later."

"Good Lord. Is she okay?"

"No."

"Are you okay?"

"I'm not sure."

"Is there anything we can do?"

"Thanks, I'll let you know. Just trust me on this for now, please. I really have to go. I'll call you when I know more."

Gannon scanned the house and saw Cora on the edge of a chair, being offered water and comfort by paramedics. They'd been monitoring her vital signs from the get-go.

Watching her now, he battled his emotions.

Am I scum? His sister had called him for help. Was he being a brother and an uncle, or was he being a reporter? Why did he feel a greater obligation to his job than to Cora? *Because it didn't feel like she was his sister.* At times he felt that she was a stranger. Then there were warm flashes, when he'd recognized the same gentle spirit who'd guided him when he was a boy.

His big sister, Cora.

And he wondered what their lives would've been like had she not run off and devastated their family. But dwelling on it made him angry. His thoughts shifted when Cora indicated that she wanted to talk to him alone.

The paramedics gave them privacy.

Cora gripped his arm.

Since this had happened, she hadn't slept or eaten. Her eyes were reddened from tears. She pulled him closer. Her lower lip started trembling.

"Am I being punished, Jack."

"What do you mean?"

"For my past. In the worst times of my life I had to do things to survive—awful things, Jack."

"What things? Tell me. Maybe it will help find Tilly."

"No, it's not like that."

"If it has something to do with why you cut yourself off from us, then tell me. I need to know. I *deserve* to know."

"I can't." Her face contorted with fear. "What if I never see her again?"

"Take it easy."

"This is not about me, not about my mistakes. It's about my daughter."

"I know, I know. You're upset. Maybe you should rest."

"You have to help me find her before it's too late, find out who took her and bring her back!" She collapsed onto his chest.

"It's all right," he whispered, looking down at her. He held her until she calmed down. When the paramedics returned to check on her, Gannon met Hackett's stare. He'd been watching.

He took Gannon aside.

"Saw you on your phone, Jack. Mind telling me who were you talking to and what you told them?"

Gannon considered his question.

"My boss needs to know where I am."

"That right? Listen, you'd better give serious thought about your role here. For some reason, your long-lost sister thinks having you here now is important."

"She was scared and she called me. The situation brought us together."

"That's fine—you're family. But your actions could be counterproductive to our efforts. Anything you learn here is privileged. Sharing it outside the investigation could undermine our work, force us to look at excluding you from the house and consider obstruction charges. You got that?"

"Oh, I get it."

"Good."

"We have the same goal—the safe return of my niece."

"As long as we're on the same page, Jack."

"We are—the one that says you do your job and I'll do mine."

Hackett glared at Gannon until a heart-stopping shriek cut through the impasse. Paramedics were struggling to stem Cora's rising hysteria as she moaned to everyone.

"Please, bring my daughter back to me! Please!"

9

*T*ick. Tick. Tick.

The clock on the wall of the FBI's office was all Cora could hear.

Time counting down on Tilly's life.

Or was that Cora's heart racing under the fierce light of cameras?

Some fifty news people had gathered for the press conference at the FBI's Field Office. They adjusted lenses, tripods, checked BlackBerry phones, made notes and last-minute cell phone calls while Cora and other officials took their places in front of the crowd.

The announcements would start momentarily.

Prior to arriving, Cora had slept for an hour but adrenaline still rushed through her. She'd refused sedatives from the paramedics and had managed to eat saltine crackers to quell her stomach butterflies after she'd agreed to make a live statement to the press.

Hackett and Gannon had convinced her that it was critical to reach out to the kidnappers and that this was the best way to speak directly to them, to Tilly, to Lyle, and to get the whole world looking for them. It could lead to a break in the case. Her plea would be distributed everywhere on the air and online.

Jack had helped her compose a few sentences. They

were printed in large font on the folded sheet of paper she
now held in her hand.

Cora clasped her hands over it to steady her nerves as
a thousand disconnected thoughts shot through her mind;
her fear for Tilly juxtaposed with the absurdity of deciding how to dress for the press conference.

What do I wear to plead for my daughter's life?

She'd decided on her charcoal jacket and matching
pencil skirt, what she would have worn to work or a funeral. *What about makeup?* A female FBI agent had
offered to help fix her face, but Cora had declined. Somehow it seemed wrong.

My daughter's life is at stake.

The conference began.

Gannon was standing a few inches to her right and the
Special Agent in Charge of the Phoenix FBI was a few
inches on her left, gripping the podium. She noticed his
wedding band but had forgotten his name. Lewis something. He'd given it to her with a crushing handshake.

As the agent spoke, Cora struggled against a state of
unreality. *Her child had been abducted by a drug cartel.
How could this be happening? She was a single mother,
a secretary. She wanted her daughter back. She thought
she knew Lyle. Where was he? Was he dead? Five million dollars! What had he done?*

What had she done?

The kidnappers' warning flashed.

*"Lyle must return our money or your daughter will die.
And if you go to the police, your daughter will die...."*

Cora heard her name.

The FBI man finished his opening remarks and had
turned to her.

"Now, Tilly's mother, Cora Martin, will make a brief
statement. But please—she will take no questions."

He gestured and she stepped in front of the cameras.
The intense light glared like a judgment. Beside the
podium she saw the tripod bearing enlarged photos of

Tilly and Lyle. Next to it stood another tripod bearing a sketch of one of the suspects and a picture of Lyle's pickup truck.

This was real.

Cora's mouth went dry. She glanced at her brother. He nodded encouragement.

She had to do this for Tilly.

Cora unfolded her paper. The cameras tightened on her, the lines on her face, her bloodshot eyes: the anguished mother. News networks were broadcasting live with Breaking News flags. Some carried a graphic at the bottom of the screen: Drug Gang Kidnaps 11-year-old Girl From Phoenix Home Demand $5 million.

Cora started.

"To the people who have my daughter, Tilly, I beg you, please, do not hurt her and please return her to me." Cora stopped, then resumed. "Sweetheart, if you can see me or hear my voice, I love you. We're doing everything to bring you home safely."

She paused, kept her composure and continued.

"Lyle, if you see this, please help us. Go to the police, wherever you are. Please. We need your help. And I beg anyone who has any information to please contact the police. Thank you."

As the agent took her shoulder and Gannon helped her retreat from the podium, several reporters fired questions. Above them all, they heard the voice of Carrie Cole, a news celebrity known across America for her nationally televised crime show based in Phoenix.

"Mother to mother, Cora! One question, please!"

Cora stopped, looked at the famous face and lifted hers, inviting the question.

"I know this must be a horrible, gut-wrenching time. No one can know what you're going through, but please share with us the last words your little girl spoke to you and when?"

Cora glanced at the FBI and her brother. The FBI man nodded.

"It was early this morning, after the kidnappers took Tilly. They called me and put her on the phone."

"What did she say to you?"

Cora hesitated.

"'Mommy, please help me!'"

Cora covered her face and turned away sobbing. The reporters shouted more questions, but the agent raised his palms and resumed control.

"To recap and conclude, as you know we've just issued a national alert. The FBI is asking for the public's assistance in locating Tilly Martin and Lyle Galviera. I want to stress that Mr. Galviera is not a suspect but a person of interest. He was last known to have been destined by air travel for California on business. He has not been located. All vehicles registered to him have been located except for his red Ford F-150 pickup truck pictured here. You have details. We are also seeking any information concerning the unknown suspects fitting the artist's sketch and details. There is still no description of the suspects' vehicle involved in this case. That is all we can release for now. Anyone with information is strongly urged to call the Phoenix FBI or your local police. We'll keep you apprised of any developments. Thank you."

10

New York City, New York

At that moment, at the World Press Alliance headquarters in midtown Manhattan, several senior editors had extended the late-day story meeting to watch the news conference on the large screen in the main boardroom.

"Am I wrong, or did I just see one of our reporters participating in an FBI press conference, in violation of WPA policy that we don't align ourselves with police?" said George Wilson, chief of all of the WPA's foreign bureaus.

No one spoke. A couple of the other editors consulted their cell phones for messages. One made notes on a pad.

"Am I the only one who has a problem with this?"

It was known that Wilson, a pull-no-punches journalist, had a prickly relationship with Gannon. Wilson swiveled his chair, turning to the head of the table, taking his issue to Melody Lyon, the WPA's deputy executive editor.

"Mel? Are you aware of the perception here?"

Lyon arched an eyebrow. She was a legendary reporter who'd spent decades covering the world's most turbulent events and was the most powerful person in WPA management after her boss, Beland Stone, the WPA's executive editor.

"I'm well aware of the perception. As I said in my memo to senior management, Jack advised me of his situation and is keeping me apprised. Henrietta Chong from our Phoenix bureau staffed the conference and will cover the story for us."

"Gannon's supposed to be in Mexico on foreign features. We're led to believe he's on the brink of delivering an exclusive. Then he abandons the assignment because of this cartel kidnapping of his niece," Wilson said.

"Yes, I alerted you when he informed me that his situation had changed," Lyon said.

"I never knew all the details until now. None of us did, Mel."

"I recognize this puts him in a potential conflict, but that's not our main concern right now."

"You seem to be missing the greater point," Wilson said.

"Which is?" Lyon was twisting a rubber band in her hand.

"Look at the optics. While on assignment covering cartels in Mexico, Jack Gannon suddenly surfaces in Arizona in the eye of the kidnapping story involving cartels, drugs, five million dollars *and his family.* It implicates him and by extension implicates the WPA and threatens our credibility." Wilson muttered, "Remember who hired him."

"What was that?"

Unease rippled around the table.

"It's no secret that many of us were opposed to Gannon's hiring," Wilson said.

Lyon had stood alone with her desire to hire Gannon after he was fired from the *Buffalo Sentinel,* where he'd become embroiled in a scandal over a source there. Everyone had rejected him but she'd sensed something about him, about his news instincts, his passion, his ability to dig. He was as uncompromising as truth itself.

"I resent what you are implying. No one has been charged in this case."

"Not yet."

Lyon slapped her palm on the table.

"Stop this bullshit, George!"

The air tensed as she continued.

"When reporters find themselves in trouble or victims of circumstance, their news organizations stand behind them. Look at the cases of the *New York Times,* the *Wall Street Journal*, the *BBC*. And look at what we just went through in Brazil." Lyon paused. "Gannon is a WPA employee. His niece has been abducted by a drug cartel. And you're damned right—by extension that implicates the WPA. But at a time like this the WPA does not consult its policy, George. It looks into its heart and makes the easy, moral choice to do what's right. Because at a time like this, we're talking about the life of an eleven-year-old child. Is that clear?"

Lyon let several moments pass.

"We will stand behind our reporter as this tragedy unfolds. Is that understood?"

Murmurs of agreement went around the table then bled into talk of updates and other business before Lyon ended the meeting. She stayed behind, alone in the room, and replayed the Phoenix press conference.

Looking at Cora, at Tilly's picture, Lyon saw the family resemblance with Gannon as she watched.

This is a hell of a way to find your long-lost sister, Jack.

11

Phoenix, Arizona, Mesa Mirage

Cora was terrified by what she had done.

Now that she had defied the kidnapper's orders, would they carry out their threat to kill Tilly?

Forgive me, Tilly. I didn't know what else to do.

Cora also feared that her appeal to find Tilly would resurrect her dangerous secret and make things worse.

Returning home after the press conference, she was exhausted, as if a lifetime had passed since Tilly was taken. FBI crime scene experts were still processing parts of her house and agents had set up additional lines to run off Cora's home and cell phones.

Hackett opposed talk of sealing her entire home as a crime scene. He wanted her in the house in case, by some miracle, Tilly got free and called. Or the kidnappers called, or Galviera surfaced. The FBI would be listening and ready to take command of her line, or clear it.

As expected, the press coverage had yielded a steady number of tips to the FBI's hotline. They were screened by analysts at the Phoenix office and assessed by agents for follow-up.

But most leads lacked detail. One caller said: *"I saw that missing kid. She was walking near a Wal-Mart, or Target? Not sure which, but check it out."* Another said, *"I saw a dude with a scar like the kidnapper's in a bar."*

One email said, This was foretold in the Book of Revelations. And then there was a woman claiming special powers who wanted to *"spiritually channel your visions on the kidnapping."*

Tilly's distraught friends and neighbors called. So did people from her church. All offered Cora kind words and prayers. Other support was more tangible, like the swift help that came from the American Network for Vanished and Stolen Children. The Phoenix chapter worked with police, creating flyers and marshaling volunteer search parties at the Mesa Mirage Shopping Center. News cameras recorded the response to Tilly's kidnapping from her schoolteachers and worried parents. They quoted criminologists, expert on the nature of drug cartels.

The press also kept a vigil at Cora's home.

Satellite trucks and media vehicles lined her street in front of her bungalow. Some two dozen in all, but the number grew along with the requests for interviews. All the networks wanted Cora to appear on breakfast and prime-time news shows. Their enquiries were handled by advisors from the volunteer group, one of them a retired news assignment editor.

"Cora's not making any more statements today, folks," he said. "The next media briefing might be tomorrow, if the FBI has any updates."

Though Cora's number was not listed, some news organizations managed to obtain it. Those that tried to call in to Cora were deflected by the FBI, except for one reporter outside, standing among the pack.

She didn't call Cora.

Inside the house, Jack Gannon's cell phone rang.

"Gannon."

"Jack, this is Henrietta Chong with WPA's Phoenix bureau. Melody Lyon in New York gave me your number and told me to call."

"Did she?"

"I am so sorry about what's happened to your niece. I hope she comes home safe."

"We all do."

"I hate doing this, but you're going in the story. AP and Reuters are making reference to you being Cora's brother. We have to do the same."

"I figured."

"Jack, New York wants me to interview Cora. Can you help me with that?" Then she clarified, "Melody wants me to talk to her, exclusively."

After a long pause, Gannon told Henrietta he would have to call her back. Hanging up, he looked across the room at Cora resting on the sofa and approached her with the request. After considering it, she said, "Just two minutes over the phone."

At that moment Hackett materialized, eyeing Gannon.

"Two minutes with whom and for what?"

"A short interview with the WPA," Gannon said.

Hackett weighed it. "As long as she only repeats what she said earlier. I'll be right here, listening."

Gannon called Henrietta Chong on his phone, then passed it to Cora. As he watched and listened, ambiguity gnawed at him. He knew he was exploiting his sister. But he rationalized it. After all this time, she'd called him. Some twenty-two years had passed between them. There was so much he didn't know about her and it had kept him ambivalent toward her, torn over whether he should be consoling her or questioning her account of what was really at work with Tilly's kidnapping.

Why had Cora asked him if she was being punished for past sins? What did she mean?

I knew dealers.

What had happened in her past? Was this somehow linked?

At that moment an agent rose from the worktable where

he had been listening to his cell phone while working on a laptop. His face taut, he tapped Hackett's shoulder.

"We just got something."

12

Thick dried mud covered all but the first two numbers of the license plate on the back of the truck.

Vanita Solaniz could not read the rest of it but was convinced the pickup that had wheeled into the Burger King parking lot was the one the FBI was looking for: a metallic red, 2009 Ford F-150 with a regular cab.

As an assistant manager at Clear Canyon Auto Parts, Vanita knew cars, trucks and vans. A few hours ago, she and her customers at the shop halted their business to watch the TV above the counter when the news broke about the little girl who was kidnapped by a drug cartel from her home in Mesa Mirage.

"My lord, that just breaks your heart, doesn't it?" she said.

One old-timer shifted the toothpick in the corner of his mouth, then said, "A damn shame. I got a granddaughter that age."

For the rest of the afternoon, with every commercial break, the TV news repeated details on the case and the F-150. Vanita watched when she could, hoping for a good ending to the story. Nothing new had happened when her shift ended and she headed for her apartment near Escalente Park.

Vanita's welder boyfriend was out of town. They had

no food in the house, so for supper she'd decided to treat herself to her favorite: onion rings and a shake at Burger King. After getting her order at the drive-through, she parked her car in a shady corner of the lot, dropped the windows and caught a sweet breeze.

That's when the Ford pickup rolled into the spot in front of her.

Hey, it's a metallic red 150, like the one on the news, Vanita thought, munching on her rings. From the tailgate's style she knew it was a 2009. The driver got out, a man wearing a ball cap and sunglasses. His passenger was a girl who looked about ten or eleven. She wore a sun hat and sunglasses. The man took her hand and they entered the restaurant.

An icy feeling shot through Vanita.

She looked at the Arizona plate, making out the first two numbers.

Five, then seven.

Vanita stopped eating.

She clawed through her bag for the blank order form where she'd jotted the pickup's plate from the news.

Oh my God.

Vanita grabbed her cell phone, called 911 and reported the details to the Tempe police, repeating her location. "It's them! Send somebody! It's on East University."

The Tempe police dispatcher kept her on the line while she alerted the FBI. A moment later the dispatcher told Vanita, "Police are on the way. Keep your eyes on the vehicle, your line open and *do not move*."

Hackett drove and Bonnie Larson relayed information over the phone to a Tempe police detective who'd turned up his radio.

"Tempe's on the line with the caller now," Larson said. "The vehicle description fits Lyle Galviera's pickup."

"And the man and the girl?"

"They match the general description of Tilly and Galviera."

As they wove through traffic, Hackett shook his head, uncertain what to make of this break. *If it was Galviera, what was he doing with Tilly? Had the kidnappers released her?*

"Advise Tempe not to send any marked units into the area," he said.

"They're only sending unmarked cars, no lights, no sirens."

"We don't want to lose them."

"Tempe's dispatching marked units to set up a one-block perimeter to stop the suspect vehicle if he flees."

In Mesa Mirage, Cora waited in agony.

The investigators who'd stayed behind with her had few updates.

It was torture, as it had been watching Hackett and Larson scrambling from her home a few minutes ago when she'd begged them to tell her what was happening before they'd left.

"We have a lead on a truck that looks like Lyle's," Hackett had said.

"Take me with you!"

"No, we don't know what to expect. We urge you to stay here." Cora turned to Gannon as Hackett added, "I can't prevent you or your brother from leaving your home. You're not under arrest, but you could jeopardize things. That's why I'm not giving you details on the location. It's for your own safety."

"All right." Gannon nodded and the FBI agents left.

"But, Jack," Cora pleaded, "one of us should be there."

"Hang on. I'll try to find out where it is."

Gannon started to call Henrietta Chong when his cell phone rang.

"Jack, this is Henrietta, there seems to be a lot of

activity coming out of the house and the TV guys listening to police scanners say that something's going on in Tempe but police are being cryptic on the air."

Gannon turned away and kept his voice low.

"Can you get an address from them for me, Henrietta? I'll fill you in."

When she called back with the address, Gannon asked Cora for the keys to her car.

Now, as Gannon drove alone in Cora's Pontiac Vibe, the GPS system indicated he was about two blocks from the Burger King. His phone rang. It was Chong, about six blocks behind him with a WPA photographer.

"Jack, the whole pack is headed to this place. What's going on?"

"They may have found Lyle Galviera's truck."

The knot in Vanita's stomach was tightening.

It was twenty-five, maybe thirty minutes since she'd called police. Every minute or so, the 911 dispatcher asked for an update.

"The truck still hasn't moved," Vanita said.

"Thank you."

But Vanita worried. Were police here? If they were, they did a good job of keeping invisible. What if the man and girl had slipped out of the restaurant? What if they got away?

Vanita couldn't stand it any longer.

With her cell phone pressed to her ear, she left her car and entered the busy outlet. She threaded through the dining room, unable to find them, concern mounting until she spotted them in a corner booth.

"I see them," Vanita told the dispatcher. "They're done eating and getting ready to leave by the door near their truck. You have to do something fast!"

The dispatcher relayed Vanita's alert to Phil Zern, the Tempe police sergeant in charge. Plainclothes detectives were positioned in the lot, some in cars, some on foot. There was no time for SWAT to set up and too many people around.

This would be a rapid takedown.

"Everyone on position, stand by," Zern said, "on my order."

A few seconds later, as the man and girl neared their truck, a siren yelped and an unmarked police car, dash light and wigwag grill lights flashing, roared from nowhere to within inches of the truck, boxing it in.

At the same time, detectives, guns drawn and badges displayed, approached the man while a voice over a loudspeaker shouted orders.

"Police! Get down on the ground—now!"

"Why?" The startled man put his hands up and looked to the girl. Two female detectives had grabbed her and were pulling her away.

"Daddyyy!"

The man was handcuffed.

"What the hell are you doing? What's going on?"

Hackett and Larson, watching from the far end of the lot, trotted to the scene. Beyond them, news crews scrambled to record it. Some people in the restaurant began taking pictures with their camera phones. A few hurried to the parking lot, where a crowd gathered. Vanita introduced herself to a detective who told her to wait near his car.

Gannon arrived and approached the scene.

Afraid and confused, the little girl was placed in the front seat of a police car. Hackett and Larson showed their ID, then compared her to the photo of Tilly Martin. *Not even close,* Hackett thought.

"What's your name, sweetheart?" Larson asked.

"Melissa Hanley," she said through tears. "Are we in trouble?"

A few yards away, Melissa's father, Doug Hanley, demanded to know why he was arrested. A detective wiped the mud from his plate.

This was not Lyle Galviera's pickup truck.

It took Tempe Police and the FBI over half an hour to sort out and confirm that Doug Hanley was Melissa Hanley's father and that they lived in Kingman, where Hanley was a carpenter and Melissa's mother, Rachel, was a bank teller. Doug and Melissa had driven down to Tempe to get Rachel, who was visiting her mother, Melissa's grandma.

Police apologized to Hanley for the alarm and inconvenience caused by the arrest but stressed that under the circumstances it was the right call. Zern asked Hanley to consider what he would want police to do if Melissa were taken under the same circumstances as Tilly Martin.

Gannon called Cora and told her what had happened.

Night was falling when he returned to his sister's house.

In the wake of the takedown in Tempe, the FBI hotline continued receiving tips, most of them vague. A funereal air enveloped Cora's home as the darkness outside deepened.

She'd refused food, sedatives, even rest.

Sitting alone, she stared at photos of Tilly. Between news reports and talking with the WPA, Gannon watched Cora, studying her anguish as time swept by. Seeing her suffering had inexplicably resurrected the pain he'd shouldered when their parents were killed.

He'd gone to the crash site.

He'd arranged the funeral.

He'd shaken with rage against Cora because their parents had died looking for her. They'd died not knowing anything about her life since the night she'd run off and destroyed their family. And there she was, flipping through memories of the life she'd created away from the family she'd devastated.

There she was, subjecting him to it.

He went to her.

"I have to know," he said.

"Know what?"

"Why didn't you come home? Mom and Dad died searching for you. They never knew they had a granddaughter. Why didn't you come home?"

She met his stare with a vulnerability that bordered on near defeat.

"Please, Jack, don't push me on this now."

"I deserve to know."

"I can't tell you. I can't. Stop asking me. This is not about me, Jack. You have to help me find Tilly."

Gannon said nothing as one of the TV news reports pierced the tension. A commentator on Tilly's case observed how most kidnappings involving cartels are revenge actions.

"I'm afraid to say but they almost always end horribly."

Later that night about an hour after Cora fell asleep, she woke.

It was precisely the same time the kidnappers had entered her home. Realizing it had now been nearly twenty hours since Tilly was taken, Cora was overwhelmed with fear and released a long, anguished scream.

"Tillyyy!"

Startled from sleep in the sofa chair where he sprawled, Gannon was haunted by how his sister's wail was identical to the one he'd heard in the morgue in Juarez.

13

The whine of the meat saw's electric blade filled the night air.

Rising from the Golden Cut Processing Plant, it echoed over the forgotten piece of industrial wasteland occupied by the plant, the Coin-O-Clean Car Wash, Odin Tool & Die and the Sweet Times Motel.

Several years back, the Sweet Times had been a favorite of truckers. Sitting across from the Golden Cut, the motel had been lovingly cared for by the original owners, a retired Navy cook and his wife.

It had offered guests a small restaurant, and flower gardens everywhere.

But the restaurant was gone and the little gardens died long ago, leaving dirt patches that encircled the property like a disease. Chipped paint ravaged the motel's exterior walls. Nearly half of the doors were fractured from being kicked in and the neon sign only lit the word *Time*, as if it had run out on a dream. The motel, now a refuge for down-and-out hookers, crackheads and outcasts, was managed by an embittered alcoholic with green teeth, who told every guest, "I don't give a rat's A what you do in there—it's sixty bucks cash for every twenty-four hours up front."

Several beer cans bobbed in the pool's brown water,

near the shallow end and Unit 28. This was a deluxe suite of adjoining rooms. Inside, the lights had been dimmed. The two male guests were surfing TV channels, monitoring news reports on the kidnapping of Tilly Martin. The screen's glow flickered on their faces and the room.

An assortment of empty take-out food containers and a bag of fruit covered the small table. The desk near it had an array of prepaid cell phones. The phones would be used for one call then destroyed.

Two police uniforms hung in the room's closet, ready for use. Under one bed, there were two AK-47 assault rifles and four Glock-20 semiautomatic pistols. At the edge of one of the two beds, there were three portable digital police scanners. Their volumes were low but the men were listening. They understood the codes.

Now, as they watched the TV news reports, their concern continued to grow. It seemed all of Phoenix was looking for Tilly.

"You did not answer me, Ruiz. What do we do now?" Alfredo, the younger man, asked in Spanish. "The bitch disobeyed the order and went to police. Now she's got the damn FBI involved!"

As with Alfredo's other questions, Ruiz's response was silence.

Until now, Ruiz had hidden his anger over the situation. This time, he reached for his knife. The glint of its blade reflected in the TV light as he cut into a large apple. He placed the first slice carefully into his mouth and chewed slowly.

Chewing helped Ruiz think.

He knew Alfredo was less experienced in these matters and therefore worried. Let him ramble with his questions.

"So what are we going to do, Ruiz?" Alfredo opened a soda. "In Mexico, a case like this is business. People don't trust police. They don't go to police."

"Alfredo—" Ruiz pointed the knife at him "—you

knew this one would be different, or did you forget that after you took your extra advance payment."

"Yes, but she went to police."

"It was to be expected."

"So what do we do? This creates a problem for us, for the operation. It is our job to set up the arrival of the *sicario,* to make sure everything goes smoothly for him. And now— " Alfredo thrust his finger at the screen as the clip of Cora's press conference plea and photographs replayed. Again, the entire screen filled with the artist's sketch of one of the suspects—the one resembling Ruiz. "And now your face is shown over and over for all of America and the world to see, Ruiz!"

Ruiz stared at the sketch. Once more he listened to the details about his description and his scar. He scratched his growth under his chin. He had not shaved.

"Ruiz, you and I know they will check your scar with the databanks and sooner or later they will know who we are. We have to do something."

Ruiz cut another piece of the apple and chewed.

"I think we should pull out of the operation," Alfredo said.

"No," Ruiz said. "We've not been ordered to abort. We've heard nothing, which means we continue."

"Continue? And do what? Where is Galviera? We have nothing set up for the *sicario.* We're not even close. They told me you were the best. I don't think so. Tell me, what is your next move?"

Ruiz turned to Alfredo. He'd insulted Ruiz's pride.

Ruiz was seething. His anger was directed at Cora, but Alfredo's fretting fueled it. Now, watching Cora, over and over, pleading to the camera while standing next to a sketch of his face, a good sketch, Ruiz grew furious.

All they'd asked was that she find Galviera so they could retrieve the money. That was all. The kidnapping was their leverage, their insurance that Cora would act quickly.

But does she find him?

No, she goes to the FBI. This woman did not know her place. She did not know the price she was going to pay for her disrespect.

"Ruiz, what are we going to do?"

The muscles along Ruiz's jawline pulsed as he turned to the open door and Tilly Martin, bound and gagged on the bed in the next room.

14

Tilly sat upright.

The one with the knife was approaching her room.

What was he going to do?

Tilly tried to keep calm but fear pulled her down, the way Lenny Griffin had held her underwater that day at swim class.

She had thought she would drown.

She'd struggled but couldn't breathe. Heart slamming against her chest, lungs bursting, alarm screaming in her ears, she kicked, scratched and gouged Lenny until she broke free.

All the jerk did was laugh.

But his smile had vanished after Tilly landed a swift punch on his face. She was glad that she'd retaliated, giving him a shiner and a guarantee that she would always fight back.

But Lenny Griffin was a stupid twelve-year-old boy.

The monster in her doorway now was a grown man with a knife, a creep who was obviously a fake cop. Because real police officers, like Deputy Sheriff Taylor, who had visited her school, didn't do the things this creep and his friend, Creep Number Two, were doing. Real police didn't take kids from their homes at night and stuff them in suitcases.

What were they going to do to her now?

Creep Number One, the one called Ruiz, just stood there, leaning on the door frame, cutting into that apple with his big knife, looking at her and chewing.

Tilly hated them.

Ruiz and Creep Number Two, the one called Alfredo, had been watching their TV and arguing for a long time. Then they stopped. Now Ruiz was just standing there, looking at her.

She was scared.

What were they going to do to her?

Her mouth was gagged, her teeth clamped on a twisted bandanna tied behind her head. Her hands were bound with duct tape. Her eyes filled with tears as she scanned the room.

That big black suitcase was in the closet.

Her coffin.

Please don't put me in there again.

It was so dark in there. When they'd taken her from her mom, they'd scrunched her in the suitcase. She could feel them lift her into the trunk of a car. Then they drove.

She was trapped in a nightmare.

Seeing her mom tied up in the kitchen was horrifying. Tilly felt so helpless. All she could do was say her mother's favorite prayer from church over and over.

Hail Mary, full of grace…pray for us sinners, now and at the hour of our death…

Tilly didn't know where they were driving or for how long. But when they stopped, they lifted the suitcase, with her in it, from the trunk, rolled it inside and let her out here, in this scuzzy place.

A hotel, she guessed.

The place smelled like cigarettes and BO. The toilet never stopped hissing. The air conditioner hardly worked. She didn't know where they were. The creeps had removed the telephone and phone book. They left the TV on a kids' channel with cartoons for babies and kept the sound low. She tried to sleep but it took hours for the aching in her legs, shoulder and neck to go away.

They gave her teen magazines, pizza, chips, chocolate bars, cookies, soda and stuff. They didn't hurt her or touch her or yell at her or anything. They kept her tied up and sometimes they asked her about Lyle Galviera, her mom's boss, if she knew where he was.

As if she would know.

Tilly just shook her head, which made her chain jingle a bit.

For, in addition to gagging her and binding her hands, they'd put a metal clamp on her ankle. They secured it to a long dog chain and locked it to some steel pipes, so she could get up and go to the bathroom and stuff.

The chain clinked a little now as she trembled under Ruiz's gaze.

Just then, sound from the creeps' TV in the other room spilled into her room. Her heart swelled. Oh my God, that was her mother on TV!

"Sweetheart, if you can see me or hear my voice, I love you. We're doing everything to bring you home safely...."

It filled her with hope, like when Lenny's grasp on her had loosened.

I hear you and I love you, Mommy!

Ruiz kept his attention locked on Tilly and ordered Alfredo in Spanish to shut the TV off. Then he cut the last piece from his apple and took his time chewing it before tossing the core in the overflowing trash can in the corner.

Ruiz stood at the door, his tongue methodically probing his teeth for the apple remnants. Then he carefully wiped the serrated blade clean against his jeans and began tapping it against the palm of his hand.

"It appears your mother has disobeyed my order."

His voice sounded friendly, but Tilly knew it was

phony, because he was breathing hard. Under that fake nice voice, he was pissed.

Tilly was not fooled.

The man was holding a knife.

He just stood there, tapping it in his hand, staring at her for the longest time as if watching some plan play out in his mind. Then he went to the curtains and using his knife, parted them slightly to look at the Golden Cut Processing Plant across the street, listening to the meat saw echoing in the night.

Then he turned to Tilly.

He touched the tip of the blade in his palm.

He'd reached a decision.

"Remember, it was your mother who forced us to take this next step. For the action we're about to take, I will beg your forgiveness."

Tilly didn't understand. Then Ruiz said, "Alfredo, come in here. I am going to need your help."

The chain chinked as Tilly tensed.

"Your mother does not appreciate who she is dealing with. We will give her a lesson she will never forget."

DAY 2

15

The flowers were yellow.

There were almost two dozen daffodils, carnations and roses arranged in a yellow ceramic vase with a yellow ribbon and a card for Cora Martin.

The vase was belted to the front passenger seat of the cab that had pulled up this morning to the tangle of police and news vehicles outside Cora's house.

Since her televised appeal yesterday, people from across the city had brought her balloons, stuffed toys and notes of support. After passing their gifts to police at the line, most well-wishers spoke to the media, offering their teary consolation for Cora.

The cabdriver who'd delivered the yellow bouquet stopped to talk to insistent reporters after he'd handed the vase over the tape to a sheriff's deputy. *"Sir, just a few words please, sir!"* The deputy gave the vase a quick inspection before taking it around the back to investigators who were checking each item.

The female Phoenix police officer who'd accepted the flowers passed a wand over the vase then delicately probed the stems with latex-gloved fingers. A detection dog from the K-9 unit sniffed the bouquet before the flowers were taken inside. The FBI agent who'd received them started to set them in the living room with the other items but reconsidered.

She saw Cora on the sofa, hands cupped around a mug of coffee. Her hair was pulled back and her sleep-deprived eyes brimmed with sadness as if she were gazing into an endless pit.

"These look pretty, don't you think, Cora?"

The agent glanced at Gannon, who was standing nearby, checking his cell phone messages, then she set the vase on the coffee table. The fragrance generated a weak smile from Cora.

"All yellow," the agent said, "for hope."

But Cora feared she was running out of hope. Aside from last night's false alarm at the Burger King in Tempe, the FBI had received no strong leads on Tilly.

Where was she? Why hadn't Lyle called? Where was he?

And she'd heard nothing from the kidnappers.

The alarm ringing at the back of Cora's mind grew louder, filling her with doubt. Had she been wrong to go to the police? The way she'd been wrong about so much in her life, running away from her family and making so many mistakes. But that was the past. She'd left it behind and had been rebuilding her life, piece by piece.

Why was this happening?

Was it somehow tied to the unforgivable act she'd committed all those years ago? *Stop.* It made no sense to think like that because it had nothing to do with Tilly's kidnapping.

But what if karmic forces were at work?

Guilt began to tighten its grip on her.

"Are you going to open it?"

The agent indicated the envelope that Cora still held in her hand. She opened it to a simple white card, with an embossed garden scene. She unfolded it, expecting, as with the other cards, an expression of sympathy or something encouraging.

She stopped breathing when she read:

You called police. You pay the price. Remove the flowers and look in the water. Find GALVIERA or more will come!!!

Cora couldn't move.

"Is something wrong?" Gannon had been watching her.

Cora's hands trembled as carefully she lifted the flowers from the water. She was afraid to look but forced herself to pick up the vase, tilt it and slowly peer into the water.

Shock hit her like a sledgehammer to the chest.

Her stomach lurched as she felt the earth move under her.

"What is it?" Gannon said.

"Are you all right?" the agent asked.

Cora dropped the vase. It shattered on the coffee table.

"Oh Christ!" said the agent, incredulous, staring at the two white orbs that had fallen from it to the floor. They looked like small boiled eggs. Each had swirls of pink fleshy strands and blue irises.

Eyes.

"My baby!!!"

Cora released a raw heart-stopping shriek and began flailing at the air.

"Jesus!" Gannon rushed to her.

After reading the note without touching it, Hackett seized a radio and called to officers outside in the front yard.

"Eight-sixty. Who made the last delivery? The yellow flowers in a yellow vase, who brought that?"

"Seven-O-one. Cabdriver with Flying Eagle. He's out front talking to the press."

"Grab him!"

"Say again eight-sixty?"

Cora's screams had interfered with Hackett's transmission.

"Grab him now! Keep it low key and bring him around back!"

Cora screamed and screamed until she passed out.

Eventually, Gannon and the others got Cora to her bedroom.

Paramedics were called to tend to her while FBI crime scene experts cleared the living room and began investigating the note, pieces of the vase and its grisly contents.

Outside, at the back of the house, Hackett and Larson went at Velmar Kelp, the taxi driver who'd delivered the flowers.

"Like I told you, I just delivered them," Kelp repeated. "I stopped for coffee at Zeke's Diner on the west side, at Central and Eighty-Second Avenue and this guy came up to me, all busted up about the missing girl and whatnot and gives me two hundred bucks to deliver them," Kelp said. "What's going on?"

"It looks like you're involved in the kidnapping, Velmar."

"What? You're crazy."

"A shit storm is about to come down on you so you'd better give us the truth now."

"I just delivered the flowers for some guy on the street, I swear!"

"Did this guy have the address?"

"No. I got it from my dispatcher, from First Eagle bringing fares to the house here, you know, news people. And the *Republic* story today gives the street and whatnot."

The FBI refused to let up.

Did Kelp get the guy's name, a card, a phone number? What did he look like? Any scars? Tattoos? What about his clothing? The way he spoke? Show us the cash he gave you. Were there witnesses? Did he ask for a receipt? Was anyone else with him? Did he get into a vehicle?

Their questioning grew into an unyielding interrogation until they convinced Kelp to ride with them to Zeke's Diner where he'd received the flowers. Supported by Phoenix detectives, FBI agents canvassed the area and searched for security cameras, all while pressing Kelp for more details.

They demanded he volunteer his fingerprints.

At Cora's house, the FBI evidence team processed the vase and note for latent prints. It was when they undertook the gruesome task of examining the eyes that their interest deepened. Something ran counter to the assumption. Something was different. They needed to conduct more tests but one of the forensic experts said: "These are characteristic of *Sus scrofa,* recently isolated."

It took a sedative and several hours to calm Cora.

By the time she woke, Hackett had returned and was with Gannon and a few other people in her room. Taking stock of their faces, Cora braced for the worst.

Tilly was dead.

"Cora," Gannon started.

She stifled a guttural moan.

"It's not what you think," he said.

"The eyes are not human," Hackett said.

She blinked in confusion.

"They were removed from a dead pig. They're pigs' eyes."

"Pigs' eyes?"

"They can't belong to Tilly, or anyone else," Hackett said.

Overcome with relief and fear, Cora buried her face in her hands.

"They just wanted to pressure you, send a message," Hackett said.

"To prove they're evil fucking bastards?"

"Cora," Hackett said, "we still need to collect your fingerprints."

She stared at him.

"My fingerprints? But you already have Tilly's. Why do you need mine? How will my fingerprints bring Tilly back?"

"We have to process the prints of everyone who touched the vase, the card and other things," Hackett said. "We talked about why we needed your prints at the outset when ERT started their work."

She remembered but said nothing.

Hackett then indicated the fingerprint analyst next to him with a laptop.

"We've got an electronic scanner. No ink, no mess. It won't take long."

Cora hesitated and Gannon tried to help the situation.

"I gave mine. Cora, it's routine."

"To create elimination prints," Hackett said. "To help isolate prints that should not be present."

Cora still hesitated.

Hackett and Gannon exchanged glances.

"Is there some reason you're reluctant?" Hackett asked. "We want you to volunteer your prints but we can get a warrant for them, if we have to."

"No," she said. "I'll give them."

"Good," Hackett said.

The technician set things up on her kitchen table, positioning Cora in a chair. But when she placed her fingers on the glass platen, raw, exposed, her mind thundered with a memory and her fingers trembled. "I'm going to need you to relax," the analyst said.

"Sorry, I'm still a bit jittery from everything."

"I understand."

"Maybe if I took a hot shower, it might help me relax."

The tech nodded and she took her hand away from the scanner.

Cora was coming apart.

In the shower, she tried in vain to hide from everything, contending with her guilty heart. Needles of hot water stung her, like the sting of mistrust she felt whenever Jack looked at her.

Steam clouds rose around her and carried her back to the point when her life first began to darken. Cora was sixteen and her friend Shawna had convinced her to go to a party downtown.

"There's going to be older college guys there."

Cora had never done anything wild like that in her life.

"Time for you to bust out, girl," Shawna told her.

At the party, the people were older. Way older. There was talk that some were ex-cons on parole. Cora was uneasy and begged Shawna to leave. But Shawna was having fun and kept passing Cora these fruit drinks the older guys kept making.

Cora started feeling woozy.

Someone took her into a bedroom, told her to lie down...don't worry you'll be fine...relax...the walls started spinning...the bed was flying and she felt someone undressing her...she couldn't resist...couldn't move... the first man stood over her, climbed on top of her...when he finished another man followed him then another as she faded into oblivion...

Cora didn't know how she got home that night.

Did someone look in her wallet for her address and drive her?

When Cora woke and realized what had happened to her, she climbed into the shower and scrubbed herself raw. She wanted to peel off her skin.

She wanted to kill herself.

How could she have been so stupid?

Shawna never knew. She'd left the party earlier, thinking Cora had left without her. Cora never told anyone what had happened. Not Shawna, not her mother, not anyone.

She was too ashamed.

She wanted to apologize to her parents, wanted to make herself invisible. She wanted to die.

In the time that followed, Cora thought she could handle it, but she couldn't. She'd turned to drugs. It was the only way she could survive. Her mother and father tried to get through to her, tried to help her.

"What's wrong with you, Cora?" Her mother sensed something had happened. "You've changed. Tell me, what's wrong?"

Cora was so ashamed she could never bring herself to talk about it and soon grew angry at her mother's concern, her prodding. It led to one argument after another, until the last one before she left home at seventeen.

With Rake.

A nineteen-year-old heroin addict who'd convinced her that her destiny was to live with him and his friends in a drug-induced splendor by the sea in California. She was so stupid. After Rake vanished, there were other addicts. For years she drifted in a drug-addled haze.

Then came that night, that horrible rainy night in California.

She'd struggled to blot it out of her mind, to never think of it, or all the events that came later that had cast her into a pit so dark she thought she would not survive. It was while she was lost in the darkness that she'd become pregnant with Tilly.

At that time Cora never realized that Tilly was her tiny point of light. She was too terrified. She didn't know what to do. She couldn't go home. Ever. She was ashamed. She was scared. She went to a clinic.

But she couldn't go through with it.

She went to a church and prayed and soon it dawned on her that this was her miracle. This was her reason to start over. She'd been given a second chance with this baby.

This new life.

But it always came back to that awful night in San Francisco.

The incident was always there. Close to the surface, breaking into her thoughts like flashes of lightning.

Don't think about it.

The blood.

Stop.

So much blood.

Stop.

Blood on her hands.

Now she was being punished for the sin she'd committed that night.

Cora was so afraid she couldn't breathe.

Forgive me.

Standing in the shower Cora stared at her hands.

Were they still red with blood?

Overcome, she fell against the shower wall and slid to the floor, lost in a whirlwind of confusion.

She could not let anyone find out about that night in San Francisco. She had to protect Tilly.

How did this happen?

Where was Lyle? How could he do this?

She could not survive without Tilly.

16

Lyle Galviera swallowed hard.

This was the last one. It totaled $1,153,280.

All bound with elastic bands in brick-sized bundles of tens and twenties and stuffed into six nylon gym bags.

He was careful to keep his back to the security camera as he zipped the last bag closed. He set it with the others in the self-storage unit, a corrugated metal five-by-five space he'd rented from JBD Mini-Storage at the edge of Phoenix. He snapped the steel lock, tucked the key in his boot and exhaled.

*The unit was air-conditioned but Galviera was sweating because the plan, this critical plan, had gone to hell when someone had kidnapped Tilly.

Why? She had nothing to do with anything.

Why, goddamn it? Goddamn it. God-fucking-damn it.

Dragging the back of his shaking hand across his dry mouth, he forced himself to keep cool. He had to fix this. All right, what could he do right now?

Stick to the plan.

It was all he had.

Adjusting his ball cap and dark glasses, he returned to JBD's security office. When the acne-faced kid at the counter saw him, he stopped bobbing his head, tugged at his earphones and ceased playing a game on his cell phone.

"I forgot to give you some of our data, Mister..." The kid had to consult the clipboard with Galviera's information. Galviera had rented the self-storage unit moments ago for fifty a month using a counterfeit driver's license. "Sorry, Mr. Pilsner, here you go."

Galviera accepted the brochure.

"And sorry, dude...I mean, sir...I also need you to sign the release that you understand our rules."

Galviera glanced at the sheet and took up the pen.

"Only you have 24-7 access to your unit at JBD," the kid said, "unless you give someone else your gate code, your keys and unit number. JBD has no access to your unit. As the tenant, you're responsible for your unit and anyone you give your information to."

"Fine." Galviera signed. "Thanks."

His knees nearly buckled walking to his battered Grand Cherokee. He had just finished securing $5.1 million of drug cartel cash in several locations. Before Tilly was kidnapped he was supposed to meet his cartel people to finalize his share of his biggest and last deal.

The kidnapping changed everything.

Am I caught between two cartels?

Somehow Galviera's people had to fix this. They had to help find Tilly.

Alive.

But things kept changing so goddamned much.

If this didn't go down right, he was a dead man.

As he drove, he tried to think.

Today was Tuesday, or was it Wednesday? He wasn't sure. Last Friday, according to the original plan, he was to fly from Phoenix to California, ostensibly for Quick Draw company business. No one knew the truth: that he was really flying to L.A. for his last deal with his cartel partners.

But before boarding his flight in Phoenix, Galviera,

as instructed, went to a pay phone, deposited a stream of coins, called a temporary number and checked in with Octavio, his chief cartel associate.

"The situation has changed," Octavio had said. "We've learned that a competitor is now disputing ownership of our routes and demanding payment."

"What? What do you mean?"

"You are likely being followed."

"Followed? Jesus Christ! You said there'd be no complications!"

"Listen to us."

"No, *you* listen. I'm the one holding the goddamned money. I'm the target. You guaranteed no complications. I did not sign on for this bullshit. What do I do now?"

"You shut up. You listen. And you live."

Galviera listened.

"We must take very specific action. We've made arrangements. Abandon your flight to L.A. and drive to San Diego immediately. On the way, stop at a public phone and call the number I give you, at the time I give you. Tell no one. Before you leave, get rid of your cell phone."

Galviera got to his pickup truck and headed alone for California. Octavio had advised him to stop in Yuma, where a "friend of ours" had exchanged Galviera's F-150 for a Grand Cherokee, gave him paperwork for it and counterfeit ID.

"In San Diego, collect the cash. All of it," Octavio said.

"All of it?"

"All of it. Then drive back to Phoenix. Break up the total and secure it in the locations we'll provide. Then you will meet us in the Phoenix area at the specified address on the specified date and time we will give you. Do not deviate from our instructions."

Galviera followed them to the letter.

Making the six-hour drive across California and

Arizona loaded with over five million in cash was unnerving, but it went OK. It was after he'd returned to Phoenix and was in the process of storing the money that the news broke of Tilly's kidnapping and the link to him.

Who was behind it?

How did they know Cora worked for him? How did they know how to find Cora's home? How did they know she had a daughter? Christ, they'd better not hurt her. How did everything turn to shit?

Now, as he drove to the meeting place, the knot in his gut tightened.

Galviera saw himself in the mirror, gaunt and looking like something that should be flushed. How had his life come to this? Hell, he sponsored three Little League ball teams. He'd worked hard for his piece of the American dream.

Now he could lose it all.

His father, a bus driver, had died, leaving his mother to support him by cleaning offices before she died from a heart attack. Galviera dropped out of college to work full-time as a bike-riding courier. Then he got a truck and started his own business delivering packages by day, pizzas at night. He built it into a major regional courier company but then married a nutcase, who preferred ferrets to children.

When she caught him cheating with an office worker, she got an asshole lawyer and tried to steal his company. It forced Galviera to hide assets, get creative with numbers. He kept his company, but the battle left him poorer and bitter.

He vowed to never get married again.

The stress of his divorce led to his gambling addiction, which he'd kept hidden. It was his lame bid to try to recoup some of what he lost in his divorce settlement. He ran up heavy gambling debts but had always cleared them.

Along the way he'd hired Cora from an agency. She

was pretty, but unlike most of the empty-headed agency bimbos, she had brains and a mature attitude.

He liked her. Really liked her.

She'd had a hard life but was a strong, independent single mother. He liked being with her and he liked Tilly. She was a smart, sharp kid. He liked having them in his life.

They made him feel whole.

Sometimes he and Cora talked about marriage but he was gun-shy.

"Not sure I'm ready to go down that road again," he'd always tell her.

Around the time the economy tanked, Galviera made some bad investments, just when company bills were mounting. He was facing an overdue $1.9-million payment. If he couldn't make it, he'd lose Quick Draw. He kept negotiating extensions but time was running out.

Quietly, he asked around for financial help.

His out-of-state bookie knew a guy, who knew a guy who knew people who were interested in an arrangement that could help him.

A meeting was set up in a hotel in Tijuana.

The investors wanted a very confidential off-the-books arrangement to have Galviera's company deliver religious items made in convents and monasteries in Mexico to select addresses in the U.S.

The deal would involve special codes, contacts and payments. In a short time, it would earn Galviera a lot of cash. The beauty of the plan was that Galviera's clients would handle everything—customs and inspections, any "difficulties" that might arise.

The truth: he was dealing with a drug cartel.

To agree meant a pact with the devil.

They smiled and assured him there would be no complications. They assured him they would take care of all risk. They assured him that with sufficient notice, he could end the arrangement for any reason at any time.

In desperation, Galviera took the deal.

And it went well.

The shipments flowed, and he collected and secured cash payments according to the instructions he was given. For his work, his first earnings totaled $976,000. A second payment a month later, was $1,034,000. The next was going to be just over two million dollars. All of it tax free. With the two million to come, Galviera would clear his debt, end his partnership with the cartel and focus on his company.

That was his plan before Tilly was kidnapped.

He'd never expected this to happen.

There were to be no complications.

Goddamn it. God-fucking-damn it.

Now, as he adjusted his grip on the wheel while pulling up to the Broken Horses Bar, he checked the time. Fifteen minutes to five. Octavio and his partner specified meeting here at five.

The building's chugging air conditioner dripped water over a fractured metal door that creaked when Galviera entered. He kept his dark glasses on, letting his eyes adjust to the lack of light while he dealt with the stench of stale beer and hopelessness.

A large TV on mute loomed over the wooden U-shaped bar where several pathetic cases were perched. There were a few wooden chairs and tables on the main floor, while along the wall, high-backed booths offered privacy.

Galviera ordered a beer at the bar and carried it to the booth, where he took a long pull and did his best to keep himself from shaking.

Christ, the TV was tuned to FOX. They were showing his face as a "person of interest," up there for the whole goddamned world to see.

He lowered his head.

Adrenaline surged through him.

He had to do something.

But what? What could he do? If he went to the police

now, while sitting on five million in cartel money, he was a dead man.

That would seal Tilly's fate.

Be calm. Stay cool. He had to fix this.

Stick to the plan. That was all he could do.

He glanced at the time. Damn. It was flying. Now it was fifteen minutes after the hour and no sign of Octavio.

What happened to them? They were never late.

Galviera took another pull of his beer.

His hands were shaking. He was a mess. He needed those guys to walk through that door so they could take care of the money, so he could give them their share and fix this.

They could deal with the people who had Tilly.

It had to be their competition, whoever that was.

I'm trapped between two cartels.

Octavio could give them their cut, convince them to release Tilly unhurt on the street or something—like that other kid, a few years back in Houston. Just let her go, no questions asked.

Everything would be settled.

It was now thirty minutes after the hour.

As Galviera eyed the clock over the bar, his Adam's apple rose and fell with each passing minute. Thirty-five minutes after the hour, forty, forty-five.

No sign of Octavio and his partner.

At the top of the hour, the news came on. A few stories in, Tilly's face appeared on the screen.

Staring at Galviera, imploring him to do something as the minutes ticked down.

17

Mesa Mirage, Phoenix, Arizona

The incident with the eyeballs was horrifying.

Tension in Cora's home mounted as the investigators hammered away at the case. Watching her go to pieces as she reckoned with the rising stakes in her daughter's kidnapping, Gannon struggled with the questions that were plaguing him.

Who was Cora?

Was she just his sister, with a niece he'd never met— and might never see? Or an ex-drug addict with secrets, caught in a deal gone wrong?

At times he found himself looking upon her as the detached journalist, trying to determine what was true. Was Cora a victim in this thing, or a player? Again he came back to her reference to "karma," which made him question if the kidnapping was tied to her years as a drug user. And her reluctance to volunteer her fingerprints was another question.

But when Gannon considered what he knew, the picture clouded.

Seeing your child kidnapped, then believing her eyeballs had been delivered to you was beyond comprehension.

In his years as a crime reporter Gannon had seen so many people collide with unimaginable horror. Through it all, he had come to learn that there was no guide on the proper way to react. People blamed others, or themselves. They looked for the guilty, or they looked guilty.

Reason and truth were always fugitives.

So at times he found himself looking upon Cora as more than a former drug addict who'd devastated his family in Buffalo over twenty years ago. She was no longer lost to him. She was a near-middle-aged single mother, who had made mistakes, who had human failings.

The person he needed to forgive.

For at seventeen Cora had been his best friend, the guiding light who'd nurtured his dream to become a writer before she ripped his life apart. Yes, she'd resurrected years of pain, but they'd found each other. And seeing what she had become underscored what he had become—a loner, a truth-seeker.

Gannon's regard for her whipsawed with each passing minute.

He loved her. He hated her. He ached for her. He suspected her.

Now, as he checked his cell phone for messages, he grappled with the old wound that Cora had carved into him, realizing that it ran so deep he didn't know where he stood. Didn't know where to place his trust, his instincts or his love.

Of one thing he was certain: he was in the middle of a huge story.

Up to now, he'd been swept up by events. It was time he took journalistic control of matters, time he started digging into the case. With an eye on the investigators at work, he'd placed a call on his cell phone to a number in Buffalo, New York.

It rang several times.

"Clark Investigations," a female voice said. "Please leave a message and I'll get back to you."

The voice belonged to Adell Clark, a former FBI agent

who ran her own one-woman private investigation agency out of her home in Lackawanna, where she lived with her daughter.

Several years back, Gannon had profiled Clark after she was shot during an armored-car heist. They became friends and Adell became one of his most trusted sources. Hell, she was his *best* source. After Cora's press conference, Gannon had texted Adell, asking her to poke around within her connections—and she had plenty—for anything that might help him on this case.

Her message cue beeped but he didn't leave one, deciding to call her back later. He tried another number.

"WPA, Henrietta Chong."

"Henrietta, it's Gannon. Are you hearing anything new out there on my niece's case?"

"Sorry, nothing new, Jack. Say, what's up with that cabdriver? The word going around is that he dropped off a note from the kidnappers or a message or something?"

"*Or something* would fit for now."

"Can you tell me more?"

"No, I can't. Keep me posted if anything breaks."

Gannon then called WPA headquarters in New York and updated Melody Lyon, leaving out the eyeballs part, telling her nothing new had happened since the takedown in Tempe. As he was hanging up, his attention went to the FBI agents.

Hackett had called a quick huddle around one of the worktables. By their body language and the tension in the air he could tell there'd been an important break. A couple of agents were typing rapidly on laptops, while others were making cell phone calls.

Once more, Gannon heard someone say "EPIC," the term for the El Paso Intelligence Center, and guessed that something critical to the investigation had suddenly arisen from there.

The unfolding scene was not lost on Cora, who'd been watching from across the room.

"Something's happening," she said. "What is it, Jack?"

Hackett approached them, hands extended to quell expectations.

"There's been a development but we're not sure it—"

"What?" Cora repeated. "Did you find her?"

"I can't release details at this time because—"

"Jack!" Cora pleaded. "What's happening?"

"Let him finish, Cora," Gannon said.

"We've had a lot of tips and this newest one is cross-jurisdictional—"

"Cross-what? What's that mean?" Cora was frantic. "Is my daughter dead? If she's dead, you tell me right now!"

"All I can tell you is that we have a lead that requires more investigation and it's going to take time. I know it's frustrating—" he glanced at Gannon "—but I'm sorry, that's all I can release right now."

"No, that's not acceptable!" Cora said. "I have a right to know what's going on! You tell me what's happened!"

As Gannon and another detective tried to get Cora to rest, Gannon's cell phone rang. He excused himself and went to a quiet corner to take the call, expecting Adell Clark or Henrietta Chong.

"Gannon."

"Jack, it's Isabel Luna."

"Yes."

"Something has come up near Juarez, something very important."

"What is it?"

"Jack, it's related to your niece's kidnapping."

"Did you find her? What is it?"

"All I can say is that it's tied to the kidnapping. I'm sorry, that's all that was revealed to me."

"Was it the kidnappers who called you? Who's your source?"

"I can't tell you any more at this moment."

Gannon shot Hackett a look over his shoulder, thinking the two matters were linked.

"Isabel, tell me what you know. Maybe I should pass it on to the police here."

"No, tell no one about this! Because I have also learned that the task force investigating your niece's case may have been infiltrated by a cartel."

"What? I don't believe this. Are you certain?"

"My sources here have heard this."

"Jesus."

"Jack, I think it's very important for you to return to Juarez immediately. There's something you need to see."

18

Dust clouds trailed the white 1999 Chevrolet Blazer slicing through the eroded stretches and dried arroyos of scrubland some thirty miles outside of Ciudad Juarez.

Out here, the police scanner mounted to the dash was picking up mostly static. The driver, Arturo Castillo, a news photographer with *El Heraldo,* adjusted it and glanced in the rearview mirror.

Jack Gannon was in the backseat searching the desolate expanse for a hint of what awaited him. After Isabel Luna had called him in Phoenix, he'd left for El Paso with Cora's pleas echoing in his ears.

"Don't leave me, Jack, please!"

"I have to check something out."

"What? Where? Why won't you tell me?"

Hackett was out of earshot but eyeballing him from across the room, where he was working with the other investigators, watching coldly but not interfering.

"Cora, let me check this out. I don't have details, just a lead from a good source."

"Jack, please don't go. Something bad has happened. I feel it."

A few hours later, when his jet landed in El Paso, Gannon made his way across the border to the offices of *El Heraldo.* Luna, true to her word, had arranged to rush him to "a location in the desert." Now, as the Chevy Blazer bumped along the dusty road, Gannon shifted his attention to Luna. She was sitting in the front passenger seat and when she'd finished sending a text message on her phone, Gannon came back to the question he'd asked earlier.

"How solid is your information?"

"My source is unassailable."

Twenty minutes later, Castillo, guided by the odometer reading and directions Luna gave from her notebook, shifted the transmission of the Blazer into four-wheel drive and headed off road and over the parched grassland.

Two miles in, they came to a fast-flowing irrigation stream. Castillo chose a narrow bend and carefully forded it. The water rose to the running boards as the Chevy wobbled over the stony bottom.

After they'd gone another two miles, a small ranch came into view. As they got closer, Gannon discerned a rickety house that looked as if it was about to collapse and a ramshackle barn. The place appeared to have been abandoned for years…until now. A handful of police vehicles were concentrated at the barn, which was encircled with police tape.

Luna, Castillo and Gannon approached the four uniformed officers leaning on the cars just outside the police tape.

"We are from *El Heraldo* and the World Press Alliance," Luna said in Spanish as the three showed their ID. Tapping her notebook against her hip, she added: "Let me speak to the person in charge here."

A hot breeze kicked up grit as Luna stared into the implacable reflection of the first officer's sunglasses. A long, tense moment passed before he spoke into his shoulder microphone.

A terse response crackled over the radio. Then, in a move that surprised Gannon, the officer lifted the tape for them to approach. Through the gap-toothed boards of the barn, he saw a car was parked inside.

A man in blue jeans, a polo shirt and cowboy boots, with a badge clipped on his belt near his sidearm met them at the entrance. As he handed over his ID, Gannon noticed the blue latex gloves he was wearing. Taking stock of Gannon, Castillo and Luna, the cop spoke in Spanish with Luna. Gannon soon figured that this cop was asking questions as Luna responded with string of *sí…sí…sí*'s. Gannon guessed they were questions about him, as this cop—save for a quick scan of the empty horizon beyond them—never took his focus from him.

The detective was in his late thirties, about six feet tall with a firm build. He had a few days' growth deepening the craggy features of his face, accentuating his piercing hooded eyes.

"Come inside," he said in English. "Follow me on the path marked on the ground by tape."

What was going on? This press access to a crime scene was astounding. As Gannon struggled to figure it out, he was assaulted by the stench of excrement mingled with putrid meat. Something was humming. Flies. Blinding beams of sunlight gleamed through the barn's walls and Gannon needed a few seconds for his eyes to adjust. Several other men in plainclothes were reviewing notes and items by an open barn window.

Gannon saw that the car was a four-door Chevy Caprice, late model with Texas tags…a rental, maybe? The windows were tinted and reflected the flash from Castillo's camera as he began taking pictures.

The detective opened the driver's door. The keys were still in the ignition and the indicator chimed softly.

Pong. Pong. Pong.

The outrush of foul air was overwhelming. From what Gannon could see, the driver was resting clumsily on the steering wheel and his passenger was leaning against the window.

Pong. Pong. Pong.

As Gannon heard the buzzing of insects and studied the spaghetti-lace pattern of black and browned blood everywhere, he realized that both corpses were headless.

Pong. Pong. Pong.

Flies from inside the car swarmed Gannon. One tried to go up his nose and he felt bile erupting along his throat.

Pong. Pong. Pong.

Staggering, he drew a deep breath and dragged the back of his hand over his mouth.

"Are you going to be okay?" Luna asked.

Gannon swallowed hard, hurried out and doubled over in the shade side of the barn, letting sweet-smelling breezes do their work, inhaling fresh air until he felt well enough to stand and face Luna and the detective.

"This is my stepbrother, First Sergeant Esteban Cruz."

"We have Coke and bottled water, Jack," Cruz offered.

Gannon said he was fine.

"This is your case?"

Cruz nodded as Gannon glanced around warily.

"Don't worry. It's safe for us to talk here," Cruz said. "These men are not corrupt. Each can be trusted."

"So what happened? What have you got here?"

"A ranch hand from the next property was out here yesterday morning hunting rabbits when he found them."

"Who are the victims? What's the link to my niece?"

Cruz unfolded a piece of thermal fax paper and gave it to Gannon. It was a photocopy of Lyle Galviera's business card, front and back. The back bore handwritten numbers...possibly codes or accounts.

"We found this on one of them," Cruz said.

"Is one of them Lyle Galviera?"

Cruz shoved a stick of gum in his mouth and shook his head.

"So who are they?"

"We think they were Galviera's cartel partners. We fingerprinted them late last night."

"Why are you telling me this? Why call me down here?"

"To help you understand the gravity of your situation," Cruz said.

"Is it more serious than what is in there—than having my niece kidnapped by monsters?"

"To begin with, we believe that someone involved in the multiagency investigation of your niece's abduction in Arizona may be on a cartel payroll."

"Yes, Isabel said that on her call. So what are we dealing with?"

"Those two dead men are ex-U.S. law enforcement. The one in the driver's seat is Octavio Sergio Salazar. He was fired from the LAPD a few years back for alleged corruption involving drug shipments in California. The other, John Walker Johnson, was fired from U.S. Customs. He was alleged to have taken bribes in exchange for border access. Not long ago, Salazar and Johnson began double-dealing with cartels that were warring with each other."

"So what happened?"

"Our ex-cops went rogue to start carving out their own U.S. routes while dealing with at least two cartels. We're not sure which ones. We think that Lyle Galviera was partnered with the ex-cops, using his courier company, and that he's holding the missing millions for Salazar and Johnson. And we think the cartels believe the cash was stolen from them."

"Where did you get all this intel?"

"There are a number of longstanding investigations on both sides of the border. When your niece was kidnapped, people in police intel on both sides of the border started connecting dots."

"Does the FBI know what you've told me? They should

be told so they can find my niece and get her out before all of this explodes."

"They've been told. In fact, several U.S. federal agents are due at this scene at any moment because of the U.S. link. But Isabel and I wanted you to know the truth, to ensure it stays pure, because of the suspected infiltration of U.S. and Mexican police by cartels."

"The people who have Tilly have given my sister five days to find Galviera. We're losing time. Do you know where he is?"

"No."

"He could be dead somewhere."

"If that were true," Cruz said, "we would know. The cartels would want the world to know that death is the price for stealing from them."

"So he's likely out there with five million dollars and scared to death."

"It's only a matter of time before the cartels find him."

"You think they know where he is?" Gannon asked.

"The bodies have been here a few days. Salazar and Johnson were probably killed before your niece was taken."

"That gives you a bit of a timeline then?"

Cruz nodded.

"There's more. Before they were killed they were tortured. We think they were lured out here and probably tortured for information about Galviera and the money. This was a double execution by a *sicario*."

"An assassin?"

"Yes. And we found this." Cruz glanced at Luna before showing Gannon a crime scene photo copied on his cell phone. The picture showed a small glass that looked like it was used for tomato juice.

"I don't understand."

"This is the signature of The Tarantula."

"The Tarantula?"

"He's a top assassin. He started professionally killing as a boy. With each high-profile killing he is known to toast La Santa Muerte, the goddess of death, with the blood of his victims."

Gannon exhaled.

"This was a message killing," Luna said. "The cartels have a complex structure for message or revenge killings. The cartel first does all the groundwork, setting up everything for the assassin to arrive and carry out the key executions. It's very ritualistic and disciplined."

"So this goes beyond getting their money back?"

"Yes. Having The Tarantula involved means cartel bosses want the world to know that everyone connected to this theft of the cartel's money will die," Luna said. "If the cartel finds Lyle Galviera first, they will torture him for information on their money, then kill him. And then they will have no use for your niece. Because she can identify them, they'll kill her, too."

"Given that they've already found and executed these two competing cartel members," Cruz said, "it won't be long until the cartel finds Galviera. No matter what happens, Galviera and your niece are marked to be revenge kills."

19

Hours later, as his jet lifted off from El Paso International Airport, Gannon recalled something the Irish writer Oscar Wilde had said about there being only two tragedies in life.

"One is not getting what one wants, and the other is getting it."

That pretty much covered it for him. As the wounded brother, there were times in his life that he'd ached to see his sister again, was willing to give anything to find Cora.

Well, he'd found her.

And as the hard-driving reporter, he had been hell-bent on finding a drug cartel assassin to write about; he had begged Isabel Luna to help him.

Well, they'd found one: a blood-drinking death-toasting killer called The Tarantula.

And he's coming for my niece.

When the plane leveled off somewhere over the Rio Grande, Gannon opened his laptop and clicked to the missing poster of Tilly. Her eyes sparkled as they met his. She looked so much like a younger version of Cora, her face radiating innocence and hope as she implored him.

Help me. Find me. Before it's too late.

He was her uncle. He was her blood.

Man, after the horror with the eyeballs, and then seeing those headless corpses in that car a short time ago, the thought of a cartel hit man targeting Tilly…. Something caught in Gannon's throat. He turned to the window, looked beyond the clouds and back on the few hours he'd just spent in Mexico.

After they'd left the desert crime scene, he, Castillo and Luna returned to *El Heraldo*'s newsroom, where he had called Melody Lyon in New York. Absorbing the grisly details she'd said: "We need to get this story on the wire now, Jack."

"I'll write it here, but we have to hold back on some of it."

"Why?"

"Because we're way too close to this. I need to protect sources."

Lyon weighed his point.

"I'll let you write it the way you think it needs to be written, *this time*."

"Okay, but can you get Henrietta in Phoenix to seek FBI comment?"

"Fine, just ship me the story ASAP. And Jack? Are you still there?"

"Yes?"

"Are you sure you want to stay on this? I can put other people on it if it ever becomes…becomes…"

"Becomes what?"

"If it ever becomes too much for you, Jack."

"I'm in too deep, Melody."

She let a moment pass before speaking. "We're praying they find Tilly safe and bring her home."

"So am I."

Turning from the window back to his laptop, Gannon called up the story he'd sent earlier to headquarters and reread it, fighting to distance himself from the fact he was writing about his own family.

The execution murders of two former U.S. law enforcement officers who were found beheaded in the Mexican desert may be tied to the recent kidnapping of an 11-year-old Phoenix girl, according to police sources.

That was how it began, a tight nuts-and-bolts exclusive that provided few details. It did not report the victims' names or anything on the assassin. Gannon had filed it from Juarez before returning to El Paso for his flight. By now his story should've gone around the world on the WPA wire and been posted online everywhere with Castillo's crime scene photos, the ones suitable for family viewing—police vehicles near the barn.

Luna was writing a similar piece for *El Heraldo*.

The story beat the Associated Press, Reuters, all of Gannon's competition. It was a WPA win that should make New York very happy, especially George Wilson, head of all foreign news. It would satisfy Gannon's employer, whose resources he needed to find his niece.

His niece.

Suddenly he was jolted by another concern.

Should he have alerted Cora that the story was coming, explained what he knew so that she could brace for it? But it would've been a risk to call her. He couldn't ignore suspicions that the task force had been infiltrated by people working for the cartel.

No, he had no other option but to get the story out.

For the rest of the short flight, Gannon considered how the execution in the Mexican desert of two American ex-cops would bring more to bear on Tilly's case. Now as the landing gear rumbled down, he searched the blurring ground for answers. There had to be something he was overlooking, something he could dig into. He had to do more to find Tilly, and he had to do it fast.

Time was working against them.

* * *

The story was getting bigger.

The first thing Gannon noticed as his cab approached Cora's house was that there were more news people out front, including a few satellite trucks from Los Angeles, Tucson and Las Vegas.

"Hey, Gannon! What about the executions in Mexico?"

He gave the pack an apologetic wave and went to the back door.

"Come on, Jack, give your pals here a break!"

In the ride from the airport to Mesa Mirage, he'd checked his BlackBerry for developments. His WPA story was the big one. The *Los Angeles Times,* Yahoo and the *New York Times* had already put it up on their sites. The *Arizona Republic* had posted it, too, along with a news features on ever-widening neighborhood searches for Tilly and prayer vigils by church groups.

The moment Gannon stepped inside Cora's house, she rushed to him.

"Why didn't you call me?"

"I couldn't."

"You should've warned me, Jack! I was going out of my mind! Oh my God, is it true? Are the murders connected to Tilly? Who are the officers?"

Mounting worry had deepened the lines carved into her drawn face. He started to take her aside.

"We need to talk," he said.

"No." He felt a hand on his shoulder. "*We* need to talk."

Gannon turned and met Hackett's scowl as the FBI agent backed him into a corner and dropped his voice to a menacing level.

"How did you learn about the homicides in Mexico, Gannon?"

Hackett's question went beyond concern over a press leak.

That Gannon knew about a major break at the same time the FBI had been informed underscored Hackett's worst nightmare as the lead investigator: *The sickening possibility that had dogged him with that memo on cartel infiltration of U.S. police ranks.*

In the icy silence that passed between them, each man knew. By Hackett's body language, by the fury behind his eyes, Hackett telegraphed his fear of a potentially compromised investigation. It was there slithering in the air, that someone, anyone, among the half dozen agencies involved in the case, including those in Texas and Mexico, could be on a cartel payroll.

It rattled Hackett that Gannon had gotten so close.

"I don't expect you'll give up a source," Hackett said, "but I'll warn you, if you jeopardize our case I'll charge you with obstruction."

"It would be better if you accepted that you have your sources and I have mine. And we both want the same thing."

"Just watch yourself."

"Excuse me, I'd like to talk privately with my sister."

"Listen up—if you have information relevant to this case, you'd better share it."

Gannon made a point of lifting his chin to inventory the agents and officers in the house.

"Right, why don't you tell me about the two dead 'cops' in the desert, Agent Hackett? Then we could talk about sharing, about trust."

Hackett grimaced then left.

Cora was alone in her bedroom, looking at pictures of Tilly. Gannon's stomach tensed after he'd shut the door. *Trust.* Did he trust her? Could he trust her? She touched her tears that fell on the photos in the laminated album.

"Cora, I need you to help me find her."

She nodded.

"We have no time. I need you to tell me the truth about everything."

"I've told you everything."

"I think you're holding back."

"I told you I made a lot of mistakes in my life."

"Stop the bullshit! I have seen what they do and what they are going to do to Tilly. You have to tell me everything so I can help."

"Oh, God!"

"Why did you call me?"

"Because you're a good reporter and I thought you could help me find the people who took Tilly, so we could bring her home."

"Are you part of this?"

"No!"

"Cora, what did you mean when you said you're being punished for past sins, that it's karma? What the hell do you mean?"

"Jack, I—I don't know—"

"Stop this! They're going to kill Tilly!"

"I know. I have to protect her. We have to find her."

"Then tell me something that could help, damn it, Cora!"

"Maybe Tilly's father knows something."

"I thought you said he was out of the picture?"

"He is. I haven't seen him since I was pregnant."

"Why do you think he could help?"

"He's a police officer with the LAPD."

20

Mesa Mirage, Phoenix, Arizona

They'd met when she was working as a waitress at a North Hollywood bar and still messed up on drugs. Ivan would talk to her. He was a tough patrol cop, divorced because of the job. Cora dated him. Then she got pregnant. It took a long time before she could bring herself to tell Ivan.

His reaction was seared into her memory.

He drove her to a clinic somewhere around Wilshire Boulevard, slapped five hundred dollars in her hand and told her to "take care of it." She got out and he drove away.

The clinic was a decaying building that smelled like a veterinarian's office where they put down dogs and cats.

Cora was so afraid.

"You're too far along," the nurse said.

Cora took it as a sign. Overwhelmed, she went to a church and prayed until she'd reached the decision to keep her baby. This was her one chance to save herself. She took a city bus to a community support agency. They counseled her, helped her get clean for her baby. It was hard, very hard, but she had Tilly alone.

And she raised her alone.

Cora never saw Ivan Peck again.

Later, she'd bumped into one of the girls from the bar who told her that Ivan was a cheating asshole who was married when he was dating Cora. *Everyone knew. Didn't she know?* And this girl had also heard that Ivan got caught up in some kind of cop scandal.

"Scandal? What kind of scandal?" Gannon had asked Cora.

"I don't know."

"Was it corruption, use of force, what? Was it in the papers?"

"I don't know."

"Ivan Peck may be linked to Salazar, the dead guy in the desert. He was ex-LAPD." Gannon consulted his notebook. "Did you know a cop named Octavio Sergio Salazar?"

"No."

"I need to contact Peck."

"Why, Jack?"

"Maybe Peck knows something about Salazar, something that could help. Do you have any idea if he's still on the force?"

"I don't know."

"Think, Cora!"

"Jack, it was more than eleven years ago, I don't know."

"I need to find him."

Gannon immediately dug into Ivan Peck's background.

He called his best source again: Adell Clark, the ex-FBI agent turned private investigator in Buffalo. This time he got through.

"Jack, I am so sorry," Clark said. "I've been tied up with an insurance fraud. I got your messages. I saw the news out of Phoenix. It's just awful. It breaks my heart. I want to help. Tell me what you need."

Gannon confidentially related every aspect of the case to Clark.

"I need all I can get on Octavio Sergio Salazar and John Walker Johnson. But first, I need everything you can get on Peck right now. I'm assuming he's alive. Adell, I need to confront him face-to-face to find out if he can help us. He's Tilly's father. He's got a stake in this. I know I'm grabbing at straws but we're running out of time."

"Okay, I've got some friends with the LAPD. I'll make calls and get back to you as quick as I can."

Before ending the call, Gannon gave Clark both names Cora had used and her date of birth then asked Clark to check if his sister had any arrests, warrants or convictions.

He then requested urgent help from the WPA news library. Then he went online and used every database the WPA subscribed to, to search for more on Salazar, Johnson and Peck. He scoured property records, state and municipal records. At the same time, he searched news archives for anything on an assassin known as The Tarantula. He texted Isabel Luna in Juarez and pressed her for updates on the executions in the desert, the cartels, anything.

Nothing new, Luna responded. Will alert you when I know more.

The news library got back to him with more on the ritualistic worship of the bogus La Santa Muerte, or "Saint Death." By collecting the blood of their victims to honor the "narcosaint," the hit men believed she would protect them while they exacted vengeance on their enemies. The images of the corpses in the barn flashed in Gannon's mind when his cell phone rang.

"It's Adell. I got nothing on Cora. I'm still working on Salazar and Johnson but I have more on Ivan Peck. Ready?"

"Okay, Adell." Gannon pulled out his pen and notebook.

"He'd been on the job roughly ten years by the time he'd met Cora. He left the department about a year ago.

In all, he had twenty years with the LAPD, starting as an officer on a foot beat, then a black-and-white patrol. He was with SWAT, working his way up the officer ranks until he made Detective I."

"Any problems?"

"Hold on. He'd been assigned to the Vice Division then worked Robbery, Homicide, Gangs and Narcotics. He was decorated, received the medal of valor."

"For what?"

"It's posted on their site. He was off duty, traveling on an L.A. freeway, when a school bus blew a tire, rolled and caught fire. He helped lead the rescue of twenty children, their teacher and driver. They all survived."

"So he's an all-star—apart from cheating on his wife and impregnating my sister."

"Well, it was sometime after Cora that he actually did get divorced. His ex claimed he hit her, punched her one night after she'd asked him about his affairs. That triggered a slow downfall, which led to his troubles on the job."

"What kind of troubles?"

"He was suspected of being…under the influence is the term I got, of some of L.A.'s gangs, notably those with ties to the Tijuana cartel."

"Really?"

"Over his last years with the department, it was alleged he stole narcotics, used excessive force and beat suspects."

"Bet he didn't get a medal for that. Was he ever charged?"

"No. He went before a Board of Rights, at least four times. He was written up, given temporary desk duty, never charged or threatened with termination. They never had enough evidence. After he clocked in twenty years, he hung it up, took his pension."

"Where is he?"

"He runs his own detective agency in downtown L.A."

"Can you give me the address?"

"I've got it right here."

DAY 3

21

Gannon's motel was on West Olympic Boulevard, at the edge of Koreatown, a mile from the Staples Center.

It was just after midnight when he arrived in L.A.

"You gotta be real careful down here this time of night, man," his airport shuttle driver, who was missing a front tooth, warned while unloading Gannon's bag in the lot.

Sirens echoed and a police helicopter whomped above while raking its light over the next block. The noise faded by the time Gannon had checked in to his ninety dollar a night "suite." The stained carpet was damp and smelled of disinfectant and foot odor.

He didn't care.

He'd stayed in worse. This was his life: hotels, motels, airplanes, fast food and deadlines. He strained to remember the past few days. He'd lost track of time after being in Mexico that morning, before returning to Phoenix. Then, once he felt he was armed enough with information on Ivan Peck, he flew to Los Angeles. Before he'd left, he told Cora what he was doing. She seemed anxious.

Is there more to her history with this guy than she's telling me?

Gannon would find out soon enough.

He was only going to be in the city a few hours and needed a room near downtown, something cheap because he was paying for this trip. It was easier to do that than try to explain why he had to fly to California to pursue a long shot lead on Tilly's father.

Gannon tossed his bag on the bed, fired up his laptop to check for emails and consulted his BlackBerry for texts. Something new had come through from Adell, more information on the two guys murdered in the desert.

Jack,

Got this on John Walker Johnson: Ex U.S. Customs, alleged but never proven that he stole seized property while working the border at Juarez. Suspended, resigned.

On Octavio Sergio Salazar: Ex LAPD, left the job after being on leave for psychological problems after shooting a suspect.

On Ivan Peck: Additional info on one of his alleged offenses before the Board of Rights. Accused of planting drug evidence against an LA gang member with ties to Mexican cartel. Complaint dead-ended. No evidence.

More when I have it— Adell.

Gannon sat on the bed and closed his eyes to concentrate on the latest intel, especially the data on Peck. It could be relevant. It could be useless. Nothing was simple when something like this was unfolding. It was never tied together neatly like in books and movies. Gannon didn't know what fit, what to ignore or what he should follow. All he knew was that he had to do everything he could to find his niece.

That was all he thought of until he fell asleep.

Peck's agency was called Ivan Private Investigations.

It was tucked in a warren amid a low brick building downtown in L.A.'s fashion district.

To get to it, Gannon had to navigate the vendors hustling knockoff sunglasses, shoes and handbags to the throb of loud rap. Then he bypassed a homeless man camped out on a bench and a few weirdos left behind by the mother ship.

The sign at the door directed Gannon to ascend the narrow stairwell above the tattoo shop and "…ffel's Canteen"—letters were missing—to the second-floor office.

Before flying to Los Angeles, Gannon had gone to Ivan's website. He'd sent an email from an anonymous online account WPA used to confirm Ivan Peck would be in his office the next morning to meet a potential client who wanted to check on someone's past.

Will be in from 9 am to 1 pm – IP, was the response.

The creaking door announced Gannon's arrival in the dimly lit office. The musty air was in keeping with the pale walls and scuffed hardwood floor. A woman in her thirties sat at a standard police-issue steel desk and looked up from her *People* magazine.

"May I help you?"

"I'd like to speak with Ivan Peck."

"Do you have an appointment?" Her eyes flicked to the half-opened door of a small room.

"No."

"Hang on," a male voice said over the rush of water in a sink. It came from the small room. A large man emerged, holding a glass coffee decanter. He positioned it into the dual coffeemaker on the credenza, pressed a switch then poured a mug of black coffee from another near-empty decanter.

"I'm Ivan Peck. And you are?"

"Jack Gannon."

"Want a coffee?"

"No, thanks, I'm good. I was hoping to talk to you."

"I got some time."

Peck led Gannon to a large office where Venetian

blinds filtered the morning sunlight on the drab walls. Olive file cabinets were secured with large padlocks. Gannon smelled onions and bacon wafting up from the canteen below as Peck hooked his foot around a visitor's chair, offering it to Gannon. The chair was before the large dark wood desk. On the desk were a pack of Marlboro Reds, a file folder, a legal pad, a pen and a holstered pistol.

Peck wore a powder-blue dress shirt, the collar button undone. His navy tie was loosened and shirtsleeves were rolled to the forearms. He filled out the shirt as if he were made of stone. He stood about six four, had a few days' salt-and-pepper growth and short, silver cop hair.

His face was void of emotion as he lowered himself into his high-back swivel chair and took a hit of coffee. Then he shook out a cigarette and, without consideration for Gannon, lit it with a match and took a long pull.

"Gannon? The name's familiar. What can I do for you?"

"I want to look into someone's background."

"Who?"

Gannon set a recent photo on the desk for Peck to see.

"That's my sister. Cora."

Peck picked it up, held it before him. Then Gannon set another photo on the desk.

"That's her daughter, Tilly."

Peck studied both photos, shot Gannon a look and passed the photos back.

"You know who they are, Ivan?"

"I know who they are. I see the news."

"Tilly's your daughter."

The little muscles in Peck's jaw started pulsing. He locked Gannon in a gaze for a long, icy moment before he got up, shut the door and inserted himself between the desk and Gannon. Towering over him, invading his space.

"What the fuck do you want?"

"I want you to help me find Tilly."

"And why would I do that?"

"Just over eleven years ago, you fathered a child with my sister, Cora. Just over two days ago, Tilly—your daughter—was kidnapped by a cartel holding her for a five-million-dollar debt they say is owed by Cora's boss, Lyle Galviera. They say they will kill Tilly if they are not repaid. In connection with this, Octavio Sergio Salazar, an ex-LAPD officer, and John Walker Johnson, ex-Customs, were found murdered in the desert outside Juarez, Mexico."

Peck stared at Gannon for several moments, then returned to his chair and his cigarette, dragging on it while keeping his eyes on Gannon. He leaned back in his chair, swiveling like a ruler on a throne as Gannon searched for resemblance to Tilly.

"What's any of this got to do with me?"

"I think you might know something."

"Why would I know something?"

"You were a cop. You worked in drugs."

"That's quite a leap. I still don't see why I should care."

"Tilly's your daughter. Cora says you dated her when she was a waitress at a bar in North Hollywood. You wanted her to have an abortion then walked away."

Peck studied the tip of his cigarette.

"Okay, the fun's over. I'm not her father. I'm not anyone's father. I got a low count, which is partly why I'm divorced." He took a few last pulls.

"Then why did you give her money and drive her to a clinic?"

"Because she begged me." Peck stubbed the cigarette in an LAPD ashtray. "Gannon? You're a reporter, right? I've seen your name in the *Times* with the Associated Press or some wire service."

Gannon didn't respond.

"Jack, let me tell you something about your sister. She was not a waitress at that bar. She was hooking there. Yeah, I banged her. Despite being a tripped-out whore, she was a fine piece of ass."

Gannon's gut spasmed as if he'd been punched.

She was hooking...a tripped-out whore...a fine piece of ass.

The insult burned through him but Gannon refused to believe it. A memory pulled him back to his childhood in Buffalo.

Here he is with Cora, Mom and Dad at Mass. Here's Cora receiving Communion, crossing herself, genuflecting.

A tripped-out whore...

Cora had had her troubles but she was not a prostitute. She couldn't be. She would never do that. How could she do that? She was a waitress. This prick is trying to humiliate me.

But Cora was an addict and addicts turn tricks.

Was it true?

Oh Christ, images of this douche with his hands all over Cora.

Maybe Peck was just trying to knock him off his game.

"That's right, Jack, your sister was a sweet piece of tail, and that's the truth about her."

Peck glared at Gannon. His words were meant to wound him and the detective was assessing their impact.

Gannon struggled to focus.

Don't flinch. Rise above the blow. Use the pain.

"You know," Peck added, "I saw Cora on CNN begging for her kid. Got to admit it's a heartbreaker and with these cartels, well, there's not much hope. Tragic for the kid and I'm sorry for that." Peck reached for his Marlboro cigarettes. "But the whole time, I'm thinking that while Cora's still looking good after all these years.

I admit, I'd still tap that again." He winked at Gannon. "But I'm thinking, after all these years, that stupid bitch is still messed up with drug shit. I mean, I heard she got into trouble way back. She is one stupid bitch."

Gannon was a heartbeat away from leaping across the desk.

But he held his ground because this was Peck's world. Gannon knew enough about hard-asses and assholes, knew that Peck wanted him to take his shot so he could physically destroy him. Gannon had no cards to play except one—which would take him over an ethical line as a reporter, but he had no choice.

"She looks like you," Gannon said.

"What?"

"Tilly. You can see the resemblance. It's there."

"What?"

"I'm with the World Press Alliance. WPA stories go around the world, you know. Now, I'm thinking about a story—just thinking about one—that would suggest that the anguished mother, Cora, has named you as Tilly's father, an ex-cop with a number of blotches on his record. Use of force and, oh right, some tie to cartels and planting evidence. Right, that would be a good one. I'm just thinking about a story that implicates you in the abduction and likely murder of your eleven-year-old alleged daughter. Should be good for your business, your life, whatever would be left of it after the hellfire that would befall you. Oh, and I kind of let my editor know about you already, in case I end up in hospital, or worse."

Peck's jawline pulsed again.

"Now, Ivan, you're a smart man. You know that old ditty about the pen being mightier than the big, bad asshole with a gun. You can work with me, or you can work against me. I do not give a damn because the only thing that matters is the life of an eleven-year-old child."

The detective eyed Gannon for several cold moments. While the wheels turned, Gannon asked him, "What about Octavio Salazar or John Walker Johnson? Can you help me out there?"

Peck stared at Gannon.

"Oh, I'm going to help you, Jack." He reached for a pen and jotted something on the notepad. "I'm going to give you a name."

Peck tore the page from the pad. Gannon looked at the name.

"Vic Lomax."

"Back in the day when I worked Vice, we knew Lomax as a piece-of-shit pimp. Your sister's pimp. I recall hearing that she got into some trouble with him way back. Word is he's in Las Vegas now. He's a major casino exec and allegedly a player with one of the big Mexican cartels. Lomax is a powerful guy. You do not want to fuck with him. So you go try your little game with him, sport. See where it gets you."

22

Phoenix, Arizona

Hackett eyed the clock, then observed the investigators settling into their seats at the table in the large conference room at the FBI's Phoenix headquarters.

As he waited to lead the case-status meeting, he was stabbed by his recurring concern.

Was there a traitor among them on the cartel payroll?

That question ate at him as he inventoried the walls, covered with photos and plaques from allied police agencies across the country and around the world. None of it meant anything when you were betrayed.

If you were betrayed.

But Hackett had no proof his case had been infiltrated. All he had was his growing unease, underscored by the latest reality: the two corpses found in the Mexican desert were ex-cops from the U.S. Their gruesome murders appeared to be linked to Tilly Martin's kidnapping by a cartel that had set a deadline for payment of five million dollars.

They were losing time. People at the table were ready.

"Let's get started," Hackett said. "We want to update everyone quickly, then get back to our assignments. First we'll do a roll call of everyone at the table and on the line.

My partner, Bonnie Larson, will then bring everyone up to speed. We'll brainstorm, hit next steps and get back to it."

The Phoenix P.D.'s Home Invasion and Kidnapping Enforcement Task Force; the Maricopa County Sheriff's Office; the Drug Enforcement Administration; U.S. Immigration and Customs Enforcement; Bureau of Alcohol, Tobacco, Firearms and Explosives were among the agencies supporting the growing investigation.

Also participating was the DHS Border Enforcement Task Forces, which, under an exchange agreement with Mexico, was embedded with Mexican police officers. In addition, there were analysts on the call from the El Paso Intelligence Center, Juarez police, agents from the U.S. working in Juarez and Mexico, and Mexican agents posted to the Mexican Consulate in El Paso.

The roll call ended and pictures of Tilly Martin, Lyle Galviera and other key players, charts and maps emerged on the room's large monitors, and through a secured encrypted internet channel. Paper rustled as people flipped through a two-page summary. As Larson updated the case, Hackett came back to his fear.

The crime now bled into Mexico, taking on an international scope, requiring more agencies be brought into the loop. Having more players, most of whom were strangers to Hackett, not only increased the risk of corruption, it gave the case a high profile and increasing political pressure.

Prior to the meeting, one of the FBI's Assistant Special Agents in charge of the Phoenix field office had pulled Hackett aside.

"A few minutes ago, the boss got a call from NHQ. The White House has let the Director know of its interest." Hackett's supervisor put his hand on Hackett's shoulder. "Earl, you can appreciate that we all want this thing cleared ASAP, whatever it takes."

Now Larson was concluding with a quick summary.

To date, they'd received nearly two hundred tips from the public. All were being screened and sorted by Phoenix P.D. and the county, with potential leads flagged for the FBI. Cora's home in Mesa Mirage was still being processed. Nothing significant had arisen from her computer, phone or bank records. The forensic experts were still analyzing items in the home for latent prints. There were impressions on the duct tape but the quality was subpar and they were still processing it. And crime scene people were still going through Lyle Galviera's condo and his computer, phone, bank and credit card records.

As Larson finished her update, Hackett elaborated on the facts, suspicions and theories the FBI had gathered and formed from intelligence collected from all agencies and sources so far.

"Among his many longstanding financial troubles, Lyle Galviera had to make a critical two-million-dollar payment in one month or lose his company. So to save his company, he goes into business with Salazar and Johnson, who were tied to Mexican cartels."

"What do we know about Salazar and Johnson?" a Mexican drug agent asked over the line from the Mexican Consulate in El Paso.

Hackett paused. He hated sharing intelligence.

"John Walker Johnson was ex-U.S. Customs. It was never proven, but it was alleged that in addition to stealing seized property while working the border at Juarez, he received a single three-hundred-thousand-dollar payment by a cartel to allow one truckload of dope to cross. He denied the allegation and resigned. The IRS said it lost the trail of the alleged payment through offshore bank accounts."

"And Salazar?" the agent asked.

"Octavio Sergio Salazar was an LAPD patrol officer who shot a suspect during an armored car robbery. He left the job after being on leave because of psychological problems. Salazar became despondent, then claimed he never received his full compensation benefits and launched an unsuccessful lawsuit against the city.

"Our intel indicates that Salazar and Johnson met in Arizona through connections, and began dealing with the Norte Cartel."

"As you know, Agent Hackett, the Norte Cartel is at war with other cartels to expand its U.S. territory," the Mexican agent said.

"We're aware. We think that in attempting to set up their own rogue network in the U.S., Salazar and Johnson made the grave error of ripping off the Norte Cartel.

"We believe that when Salazar and Johnson went to Juarez to formally put their network in play, the Norte Cartel executed them and went looking for Galviera and their money. Galviera went underground with the cash. Evidence was found at the crime scene linking Salazar and Johnson to Galviera. And we checked the ESN's on the prepaid cell phones used by Salazar and Johnson. They were used to call numbers of a prepaid cell phone in Phoenix in the days before Galviera disappeared."

"So why did the cartel take Tilly Martin?" a Phoenix detective asked.

"We have not yet determined precisely how the cartel located and selected someone close to Galviera. But that is their method. Somehow they learned that Cora was not only his secretary, but his girlfriend. Posing as cops, they grabbed Tilly to pressure Galviera to surface with their cash."

"How do we know Galviera is not dead?" one investigator asked.

"We think the cartel would have displayed him as a message," Hackett said. "They're big on that."

"This gives us reason to believe Tilly is still alive, too," a female DEA agent said.

"Yes, it does," Larson said.

"But for how much longer?" Hackett said. "As we've seen with the eyeball incident and the severing of heads in the desert, these guys have turned torture into an art form."

Another grim-faced veteran DEA agent shot Hackett an icy stare.

"Let's see if I've got this, Earl. We have no leads on where Tilly is?"

"Nothing solid."

"We have no leads on where Galviera and the money are?"

"No."

"Tell me something about Cora's brother, Jack Gannon, the newswire reporter. Didn't he have some tie to Mexico? How did he get on the desert murder story almost as fast as your team, Earl?" The agent's gaze went around the room.

"We checked him out. He was on assignment in Mexico at the time of the kidnapping. He's a well-respected journalist who was nominated for a Pulitzer. He's broken a few big stories, including that one about a Buffalo cop under suspicion and a threat against the U.S."

"Well, if that's the case, if I were you, Earl, I'd be concerned about the things he may know that you don't."

The DEA agent had hit a nerve. Hackett knew Gannon had gone to Los Angeles and was concerned Gannon might have information he was not sharing with the FBI. But he'd be damned if he was going to admit it here and now.

"We can't prevent him, or the press, from investigating this case as a journalist," Hackett said. "He's obviously got a stake in it."

"And what about his sister?" The DEA agent held up the summary. "Your sheet here says she's a former addict. Hell, that's got to raise a few red flags."

Larson noted that checks were done for the drug dealers Cora Martin, aka Cora Gannon, had admitted associations with some fifteen years ago. "The subjects were known by the street names of Deke in Boston and

Rasheed in Toronto. Boston P.D. and the Toronto Police Services have found nothing so far," she said.

"We're pursuing other avenues of investigation. It would be premature to discuss them now." Hackett shot a look around the room. "I think that wraps it up at this time."

The meeting broke up.

Investigators gathered files, notebooks, cell phones and BlackBerries and shuffled from the room, leaving Hackett alone. He ran his hand across his face, chewing on his anxiety, which encompassed his mistrust of Gannon and his suspicion of Cora.

They got clear fingerprints from her. So why did she hesitate to volunteer them at the outset?

As far as they could determine, Cora was never arrested, or charged. So why hesitate to give up her fingerprints?

Every cop knows that at the outset of a crime, everyone connected to it lies, covers up or hides some piece of the truth.

Everyone.

Tilly's enlarged photo stared at Hackett from the monitor.

Sitting there, it suddenly dissolved into the face of the red-haired medical student, Betsy.

Hackett blinked and saw Tilly's face again.

Maybe he was exhausted.

All he wanted was to find her alive and arrest the people responsible, because standing over the casket of another innocent victim murdered on his watch was something he could not bear.

23

Lago de Rosas, Mexico

A hard day's drive south of Juarez on a windblown road, stretching before the lonely sierras, the bean fields, and abandoned mines, was the hamlet of Lago de Rosas.

It was a speck on the map, forgotten by the nearest, still-distant towns. Few in this remote region paid much attention to the seventeen hundred campesinos, impoverished descendants of field workers, farm and ranch hands who lived, toiled, prayed and died here.

For Lago de Rosas was little more than a faded memory, a dusty cluster of tumbledown shops, and ramshackle adobe houses. They lined tired dirt streets that huddled around the community's church, built of white stone by Roman Catholic missionaries in early 1800s.

But like the hamlet, it was decaying.

Its bell tower was eroding. Inside, the floors were cracked. The carved pine pews were split. The chipped walls were barren, punctuated by stained-glass windows with graphic depictions of Christ's suffering at the Stations of the Cross. Lit by the sun, the images came alive; Christ's blood flowed in crimson streams that carried the promise of salvation from the torment of human suffering.

Father Francisco Ortero adhered to this belief. It's what sustained him every day, he thought as he left the small rectory and walked under the punishing sun through the earthen courtyard to the church.

Evil thrived in Mexico's violence and he had witnessed too much of it.

For some thirty years, Father Ortero had been posted to parishes throughout Ciudad Juarez. He was on the front line as the city evolved into the primary battlefield for the country's drug wars. In that time, he'd seen children he'd baptized fall into the drug world; a world where friends became enemies; a world that pitted brother against brother.

He saw the city's streets turn red with blood.

In that time, he'd sermonized in his church about the dangers of living the life of the *narcotraficantes*. He counseled families of victims, tried to reach out to gang members, went to prisons to talk to criminals and urged them to return to God.

But his parish, his city, his country continued hemor-rhaging.

Father Ortero had lost count of how many roadside shootings he'd hurried to in order to offer the sacrament of the dying, or how many hospital beds he had been called to in order to hear a last confession, or how many times he performed a funeral mass.

When Father Ortero's friend, a community leader, was murdered several months ago, he shook with rage. He couldn't explain why this death had angered him more than any of the countless others.

Perhaps he'd reached a breaking point?

For he believed he was a soldier in a war against evil.

And he refused to accept that God could let evil tri-umph.

In the wake of the murder, the priest had called out from his pulpit for anyone with information to step forward, to let the world know who the killer was. *Or take care of matters the narco way.* When word of his outbursts reached his diocese he was summoned to his bishop's office.

"This kind of vengeful talk is not the way of the church. It is dangerous, Francisco. No one knows that better than you," the bishop said. "The cartels will threaten you, or worse. I think it is time for a quiet reassignment, for spiritual and safety reasons."

Without any fanfare, Father Ortero's bishop posted him to the smallest, poorest community in the diocese with orders to "heal and rest."

This was how he came to be the exiled priest in Lagos de Rosas.

Father Ortero's keys jingled as he unlocked the church door and went inside and prepared. In the sacristy, he kissed his purple stole, put it on over his white clerical shirt and glimpsed himself in the small mirror under a cross. Nearly sixty-three, he still had the strong posture of the boxer from his seminary days when he was an Olympic-caliber middleweight.

He never feared a fight.

Father Ortero accepted that Lagos de Rosas would be his last posting, that he would retire with this parish. Die here, perhaps. He accepted that fact, but acceptance was absent from his face. Behind his placid, priestly mask, his eyes carried an underlying sadness, flagging unhealed wounds and a brewing storm of unresolved anger.

He shifted his thoughts and walked through the church. The air smelled of wax. Someone had lit the votive candles. A few parishioners were in pews, on their knees, their rosary beads clicking softly as they prayed.

He checked his watch before entering one of the confessional booths. The latch for the half door clacked. He drew the curtain. The small red ornate light above the confessional went on. For the next two hours, as was the case every weekday, according to the sign posted at the front of the church, Father Ortero would hear the confession of sins.

Over that time, several people came in and out of the church. Children held their tiny hands firmly together at their lips, prayerlike. Adults were less formal. One by one they entered the darkened booth, knelt and whispered their confessions.

They were the usual trespasses: A boy stole a peso from his mother's purse. A mother had slapped her daughter during an argument. One man had lusted after his neighbor's wife. Between confessions the priest used a small light to read the Bible, making notes for his next sermon.

As the two hours came to a close, Father Ortero peeked through the curtain. The church appeared empty. He decided to finish reading his chapter of Scripture, then end the session.

As he reached the last few paragraphs, someone entered the confessional. He saw the silhouette, but heard nothing.

"Go ahead," Father Ortero encouraged.

Silence.

"Don't be nervous. God is present."

Silence.

"How long has it been since your last confession?"

Silence.

"I'll help you begin. Bless me, Father…"

"I've been searching for you, Father Ortero."

The priest was taken aback. The unfamiliar voice was that of a young man.

"You've found me, my son. How can I help you?"

"I am a *sicario*."

Ortero cleared his throat, his knees cracked as he stiffened in the booth.

"Do not think about looking at me, Father. It would be a mistake to try to identify me."

"The seal of the confession offers anonymity," he said, "even for *sicarios*."

"It is what I am."

"Do you wish to confess?"

"I wish to negotiate."

"What is there to negotiate?"

"Recently, police have found two bodies in a barn on a ranch south of Juarez."

The priest was aware, having read a news story.

"That is my most recent job."

"Confess. Surrender. I will help you turn yourself in."

"I have searched for you because you are known to have reached out to narcos. You are respected among the *narcotraficantes,* some of whom would enjoy seeing you in your grave."

"If it is God's will."

"Today, I am as close to God as you will ever get without dying. I have killed nearly two hundred people. I am the last thing they saw before death. There has never been anyone like me and there never will be anyone like me."

"What is it you want to negotiate?"

"I am haunted by the ghosts of people I have killed. They torment me, telling me that rival *sicarios* are coming to kill me and that because of my sins, I will not be permitted to enter heaven, that I am doomed to burn eternally in hell unless I do something about it."

"Change your ways and surrender."

"I want to walk away from this life."

"Then do it. Confess to police now, call the press to report it for history."

"I need to walk away according to my terms."

"What are your terms?"

"I will quit the *sicario* way, but first I must finish one final cartel job in a few days. I will be paid a lot of money for this. I will give half of the money to this church, your church of Lagos de Rosas, for this pitiful stain of a village. Think of all the good you could do. A new school, or clinic? In exchange you will absolve me of my sins so that I will gain entry to heaven. That is my deal."

"Entry to heaven is not purchased with blood money. The way to heaven is truth."

"I have told you the truth. Help me." Silence passed and the young man repeated, "Help me. I cannot sleep. I am tortured by the dead."

"Turn yourself in."

"You must absolve me."

"I can't."

"As a priest, you are bound by your oath to God. Absolve me."

"You are not truly repentant. You are a frightened braggart. There can be no benediction."

A tense moment passed.

Then Father Ortero felt movement before the curtain whisked in the adjoining box. He leaned forward in his confessional seat, parted his own curtain to see a shadow exiting the empty church.

Flames of the votive candles trembled in the air that trailed its passing.

24

The airline agent behind the ticket counter grasped that Gannon needed to be on the next flight to Las Vegas.

"You said one way?"

"Yes."

"Nothing to check in?" Her keyboard clacked.

"Nothing."

A printer hummed, then she handed him his boarding pass. "Your flight boards in twenty minutes. The security lines are good. You should make it." She reached for a walkie-talkie. "I'll alert the gate agent."

"Thanks."

After trotting though Terminal One at LAX and clearing passenger screening, Gannon arrived at his gate, where the agent there confirmed his pass and seat.

"Thank you, sir. We'll commence preboarding in ten minutes."

Gannon used the time to call Cora on her cell phone in Phoenix.

"Hello."

"It's Jack. Are you free to talk?" But it didn't matter if Hackett was near her, he could not hold off pushing her for more information.

"Yes."

"Ivan Peck says he is not Tilly's father."

"He's lying."

"He says he can't father children."

"He's lying."

"What proof do you have?"

"He was the only man who…the only one who…"

"Just tell me the truth, Cora!" Heads snapped in his direction; people stared at Gannon. He moved to a private area and dropped his voice. "He said you weren't waitressing in North Hollywood." He paused. "Cora, he said you were a hooker."

As the word hung there, he heard her break over the line and it tore him up inside. He clenched his eyes as memories pulled him back to Buffalo, to when they were just kids. It was his bedtime. Mom and Dad were working extra shifts. He'd taken his bath, gotten into his pajamas, combed his hair, brushed his teeth. Now Cora was reading Paddle-to-the-Sea *to him, the part where the forest was burning and flames covered the entire page. Everything was on fire. And now here he was standing in LAX, swallowing bile because his sister, his big sister whom he'd worshipped, had been a prostitute.*

Even with his eyes shut, everything was on fire.

Cora was crying now.

"It's all right," he said. "Just tell me the truth. Tell me how you are certain he is Tilly's father."

"He refused to use protection. He paid double. He was the only one. I was an addict, Jack. I needed money to survive. I was in hell. I was messed up. You could never understand how much shame I felt, why I could never go home again."

Gannon searched the preboarding area in vain, looking for the right words.

After a moment, Cora found a measure of composure and continued.

"Peck is Tilly's father. Damn it, did you not see the resemblance?"

"No. Maybe. I don't know. Look, he gave me a lead, so I came here, straight to LAX."

"A lead?" Hope rose in her voice. "What is it?"

"A guy you used to know. He's in Las Vegas now."

"Who?"

"Vic Lomax."

"Lomax. No. No, Jack!"

"Listen, Cora, I realize Peck may have been feeding me bullshit. I know this is a long shot but he said Lomax was tied to cartels. He might get us closer to people who have Tilly."

The gate agent announced the first boarding call for his flight over the public address.

"Are you flying to Las Vegas now?"

"Yes."

"Don't. I'm begging you to stay away from Lomax."

"Why?"

"He's a dangerous monster, Jack. Stay away from him."

"We don't have many options here."

"Lomax is not one of them. He's in the past, buried, dead to me, Jack."

Confusion and anger began churning in Gannon's gut.

"What's wrong with you?" he said. "Tilly's life is on the line. We have to try everything. Lomax might know something!"

"Do not go to Lomax!"

"What the hell's going on? You begged me to help you. Are you telling me everything? Are you playing me? Are you involved in this, Cora? Tell me the goddamn truth!"

"No!"

"Then what the hell's wrong with you?"

"Jack, please." Cora swallowed. "In all those years, with everything I went through, my life was a nightmare.

It's *still* a nightmare. If I lose Tilly… I'm so sorry. I just don't know anything anymore."

The long-distance static between them carried her sobs until Gannon heard another boarding call.

"I have to go, Cora."

25

The sedate, upscale community of Tall Palm Rise was east of The Strip, between Flamingo Road and East Sahara Avenue.

Big celebrity names, casino execs and a few mobsters had once lived in this enclave of custom-made luxury homes, bordered by golf courses, country clubs and palm groves.

It oozed retro grandeur.

Gannon's cab rolled by the coral-colored stucco houses. Their butterfly roofs crested the high stone-and-shrub privacy walls. Some remained hidden by the fruit and palm trees. Most had fenced yards equipped with security systems that kept visitors under surveillance.

This was where Vic Lomax lived.

A long way from pimping in North Hollywood, Gannon thought.

From the moment he'd left Peck's office in Los Angeles for Las Vegas, Gannon had launched an all-out investigative offensive on Victor Lomax. In the short time he had, Gannon worked his sources, texting Isabel Luna and Adell Clark.

In the taxi to LAX, he used his BlackBerry to search every WPA database he could for records and learned that Lomax held controlling interest in the World of Dreams, a Las Vegas casino-hotel. Soft news stories had portrayed him as a philanthropist involved in local, state and national charities.

There were pictures.

Cora was right, the guy looked all wrong. Like smiling was painful. Like being in human skin was alien to him. Yet there he was, grinning with Hollywood stars, handing out big checks, including one for a shelter for abused women.

"Be careful, Jack," Adell had cautioned him over his phone after he'd landed in Las Vegas, as he walked through Arrivals. "I called in a lot of big favors—retired FBI, DEA and Las Vegas Metro. Told them this was all about behind-the-scenes work to find your niece and that I needed their best intel on Lomax ASAP."

"And?"

"This guy is scary. He's come up in a number of investigations but there's never been enough to take to a grand jury."

"Bottom line?"

"The DEA and IRS suspect Lomax is using his casino to launder money for one of the cartels."

"That's not surprising."

"There are rumors that Lomax performs other services for the cartel, that he makes bodies disappear in the desert."

"You find anything linking him to Salazar or Johnson?"

"No, but Lomax has entertained major cartel figures at his casino."

"Then he'd likely know something about Tilly's kidnappers."

"It's possible. Listen, I think the best place to find him is his casino."

"No, I'm going to his home."

"Are you nuts? You *do not* want to show up at his home."

"I want his attention."

"Jack, don't do it. It's too dangerous."

"Thanks, Adell."

Gannon had ended the call, gotten into a cab and checked his bag at a cheap airport motel before heading to Tall Palm Rise.

Now, as his cab reached Lomax's address, Gannon reached for his wallet. He paid the fare, tipped the driver, then held out two twenties. "You get one now and the other when I get in after you wait down the street. Not sure how long I'll be, but wait." Gannon slid on his dark glasses.

"I'll give it as long as I can," the driver said.

Lomax's house was 28 Ripple Creek Path, a single-story pale yellow stucco frame. It had an extra-large carport and gurgling fountain in the circular drive. The house sat on an acre lot hidden by shrubs, trees and professionally maintained landscaping. It was fully fenced, protected by high stone walls and a double wrought-iron gate, with an intercom embedded in the right stone column.

Gannon pushed the intercom button and waited.

A mechanized whirr sounded as the security camera atop the right column tilted slightly to record his visit.

"Yes?" a female voice asked through the intercom.

"My name is Jack Gannon. I am a reporter with the World Press Alliance. I want to see Mr. Lomax, Vic Lomax."

"He's not here. I suggest you try his office at World of Dreams."

"I suggest you give him a message. Tell him his North Hollywood past has caught up with him. Tell him he's going to be named in a news story about the kidnapping of a child by a drug cartel. Tilly Martin is my niece. Tell him he can meet me face-to-face in the next ninety minutes at the Loaded Dice diner on Las Vegas Boulevard to comment on the story. Otherwise, the story goes out with his name, his picture and the allegations."

"Who the hell are you?"

Gannon removed his dark glasses and stared at the camera.

"Jack Gannon. World Press Alliance, the newswire agency. Take my picture. I'll wait at the diner for ninety minutes for Mr. Lomax. Then the story goes. Tell him that, now. Got it?"

A mechanized whirr sounded again as the security camera pulled tighter on Gannon. He waited, replaced his glasses, then walked to the waiting cab, reaching for the twenty to give the driver.

Did he just make a mistake?

Gannon glanced at the big clock above the counter of the Loaded Dice diner. For the better part of an hour, he'd subtly scrutinized every customer who'd entered the diner, concluding that they were tourists, rollers or local characters. No one resembled Vic Lomax.

What if he struck out? What next?

As the waitress topped up his coffee, he was assailed by images of Cora's past. He saw her with Ivan Peck— *"she was a fine piece of ass"*—with Vic Lomax and other scumbags and creeps.

My sister.

He considered his mother and father and the sleepless nights they'd spent sitting in the darkened Buffalo kitchen, sick with worry, not knowing if Cora was alive.

Knowing the truth would have killed them.

After picking over the remainder of his cheeseburger and fries, Gannon stared at himself in the black surface of his coffee. He needed to shave. The past few days had been mashed together, Mexico, Phoenix, Los Angeles and Las Vegas. Where did he go from here?

He checked his phone again.

No texts from Luna or Adell. One word from Lyon in New York.

Update?

Chasing a new lead. Tell you more when I can, he responded.

Cora texted him: What's happening, Jack?

Not sure, we'll talk later.

Then he looked at Tilly's picture again. It was like looking at Cora. Memories started to swirl until the waitress arrived to remove his plate. Two hours had passed. It was time to go. He paid the bill, then went outside to flag a cab to the airport.

"Got the time?" a voice asked.

Gannon turned to a large man who'd materialized on the sidewalk, just as an SUV with tinted windows halted beside them. The rear passenger door swung open. Sitting inside, a man with a jacket on his lap tugged it back to let Gannon see a gun barrel.

"Get in," the stranger behind him said.

26

The SUV traveled southbound along Interstate 15.

Gannon was positioned in the rear seat, between the large man and the man with a gun. Another man sat up front with the driver.

No one spoke.

They had to be Lomax's people. *Be calm.* He inhaled and tried to control his breathing. *Think,* Gannon told himself. *Is there anything you can do here?*

The large man was rough as he patted Gannon for a weapon. Then he took Gannon's BlackBerry and wallet and passed them to the guy in the front passenger seat. He studied Gannon's ID, made a call and spoke in muted tones.

Gannon felt the highway clicking under them as they traveled beyond the city, then turned onto a secondary road, then turned again onto a back road. Fewer and fewer buildings dotted the landscape. Before long, the area had grown desolate. The SUV jiggled when they turned off the road and cut across the desert, coming to a ridge that descended into a low valley that looked like a dried riverbed.

They stopped and jerked Gannon out of the SUV.

The heat was intense as they led him several feet away.

He heard the tail door open. A shovel clanked on the cracked earth.

"Start digging, asshole," one of the men said.

Gannon looked at his captors, stone-cold behind their dark glasses. One stepped forward, seized the shovel and scraped a six-foot-by-two-foot square in the surface, then put the shovel in Gannon's hand.

One of the men directed Gannon with his gun hand.

"Dig down three feet."

Gannon's stomach spasmed as all the saliva evaporated in his mouth. He barely felt the shovel as he started digging.

"My news organization knows where I am and who I went to see," he said.

The air exploded and Gannon flinched as the gunshot echoed.

"Shut the fuck up and dig," the gunman said.

Gannon started digging.

Odd, he was not afraid. He was at peace. If this was how it was going to be, then this was how it would be. But he would not go down without a fight. He considered charging the gunman with the shovel, swinging that blade at his throat, but no doubt the others were armed, too. They were standing too far apart. At best, he'd get a shot at two of them, he figured as the sweat dripped from his face, making blotches in the sand.

Gannon was down a little over two feet deep when, out of the corner of his eye, he saw a dust cloud. He heard the crunch of tires, then saw an approaching vehicle.

Another SUV.

The gunman took the shovel from Gannon.

"Get on your knees and face the hole."

Squinting against the sun, Gannon saw doors open. A man in a white suit got out of the vehicle and approached the group. His dark glasses were locked on Gannon as he took Gannon's wallet from one of the men. He went through it quickly and nodded to the gunman, who then pressed the barrel hard against Gannon's head.

The new man removed his dark glasses.

Vic Lomax.

His face seemed as if it had been broken; his eyes were asymmetrical, as if one had migrated down and the other was sunken. His upturned shark's mouth twisted into a sneer and Gannon's head snapped when the back of Lomax's hand flew across his face.

"Who sent you, Gannon?"

"Nobody sent me."

"Don't lie."

"Nobody sent me."

"You go to my home. You threaten my family. You know, I scrape shit like you off my shoe. Did that old skank of a sister send you?"

"No."

"Some shit-for-brains cop?"

"No."

"Why come to me about this kidnapping shit that's all over the news?"

"To beg for your help to find my niece."

Still breathing hard, Lomax's nostrils flared as he glared at Gannon.

"I only know what's in the news and it looks like a lost cause."

"I'm begging you, please."

"Your stupid bitch sister never learned. She's at it again. You ask her why she got herself tied up with this Galviera asshole, who seems to have pissed off the wrong people."

"Just help me. A name, advice, anything, and I'll go away, I swear."

"I can make you go away—" Lomax snapped his fingers "—like that."

The gun bored into Gannon's skull.

"Please, she's eleven years old."

"I got nothing to do with this. Bet you didn't know that your bitch sister got into trouble with a cartel a long time ago. Ask her if it's got anything to do with this kidnapping shit."

"What kind of trouble?"

"The worst kind." Lomax gave it a few seconds to sink in. "You ask her what she and Donnie Cargo did in San Francisco all those years ago. When I first heard about it, I told them to hide, stay out of the mix. I told her this would follow her all of her life. Well, now it's caught up to her. So you talk to your sister, asshole, because I'm thinking that if your niece is not dead yet, she will be. And the only person Cora can blame for that is Cora."

27

Lago de Rosas, Mexico

The old woman was dying.

At her son's request, Father Francisco Ortero's weekly visits had become a daily ritual, now that she was so close to death.

She lived with her family at the hamlet's edge in a shack built of wood salvaged from pallets discarded by the fruit warehouse in the next town. The priest always declined the family's invitation to supper, not wanting to further strain their meager means.

He always arrived when the woman's daughter-in-law was washing her battered pots and pans, or taking dried linen down from the line. The little house was well kept and the corner of it where the old woman was confined to a narrow bed smelled of fresh flowers.

She always took Holy Communion from the priest, who would talk with her into the evening, telling her that she would be with her husband soon, for it was his job to prepare her to meet God. His words comforted her and she smiled.

When Father Ortero left, the moon was rising, washing the dirt road in blue as he walked back to the rectory. Finding peace in the evening, he looked back on his day. His foremost thought was the *sicario* who'd entered the confessional. While he had always expected some repercussion for the outspoken stand he had taken in Juarez against the *narcotraficantes,* the encounter was unexpected.

A cartel assassin had come to him—not for blood, but to confess.

The priest wondered if he had done enough to guide the killer back to God. Should he somehow alert police investigating the double murder south of Juarez? Wouldn't that break the seal of the confession, violate his vow? Perhaps he should talk to his bishop. His questions fell into the silence that cracked with the long, wild cry of a coyote, reminding him that primitive forces were near.

No one else was on the road tonight.

It was a lonely walk, his only company being his thoughts and the mournful wail of the predator in the darkness. This one was likely hunting mice or lizards. While coyotes were common here, they did not attack humans. He was not concerned. He'd walked this road many times and was often serenaded by coyotes.

Thud!

A stone hit the ground and rolled behind him. Instinctively, the priest stopped and turned.

Nothing was there.

When he turned back, a figure was standing before him, a few feet away, blocking his path. He was slender, taller than the priest, who stood five feet eight inches. A young man, judging by his build and his posture.

A bandanna covered his face, allowing the priest to see only his eyes and short hair. He wore jeans, a T-shirt and a shoulder holster that cradled a semiautomatic handgun.

"Father Ortero."

Immediately, he recognized the voice.

"Do you remember me?"

"Yes."

"I asked for you in the town. They told me I would find you here tonight. Don't be afraid."

"As I recall, you are the frightened one."

"You insult me. I have killed men for less."

The priest extended his arms, opened his palms.

"Go ahead. Guarantee your seat in hell."

The moon was ablaze in the *sicario's* eyes.

"I have given more thought to my situation, my offer to the church and what you said."

"You wish to confess here, now, and surrender to police?"

"I need to understand redemption and salvation. If I am truly repentant and I make my generous donation, will I receive absolution?"

"How old are you?"

"I am twenty."

"You are naive to think you can manipulate favor with God."

"I am sorry for my sins and I am willing to give the church more money than it will see in a thousand years."

"You murder two hundred people and you expect to buy eternal salvation with blood money?"

The *sicario* fell to his knees.

"My nightmares torment me and a rival gang wants to kill me. I must be absolved. I now know that Santa Muerte is a false saint. I leave my calling card now for effect only, to impress police. But I know she cannot protect me. I must make things right with God. I have given more thought to what you said."

"You will confess and surrender?"

"In a few more days, I will finish my next job, the one that pays large. Then I want you to arrange for me to tell my story to a trusted journalist, so police cannot twist it. Then I will surrender if I can work a deal with police."

"What sort of deal?"

"I want to go into witness protection in the U.S. or in Canada, in exchange for information I will give them about cartels, very important information that could end a lot of bloodshed."

"What is this next job?"

"I don't know. I will be told details later."

"Why not surrender now, end the killing now?"

"I need the money from this last job for my new life and to give to the church. Can you help me do this?"

"I do not like your proposal."

"It is not for liking. Can you help me?"

"Yes, I can help you surrender."

"And can you assure me absolution and save me from eternal hell?"

"Determining the destination of your soul is for God. I can assure you that if you go back on your offer, if you fail to surrender and atone, your soul will remain outside of God's light forever."

"I give you my word. I will surrender. I will be in contact."

The priest's rectory had one of the few phones in Lago de Rosas and the *sicario* took the number from Father Ortero before vanishing.

The priest stood alone.

He cupped his hands over his face. His heart was still racing as he tried to comprehend what had transpired. Did it even happen? It was as if the *sicario* were never there.

As the priest resumed walking, a desert wind tumbled across the land carrying with it the long rising howl of the coyote. It turned into yapping that fell into a growl, triggering a sudden high-pitched scream of something dying out there in the night.

28

It didn't add up.

As night fell, Percy Smoot wet the tips of his nicotine-stained fingers with his tongue and counted the cash at the Sweet Times Motel register.

Worn and torn fives, tens and twenties piled on the front desk. When he finished counting, the total was four hundred and eighty dollars.

Percy pushed aside the long strands of greasy hair that curtained over his face. His bloodshot gaze traveled over his bifocals to the heap of bills as if waiting for the total to change.

It should be five hundred and forty.

He shifted the toothpick clamped in his mouth and scratched his gut, which stretched the mustard stains on his Cardinals T-shirt. He then flipped through his registration cards. Nine units rented at sixty a pop, which meant he should have freakin' five hundred and forty in cash.

So why did he only have four eighty?

Somebody didn't pay.

If Percy came up short, that peckerwood owner, Lester, would accuse him of dipping into the till again and take the difference out of his paycheck.

Percy would be damned if he'd let that happen.

Fact was, somebody didn't pay. Question was, who?

He was certain he'd collected from everybody.

He rubbed the three-day growth on his chin, thinking, then drank from his mug of bourbon-flavored coffee. He looked at the nine empty key pegs on the wall. He definitely had rented nine units. *So, let's take a look at them cards again.* One by one, he snapped through the registration cards, trying to recall the face that went with each unit. Names meant nothing; no one ever used their real name here. Percy didn't give a rat's A, as long as they paid cash up front.

Every now and then, he'd cut some slack with his regulars.

But this time, someone must've got by him. *Here we go, the guilty party: Unit 28. It was those two shifty guys.* He tapped the card and it started coming back to him in pieces. They'd come in when Percy was half-asleep. They said something about paying later. He wasn't sure. All he knew was that they freakin' owed him.

All right. Percy sniffed, took another shot of his "coffee," reached for the motel phone. *Unit 28's going to cough up sixty bucks fast, before Lester shows up to collect today's cash.*

As he extended his forefinger to dial, he released a volcanic belch and blinked. Whoa, that was a bad one, Percy thought, assuring himself that he had pressed the right buttons for Unit 28.

The line rang twice before it was answered.

"What?"

"This is the front desk, sir."

"So?"

"It appears your account is open and we request that you settle it now."

"What?"

"Sir, you have an outstanding payment of sixty dollars cash."

"I paid you, you drunken asshole."

"That's not what our records show, sir."

"Fuck you." The line went dead.

Percy cursed and steadied himself on the desk. *All right, if that's the way we're going to play it.* He reached under the desk for his bottle and added more bourbon to his coffee. He took a big gulp, gritted his green teeth, then grabbed his baseball bat from behind the door.

Nobody rips off this old dog, Percy told himself, tapping the bat to his palm, ready to settle matters. Walking by the shit hole pool was a hazy reminder that he was a far cry from his old job at the Biltmore, before his wife died and he hit the juice.

Yeah, well, those days are gone.

His current problem crystallized when he got to Unit 28. He remembered. It was a deluxe suite with adjoining rooms but he'd only charged the two guests sixty bucks. He should've charged one-twenty. He hammered the bat on the scarred door. Nothing happened for a long moment until he felt a slight vibration, indicating movement inside.

He pounded again.

"Open up, hotel management!"

The lock and handle clicked. The door opened a crack and a man's unshaven face appeared behind the security chain. Percy brought the tip of his bat to within inches of it.

"You owe this establishment sixty dollars cash."

Questions surfaced in the man's dark eyes as he assessed Percy.

"I think you have made a mistake."

For a second, Percy thought the man's voice differed from the guy he'd just called but he dismissed it, hawked, spat and fixed his grip on the bat.

"Pay me now, or I call the cops to kick your ass out."

Unfazed, the man contemplated Percy as if he were an insect that had crawled under his boot. A moment passed before the man came to a decision.

"It's possible my friend did forget to pay. Sixty dollars, is it?"

"Damn straight."

"Wait."

Remaining at the door, the man shifted his weight as if searching for his jean pockets. Percy's ears pricked up at the jingle of a long chain coming from the adjoining room.

"Do you have a dog in there?"

The man shook his head.

"Because we have a no-pets policy. I might have to charge you extra for any damage."

"No dog."

"I don't give a rat's A what you two do to each other in there." Percy scanned what he could see through the sliver the opened door made. It was very dark but he glimpsed the wall mirror, reflecting the adjoining room. The inside partition door swung open ever so slightly and there was a diffusion of light, as if someone had moved inside.

Then everything became still.

Too still.

What was going on there in the other room?

In that instant Percy sensed something was not right. The man at the door, reading the first stage of alarm rising on Percy's face, tightened his grip on the Glock he was holding behind his back. The moment was telegraphed to the door man's partner, sitting on the edge of the bed with one hand over Tilly's mouth, the other holding a knife to her throat.

"Here, this should cover it."

The door man gave Percy several crumpled bills before closing and locking the door, leaving Percy to count off one hundred dollars.

He lowered his bat and shrugged.

As he returned to the office in his alcoholic stupor, he threw a parting look over his shoulder.

Something was not right in Unit 28, not right at all.

29

Twenty-five thousand feet over Nevada, Gannon gazed out his window, contemplated the sun setting over the desert and his close call with Vic Lomax.

After weighing the downside of murdering a reporter who was investigating a high-profile case, Lomax had instructed his goons to return Gannon intact to Las Vegas.

The ordeal resurrected other threats Gannon had faced in Texas, Brazil and Africa. That his job could be dangerous was a given, but this time it was his niece's life on the line and he had to do everything he could to save her. He was unearthing pieces of Cora's past, but those pieces spawned questions that might, or might not, be crucial to finding Tilly.

Who is Donnie Cargo?

What did he and Cora do in San Francisco? Was Cargo tied to Salazar and Johnson?

Those questions had troubled Gannon when he'd arrived at the Las Vegas airport, where he'd first considered flying to San Francisco. Before buying a ticket he'd launched a quick online search on Donnie Cargo but had found nothing.

Was Donnie Cargo even a real name?

He'd asked the WPA library to help and he'd contacted

Adell Clark and Isabel Luna, requesting they check for anything on "Donnie Cargo." It was not looking good and Gannon feared his luck at finding people fast may have run out. With little more than Lomax's accusation, he decided to return to Phoenix and confront Cora, again.

She had texted him minutes before he'd departed.

Jack, what's happening? Did you find Lomax?

Yes. We have to talk.

Call me.

No time. We'll talk when I get back.

Now, as the lights of Phoenix wheeled below and Gannon's plane began its descent, he returned to Lomax's allegation.

"Your bitch sister got into trouble with a cartel a long time ago…the worst kind…you ask her what she and Donnie Cargo did in San Francisco."

In the time Gannon was gone, Cora had remained lost in her pain.

She had not slept or eaten. The deeper Jack dug among the ruins of her old life, the more dangerous it got.

In finding Peck and Lomax, he'd exhumed demons that would drag her back into the pit of her past.

What did Lomax tell Jack?

It could guarantee that I never see Tilly again.

Forces continued mounting against Cora. Images of the gruesome delivery of eyeballs and those of the headless corpses of the two ex-officers found in the Mexican desert, tortured her. The FBI still had nothing on Lyle or the money. They had no leads on the kidnappers, or any trace of Tilly.

Was she still alive?

Cora prayed but hope seemed as distant as a dying star.

Now she heard the sound of rising voices in her living room. Recognizing one as Jack's, she went to her bedroom door, stopping when she saw him arguing with Hackett about where he'd been.

"I'm warning you, Gannon, if you're withholding information or interfering with this investigation—"

"You want to spend time violating my First Amendment rights instead of finding my niece? Want me to alert the WPA's lawyers in New York?"

"I want you to think about what you're doing. If you—"

"I have a right to talk privately with my sister."

Gannon entered Cora's bedroom, closing the door behind them.

"What did you find out?" Cora asked.

He struggled to keep his voice low as he spat back with a question.

"Are you involved in any way?"

"No!"

"Do you have, or have you ever had, a connection to any cartel that could be linked to this?"

Cora couldn't answer him.

"All right, so far this is what I've got," Gannon said. "You ran away with a drug addict, destroyed our family, became a prostitute, got pregnant, left the life and cleaned up. Then your daughter is kidnapped by a drug gang because your boyfriend owes them five million dollars and you want everyone to believe that you and your past have nothing to do with this?"

Her face crumpled and she covered it with her hands.

"What are you keeping from me, Cora?"

Could she tell him? Could she spell out every devastating mistake she'd ever made? Several anguished moments came and went.

"Cora?"

She didn't respond.

"You called me, remember? I'm putting everything on the line for you."

"It's not about me, Jack. It's about finding Tilly. I called you to help find who took her, help me bring her home."

"Then tell me everything! For Christ's sake, Cora! I get more help from the scum in your past than I do from you!"

"I have to protect Tilly!"

"From what? What could be worse than this? I don't understand you!" Gannon saw that she was contending with a whirlwind. He softened his approach. "You were my hero, Cora. My big sister. I worshipped you. It's because of you I became a reporter."

"Jack, you have to trust me. It's not what you or Hackett think. I am a good person, a good mother. I did terrible things to survive a long time ago. I'm not perfect...I made mistakes. I was a seventeen-year-old addict when I ran away. It was stupid but I had my reasons."

"Yeah? And what were they?"

Fear, horror and shame.

Two life-changing incidents were buried in Cora's past; events she never spoke of, or dared to revisit. She'd kept them secret for decades. That's how she'd survived, if you could call it that. But now, in order to help save Tilly, she would have to exhume one of them for Jack.

Only one.

The other must never be revealed.

Cora swallowed hard, hesitated. The pain was unbearable, the shame overwhelming. It hurt so much to even form a thought around the right words. But she had to do it. She'd have to tell him about the night that changed her forever.

The night that made her less human.

"When I was sixteen, I went to a party. Somebody put something in my drink and I was gang-raped."

Gannon stared at her for the longest time.

His big sister.

Memory carried him back and he no longer saw Cora, the damaged woman before him. Suddenly he saw his sister at the kitchen table of their Buffalo home, blowing out candles for her fourteenth birthday party.

She glows in that pretty yellow dress Mom had made.

Glows like an angel.

Looking upon her now, in the wake of her painful revelation, his heart broke for her. His eyes stung and slowly, his shock gave way to rage. He wanted to drive his fist through something, wanted to attack the violation of his sister.

"Who were the assholes? Do we know?"

She shook her head.

"Jesus, Cora, I'm so sorry. I…I never…realized."

"This is the first time I ever told anyone. I never told Mom, Dad, anyone. That was a mistake. I turned to drugs. That's how it all happened. The night I ran off, after my biggest blowup with Mom and Dad, Dad told me to never come back. It was like a knife through my heart. I was garbage to them."

"That was never true, Cora. They did everything they could to find you, to bring you home. Mom told me how Dad regretted saying what he said to you every day of his life after you left. They loved you."

"I know. I don't blame them. I was horrible to live with. I was stupid, so messed up. And after I left, I made one mistake after another for over a decade. I was a failure and nearly destroyed myself. But it all changed when I had Tilly. She was my salvation. When I had her, I turned my life around. Then this happens. I don't have anything to do with cartels, or any of this."

"Is that the whole truth? Are you telling me everything?"

"You want the whole truth? Okay. Deep down, I am out of my mind with fear that maybe somehow, in some way, this could be connected to my past. But it's not about me. My past is behind me. I'm a single mom, a secretary at a courier company. I never knew what Lyle was up to. I loved him, trusted him with my heart and he betrayed us. That's the absolute truth, Jack."

He rubbed his haggard face, then his eyes.

"Not all of it."

"What do you mean?"

"Who is Donnie Cargo?"

The name tore her wide open. Jack was getting too close to her last secret. Lomax must've told him about Donnie. Cora looked at him. Or rather, she looked right through him, as though he wasn't there, trepidation clouding her gaze. The name pierced her the way lightning pierces the darkness, hurling her back to that night in San Francisco and…

Rain.

A downpour. She's maybe nineteen and her life's a blur, like the city with its twinkling lights drowning at night. Donnie's driving, Vic is with her in the back and she's tripping, totally wired on crack. It's a pretty city, cable cars climb halfway to the stars. Donnie and Vic picked her up. You're coming with us. Donnie Cargo brags that his nickname means shipment because he moves the supplies. He doesn't have a real name. She doesn't care. He's always jittery, always sweaty. You're coming with us on an errand. That's right, Vic says. Got to take care of business, then we'll have a little party. Vic throws good parties, has good drugs. She owes Vic. She works for drugs. A little of this and a little of that. Anything for drugs. Vic owns her because she owes him. Vic's the boss. Vic the prick, Vic the psycho. Vic has more enemies than friends. What does she know? She's a tripped-out street ho from Buffalo. What does she care? All she wants to do is party. Kick ass, die young. You're coming with us on a little errand before Vic's party. They float through Golden Gate Park, the Haight. I was born late, she says. I should have been a hippie…flowers in my hair…rain fallin' on my head… Where are they now? Eight miles high. Where we going, boys? Where is this place? I'm a stranger here. Projects, blighted row houses and gloomy alleys. Vic says I got to send a message to a guy. A streetlamp hits on the chrome of the gun tucked in Vic's waist. A gun? Cora's upright like a shot. What the fuck? A gun? Donnie, let me out! He smiles. Be cool. Let me out now, you crazy mothers! Vic says be cool. Cora, baby, dial it down. Cora…Cora…Cora…

"Cora, did you hear me?" Jack squeezed her shoulders hard. "I said, something's going on."

"What is it?"

He opened her bedroom door to a surge of activity among the investigators in her living room. The air sparked with tension, as an agent, cell phone pressed to his head, passed on information to Hackett,

"Phoenix P.D. emergency dispatcher's got a caller now in real time who says he's got a location on our suspects!"

"Can she patch us in to listen to the call?"

The agent spoke into the phone, then gave a big nod.

30

"Sir, can you confirm if the people are still in the unit?"

The Phoenix police emergency operator listened for the caller's response through her headset. Pumped with caffeine for her night shift, she concentrated amid a multibutton telephone console, radios and monitors with colored geocode maps, her fingers poised over a keyboard.

"Sir?"

"Yes, they're there."

The operator resumed typing.

Her rapid-fire staccato updates shot across computer screens in patrol cars, alerting them to a report of a possible kidnapping/hostage-taking in Unit 28 of the Sweet Times Motel.

Immediately procedures were set in motion for a rescue operation. Radio silence was maintained in case the subjects were monitoring emergency traffic on scanners. All communication was made through secure cell phones or by text, as police cars took up positions just out of sight of the motel. More units were dispatched to the area with orders not to use emergency lights or sirens.

"Sir, can you see the room from where you are now?"

"No, not from the office here."

"But you saw them?"

"Yes, half an hour ago, maybe. I was at their room talking to one of them about their outstanding bill. Then I turned on the news and seen another report on that kidnapped girl, then I realized what I seen in the mirror. At first I thought it was a woman—it was dark—but there was a guy holding his hand over her face. I seen a bitty piece of them in the mirror. I heard a chain, like a dog's chain, and the guy at the door looked like the police sketch on the news. And later it hit me after I watched the news report—oh boy, that's them all right."

The operator's supervisor stood over her workstation. He was also wearing a headset and listening. He had another line going directly to the FBI. The supervisor pressed a button that let the FBI and Hackett's team in Mesa Mirage listen in on the motel caller to the 911 operator.

"Sir?" the operator continued. "Sir, I need you to listen to me carefully. Did you see any weapons?"

"I think I saw a knife."

"Can you describe the vehicle belonging to the subjects?"

"No, they parked around the side. Want me to look?"

"I need you to stay on the line. Can you do that, sir?"

"Yeah."

"Okay, good. We've got people rolling."

"Hey, there's a reward for this, right?"

Forty-five minutes after the 911 call, the heavy-duty van used by the Phoenix Police Department's Special Assignments Unit creaked to a halt in the Golden Cut Processing Plant's larger shipping lot behind the plant. The lot was near the Sweet Times Motel but not visible from any unit.

A dozen SAU squad members stepped out, equipped

with rifles and handguns, each wearing helmets, armor and headset walkie-talkies. They huddled around the hood of an unmarked patrol car. Tate Halder, the squad sergeant, switched on his headlamp, unfolded a large sheet of paper and sketched a map of the motel property based on an attachment emailed to him by the records department.

"Listen up, people. Unit 28 is here, north of the pool—"

As the squad crafted its strategy, police cars choked off traffic at all points around the motel area. Officers with photos of Tilly Martin fixed to clipboards recorded plates and checked vehicles leaving or attempting to enter the zone.

SAU Lieutenant Chett Gibb and negotiator Rawley Thorpe had entered the motel office. After interviewing the 911 caller, motel manager Percy Smoot, Gibb took no chances, despite Smoot's booziness. Gibb sent plainclothes officers to escort all guests, with the exception of Unit 28, from their rooms and quietly lead them out of the line of fire.

When FBI Agents Earl Hackett and Bonnie Larson pulled into the Golden Cut parking lot, they were directed to the motel office. They shook hands with Gibb and Thorpe, who acknowledged Smoot's condition.

"All right, what do you have?" Hackett asked.

"Mr. Smoot here is convinced Tilly Martin is being held hostage by two men who fit the description," Gibb said.

"Did you talk to her?" Larson asked Smoot.

"No, ma'am, but I saw her in there, even though it was dark. I think they got her chained."

"Have you had anything to drink today, sir?" Hackett asked.

"Couple sips for medicinal reasons. But I am telling you, I know what I seen a little while ago."

"Thank you, sir," Hackett said, pulling Gibb and Thorpe aside. "What's next?"

"Halder's squad makes a dynamic entry, kicks the door, goes in with flash bangs."

"You've ruled out calling in?" Hackett asked.

"Can't risk them grabbing the girl, using her as a shield."

Gibb raised his walkie-talkie and checked with Halder.

"What's your status, Tate?"

"Good to go."

Without making a sound, two squad members scouted the hot zone surrounding Unit 28. The motel had been cleared of life and the night held an eerie quiet, conveying a false sense of calm.

Tension filled the air, as if a shotgun had been racked.

Using a stethoscope device, they heard the sound of Unit 28's TV and air conditioner. No other movement, as they waved in their team.

Pressed against the chipped exterior walls, the squad inched toward the door with one member leading as point, another as rear cover.

For an instant, Halder recalled how a barricaded gunman shot a squad member during an arrest at a school shooting last year. The officer survived; the gunman didn't. Checking his grip on his weapon, Halder forced his thoughts back to the operation.

His squad was made up of battle-tested veterans.

Each one was ready.

At that moment, Jack Gannon and Cora arrived in Cora's Pontiac Vibe at a police checkpoint at the outer perimeter, far from the motel.

They got there without Hackett's blessing.

Indifferent to their pleas at the house, Hackett had

refused to give them information on the motel tip, again, because he didn't want them at the scene. It didn't matter. Gannon had been alerted by a WPA photographer who was among the press pack keeping vigil outside Cora's home. The photographer was standing near a patrol car when he'd overheard two officers discussing the dispatches they'd read on their terminal.

As Gannon expected, the breaking news was not exclusive to the WPA. Other media outlets had also learned of it through their sources and once they spotted Cora at the police line, they moved in for her reaction. Microphones were thrust at her and news cameras closed in as reporters fired questions.

"Is your daughter in the motel?"

"Are these the kidnappers?"

"Cora, please tell us, what thoughts go through your mind at this time?"

Her heart racing she glanced at Jack, who gave a little nod.

"I'm terrified," she said. "I can't take it anymore. I want Tilly home, safe."

Beyond the motel's pool and across the courtyard, SAU sniper Paul Mulligan lay flat on his stomach in the shadow of a trash bin, one eye squinted behind his rifle.

The window and door of Unit 28 filled his scope.

Mulligan's accuracy was rated at ninety-eight percent.

The room's curtains were almost completely drawn. Concentrating on the dark interior, Mulligan detected no movement and whispered his report to Tate Halder and their lieutenant, Chett Gibb.

After a last run-through, Gibb green-lighted the squad.

"Go!" Halder said.

The battering ram popped the door, followed by the deafening *crack-crack* and blinding flashes of stun grenades as the tactical team stormed the room. Flashlight beams pierced the fog as the heavily armed team swept the rooms in choreographed tactical maneuvers to detect and neutralize any threat.

Bedroom number one: empty. Bathroom: empty. Closets: empty. Bedroom number two: empty. Bathroom: empty. Closets: empty. The ceiling, floors and walls were tapped for body mass.

They found fast food take-out containers heaped in the trash.

"What the hell?"

Halder and the others looked at a long silver chain fixed to an open handcuff near the bed.

"We just missed them, Tate." Hawkins, the squad's point man, touched a take-out coffee cup. "It's warm."

Halder reached for his radio.

Less than half an hour after Halder's squad cleared Unit 28, the FBI's Evidence Response Team began processing it. Time passed at an excruciating pace before Cora's cell phone rang.

It was Hackett. After learning Cora and Gannon were at the tape, he advised them to proceed to the motel.

"Need you to look at something."

Cora passed her phone to a Phoenix officer, who nodded a few times and said, "Right away." Then Cora and Gannon went to the Sweet Times office. Hackett showed Cora a photo on his cell phone of a small shirt.

"They found this on the bed," he said, zooming in, enlarging it.

Cora and Gannon studied the shirt's unicorn pattern.

"Oh my God, that's Tilly's pajama top!"

"There's no mistake?" Hackett asked.

Cora touched her fingernail to a small tear on the cuff. "I did that on the dryer door. That's hers," Cora said. Looking at Hackett, her eyes filled with anguish. "Did you find her?"

31

Hail Mary, full of grace...pray for us sinners, now and at the hour of our death...

Can God hear me in my dark coffin? Tilly asked.

Drenched with sweat, almost drowning in fear—*drowning, like when Lenny Griffin held her underwater.* Her heart was pounding with the *thump-thump* rhythm of the wheels on the highway.

Where were they going? What were they going to do?

She was buried in darkness.

The creeps had moved so fast after some angry guy had banged on the door. Tilly's first thought—her hope—was that real police had come to save her. The banging had surprised her kidnappers. Ruiz, the one whose English was good, told Alfredo, the dumb one, to hold her.

She had tried to claw off her gag, to scream for help to whoever was banging on the door, but Alfredo had one hand around her mouth and held a knife to her throat with the other one. The guy at the door sounded mad and from what she could glimpse through the crack, he had a bat or something.

Ruiz calmed him down.

But when Tilly saw the gun behind his back, she

thought, *"Oh no, he's going to shoot the guy at the door, then kill me, too."* She got so scared she peed a little.

Ruiz gave the angry guy money and he went away.

Then—*bam!* They moved so fast.

They didn't even put on the phony cop uniforms, staying in their jeans and T-shirts as they collected all their stuff in travel bags. Then they unlocked the chain from her leg, cut the tape on her wrists, making her get dressed, go to the bathroom with the door open, all the while barking: *"Hurry up! Faster!"* Then Alfredo tightened her gag and retaped her wrists. But he didn't notice how she'd held them apart slightly, getting some play that allowed her to wriggle them a little.

Then she was forced back inside the big black suitcase.

My coffin.

They zipped it shut, rolled her to their car, hefted her into the trunk and drove. Tilly couldn't make sense of her nightmare. Why were they doing this to her? She didn't really understand why they were so mad at Lyle. He was nice to her, he worked so hard at his business and her mom was in love with him.

Tilly liked Lyle a lot and hoped that one day they'd be a real family.

Why can't they just leave us alone?

Tilly missed her mom so much. She loved her so much and wanted to be home with her now, *so much.*

What if the creeps kill me?

What if I never see Mom again?

Tilly tasted the salt of her tears seeping into her gag and held her breath when she felt the car slow down. As the highway noise decreased she heard the muffled voices of the creeps. They were fighting. The car continued slowing until it stopped dead and the motor shut off.

Tilly heard a door open and the car dipped with the weight shift of someone getting out. She heard more arguing in Spanish. Then a small noise at the side of the car, the squeak of something twisting, the knock of metal against metal, the rush of liquid and smell of...*they'd stopped for gas.*

Yell. Scream. Make noise! Someone would hear and call police!

No!

What if no one heard? They were already angry.

Tilly did not move, except to brush her tears. That's when she discovered that her sweat had dissolved some of the adhesiveness of the tape. She wriggled her wrists and felt her bindings slip ever so slightly.

She worked her wrists a bit more.

The tape remained secure, but little by little Tilly could feel her bindings loosening.

32

Black Canyon City, Arizona

Some forty miles north of Phoenix, the white Ford sedan with Tilly Martin captive in the trunk exited Interstate 17.

Dangerously low on fuel, Tilly's captors had driven into Black Canyon City, looking for a service station. Ruiz was behind the wheel, concentrating on scanners and radio news reports, while Alfredo nagged him about their predicament.

"I don't like this," Alfredo said. "We should call the bosses, end it now."

"Shut up."

"But it's not good, Ruiz."

"You are like an old woman. Do you have any balls?"

Ruiz questioned the wisdom of the bosses in Mexico who'd selected Alfredo for this job. He lacked the ability to think quickly on his feet. If the jackass came within a hair of becoming a liability, Ruiz would remove him without hesitation, probably with the Glock-20 he had under his seat.

Black Canyon City sat in a valley carved out before the Bradshaw Mountains foothills. It used to be a stagecoach station. All seemed peaceful in the night as sleepy frontier storefronts flowed by. Ruiz focused on the scanners and radio news. Hearing nothing on their motel, he resumed analyzing what had happened in Phoenix. Yes, they'd been caught off guard but Ruiz had kept his cool. Reading the unease in the stinking motel manager's face, he'd seized their only option.

Leave.

Ruiz was lucky Alfredo hadn't gone to the door. Alfredo would have shot the manager, because Alfredo was stupid. The jackass had left the tank empty. He'd shown his lack of professionalism by ignoring Ruiz's specific instructions to keep the car's tank full when he picked up take-out food, so they would be ready for emergencies like this.

Shaking his head, Ruiz pushed back his growing anger until he spotted a gas station, a one-story cinder block building with a towering cactus on either side. It had a small café, and a flickering neon sign that offered "Curios" and an invitation to See Our Rattlesnake Display!

Ruiz parked by one of the four pumps designated for self-serve, got out, twisted off the fuel cap, put it on the roof and began filling the tank.

As the gas flowed, he gazed toward the mountains silhouetted against the evening sky and tried not to think of the small human in his trunk. She was a product, nothing more. This was a job, but unlike the others, this one was going to give a brutal message.

Time was almost up.

Soon the *sicario* would be brought in and it would be over.

Like that.

Ruiz glanced at the pump's counter. A chill rattled up his spine when a blue-and-white patrol car for the Arizona Department of Public Safety with two DPS Highway Patrol officers eased up to the store. Ruiz cursed under his breath but continued filling the tank, thankful he'd told Alfredo to tighten the gag on the girl.

The officer who was driving opened his door.

Police radio chatter spilled from the car as he got out. He was a tall, well-built white boy, about thirty, trimmed moustache. He adjusted his utility belt, nodding at Ruiz. Ruiz returned his nod, then watched the officer head into the store.

The second officer was in the passenger seat, flipping through pages on a clipboard and checking the car's small computer.

At that moment Alfredo got out and began cleaning the front and rear windshields. Talking low in Spanish to Ruiz, he asked: "What do we do?"

"Pay for the gas and leave." Ruiz had finished. "Get back in the car."

Ruiz replaced the nozzle and followed the officer into the store to pay.

Alfredo watched the officer in the car. He was older, tense with his paperwork, writing, making notes, checking. Alfredo glanced into the store. Ruiz was taking a long time. The officer in the car halted his work and turned his face to the computer. Something grabbed his attention and he spoke into his shoulder microphone.

Inside the store, Ruiz was standing behind the tall officer waiting his turn to pay when the radio bleated: "Dan, you know that thing we were talking about with the girl in Phoenix? Something's up. They may have them."

"Really?" the tall officer said. "Guess you owe me ten bucks. I told you that would pop."

"They just sent a statewide."

"Well, if your piece of crap unit hadn't blown the rad, you might have been up for some OT. Now, are you sure you don't want anything? Last chance."

"Yeah, an orange soda and some of those spicy chips."

The officer went to browse the chip rack and the thin, wrinkled man standing at the cash looked at Ruiz.

"Sir, I can serve you. Just the gas?"

Ruiz nodded.

"Thirty-five dollars."

Ruiz put a twenty, a ten and a five on the counter.

"Would you like a receipt?"

"No."

"Have a nice day."

As Ruiz exited the store, he heard the tall cop's radio going again but could not make out the message, only that the tone seemed urgent. Ruiz just needed to get to his car. The officer paid for his food, then followed him out the door, watching him, suddenly noticing something about the white Ford sedan.

Alfredo saw concern in the cop's face as Ruiz got in the car.

Eyeing Ruiz and the car, the tall officer set his food on the ground and walked directly toward them. In a heartbeat, Ruiz turned the key, started the engine.

"Excuse me," the officer said as his partner got out of his car to see.

Ruiz's mind raced as he gripped the transmission shifter.

"Hold on there, sir!"

The officer was almost at the car. Alfredo whispered to Ruiz to pull out as Ruiz dropped his hand between his legs to feel the grip of his gun under the seat.

"Don't move!" the officer said, going toward the trunk.

"Jesus. Just go!" Alfredo cursed Ruiz, who sat calmly, watching the officer reach above the trunk, then step to the driver's window.

He held up the gas cap.

"You forgot this."

"Oh." Ruiz smiled. "Thank you."

"We wouldn't want you spilling gas all over the highway." The cop replaced the cap, tapped the trunk to signal all clear. "Drive safely."

DAY 4

33

At 5:00 a.m., at the edge of Juarez, in a squalid house on a hilly dirt street of decaying adobes, burned-out cars and yapping dogs, Angel Quinterra lay in bed, waiting in the stillness.

He had not slept.

Again, as with every night, he was visited by the faces of the dead, telling him that death was coming for him.

Last night, two soldiers from the cartel had picked him up in an SUV near Lago de Rosas and brought him to this place.

"Sleep here," they'd told him. "You will be called at 5:00 a.m. with instructions."

When he'd arrived, the nervous man and woman who lived in the house had said little. Angel was told to refer to the couple as his "uncle and aunt," and they gave him a small room with a bed. Above it was an ornate crucifix and a rosary draping the framed photograph of a smiling woman in her twenties.

Angel had no idea who she was and didn't care.

This run-down shack was a far cry from the palatial ranch—the safe house—where Angel had been staying. As the cartel's top *sicario*, he had grown accustomed to luxury while waiting between jobs. The cartel had placed him in the mansions of drug lords in Mexico or South

America. Sometimes he took trips to Las Vegas, New York, Rio de Janeiro, or London. Always first class and the best hotels. Once he went to Barcelona to watch bull-fights, then to Monte Carlo to see a Formula One race, where he stayed on a private yacht.

At twenty, Angel had enjoyed his life as a cartel assassin.

But he knew it would end and was secretly working on his exit strategy with the priest.

His cell phone vibrated with a call. It was 5:09 a.m.

"*Sí.*"

"Are you ready for work?" Thirty asked.

They never used names. Thirty was Deltrano, the number two man in the Norte Cartel. He was Angel's main contact. The head of the cartel, Samson, was known as Twenty-five.

"*Sí.*"

"You will be a student today, are you ready for school?"

"*Sí,* I'm ready."

"Twenty-five says you will take a school trip into the United States."

"Where?"

"First, go to your new school in El Paso. Don't forget the backpack your uncle has prepared for you. Everything you need for this trip is inside. Now listen to my instructions…."

Afterward, in keeping with cartel practice, Angel destroyed his cell phone. In most cases, they were only used for one call. Then the woman made him breakfast. The man explained that he and his wife worked as janitors in the U.S. Consulate and had access to government forms. The cartel had murdered one daughter and threatened to kill the rest of the family if they didn't pass blank government papers to their people, for them to make official documents.

The man gave Angel a backpack containing a new cell

phone, T-shirt, jeans, a forged student visa and other records. The records confirmed Angel was registered as a new student at Azure Sky Academy, the private religious school in El Paso. Several hundred students from Juarez crossed the bridge to attend it every day. As the sun rose, the man showed him where to catch the school bus to the border.

Angel started walking to the stop.

As dawn painted the barrio in gold, he was reminded of how people here were forced to live. The smell of sewage hung in the air. The dirty faces of children picking through garbage were an outrage.

Where was God?

It was understandable to him that the young people saw the narcos as righteous rebels, exposing corrupt politicians and police, refusing to be exploited in the U.S.-run factories, battling oppression, injustice and rising above poverty. To many, the narcos were heroes.

At the bus stop, Angel saw his reflection in the storefront glass between its security bars just as he boarded the bus. He showed the driver his papers and took a seat, still seeing his reflection through the window as the bus rolled and memory pulled him back through his life to the time he was ten years old....

They are living in a ramshackle shanty near the dump. His mother works in a maquiladora. *His father, a security guard, has lost his job to drinking. He spends his days sifting through trash, seething at his life and polishing his gun.*

He beats Angel and his mother every day. At supper he's raging at Angel's mother. "You stupid bitch! You and the boy are holding me down." She's serving him beans. "These beans are cold, bitch!" Before Angel's eyes he pulls out his gun and shoots her in the head.

She falls dead on the table, eyes wide, staring at Angel, who turns to face the muzzle now aimed at him. The barrel shakes. Angel waits for the bullet, glaring at his father. His boiling hate eclipses any fear as Angel's fingers tighten on his knife.

"Kill me, too!" *Angel screams at his father, whose face dissolves into tears, and in one swift move he thrusts the gun into his own mouth, pulls the trigger, splattering his brains on his mother's picture of the Blessed Virgin.*

Where is God?

Angel's bus drove through Juarez, picking up students. As it filled, it buzzed with chatter in Spanish and English. No one noticed him. He was alone, as he'd been in the days after his mother's murder.

He was taken in by his mother's church, where he'd learned English from the priests who delivered him into a foster home. Over the years, Angel pinballed through the system, feeling unwanted and unloved. Finally, he ran away to live on the streets of Juarez with other outcasts. He formed a gang that broke into the homes of rich people to steal whatever they could.

One night Angel and his two gang members were caught by men who were asleep inside a house they had broken into. The men took them in a van to an abandoned building where several narcos with AK-47s were gathered around a young man tied to a chair.

Angel and his cohorts were held at gunpoint while the group's leader was told what had happened at the house. He assessed the boys, considered the situation carefully, then considered the prisoner.

"This piece of excrement in the chair stole from me, too," the leader said. "Only he stole much, much more than you little dogs." The leader ordered that a handgun be placed on the ground in front of the captive man.

"Which of you dogs has the balls to pick up that gun and shoot him for me? Which of you has what it takes?"

Angel's first friend started to cry and pleaded to be freed and Angel's second friend stood there trembling. Angel looked at them, looked at the leader, then at the prisoner. Angel picked up the gun, raised it to the man's forehead, imagined his father's face and squeezed the trigger.

The explosion was deafening.

The man's head dropped. His blood dripped steadily to the floor.

Nodding, the leader smiled. "Now, shoot your dog friends. They are witnesses."

Angel looked at the leader, raised the gun to the head of the first boy, who pleaded as the other narcos held him: "Angel, please, no!"

Angel squeezed the trigger and it clicked. The gun was empty.

All the men laughed as the leader patted Angel's head. Then he looked deep into Angel's eyes, his face softening as if he'd found something sad and distant.

"What is your name?"

"Angel."

"Angel, you have the stone heart of *sicario*. From now on, you work for me."

Angel was thirteen.

That night he had found his family.

Over time he'd learned that cartels employed young assassins because they worked for less than an ex-cop or soldier, because they could get access to most places without raising suspicions and because they could be controlled.

But not Angel. He was smart; he liked killing. He was good at it, was paid well and had earned his status as a force to be feared.

Now he was twenty and felt as old as the mountains, aware death was near because rivals were not his only threat. When cartels brought in a new assassin, their first job was to kill their predecessor, who usually knew more than anyone about the organization.

It was business.

The man in the chair Angel had killed that night was

an eighteen-year-old *sicario,* who tried to steal from the cartel for his own escape.

As the school bus traveled through downtown Juarez, Angel watched the Mexican soldiers patrolling the streets. Lines of traffic started backing up as the bus neared the bridge to the United States. Soon the students got off and joined the long lines of people waiting to walk over the muddy Rio Grande on the pedestrian bridge, a virtual tube of wire security fencing.

On the American side, U.S. border agents with drug-sniffing dogs surveyed the line advancing to the checkpoint. When his turn came, Angel presented his passport and student visa. The U.S. officer examined them, checking Angel against his photo before clearing him.

It was over quickly.

Angel entered the U.S. and walked to the intersection of Sixth Avenue and El Paso Street, glancing at the greeting on the sign that said Welcome to Texas!

As instructed that morning, he reached for his phone and made a call.

"Go to the bus station. A man wearing a Dallas Cowboys T-Shirt and hat will ask you for the time. He will give you cash and new phones."

"That's it?"

"Buy a one-way ticket to Phoenix."

"What is in Phoenix?"

"Your next job."

34

A half hour east of Phoenix, in the lobby of the Grand Cactus Motel, a computer station offered free internet access for guests.

Lyle Galviera was using it to catch up on news reports posted online, a recent story on Tilly's abduction from W-Cero News.

Salazar was dead. Johnson was dead.

They were found in the desert south of Juarez.

Their heads had been removed.

Oh Jesus.

Pictures of Salazar and Johnson were shown over the murder scene in the desert. Then Galviera stared at a photo of himself over a caption: Lyle Galviera, Person of Interest. The report said Galviera disappeared with five million in cash stolen from the Norte Cartel, reputed to be one of Mexico's most powerful and vengeful cartels.

The story said two men posing as police officers invaded the suburban Phoenix home of Cora Martin, Galviera's secretary. After binding Cora and ransacking her home in vain for the Norte Cartel's cash, the men kidnapped Tilly. There were images of Tilly, images of Cora pleading at the FBI news conference.

The report ended with the Norte Cartel's ultimatum to

Cora: she had five days to find Galviera and their cash or risk never seeing Tilly again.

Time was running out.

Gooseflesh rose on Galviera's arms as he sat at the computer, transfixed.

My only cartel contacts are dead. Salazar and Johnson were going to help me process the money. I needed them to fix this whole thing, to find Tilly, to bring her home. What if Tilly is already dead? It would be on the news, wouldn't it? No, only if they found her. They found Salazar and Johnson. If the Norte Cartel found those two guys, then they were going to find me.

Oh Christ.

"Are you going to be much longer, Mister?" A boy about twelve, his face splashed with freckles, tapped the note taped on the frame:

Please Be Considerate of Other Guests and Limit Your Session to 10 Minutes. Thank You, Management.

Galviera logged off.

Still stunned, he joined the small line of people waiting to be seated inside the motel's large restaurant.

I've got to do something.

Galviera knew about the Norte Cartel but never suspected that Salazar and Johnson had been stealing from them.

He had to find a way out of this.

"Table for one, sir?"

The hostess led him through the crowded dining room. With his dark glasses, ball cap and unshaven, tanned face, Galviera blended in with the tourists. She seated him at a small corner table next to one with four grandmothers nattering about their visit to the Grand Canyon.

"My Bert always wanted to see it."

"So did my Edgar. It was so beautiful. I sent my grand-daughter in Hartford a picture."

Galviera excused himself after his chair bumped Grandma Hartford's chair. She'd used the nearest empty seat at his table for her purse and travel bag so stuffed with souvenirs it was close to tipping.

"Not a problem, dear." The old girl gave the bags a cursory adjustment.

Galviera looked at the menu for answers.

Could he stay on the run with five million dollars? Find some quiet place and disappear? How long would he last? Not long. He was not a criminal. All he'd wanted was to save the business he'd built. When the waitress came, he ordered a chicken sandwich and struggled to stay calm.

He could reach out to the Norte Cartel and give them the money in exchange for Tilly's life. *Give them some of the money.* He needed his two million. He could say Salazar and Johnson took the rest, that all he had was three million.

Who was he kidding?

Look what they did to them in the desert.

He could surrender to police. Then what? Go to jail? Lose his business? Besides, how would that help Tilly? No, he had to reach out to the Norte Cartel.

How?

With Salazar's secret cell phone number. It was all he had. The one he was told never to call unless it was life and death. Well, it was over for Salazar, but some-one would have his cell phone, either police or the Norte Cartel.

Galviera had no cell phone, no BlackBerry, no laptop, nothing wireless that could be traced to him.

His attention went to Grandma Hartford's bag.

He had noticed when he took his seat that her cell phone was atop her bag of souvenirs. She and her friends were absorbed in looking at a brochure about Superstition Mountain.

Galviera glanced around. No one would notice. He coughed, palmed the phone and went outside toward the small park by the pool. He fished Salazar's number from his wallet.

He looked at the phone and prepared to dial.

Wait!

Think this through. The police could put a trace on all calls received by Salazar's phone. They could triangulate the call signal to its origin and get on Galviera's trail so fast.

What if the Norte Cartel had the phone and they answered? Then what? What would he say—give me Tilly, I'll give you your cash and we'll call it even?

Would that work?

Not likely.

Was there any other way?

He didn't have any time. He had to make a decision now. His hands started shaking.

Suddenly the phone started ringing in his hand.

"Susie" came up on the call display.

35

Hope flickered.

They did not find Tilly at the Sweet Times Motel but they did find her pajama top. The top, the take-out food wrappers and the status of the room indicated that she had been there recently and was likely still alive.

Cora, overcome at the scene, was now resting in her bedroom.

Gannon would have to wait to pursue asking her about Donnie Cargo and San Francisco.

While paramedics watched over her, Gannon worked on his laptop in the living room, words blurring on his screen as he scrolled through the material he'd requested from the WPA news library. Like a prospector panning for gold, he reviewed stories on cold cases in San Francisco, and old stuff on Salazar and Johnson.

Nothing.

Who was Donnie Cargo? Why wouldn't Cora talk about him? Was Lomax feeding him BS? Was the incident in her past linked to Tilly's kidnapping? The creeps from her former life had taunted him about a connection. Could those sleazebags be trusted?

Gannon was at a loss.

Should he pursue Cora's secret, or Salazar and Johnson's connection to Lyle Galviera?

He looked across the room at Hackett and his task

force, remembering Isabel Luna's warning that someone among them could be on the cartel's payroll.

Did one of them tip the kidnappers at the motel?

They seemed to have gotten away with no time to spare.

Gannon's cell phone rang. The caller's ID was blocked.

"Gannon."

"Is this Jack Gannon, the reporter whose niece was kidnapped?"

It was a male voice, early thirties. Sounded sharp.

"Yes. Who's calling, please?"

"Do you protect sources, Gannon?"

"Yes, if it is crucial."

"This is crucial. I have information related to the case for you, but I have to remain anonymous and protected."

"What is it?"

"Not over the phone."

"I don't have time to waste.

"Meet me alone within an hour."

"Tell me what you have, please."

"Something on the people who took your niece."

Within fifteen minutes Gannon was driving across Phoenix.

He'd had the foresight to park Cora's Pontiac Vibe in a neighbor's back alley a few doors down and cut through backyards unnoticed. He pulled out of Mesa Mirage without being followed by any of the reporters at her house.

He worked his way to the 1-10 north, then took the Black Canyon Freeway west. His caller had provided no details, only instructions to meet him on the hour at a specific bench in the southwest area of Harmon Park. Upon arriving, Gannon parked on Pima and walked the rest of the way to the bench, carrying a copy of the *Arizona Republic,* as the caller had specified.

The guy had refused to give up any data over the phone. He sounded halfway articulate and credible, but it was a crapshoot gauging people in these situations. Odds were this was all bull. Gannon knew how some people, sickos, liked to get involved in high-profile cases.

They were a waste of time.

But a good reporter never dismissed a tip without checking it out, and with Tilly's life on the line Gannon had to follow through. Waiting at the bench, he inventoried the area: a mom with a baby in a stroller, two girls sitting on the grass in the distance playing guitars.

Gannon glanced through the newspaper and reread the *Republic*'s last story on the case. Was there anything they had that he could use?

"Jack Gannon?"

A man in his early thirties sat next to him. He wore a navy suit jacket, matching pants, blue open shirt and dark glasses. He'd recognized the voice of his caller.

"That's right. And your name?"

"Forget that."

"Come on. I didn't come here to play games, pal."

"Neither did I. This is serious shit, Gannon, very serious."

He talked rapidly, as if he'd downed five energy drinks.

"I've been watching the news. I saw you on TV with your sister. I read your news stories, even the old ones. You've been places. You're pretty good, almost won a Pulitzer."

"What is this about?"

"Jack, did they figure out how the kidnappers found your sister's house?"

"No. Well, if they did, they didn't tell us."

"They hired my firm, the firm I work for. I'm a private investigator."

"What?"

"Don't blame me. We didn't know anything at the time."

"Hold on. Back it up. Who the hell are you? What is this?"

"The only thing I'm giving you is information, so unless you want to end this now, I suggest you listen."

"Go ahead."

"A few days before the kidnapping, a woman with a Hispanic accent comes into our office, wants to hire us for a 'very urgent job.' She said she was with an export company in Mexico City that was about to enter into a deal with Lyle Galviera's company."

"Quick Draw Courier?"

"Yes. She said her people were having last-minute doubts about Quick Draw and wanted a full background on Galviera and his executive office. She said her clients had to know now before they would sign the deal in a few days. To confirm her connection to the export company, she presented me with a letter on letterhead from Mexico. I even called the number. It all checked out. Now, we're licensed to lawfully look into the conduct, whereabouts, affiliations, transactions, or reputation of any person or group."

"A background check?"

"Exactly. So in the time we have, we provide as much detail as we can on home addresses, financial, social standing, everything on everyone in the exec office— twelve people in all—and give her the report. We tell her Galviera is divorced, no kids. But his credit card records show jewelry purchases and flower deliveries, and through our calls to the florist, we learn he is dating your sister, who has an eleven-year-old daughter, et cetera, et cetera."

"Jesus."

"The woman thanks us, pays us in cash, and a short time later, your niece is kidnapped. I just about upchucked my lunch. I called the number on the letterhead in Mexico City again, and guess what?"

"No longer in service?"

"That's right."

"Jesus. You have to go to the FBI with this."

"That's exactly what I told the owners of the firm."

"And?"

"They said, look, we provided a service. What the client does with the information is on the client, not the firm."

"That's not right. Don't you have some duty to report this?"

"Exactly, I told them. I thought we were close to committing some kind of felony, aiding and abetting or something, and we should report this and cooperate."

"So what happened?"

"I was ordered to shut up and advised to forget about it."

"Why?"

"Let me tell you about the people I work for. They do some pretty sketchy work with drug dealers and coyotes, the guys who smuggle illegals into the U.S. Very, very dark stuff. I only joined them three months ago. Now, I don't want to lose my license, or go to jail, or worse. So I'm quitting today, taking a job with a friend in corporate security in Tucson."

"Wait. Why don't you go to the FBI?"

"I've got too many other issues with law enforcement."

"Where does this leave me? Who was the woman who came to you?"

"I poked around in the files and was able to get a number. I needed to clear my conscience. Here you go. You're on your own with this."

The guy passed Gannon a slip of paper, then left.

It was a telephone number in Juarez, Mexico.

36

Arriving for her shift at the Forest Valley Hospice, Olivia Colbert went to the small office and reviewed the patient notes.

She had volunteered here a year ago, determined to offer the same compassion the staff had provided her mother before her death. They took exceeding care in preparing people dying of cancer for their final days.

And they helped their families, too.

It was not easy. Facing people in pain took an emotional toll but Olivia was strong, like her mother, who'd been a nurse. Olivia was completing a nursing degree at the University of Ottawa and dedicated her work to her mother's memory.

Here we go.

Olivia came to today's notes for Mr. Montradori. She was especially concerned about him because he was alone. Since he'd arrived a month ago, Olivia had tried her best to help him. While all of her other patients had relatives, or a friend, Mr. Montradori had no one.

He was not married. He had no children. No friends.

"Been a loner all my life," he'd told her the first week. "Just me and my sins to keep me company."

He was fifty but so ravaged by his cancer he looked like an eighty-year-old man. He'd been a small-engine mechanic, fixing lawn mowers and snowblowers in his small shop in Alta Vista.

"Was wild in my younger days before I toned things down," he said. "When the doctor gave me the news, he gave me a brochure for Forest Valley. I liked the pictures. Seemed like a nice place to die."

Olivia smiled to herself, logged off, slid the keyboard tray under the desktop, collected her notes and started her duties.

The hospice was a stone building located in the eastern suburb of Orleans atop a hill, nestled among a pine forest. It overlooked the Ottawa River, Quebec and the Gatineau Hills, which turned into a patchwork quilt of color in autumn.

The building had twelve patient rooms. Seven were occupied. Olivia took her time checking on each one. She helped those facing death contend with their fears and the concept of the end. Many reconciled unsettled matters, unresolved relationships; made their peace and planned their memorials. While making her rounds, Olivia was pleased that each patient had a friend or relative with them. No patient was alone, except for Mr. Montradori.

He'd preferred it that way.

"Hello, Mr. Montradori."

Olivia smiled when she entered his room. He was in bed, watching TV news. His eyes brightened slightly above his breathing tube, his way of acknowledging that he was happy to see her, but they remained fixed to the newscast.

He never asked much of her, never talked much. He was just glad that she was near, so that he was not really ever alone. He liked news channels and old Western movies like *The Searchers* and *True Grit*. Olivia took care of that and gave him a headset so he could watch them without disturbing the others.

Olivia read over his chart and refilled his ice water, glancing at the TV. There was another report on the case in the United States, the kidnapped girl in California, or was it Arizona? She wasn't sure. Something about the desert in Mexico. They were repeating that clip of the mother at the microphones pleading for her daughter's return. Such a terrible story, it broke Olivia's heart.

Just like Mr. Montradori broke her heart.

Yesterday, Olivia had helped him decide on his final arrangements. He wanted to be cremated. That was it. Olivia had arranged for a lawyer to bring the papers later today for all the final adjustments.

"Can I get you anything, Mr. Montradori?"

He blinked.

His breathing was labored. Olivia sat next to him and took his hand. His voice rasped but he was clear.

"I need to get something off my chest, something I've been carrying for a long time, Olivia."

"Would you like me to call the priest, or the counselor?"

A long moment passed and he gave his head a very slight negative shake.

"Call the police."

Olivia thought his medication was confusing him.

"You want me to call the police?"

A single finger trembled as it rose from his free hand resting atop his blanket to indicate the TV news report on the kidnapped girl in the U.S.

"I have information on a case," he said. "That case."

37

"What the hell's the holdup?"

Phone pressed to his ear, Steve Pollard, a latent fingerprint specialist at the FBI's Integrated Automated Fingerprint Identification System, shifted uncomfortably at his workstation.

Earl Hackett had ignored procedure and called him directly.

Again.

"I'm sorry things were miscommunicated," Pollard said. "We advised ERT in Phoenix that their first submission was rejected. The prints were not legible."

"What about the others?" Hackett said. "There has to be something there to identify these guys. I can't believe that it's taking us this long to get a hit. What about the stuff from the motel? ERT found prints on all the items in the trash."

Pollard eyed his computer monitor, the split screen showing enlargements of two fingerprints.

"Yes, these newer samples are clear. We're processing them now."

"How much longer?"

Both men knew that electronic submissions typically received responses very quickly, within two hours at most. *Typically.*

"We're moving as fast as we can. We had a system crash."

"Do you grasp what's at stake here?"

Pollard glanced at the framed picture of himself with his wife and their ten-year-old son at the West Virginia Blackberry Festival. Since the Phoenix case broke, Pollard and his team had been putting in fourteen-hour shifts supporting the Phoenix investigation, going flat out to process every impression they submitted in order to get a lead on the suspects who kidnapped Tilly Martin.

He'd taped her photo next to his son's.

"I'm aware of the stakes, Agent Hackett. I'm aware everyone's on edge. We're working as hard as we can."

"Just be damned sure you alert us the instant you've got something."

After hanging up, Pollard looked out his window at the hills of West Virginia. He massaged his temples, repositioned his glasses and resumed working. Pollard's section, known as the IAFIS, was part of the FBI's Criminal Justice Information Services and was housed in a sprawling three-story modular complex, some 250 miles west of Washington, D.C.

The IAFIS used state-of-the-art hyperfast databases designed to match latent fingerprints. Pollard's job as a specialist was to analyze impressions, study comparisons and help with identification for the requesting agency.

The information Pollard obtained was processed through regional, state and national crime databases, such as the National Crime Information Center and the Violent Criminal Apprehension Program, which was a repository for details on unsolved homicides. And he could make requests through international agreements to search databases of other countries.

At the outset of Tilly Martin's kidnapping, crime scene techs had tried to get clear impressions off the duct tape the kidnappers had used to bind Cora. The techs had also tried lifting prints from the kitchen table, chairs, counters; off the furniture in Tilly's room; everywhere in the house.

But nothing was usable.

All Pollard had was the set of elimination prints, those from people whose prints would be expected in the house. Cora and Jack Gannon had volunteered theirs. Tilly's were lifted from her dresser mirror. Lyle Galviera's were taken from the fridge door in his condo.

Pollard would later compare those prints with any new ones that emerged, then run the new ones through the gamut of databases.

The development concerning the Sweet Times Motel had yielded a break. The FBI's Evidence Response Team had lifted a series of good, clear impressions from the right hand off soda cans discarded in the trash.

Pollard made a visual point-by-point comparison between the impressions on his monitor, studying the arches, whorls and loops, and compared them with the elimination prints.

He determined that some of the smaller latents matched Tilly's, confirming she had been in the motel room. Two other sets of latents were unidentified.

Now we're talking.

With the first, he started with the right thumb, which in a standard ten-card is number one. He coded its characteristics, then those of the other fingers. Then he scanned the prints and entered all the information into his computer.

Then he submitted it to the automated fingerprint-identification system for a rapid search through massive local, state and nationwide databanks for a match. Then he did the same with the second set and his computer hummed as it processed his data for a list of possible matches to study.

It would take some time. The IAFIS stored several hundred million impressions from law enforcement agencies across the country.

Pollard went to the coffee room to start a fresh pot of coffee, then returned to his workstation. The search was done. In the first set, he was given a list of three possibilities that closely matched his first unidentified submission.

He started working on it right away.

Again, Pollard made a visual point-by-point comparison with the first set of soda can mystery prints and the three offered by the database as potential matches. This was the part of the job Pollard loved, concentrating with enormous intensity on the critical minutiae points, like the trail of ridges near the tip of the number two finger. No similarities, there. That eliminated the first two candidates right off. For the last one, he enlarged the samples to count the number of ridges on the number three finger.

Pollard's eyes narrowed. All the minutiae points matched. The branching of the ridges matched. He began tallying the clear points of comparison where the two samples matched. Some courts required ten to fifteen clear point matches. Pollard stopped at twenty, knowing that one divergent point instantly eliminated a print.

All right.

He had a match on the first print.

For the second mystery print, the databases offered two possible matches.

For the next ten minutes, Pollard when through the same exacting process until he was satisfied he had a match.

Pollard then confirmed the identification numbers of the matching prints and submitted a query for each of them into a number of databanks.

It shouldn't take long. He reached for his coffee.

In about a minute, the first result came back and the hardened face of a man in his thirties stared back at Pollard from his monitor. He went to the subject's file summary. It came through a DEA database by way of Interpol and Mexico's *Centro de Investigación y Seguridad Nacional*.

The man was Ruiz Limon-Rocha, a Mexican National. The second result brought a younger face, which glowered at Pollard. He was Alfredo Hector Tecaza, a Mexican National. Pollard had their photos and abstracts of their files.

This was the break that Hackett needed. These two should be run through the Intelligence Center in El Paso.

Pollard reached for his phone.

38

Death was never far from Rosalina.

The sound of power tools and the smell of fresh-cut wood when she passed by the coffin maker's shop was a chorus to her grief as she hurried through the barrio market to her meeting.

Today, Rosalina was taking a stand against the narcos.

No mas, she promised her dead child, *no more blood.*

Rosalina's world had ended six months ago with the murder of Ivette, her twenty-two-year-old daughter.

Ivette was an aid worker killed in a drug gang's attack at the clinic where she had worked with her younger sister, Claudia. Rosalina and her husband, Ruben, believed Ivette was targeted because she and Claudia were outspoken against the *narcotraficantes.*

After her death, Rosalina and Ruben sent Claudia to live with a cousin in the country. The gangs had sent Ruben a message: they would spare pursuing Claudia through their network, if Rosalina and Ruben stole documents for them from the U.S. Consulate where they worked at night as cleaners.

Ruben agreed to comply—*"we need to be free of them"*—but Rosalina wanted to refuse. The gangsters were cowards. Thugs. She hated them and was proud that her daughters had inherited her moral backbone.

"Look at what they've taken from us, Ruben," she told him. "We will never be free of them unless we fight back. And I will fight back, even if it kills me."

For Rosalina, the tipping point was not stealing the documents but being forced to harbor a *sicario—in her home*—so he could go off and kill. The final outrage: *he'd slept in Ivette's bed.*

Now, she was taking a stand in Ivette's memory.

She was fighting back.

Not long after the *sicario* had left, Rosalina gathered her things, rushed to the local grocery and used the public phone to make a call. Then she caught a crosstown bus. Now, walking through the market, Rosalina tightened her grip on her bag. It held documents she would pass to the one person who could help.

Isabel Luna was almost trotting through the crowded market when she was stopped by the voice at her back.

"Hold on."

She turned to Arturo Castillo, the chief photographer with *El Heraldo,* who was failing to keep up with her.

"Come on, Arturo, we're late. I don't want to lose this one."

Solid leads to *El Heraldo*'s newsroom were rare these days, so when Isabel received one from a female caller claiming to have documented information on "something big" involving a cartel, she took action. She took the usual precautions in not going by herself to meet the source, in case the cartels were attempting to lure her. While traveling in pairs or small groups was no guarantee against any attack, the practice was to never travel alone and always leave details with your news desk.

In Juarez, many people went about their daily lives in trepidation, never knowing if that person staring at them was part of something suspicious, or if they should fear that car behind them.

Journalists tried not to be conspicuous. Arturo kept his cameras out of sight using a small bag, not the obvious bulging camera bag and certainly nothing around his neck.

Not for this assignment, anyway.

"Where are we going, exactly?" he asked Isabel.

"There, ahead."

She pointed with her chin, then led him past the stands and overturned wooden crates tilted to display tomatoes, bananas, potatoes, carrots, zucchini, cabbage, corn. Isabel searched the crowd and the vendors—farmers in jeans wearing straw hats or ball caps, women wearing aprons over print dresses—until she came to the vendor selling large baskets, stacked in columns reaching to the green awning.

Standing alone near it was a woman in her forties. She was wearing a white shirt over jeans, a brown-and-white sweater, and was holding a large canvas bag with a blue-and-white square pattern.

Isabel approached her and used the identifying phrase.

"Are you waiting for Isabel?"

"*Sí.*"

"I am Isabel. We spoke," she said, discreetly showing her ID. "And this is my friend Arturo. He works with me."

Arturo gave her a small smile.

The woman assessed them. She read and trusted the work of the people at *El Heraldo.* "I am Rosalina." She glanced around, comfortable in the noise and activity of the busy market. "I will talk to you right here, and quickly."

Isabel nodded and listened as Arturo kept an eye on their area.

Because of the din, there was no risk of anyone

overhearing Rosalina as she related her family's tragedy and current situation. Isabel listened without taking notes, nodding, saying little, asking an occasional question.

Rosalina explained how her daughter's killers threatened her surviving daughter in an extortion bid to force her and her husband to steal U.S. government documents and harbor a *sicario* "for something large."

"We overheard the gang members talking when they dropped off a school backpack at our home with items and the completed documents for the *sicario*. We know this young man was posing as a student when he entered."

"Which school?"

"Azure, in El Paso. I think this *sicario* is being sent on a very big and very bad job in the U.S." Rosalina opened her bag and pulled out a smaller bag with a large brown envelope. "The cartel does not know but I made copies of everything and I made notes. It is all in here for you. We know *El Heraldo* is the most courageous newspaper in all Juarez, and I am counting on you, in the memory of my beautiful daughter Ivette, to do the right thing through your connections and stop him and his cartel."

Isabel did not look at the documents in the market.

It was not the appropriate place.

Luna had to trust her instincts about Rosalina, had to trust what she heard in her voice. She saw the pain etched in her face, and her hands, scarred from solvents and nearly arthritic now from years of scrubbing toilets in office buildings.

Isabel looked into Rosalina's eyes that were brimming with anguish and burning with the same fire that burned in her own heart—the righteous fire that raged to cleanse Juarez of the poison that flowed through its streets, carrying the evil that was destroying a generation.

United by death, the two women hugged.

"I give you my word, I will do all I can," Isabel said.

39

Mesa Mirage, Phoenix, Arizona

Something was up.

When Jack Gannon called Melody Lyon at WPA head-quarters, her voice carried an uneasy undertone. She was cool to his updates on Tilly's abduction until he abruptly shifted the conversation.

"What's going on there, Mel?"

As a journalist, Lyon never shied from a tough question.

"All right, here it is. Jack, do you have anything to do with this kidnapping?"

"Me?" Gannon struggled to keep his voice low.

"Even after the fact? Like maybe your sister and her boyfriend got caught up in a bad drug deal or debt, and they asked you to help them before it went wrong with the kidnapping? We need to know."

"What is this? Are you serious?"

A moment passed.

"Mel, didn't you hear what I was telling you? The cartel behind Tilly's kidnapping hired a P.I. firm to get info on Cora in order to pressure Lyle."

Another moment passed.

"What's going on, Melody?"

"FBI agents from the New York Division just left our office. They grilled people here individually, Jack—me,

George Wilson, Al Delaney, Carter O'Neill, Beland, the people who handle your copy."

"On what?"

"Your character, your habits. They wanted to know if we thought you could be involved. They're likely going to talk to the staff at your old paper, the *Buffalo Sentinel,* too."

"I don't believe this."

"Jack, tell me the truth. Are you involved?"

"You really have to ask? You of all people know what I've been through to get here. Now you think it's possible that I've got the inclination, time and stupidity to be a drug dealer?"

"But your sister…"

"My sister and I have been estranged for over twenty years. I was twelve when I last saw her, Mel. Twelve. She's a stranger. I am getting to know her and getting used to the fact I have a niece. Hell, a few days ago I believed I had no living relatives. Under the circumstances, this is a bit of a challenge."

"I understand that, but I need your answer, Jack."

"Is someone there with you? Are you recording this for the FBI? Well, my answer is no, goddamn it! No, I am not involved. Christ, you're the one who assigned me to Juarez. Then, out of the freaking blue, my long-lost sister, who apparently had been watching my bylines over these years, calls me for help. I told you all of this."

A long silence passed before Lyon exhaled slowly.

"I believe you. But listen, if this ever comes back on you, it comes back on the WPA. And the damage to you and to this organization would be monumental."

"This is not about me or the WPA, Mel. It's about a kidnapped child and we're wasting time."

"Agreed. Let's go over the status of things again."

Lyon updated him on how the WPA was continually filing everything it could on the case from its bureaus in Phoenix, California, Texas, Washington, D.C., and

Mexico. Gannon went back to telling her about his tip on how the cartel had hired a private detective agency to locate Cora's home and that he was working to determine the location of a contact number he'd obtained.

Gannon carefully withheld any mention of his own suspicions about Cora or the allegations Peck and Lomax had made about Donnie Cargo and her troubled past. First, he had to keep pushing Cora for answers.

That was his next step.

After he finished his call he went to Cora's bedroom. A paramedic had just left it, closing the door softly behind him.

"I need to talk to her," Gannon said.

"Give it time. The sedative is still working on her. She needs to rest."

Frustrated, Gannon returned to working on his laptop, feeling the eyes of the investigators on him. He didn't care. He needed to check with Adell and Luna.

You do your job, I'll do mine.

Cora was in her bed, floating on a cloud of sedation.

Everything was going away. Everything was going to be all right. Her breathing was calm. She saw her ceiling in the soft light through her eyelids, big black wings scraping her face. She was imagining...

...her phone ringing...is it ringing now...no, it is not ringing...oh yes it is...no...please...Tilly's calling... Tilly's safe... No...Tilly, accusing her... It's because of you, Mommy...your fault...because of what you did... pictures...memories are swirling...with distortions... ears are pounding...in the rain...it's karma...going to get you...raining in San Francisco... Donnie and Vic... oh shit...what are you doing...there's a man with a gun over there... Donnie, what is it?... Vic says hold this... what...please, no...it's so heavy...Cora...stop the car, Donnie...stop the car...what just happened...running in the rain...crying in the rain...on her knees...in the

rain...stop the rain...her heart is bursting...her pulse is racing...she wants to scream...needs to scream...oh God...what...happened...the hard rain...blood...so much blood...oh God...oh Jesus...her hands...blood all over her hands...what did you do...it won't go away...it'll never go away....

40

Arturo Castillo positioned the last document in the high-speed scanner.

Across the newsroom, Isabel Luna worked at her keyboard while talking on the phone to an important source.

After their clandestine meeting with Rosalina in the market, Castillo and Luna had rushed back to *El Heraldo's* offices.

Now Luna, her handset wedged between her left ear and shoulder as she typed, was stressing the urgency of her information to the only Mexican cop she trusted: her stepbrother, First Sergeant Esteban Cruz.

"I'm sending it now." Luna signaled Arturo that she'd received his last scan. "Nine attachments, including his photo. I'm certain it's him. Stay on the line."

In the time it took for the attachments to transmit, Isabel explained how her source had obtained the documents before Cruz cut her off.

"Got them," he said.

Luna and Cruz went through each one together. Isabel blinked at the photograph. He was so young, a face to fit any one of the young men she saw in Juarez every day, yet in her heart she knew him.

"It's him," she said.

"Are you certain, Isabel?"

"Yes. Based on what I see and based on what I know, this is him. Look at him, posing as a student. He's killed nearly two hundred people. Think of all the suffering, Esteban. Look at the notes. It's the *sicario,* The Tarantula."

"This photo for the counterfeit passport is the first we've ever seen of him. This could be a big break."

"My source says he crossed into El Paso—" she glanced at the time "—less than two hours ago, maybe. They'd have a record. He could be on his way to the next killing in the U.S. We have to find him."

"I'll take care of this."

"Keep me informed, Esteban."

At his desk, Cruz cupped his hands over his face, peering over his fingertips at the revelation on his computer monitor.

A thousand thoughts streaked through his mind, but with a Herculean effort he deflected the most painful ones to concentrate on his job.

He'd led the investigation into the murders of the two American ex-cops in the desert, Salazar and Johnson. Judging from Isabel's source's documents and based on what Cruz knew from the murders, he agreed.

This was The Tarantula.

And if Salazar and Johnson were tied to the Phoenix kidnapping, as investigators in the U.S. and Mexico believed, then this could mean the cartel has dispatched their *sicario* to finish things there.

To kill the girl.

Or Lyle Galviera.

Or both.

Either way, Cruz had to act fast. How should he put this break into play? *I could take care of it myself. Cross over on police business and find him. I have friends in the U.S. who could help quickly with all I would need. I could resolve it the narco way. No, stop thinking like that. You're taking things personally and that can be dangerous.*

Besides, he was obligated to share the intel with the FBI agents working with his team on the murders. He would do that through proper channels, even though it entailed FBI bureaucracy.

He would do the same with his own bureaucracy.

But he was uncomfortable sharing the information. He feared infiltration. The information could be intercepted by someone on the cartel payroll. There was always risk everywhere. No one knew that better than Cruz and his stepsister. For a moment he pictured his father's grave in the cemetery.

Then it became clear to Cruz who he needed to call first.

The El Paso Intelligence Center was ensconced on the secured grounds of Fort Bliss in a squat light brick building with beautiful palms at the main entrance.

The EPIC's parking lot offered a view of Juarez, just across the brown shallow water of the Rio Grande. The staff often changed shifts to the echo of gunfire rising from Juarez, a reminder that while U.S. law enforcement went about its work, the cartels went about theirs.

The installation was the nerve center of the U.S. government's war on drugs and global crime. It was operated by the Drug Enforcement Administration, supported by personnel from nearly twenty federal agencies, and a number of state, county and local departments.

Using a network of cutting-edge law enforcement databases, it connected the dots in real time to help track the history of a suspected terrorist detained at an airport, or aid a patrol officer who has just made a routine traffic stop, or anything to help an investigation.

Some three hundred analysts, intelligence experts, federal agents and a spectrum of other specialists examined a galaxy of information scraps, pulling them together to provide fast tactical support to investigators across the U.S. and around the world.

One of EPIC's best analysts was Javier Valdiz, a DEA intelligence expert. A short time ago, he'd received an urgent query submitted by the FBI's fingerprint lab in Clarksburg, West Virginia. Latent prints collected at an Arizona motel identified Ruiz Limon-Rocha and Alfredo Hector Tecaza as suspects in the kidnapping of Tilly Martin.

Valdiz was coordinating queries related to her abduction when the FBI requested he analyze Limon-Rocha and Tecaza's backgrounds.

Valdiz had to be careful, as EPIC analysts, depending on their level of security clearance, had access to extremely sensitive intelligence, some of it arising from live, undercover operations.

In the case of Ruiz Limon-Rocha, Valdiz's research showed that he had been a sergeant and a member of the Airmobile Special Forces Group in the Mexican military. Research on Alfredo Hector Tecaza revealed that he had been an infantry corporal in the same branch of the military. Further EPIC analysis showed that, one year ago, Limon-Rocha and Tecaza were recruited to join the Norte Cartel by an upper-tier member.

Who brought them on?

Valdiz wondered about that just as his line rang.

"Valdiz."

"Esto es Cruz, cómo es usted, mi amigo?"

"Esteban. Very busy."

"You may not know, Javi, but I am working on the case of the two American ex-cops south of Juarez. I am not supposed to call you directly."

"For you, my door is open."

Before being assigned to EPIC, Valdiz had worked as an undercover agent until a bullet during a gun battle with a cartel put him in a wheelchair. Valdiz would have bled to death in the desert if the Mexican state cop partnered with him had not risked his life to carry him to safety.

That cop was Esteban Cruz.

"What do you need, Esteban?"

"This is urgent." Cruz explained quickly, then emailed Valdiz the attachments. "We need to get an alert out. We need to intercept this *sicario.*"

Valdiz read through the information.

"If our guy entered at El Paso and was going to fly to Phoenix, the flight itself is ninety minutes. Then add at least an hour for security screening and check-in," Valdiz said.

"They might still grab him at the airport."

"They might. But if he drove, it is a six- or seven-hour drive. We've missed him."

"Unless he took a train, or a bus."

"The border guys would have scanned the passport," Valdiz said. "We can get people to the terminals to check with ticket agents, look at security cameras. We're talking only a few hours. We can do the same at the airport. Hang on."

Valdiz took care to submit his analysis on Limon-Rocha and Tecaza to his supervisor to approve and forward to the FBI in Phoenix.

Then he turned to another monitor and launched into rapid typing, working on the alert for the *sicario.*

41

The secretary waved Hackett into ASAC Bruller's office.

Seth Bruller—Assistant Special Agent in Charge of the Phoenix Division—was standing alone at his desk, sleeves rolled up, on the telephone.

He shot Hackett a look that made it clear: he was not enjoying this end of the conversation.

"Understood…yes, sir…I appreciate that…we will, sir." Bruller ended the call, undid his collar button, loosened his tie and glared at Hackett.

"That was headquarters. They're not happy, Earl." Bruller snatched the file containing the inventory of items and material collected from the motel by the Evidence Response Team from his desk. "Damn it, where's our lead on this?"

"We're waiting for Clarksburg to process the latents," Hackett said.

"Still?"

"They've been promising it momentarily for the last three hours."

Bruller dropped the file, shaking his head. "Have we got anything else? A plate, a sighting, anything?"

"Nothing's surfaced. We're going to informants in Tijuana, Juarez, Phoenix and L.A."

"And?"

"We're leaning on them."

"Not hard enough." Bruller seized a printout of a news story. Hackett saw the logo for the WPA newswire. "What about Gannon, the brother who's running all over the place. You get anything from him?"

"Just attitude. If he's got anything, he's not saying."

"His niece's life's at stake. Why doesn't he work with us?"

"Gannon doesn't trust us."

"*He* doesn't trust *us?*"

"That's right and I don't blame him."

"What?"

"Look at the facts—Salazar and Johnson were American ex-cops."

"They were bad cops. It happens."

"And you recall that little memo warning us of cartel infiltration of U.S. law enforcement?"

"What about it?"

"I don't know what happened with the motel, Seth. It was almost like they could hear us coming. We were so close, their coffee was still warm."

"Are you saying these guys were tipped from inside the task force?"

"I don't know what to think."

"I'll tell you what to think—think about doing your damned job by looking for criminals, rather than looking for blame!" Through his glass walls Bruller saw heads turn to his office. He sat down, repositioned the two framed photos of his boys in their Scout uniforms and pursed his lips. "You say Gannon doesn't trust us. Well, I don't trust the fact he just happened to be in Mexico when all this came down with his sister. It's just a little too coincidental, don't you think?"

"The New York Division interviewed his editors," Hackett said. "Gannon's reason for being there checks out. Our people found no red flags in his background. He was on assignment in Juarez when this happened."

"What about Galviera? What did we find on him?"

"Nothing other than what we know."

"That's it?"

"It's already in the report you have, Seth. He had financial trouble. He gambled. He was going to lose his company and sought relief through Salazar and Johnson."

"And who else? Did you pursue that? Where are your informants? Who else did Galviera associate with? For Christ's sake, Earl!"

A soft rap on the open door interrupted them.

"Excuse me," Bonnie Larson said. "I thought you'd like to know we've just received confirmations from the lab and EPIC. The prints of our kidnappers belong to two Mexican nationals in the Norte Cartel."

"Get on it." Bruller reached for his phone. "I'll advise NHQ."

Returning to their desks, Larson pulled Hackett aside, dropped her voice. "Thank God I got you out of there. With all that yelling, I was afraid."

"For me?"

"For Bruller." Larson rolled her eyes. "The last time he was operational, cell phones were just a dream."

Upon examining the new analysis, Hackett's stomach tightened.

The first man was Ruiz Limon-Rocha, a Mexican National. DOB: 14 July 1980. Height: 5'11". Weight: Unknown. Hair Color: Black. Eye Color: Brown.

The second was Alfredo Hector Tecaza, a Mexican National. DOB: 03 December 1986. Height: 5'10". Weight: 170. Hair Color: Black. Eye Color: Brown.

Limon-Rocha and Tecaza were ex-military recruited by a high-ranking member of the Norte Cartel. The two dead guys in the desert were American ex-cops, believed to be working for the Norte Cartel before betraying them.

Hackett also reflected on the task force, now hitting upward of seventy people from a range of jurisdictions.

Unease gnawed at him. The Norte Cartel was known for infiltrating law enforcement agencies.

His phone rang. Bruller wasn't finished. He had a question.

"What about Cora, the mother?"

"What about her?"

"How deep did we go on her background?"

"We've been through all this. You saw our reports. No record, no warrants. She admitted to her past addiction to hard drugs but has been clean for over eleven years, since her daughter's birth."

"She admitted to knowing drug dealers."

"Yes, in the past, but her neighbors told us she is a clean-living, churchgoing single mom."

Larson's line rang. She picked up the call, then started waving frantically at Hackett.

"Right," Bruller was saying into Hackett's ear, "but her boyfriend was a money man for the Norte Cartel. We need to polygraph her. Let's get that set up."

Hackett hung up, knowing Bruller was right. He should've trusted his instinct and polygraphed Cora earlier.

"Earl!" Larson cupped one hand over the receiver. "It's EPIC. They just got a lead that a *sicario* for the cartel just entered the U.S. at El Paso. They think he's our guy for Salazar and Johnson and he's on a bus to Phoenix now. Arizona DPS is talking to the bus company and the driver. They're getting set to take it down now!"

42

Angel watched the desert roll by his window.

The bus, westbound on I-10, had just left New Mexico. It was nearly full with weary passengers: leather-skinned men in faded denim shirts, young mothers with small children, a few students, and a few grandmothers; people running away, or going home, people who kept to themselves. When they spoke, they talked softly in Spanish, their privacy protected by the drone of steel belts on asphalt.

Angel was alone.

The seat next to him was empty. He was taking in the wide-open landscape and mountain ranges, the territory where Cochise and Geronimo once rode.

But every few seconds his eyes shifted to the driver.

Something's wrong.

Angel had been watching him in the big rearview mirror and, when the light was right, studied his reflection on the windows.

It was essential to Angel's survival that he be aware of every sound, action and reaction.

Yes, he'd entered the U.S. earlier in Texas without incident. But his counterfeit documents had been scanned into computers. And the bus terminal went smoothly, but he'd noted the security cameras and an intelligent ticket agent who seemed capable of remembering faces when he glanced at him. *"Just one way to Phoenix, sir?"*

Angel took nothing—absolutely nothing—for granted as he continually assessed every iota of information to determine if it was a threat.

And now, he may have detected one.

Through the driver's body language.

A short time ago, somewhere around San Simon, something twigged. The driver had taken a call on his cell phone. Angel could not hear any of it over the rush of the wheels and the fan pushing conditioned air, smelling of fabric freshener and diesel, through the old bus. But in seconds, the driver's reaction to his call telegraphed alarm in a million ways.

While on the phone, he'd glanced into his mirror and quickly inventoried his passengers, nodding as he spoke. Angel noticed how, upon ending the call, the driver repositioned his grip on the wheel with both hands, then licked his lips. Then he dragged the back of one hand across his mouth as he constantly checked his side mirror.

As if he is expecting to see someone come up beside them.

The warning signs accumulated.

Trouble's coming.

Angel had to act but he needed to keep calm. He controlled his breathing the way he'd been conditioned since his first days as a professional assassin.

At that time, the cartel had sent him to a secret training camp, where for several hard months hired mercenaries from around the world taught him how to maintain and shoot with accuracy every kind of gun, from pistols to assault rifles. He was instructed on how to use knives, bows and employ everyday items as weapons. *Here is how a paper clip can be used to puncture an eyeball.* The mercenaries taught him self-defense, how to read and escape dangerous situations and survive as a fugitive.

They taught him the art of killing hand to hand, but not how to live with death on his conscience.

Angel had soon understood that killing was not possible for all the prospective hit men at the camp, where cartel enemies had been delivered for execution.

Some could not do it.

They could not look into the eyes of their target, a defiant man, a sobbing woman, even the pleading child of an enemy kneeling before them, and end their life. Some broke down, lost their minds.

They were the first to be executed.

Angel was different.

He held enough hate in his heart, knew the smell and taste of it, so that squeezing the trigger was a release.

An embrace.

But with time, killing had exacted a toll, and now he knew that his days as a *sicario* were numbered. He was tired of the torment, tired of living in the crosshairs, of facing eternal damnation. That is why he brokered his deal with the priest.

That is why he would bring it all to an end after this final job.

But it would end on his terms.

Not here.

Not with a white, potbellied bus driver squirming in his seat. Angel continued studying his actions for the next few miles and contemplated his options.

Since departing El Paso, Angel had used the bathroom a few times, familiarizing himself with the layout of the old bus, a Strato AirGlider, and the distribution of passengers, mentally noting which ones were using wireless laptops or cell phones, possibly watching news sites.

He was vigilant. None of the passengers, so far, posed a threat.

They were passing the Dos Cabezas Mountains and, according to the signs, nearing the exit for Willcox. That's when Angel noticed a car had materialized alongside the driver's left, then eased its way ahead of the bus, giving Angel a clear view.

It was a gleaming white Ford.

A Crown Victoria, no markings, no roof lights. But the push bars on the front bumper and back dash lights were telltale indicators of an unmarked police car.

Then the bus driver lifted two fingers in a subtle wave.

Angel very calmly collected his bag and headed to the bathroom. The passengers, many of them dozing, were oblivious to what was transpiring.

The bathroom was locked. It was occupied.

Angel waited.

Then he felt the bus decelerate.

He rapped softly on the bathroom door. Through the windows he could see the bus was leaving the interstate. Angel heard movement in the bathroom just as the public address system in the bus crackled with the driver's voice.

"Ladies and gentleman, we're making an unscheduled stop in Willcox to have a mechanical issue checked. It will not take long. Please remain on the bus and accept my apologies for any inconvenience."

The bathroom door clicked and a large grandmother navigated her way out, muttering in Spanish. Angel waited, then entered the small room, holding his breath.

Inside, Angel locked the door and stood on the lid of the toilet seat. Above the toilet, in the ceiling, was a combination vent and escape hatch. The hole was about eighteen-by-eighteen inches, covered with screen.

The hatch cover was open, tilted upward toward the front of the bus. Angel noticed the wires that likely connected to an indicator light on the driver's console. He used his small knife to cut them.

He removed the screen, hooked a long strap of his pack to his shoe then hoisted himself smoothly through the hole, pulling his pack after him. He lay flat on his stomach, keeping low to the bus roof, hanging on the lip of the hatch as the wind rushed over his body.

The bus turned on to the business loop. As it crawled along, Angel glimpsed a scattering of settlements before it approached the downtown and clusters of sleepy low-rise buildings.

Over the noise outside he could hear someone knocking on the locked bathroom door, then a man's voice, muffled but impatient.

The bus stopped at a traffic light beside a large dump truck loaded with fine gravel or sand. This was Angel's chance. Keeping close to the roof, he waited for the right moment, slid to the side and leaped into the truck.

Angel's pulse raced.

Sand stuck to his moist face and hands as he waited in the dump truck, waited for voices, for a siren, for a commotion, for an ending.

Then the dump truck jolted and its transmission grinded as the driver upshifted. The truck rolled slowly through downtown Willcox.

Angel peered over the side, saw his bus disappearing as the dump truck turned and headed out of town.

He was now two hundred miles from Phoenix.

43

Steve Pollard had to be certain.

At the FBI's crime data center outside Clarksburg, the fingerprint analyst needed to check another aspect of the Phoenix kidnapping.

Pollard's standard operating procedure was to leave no stone unturned.

He'd already identified the two kidnapping suspects, Ruiz Limon-Rocha and Alfredo Hector Tecaza. Check that off. But he was troubled by the elimination prints from the Phoenix case. Pollard had used them to compare with Limon-Rocha and Tecaza's impressions but was uncertain if the elimination prints themselves had been submitted through the network of crime databases.

Pollard was submitting them now. Better to do it twice than risk an oversight, he thought. Even though he didn't expect anything, he had to exhaust all possibilities.

After submitting the elimination prints, Pollard was about to check the daily email on success stories circulated to all the fingerprint examiners in the section. But he didn't get the chance. One of the databases yielded a hit on one of the elimination prints Pollard had just submitted. His eyes narrowed at he concentrated on the result.

What the heck?

It came out of the Violent Criminal Apprehension Program, the national database that held details on a range of violent crimes, including serial murders and unsolved homicides, some going back over twenty years.

One of the submissions had yielded a possible match from an unsolved case. Pollard sat up, went to work making comparisons.

I don't believe this.

A few minutes later he started making phone calls.

At that moment, in Texas at the El Paso Intelligence Center, DEA analyst Javier Valdiz was drafting a new intelligence note on the Norte Cartel for FBI Special Agent Earl Hackett in the Phoenix Division. This one would expand on the summary he'd sent earlier on Ruiz Limon-Rocha and Alfredo Hector Tecaza.

Valdiz worked quickly, marrying up-to-the-minute raw data with the history of the Norte Cartel. He consulted the org chart of cartels in Mexico, Central and South America and criminal networks throughout the Caribbean and their tentacles into the U.S. and elsewhere. The latest edition was complex, starting with leaders and commanders, flowing to plaza bosses, gatekeepers, soldiers, enforcers, transportation chiefs and *sicarios*. The genealogical aspect to the charts showed bloodlines going back generations, family networks, affiliations.

The Norte Cartel, also known as the Zartosa Cartel, arose from the barrios of Ciudad Juarez to challenge all existing cartels in a battle for control of the prized shipment routes into the U.S.

The Norte Cartel trafficked in marijuana, Colombian cocaine, heroin and methamphetamines. It controlled major distribution hubs in Florida, Georgia, Texas, Arizona, California, and in Chicago, New York, Montreal, Toronto, Vancouver, London, Amsterdam, Paris, Madrid and Rome.

It was effective at bribing and threatening government

officials, infiltrating police agencies and operating a near-perfect unit of elite, young, highly-trained assassins. Its membership was said to number two thousand, making it among the most powerful, deadly and vengeful of all the major narco organizations. To steal from the cartel meant grisly death. To challenge them in any way ended in torture, mutilation and decapitation, with corpses displayed as warning. The cartel had no alliances and waged war with all rivals, Valdiz wrote.

The Norte Cartel was led by Samson Zartosa aka Twenty-five, El Monstruo. DOB: Unknown. Height: Unknown. Weight: Unknown. Hair Color: Unknown. Eye Color: Unknown. Second in Command was Garcia Deltrano aka Thirty, Comandante. DOB: 16 July 1967. Height: 5'10". Weight: 180. Hair Color: Black. Eye Color: Brown.

Cartel history, intelligence and legend indicated Samson Zartosa rose from the gutter of a Juarez barrio to become one of the world's wealthiest and most-feared drug lords.

Samson Zartosa's father, a carpenter, was stabbed to death in front of his wife and their three sons by two men who'd come to their home demanding money. Samson, the eldest, was fourteen. He led his two younger brothers to find and kill their father's killers, and their families.

It turned out that the two men were thugs in a feared gang.

Consequently, the Zartosa family's stature and respect was instant. At fourteen, Samson assumed control of the murdered men's barrio gang, and in a few years built it into a merciless drug cartel.

Along the way, tragedy befell the Zartosa family three more times. The boys' mother died young of a heart attack. Eduardo, the youngest brother, was in his late teens when he was killed while on vacation in California. Hector, the middle brother, died two years ago during a gun battle with Mexican military forces that left twenty Norte members dead.

When Samson learned Hector had been betrayed by a DEA informant, he ordered the decapitation of the informant's family members. Next, through threats and bribery, the Norte Cartel determined the informant was being guarded by Mexican and U.S. officials in a mountain hideaway. On the day a convoy was to transport him to an airstrip, two hundred Norte Cartel members surrounded the vehicles, extracted the informant and executed him on the spot.

This was the last known betrayal of the Norte Cartel until the recent rogue action by Salazar and Johnson. The latest up-to-the-moment intel showed that Salazar and Johnson were working for the Norte Cartel, handling security for the San Diego and Phoenix cells, when they attempted to set up a rival route and the upstart "Diablo Cartel," using Lyle Galviera's courier company.

Their operation, said to have involved upward of five million in stolen Norte Cartel money, resulted in their murders, Tilly Martin's abduction, the disappearance of Lyle Galviera and the dispatch of a Norte Cartel assassin, believed to be destined for Phoenix.

Valdiz exhaled and began reviewing his note to clear with his supervisor when his computer pinged. He'd received an encrypted email from the FBI's fingerprint unit in West Virginia.

His attention was drawn to the subject line: Alert re Phoenix Kidnapping & Cold Case.

What's this?

He opened it and began reading when his phone rang.

"Valdiz."

"Hey there. Steve Pollard, FBI's fingerprint section in Clarksburg. I just sent you an alert on the Phoenix kidnapping."

"It's a hell of an alert."

"I've alerted ViCAP people, everybody. We need to talk about this."

"I think so. This changes everything."

44

San Francisco, California

In the hours before Donald Montradori died of cancer, he gave Ottawa detectives details of an unsolved murder that happened near San Francisco's Golden Gate Park more than twenty years ago.

His deathbed revelations set a series of events in motion.

The Ottawa investigators had recorded his sworn statement, obtained his signature and, adhering to procedure, alerted the Royal Canadian Mounted Police. The RCMP administered the Violent Crime Linkage Analysis System, known as ViCLAS, Canada's enhanced version of the FBI's ViCAP system.

The Mounties operated the program in the force's Technical and Protective Operational Facilities base. The facility sat some sixty miles north of New York State's border with Canada on Ottawa's east side, amid sprawling suburbs, a few fruit orchards and disappearing dairy land. A bison head, the seal of the RCMP, rose specter-like out of the building's soft gray stone over the entrance. Inside, RCMP Sergeant Andre Caron, a ViCLAS expert, assessed the new information, then immediately contacted Stan Delong, the FBI's ViCAP coordinator in Quantico, Virginia, who handled RCMP submissions.

Delong listened intently as Caron told him about the break in the old case.

"Shoot everything to me ASAP, Andre. I'll get that into our program right away and contact our people so it gets to the lead at SFPD. We see all kinds of stuff, but this is a hell of a thing. Thanks, Andre," Delong said.

Delong called the San Francisco FBI's ViCAP coordinator, who called Arlene Stapleton, his counterpart at the San Francisco Police Department, who immediately put out a call to SFPD Homicide Inspector Paul Pruitt.

Delong reached Pruitt on his cell phone in Chinatown. He was off duty and shopping with his wife and their daughter.

"Inspector Pruitt, this is Arlene Stapleton, SFPD ViCAP coordinator. Sorry to intrude on your time but we've received significant new information on a cold case and you are identified as the lead."

"Which case?" Pruitt raised his voice over the street noise.

"Eduardo Zartosa."

"What's the information?"

"It looks like your shooter's been identified."

"I'm coming in. I'll call my partner. Thank you, Arlene." Pruitt hung up and turned to his wife, who already knew that she was losing her husband for the rest of the day. "I'm sorry," he said. "I have to go."

"It'll be quicker for you to take a cab. We'll take the car home." She kissed his cheek. "Call me. Let me know how it goes."

In the cab, Pruitt alerted his partner, Russ Moseley, and their lieutenant.

Headquarters for the San Francisco Police Department was located at the Hall of Justice, a grim Stalinesque building rising from Bryant Street amid the low-rent units, office towers and high-tech firms in San Francisco's Soma district.

Pruitt hustled up the steps of the Hall's grand entrance

to the polished stone lobby, flashed his badge at the security check and took the elevator to the fourth floor and Room 450—Homicide Detail.

Pruitt went to the file cabinets, pulled out everything on the old murder, settled into his desk and set to work reviewing the case. In a short time, Moseley and Jim Cavinder, their lieutenant, arrived and joined Pruitt in reacquainting themselves with the ancient case.

Eduardo Zartosa, a twenty-one-year-old Mexican national, was visiting the city on vacation with friends when he was shot to death. His body was found in an alley adjacent to a parking lot in The Haight on Waller. A Smith & Wesson .38 Special, stolen from a pawnshop a year earlier, was found in a trash bin on Belvedere. The autopsy and ballistics determined it was the murder weapon. A set of unidentified latents had been collected from the weapon and submitted to ViCAP, along with other details.

Zartosa's friends said he'd left a party at an apartment to buy something to eat. There were no incidents at the party. No witnesses to the crime. Relatives arranged for the body to be flown to Mexico. Early on, Zartosa's uncle would call for updates on the case, then the calls ceased. Contact information for the uncle and friends was no longer valid.

"When's the last time anybody's looked at this case?" Cavinder asked.

Pruitt struggled to remember.

"About two years back, an old-time gangbanger facing a charge tried to barter a lead on it, but it fizzled," Moseley said.

The case was twenty years old. Over that time, it had been passed around to a lot of detectives.

The three of them gathered in Cavinder's office and reviewed the material sent by the Canadians. They watched Montradori's account of what happened the night Zartosa was murdered, with Pruitt taking notes, until it ended.

"All right, I want to move on this. I'll call the D.A. You guys better look into a flight out to Phoenix tomorrow. Hold up," Cavinder said as his phone rang. He took the call, listening for a full minute. All he managed at the end was, "Uh-huh. What? Right. Thanks." Cavinder put the phone down and started working at his keyboard.

"I don't believe this."

"What's up?" Pruitt said.

"That was the Captain. We've just got a call from the FBI crime lab. They've identified prints on the gun used for Zartosa."

"What the hell?" Moseley said.

"And the Captain says SFPD also got a call from the El Paso Intelligence Center with new intel tied to our case. I'm flipping the material to you now."

"What's with that?" Moseley said.

"This case is erupting," Pruitt said.

"Did we ever establish where Zartosa's family tree reaches?" Pruitt and Moseley exchanged glances.

"It's so old, I don't think anyone's checked, not in recent years. Why?"

"It goes deeper into that Phoenix kidnapping and it's not good. Look—" Cavinder glanced at his watch "—you guys need to get to Phoenix ASAP. Get home and pack. I'll get Shirley to check flights. I'll call ahead, tell the FBI you're coming. We need to work with them on this and we don't have time to lose."

45

Phoenix, Arizona

Hackett stood at his desk, twisting a rubber band, staring at the map of Arizona covering the wall.

This was taking too long.

His phone should be ringing, confirming an arrest.

The last word came thirty minutes ago from Arizona DPS. They had the bus stopped at the Willcox terminal.

Why was it taking so long?

The border people and EPIC had confirmed the passport for a Carlos Manolo Sanchez, likely an alias. But they had a photo. At El Paso's bus terminal, the ticket agent, aided by the photo and security cameras, assured two El Paso detectives that Sanchez had boarded the express bus for Phoenix with thirty-six other passengers.

Arizona DPS had made cell phone contact with the bus driver a few miles east of Willcox. The driver had confirmed that there were thirty-seven passengers aboard, including a passenger fitting the suspect's general description. The driver had agreed to use the ruse of a mechanical problem to make an unscheduled stop in Willcox.

DPS was supposed to grab him.

EPIC's intel indicated this was the hit man for the Norte Cartel, who was suspected of killing Salazar and Johnson in the desert.

We need this arrest. Come on. Come on.

Hackett's land line rang.

"Hackett."

"Agent Hackett, this is Sergeant Tim Walker, DPS Highway Patrol in Willcox. Our subject was not on the bus."

"What?"

"He was not there."

"What do you mean, he was not there?"

"Only thirty-six people were on the bus when we stopped it. Our people conducted a thorough search, confirmed IDs, tickets of every passenger. No Carlos Manolo Sanchez. Nobody came close to the photo. We found an open ceiling ventilation door above the bathroom."

"That's just great!" Hackett slammed the handset into the cradle.

"What happened?" Larson approached his desk.

"He slipped through our fingers. How in hell did he know to run?"

Larson cursed under her breath.

Hackett surveyed other agents working in the Bureau, considered the task force members at Cora's house and shook his head.

You never know who is on your side, he thought bitterly.

Hackett looked down at his files, including the one holding that Bureau-wide memo on cartel infiltration of U.S. police ranks. Was his task force compromised? Or was his paranoia entwined with his guilt over Colombia? He glanced at Tilly's enlarged photo on the board across the room. He could not bear to have another case end with an innocent victim's funeral.

"Did you hear me, Earl?" Larson had her hand cupped over the phone. "Bruller's calling from his car. He just heard what happened and needs to talk to you. Says it's important."

"He just wants to get in my face. Tell him I'm on another line, I'll call him back."

After Larson dealt with the ASAC, she got Hackett to focus.

"We've got work to do, Earl." She opened a folder. "Look. We've got photos for Limon-Rocha, Tecaza and now Carlos Manolo Sanchez. We can run them with Tilly and Galviera's picture, get it out in a release to the news media. Get everybody looking for these guys."

"All right."

"Good. I'll get moving on that."

Hackett then consulted the EPIC file and revisited his concerns about Gannon and Cora. If there was one thing Hackett had learned as an investigator, it was that no one ever told you the truth.

Not the whole truth.

Cora had hesitated to give up a fingerprint.

Why?

Hackett was tired of being fed BS.

In his gut, he knew that something beneath the surface was at work with Cora and he vowed to find out what it was. His mood brightened when he spotted a slim, bespectacled man in a tan suit making his way to his desk; the man who would help him find the truth.

"Oren. Good to see you." Hackett extended his hand to greet Oren Krendler. "I'll make some calls and we'll get things rolling as quickly as possible."

Krendler nodded and adjusted his glasses.

He was the Phoenix Division's polygraph examiner, a legend for having obtained more admissions than any other examiner in the Bureau.

46

"There's been a troubling break in the case."

That's what Isabel Luna's last text to Jack Gannon said. Luna gave him no other details, saying only that she would call later.

That was over an hour ago.

Gannon was hammering on his laptop and burning up cell phone minutes in Cora's living room, going full tilt at everything and getting nowhere. He'd struck out on tracing the phone number tied to the woman who'd hired the private investigation agency to find Cora's home.

He got nothing.

He called his best source, Adell Clark. She'd struck out. "I suspect it's a cartel number, Jack. Could be a prepaid phone. Or a case of phone companies being paid to act as if these numbers do not exist."

Confusion and anger welled in his chest as he reexamined the allegations by Peck, the man Cora said was Tilly's father, and Lomax, Cora's pimp. *"Your sister got into trouble with a cartel a long time ago—the worst kind."* What happened? And who was Donnie Cargo? Why had Cora refused to talk about him?

Was this linked to Tilly?

Increasingly, the FBI was looking harder at Cora. The mistrust swirling about the case was deepening.

Gannon looked at the photo of Tilly, the niece he didn't know, and tried to make sense of it all, tried to make sense of Cora. At one point, she had been the most important person in his life. Now she was alien to him.

How had their lives changed so much?

He had always figured the critical moment was that night at their home. He was eleven years old, Cora was sixteen. She was flitting between the bathroom and her room getting ready for her first official date, carefully applying makeup, spritzing perfume, putting on jewelry, dressing up.

Looking different.

That's when he knew that Cora was no longer the older kid who knew how things worked in the family, how things worked in life. She was no longer his big sister-mentor. She had been transformed into someone else. She had other priorities. In taking her first steps to becoming a young woman, she had started her journey away from him.

Leaving him behind.

Leaving him alone.

Then came the night of Cora's Armageddon with Mom and Dad—the night she left and never came back.

That was that.

And now after all these years, Cora needed him. *Needed him.* The ghostly reminders of their mother and father were surreal—in her face, her voice, every little thing; the way she moved, even the way she'd arranged her kitchen. *Canisters this way, pot holders here, the kettle there, all the same way Mom set up her kitchen.*

It haunted him.

As for what was happening, he stared blankly. He had no control anymore, no control over who he was, over the situation, the story, over anything.

All he knew was that a clock was ticking down on Tilly's life.

* * *

Cora woke and in that millisecond of torpor before the nerve cells in her brain connected, everything was right in her life.

Tilly is home. Safe. Happy.

But the instant everything registered, the terrible reality crashed on her.

Tilly is gone. It's my fault because of the life I've lived.

The sedative had enabled Cora to rest, but it was useless against her anguish. How could she live, how could she go on with her daughter stolen from her life?

How?

She couldn't make sense out of what went wrong with Lyle. She ached to talk to him.

If only she could wind back time, go all the way back to every mistake she'd made that had led to this horrible point. There would be no drugs, no leaving home, no leaving her parents, Jack, no addiction, no pain and no shame. Only Tilly and the good life they'd built together, just mother and daughter. They'd been doing fine.

Until this.

Cora groaned and thrust her face in her hands.

She had to keep going.

You have to be strong for Tilly. Tilly was a fighter.

Tilly is *a fighter.*

Cora sobbed into her pillow for several minutes before she found the will to shower and get into some clean clothes. No one seemed to notice when she padded to the kitchen to make tea. While she had no appetite, she ate some saltine crackers.

All the detectives, including Jack, were watching a TV news report. Through the forest of bodies, Cora saw it was a "Live Breaking News" report on one of the all-news networks. She glimpsed Tilly's face on the screen and nudged her way to the set.

Seth Bruller was at a podium making a public appeal

for help locating Tilly. Then he said the FBI was also seeking the "public's help locating the following individuals, who are persons of interest in connection with Tilly Martin's kidnapping."

Once more, they showed Lyle's picture. Then three more photos appeared—the faces of Ruiz Limon-Rocha, Alfredo Hector Tecaza and Carlos Manolo Sanchez.

Cora stared into the eyes of the two men who had invaded her home—*the bastards who stood in this very space*—bound her, stole Tilly.

She gasped and steadied herself against the back of a chair.

How did the FBI get their photos? Why did they identify them without telling her? Before Cora could react, the TV footage cut to a shaky live aerial angle from a news chopper.

"Now stay with us," the news anchor said. "We have just learned...have we got it? There it is. Our affiliate in Tucson is reporting out of Willcox, Arizona, east of Tucson, that a bus traveling from El Paso, Texas to Phoenix was believed to have been carrying one of these men as a passenger and was stopped earlier. Sources tell us the FBI, or rather the DPS, did not locate him but is still processing the bus for evidence. That would indicate he was on the bus and somehow eluded police."

Cora couldn't stand it.

"Did you find Tilly?"

One of the task force investigators shook his head.

"Ma'am, we just have more information on the people we're looking for."

Cora went to her brother but his cell phone rang.

Gannon answered.

"Jack, its Henrietta." Her voice was low. "I'm at the FBI news conference. New York is asking what you know about the bus and the other suspects."

"Zero. I know what's being reported."

"That's it?"

"No one's told us a damn thing."

"Okay, I'll tell them, but they're getting impatient."

"I don't care."

Upon ending Henrietta's call, Gannon had another one.

"This is Isabel Luna in Juarez. Can you talk now?"

"Hang on." Gannon raised a give-me-a-moment finger to Cora and excused himself to a quiet corner of the house. "Isabel, do you know about the bus in Willcox?"

"Yes. The suspect, Sanchez, is using an alias. The face is a true picture. It's The Tarantula." Gannon listened as Luna continued. "He is the Norte Cartel's top *sicario,* the top assassin. Based on the crime scene and their sources, Esteban and his team believe he killed the two Americans in the desert south of Juarez, the men associated with Lyle Galviera."

Gannon's breathing quickened; a picture began emerging as Luna continued.

"The *sicario* entered the U.S. at El Paso and took a bus to Phoenix. American police were advised and they stopped the bus but he got away, as the networks are reporting. Jack, we believe he was dispatched to kill Lyle Galviera."

"Jesus."

"And Tilly."

"Oh Christ."

Gannon's eyes swept the room until he found Cora and swallowed.

Could he tell her? An assassin's coming to kill your daughter. Maybe this was the time to push Cora to answer Lomax's allegation.

Luna continued, "The FBI and Arizona authorities are obviously taking matters seriously, with a dragnet, while gathering all the information they can. But *sicarios* at this level are impossible to find. They blend in like chameleons."

During his conversation Gannon noticed that Hackett, Larson and other people had entered the house through the back door, approached Cora and took her aside. They looked grave.

This could be it, Gannon thought.

"Isabel, thank you. I have to go. Please contact me the moment you have any new information."

"Of course."

Gannon joined Cora and the others.

"Sorry," Hackett said to Gannon, "we need to speak to Cora alone."

She shook her head, trying to read the faces confronting her for what was to come.

"Whatever you have to say, I want Jack with me."

"Very well," Hackett said. He turned and introduced a slender man in a well-cut suit. "This is Oren Krendler, our division's polygraph examiner."

"Polygraph examiner?" Gannon said.

"We're requesting Cora submit to a polygraph examination as soon as possible."

"A lie detector? Now?" She half turned to the TV. "I don't understand. Shouldn't you be concentrating fully on finding Tilly? I mean—"

"We talked about this earlier with you, Cora. We have some uncertainties in the case that we need you to help us clarify, so we can concentrate fully in the proper areas. This is just a tool we use to be sure our investigation is thorough. Now, it is strictly voluntary. You can refuse, but it would be helpful in our investigation of your daughter's kidnapping. It could lead to her safe return. You want to do all you can to help us return Tilly, don't you, Cora?"

Cora glanced at Jack, immediately irritating Hackett.

"I don't understand," Hackett said. "Why do you need to get direction from your brother on this, Cora?"

"Because we know what this means," Gannon said.

"Oh? And what's that, Jack?"

"You consider her a suspect."

"I didn't say that. What I said was that this is a tool. We need to clarify things so we can focus our investigation effectively."

"Do it, Cora," Jack said. "But get a lawyer first."

"A lawyer?" Hackett repeated.

"Come on," Gannon said. "You all know that if you're going to do this right, you should Mirandize her. So she should have a lawyer, and not feel pressured, since it's *strictly voluntary.*"

"Fine," Hackett said, "but we need to get moving. So get your lawyer ASAP." Hackett's phone started to ring and he turned to answer.

"Jack," Cora seized his wrist hard and whispered, "I don't have a lawyer."

"I'm going to help you, Cora."

As Gannon started to make a call himself, he overheard Hackett say into his cell phone, "Say that again. Who's here from San Francisco?"

47

Upon returning to the FBI's Phoenix Division, Special Agents Hackett and Larson were summoned to the ASAC's office.

Two men in suits stood to greet them.

"Our friends here are with San Francisco P.D., Homicide Detail." Seth Bruller flashed his diplomatic smile.

"Paul Pruitt," the first man said.

"Russ Moseley," said the second.

Hackett and Larson introduced themselves, shook hands.

"How is it looking for the polygraph?" Bruller asked.

"Good to go once she consults a lawyer," Hackett said. "Oren's ready."

"Good." Bruller nodded to the California detectives. "We need to move on this. Especially after we dropped the ball with the bus takedown."

"That was DPS, Seth. We weren't there."

"Regardless. The ball was dropped, but this new twist gets us back on track. As I told you on the phone, our colleagues are here to share some important pieces of the case. In fact, they flew to Phoenix once they'd learned of the development in their cold case and its impact on ours. Let's go to the small conference room. Kelly's put out fresh coffee."

"Coffee would be good." Pruitt reached for his briefcase.

In the brightly lit meeting room, the investigators helped themselves to the ceramic FBI mugs and coffee on the credenza, then took seats at the polished table.

"If this is going to have a bearing on the polygraph, I think Oren should be involved now to expedite things. Oren Krendler is our division's polygraph examiner. I'll get him."

"Paul, Russ, any objections?" Bruller asked.

"None."

Once Krendler joined them, Pruitt began by summarizing the homicide of Eduardo Zartosa. He distributed old reports, maps, crime scene photos, explaining how the case had dead-ended.

"It went into a deep freeze for nearly twenty years, until now," Pruitt said. "Things just started happening, cracking it wide-open, to the point where we think we can finally clear it."

Pruitt said Donald Montradori, a drug dealer known as "Donnie Cargo," was in San Francisco at the time of Zartosa's murder. Montradori, a Canadian national, returned to Canada after Zartosa's homicide and lived a quiet life until he recently passed away. Before he died he gave Canadian police a sworn statement on the crime.

"Let's view that now," Pruitt held up a flash drive.

Larson installed the drive in the meeting room's laptop and the group viewed Montradori's twenty-three minute deathbed statement.

"To me, the question is," Hackett said, "whether he's telling the truth."

"That's the reason we're here," Moseley said. "We need to be certain, just as you do."

"Montradori indicated that the high-profile coverage of your kidnapping had weighed on him," Pruitt said, "because of its connection to the old case and the fact that his conscience had never been at ease since the murder. Our receipt of the statement from Canada came at the same time your fingerprint lab and ViCAP got a hit on latents from your case, matching those on the murder weapon in our cold case."

"This is wild, Earl," Larson said, "just wild."

Hackett nodded, concentrating on the files in the San Francisco case, the photos of the murder weapon, a Smith & Wesson .38 Special, a set of clear latents obtained from it. There were pictures of other items in the file—a wallet, a ring, a crucifix and a lighter. Hackett was unsure of the importance of each to the case.

"Then," Pruitt added, "the El Paso Intelligence Center kicked out a little family history on Eduardo Zartosa. Admittedly, this aspect was lost on our people back then. But we've certainly grasped the significance of his family ties to your case now. We think we can help each other."

"What do you propose?" Hackett said.

"We don't want to get in your way," Pruitt said. "Your case is more pressing. If you're going to polygraph Cora Martin, consider weaving some of the questions we have into it. We'd need to do this delicately but we think it would also help your case."

"Sure," Hackett said.

"Then let us interview her afterward. We've spoken to our D.A. on charges and the way to proceed, depending on what we determine."

"I don't have a problem with that," Hackett said. "Do you, Seth?"

Bruller stuck out his bottom lip. "It should be fine. I'll call the Assistant U.S. Attorney and brief the office. Start working with Oren here on your approach. We need to keep moving on this."

As the investigators worked with Oren Krendler on developing a line of questioning, Hackett grew confident that this was the break they needed.

He knew that Krendler—calm, cool, nonthreatening—
was a master at obtaining admissions.

Yes, Hackett thought, something's going to pop.

But will it come in time?

48

"Why do you need the names of the top defense attorneys in Phoenix? What's happened, Jack?"

In the dead silence that followed Henrietta Chong's question, Jack Gannon realized that he'd made a mistake.

"Forget it."

"Is it for Cora?" Chong asked. "What's going on? Are they going to charge her?"

Gannon squeezed his phone, retreating from the request he'd made.

"No, no, nothing like that." *Chong's not stupid and she's not my confidante. She is a WPA reporter. What was I thinking?* "Forget I asked, just forget it. Did anything more come out of the news conference, the search for the suspects?"

"No—"

"Okay. I have to go. Thanks, Henrietta."

"Wait, Jack! What the hell's going on? Asking me to recommend a lawyer is more than weird, given that I'm reporting on your sister. It raises questions and puts me in a conflicting situation."

"Just drop it, Henrietta. Forget it, all right? Have you never had a source backpedal on you? We're under the gun, please drop it."

"What would you do if you were me?"

"Christ, forget it."

Gannon hung up. Angry at himself for not thinking clearly, he cupped his hands to his face and exhaled. He was in Cora's bedroom, trying to arrange an urgent meeting with a lawyer, a good lawyer. But he didn't know anybody in Phoenix.

Still, going impulsively to Henrietta for help on this was like putting out a fire with gasoline.

He had to regain control but he didn't know who to trust, where to turn.

The FBI was pressuring them, an assassin was coming, Cora was not telling the whole story, no one could find Galviera. He'd already seen two headless corpses. Would they find Tilly next?

Gannon resumed searching for a lawyer on his laptop when Cora stuck her head in the door. "I called Amy Henson next door. They'll let us borrow their Honda when we're ready. We can cut through the side yard by the garden shed. No press should see us."

"Great." He didn't look up from his typing. "I need more time."

It took another twenty minutes of scouring news articles on recent high-profile criminal cases in Phoenix before he found something. There was the case of a welfare mother wrongly accused of murdering her baby boy. Turned out the injuries could have been caused by a neighbor's dog. A note to that effect in an autopsy draft report was overlooked by police. And in another case, a man imprisoned for twenty years for kidnapping and murdering a college student was set free after DNA exonerated him. Both cases were handled by Augustine Goodellini, a top-notch criminal defense attorney with Goodellini, Pereira and Chance.

Gannon called the firm.

"I'm sorry, Mr. Goodellini's not available."

Gannon was connected to a senior attorney in the firm,

Lauren Baker-Brown, who, after listening to what he had to say and recognizing Cora's case, cleared her calendar and instructed them to come to their downtown offices immediately.

Gannon got Cora and they left.

"You know our prayers are with you," Amy Henson said, handing Gannon the keys to her white Honda and hugging Cora. "Good luck."

Gannon entered the law firm's address into the GPS before they slipped by the press unseen and cleared the neighborhood.

As they merged with freeway traffic, Cora started to cry.

"I'm so sorry, Jack. You're a good brother."

He said nothing as buildings flowed by them, like so many past hurts. He just wanted to get Tilly home safe, deal with the truth—whatever it was—and then get on with his life.

His cell phone rang and he passed it to Cora to read the call display.

"It says, WPA NY Lyon," she said.

"Don't answer."

The offices of Goodellini, Pereira and Chance were on North Central Avenue. The firm's reception area held an air of solemnity.

"Please be seated. I'll let Lauren know you're here," said the wispy, twentysomething man at the front desk.

Gannon and Cora barely had time to take in the polished stone floor, thick leather sofa, light wood walls and a floor-to-ceiling painting that resembled a tiger's hide.

"This way, please."

The young man led them down the hall and into a corner office that conveyed a sense of ordered diligence. Two walls of windows overlooking the city; a wall of mahogany bookcases; a neat desk, everything organized and in place; a framed photograph of a handsome man and a girl who looked about the same age as Tilly. *That's good,* Gannon thought.

"Lauren Baker-Brown." A woman in a peach suit with a pleated skirt came from around her desk to greet them.

"I know this is serious and urgent. Thank you, Chad, please close the door." Baker-Brown took her seat and provided a brief résumé. She'd been a county prosecutor seven years and private criminal attorney for six years. She was seasoned. She took up her pen and made a note of the time on her yellow legal pad. "Let's get started. Bring me up to speed."

For the next thirty minutes, Baker-Brown listened to details of Cora's situation, including a brief history of her life as a drug addict. She made notes to outline a defense, if it went that far.

"Okay, let me give Special Agent Hackett a call, then we'll talk again. You can wait in the conference room. There's a TV in there. You can watch news or whatever you'd like."

Half an hour later, Gannon and Cora were back in Baker-Brown's office.

"All right, seems we have a new wrinkle. Two detectives from San Francisco have just arrived in town. They want to interview you about your time there, once you've taken your polygraph test."

Gannon's attention pinballed from Baker-Brown to Cora.

"What happened there, Cora? Is it connected to Tilly's kidnapping?"

"Maybe," Cora said.

"Maybe?" Gannon said. "Is that the most you can tell us?"

"Cora," Baker-Brown said, "is there something more you think I should know? We could ask Jack to excuse himself. It's all lawyer-client privilege."

Cora stared into her empty hands. Her past had caught up to her.

"No, let them ask their questions. I will answer as best as I can. San Francisco was twenty years ago, a bad time."

Gannon said nothing, prompting Baker-Brown to resume steering the session.

"Here's how I see things, Cora. The FBI is either going to clear you as a potential suspect, or, acting on their suspicions that you may have been involved in your daughter's kidnapping, they will start to build a case against you, likely by tying your time in California to Lyle Galviera's dealings with the Norte Cartel. Now, in my view, based on what I could garner from Hackett, much of what the FBI has at this time seems flimsy, circumstantial, which does not bode well for them. But you say your memory of your time in San Francisco is hazy. And, you've said that, despite your past, you had no knowledge of Lyle's relationship with the cartel. That's a stretch for a jury, which would not bode well for you."

Gannon and Cora said nothing. He glanced at his sister. She was trembling, gripping the arms of the chair as Baker-Brown continued.

"To take the polygraph would demonstrate that you have nothing to hide and are willing to do whatever is necessary to help find Tilly. To refuse is your absolute right. But a refusal will stigmatize you in the court of public opinion. It creates the impression that you do have something to hide. Any innocent, concerned parent would take a polygraph in a heartbeat to find their child, that sort of thing. And believe me, even though juries are supposed to be impartial, they are in step with the emotions of a community, often by osmosis."

"I want to take the test now. Anything to find Tilly."

"All right. I will alert the FBI and we'll call a cab."

Few words were spoken during the ride to the FBI's office. Cora sniffed and twisted a tissue in her hands.

Gannon's phone rang with two more calls from the WPA in New York and one from the bureau in Phoenix. He didn't answer any of them.

The cab stopped in front of the FBI's Phoenix head-quarters on Indianola Avenue. As Baker-Brown, Cora and Gannon walked the few steps to enter the brick-and-glass building, Gannon heard his name called.

It was Henrietta Chong and a WPA news photographer, who fired off several rapid shots of Gannon, Cora and her defense attorney entering the FBI building.

Chong and the photographer were approaching them.

"Any comment on speculation the FBI now has Cora under suspicion?"

No one responded.

"Jack? Any comment on this turn in the case?"

Gannon knew this was his fault, unless Hackett had tipped them.

He shook his head, his stomach tightening.

49

Tilly Martin's face beamed at Vic Lomax from the big flat-screen TV.

It was followed by the scowling mugs of Ruiz Limon-Rocha and Alfredo Hector Tecaza of the Norte Cartel. Then Carlos Manolo Sanchez, the young one. Then Lyle Galviera stared at him. Then the replay of Salazar and Johnson, the dirty cops murdered in the desert south of Juarez.

And here again was the footage of Cora pleading alongside the FBI.

That stupid fucking bitch.

Lomax had canceled his meeting on wagering trends and revenue-per-room percentages, locking himself away in his glass-wall office overlooking The Strip to replay the latest network news reports on the Phoenix kidnapping.

This new information disturbed him. He watched, tapping one of his business cards on his chin.

Lomax knew the drug trade well and figured the young one, Sanchez, was likely a Norte hit man. This was not good. The heat was increasing, all of it brought on by that fool, Galviera, and his stupid bitch.

Cora.

Never in a million years did Lomax expect to see that skank again.

Then, after all these years, comes this shit with her kid, and her reporter brother comes right to his house.

Right to my goddamn home! I should've killed the fucker.

Now the shit keeps piling up and the Norte Cartel has gone into full vengeance mode on Galviera.

And now it's getting too close to me.

Lomax had his own operations with his own business partners.

But his connection to Cora would cost him. Those Mexican motherfuckers were going to drink Galviera's blood and cut off the head of anyone remotely linked to him. There are truths in the universe that must never be challenged, and one of them is that you do not rip off the Norte Cartel and expect to live.

No matter what he did, his connection to Cora was a liability. He had to do something to remove the risk.

The best defense is a good offense.

He turned the business card over.

A phone number was penned on the back, a very important phone number that Lomax had paid fifty thousand dollars to obtain.

He had a cell phone on his desk, one he'd taken from his casino's lost and found. He'd use it to call the number, then have a staff member toss it in the fountains at the Bellagio.

Calling the number was dangerous, but it was Lomax's only way to get his message to the very highest levels of the Norte Cartel—to its very heart.

Because the information he had exceeded any rip-off.

Lomax knew about Cora, Donnie Cargo and the mystery surrounding the murder of Eduardo Zartosa— little brother of Samson Zartosa, the head of the Norte Cartel.

Whether Lomax's information was true or not didn't matter to him.

As long as it's true enough to save me.

He held the phone steady, checked the card and started pressing numbers on the keypad.

50

The mansion stood on a craggy palm-shrouded hill with a sweeping view of the mountains, fifty miles west of Ciudad Juarez.

The only way to access the property by ground was a winding road whose entrance was gated and guarded by private security officers, ex-soldiers armed with AK-47s.

Other security officers patrolled the grounds on all-terrain vehicles and by horseback. The entire property was fenced with razor wire and necklaced with motion sensors, laser-activated trip wires and several dozen security cameras.

Ownership of the land was not listed on any government records. On paper, the estate of Samson Zartosa, leader of the Norte Cartel, did not exist.

His security was formidable.

His fortress had never been penetrated, although two idealistic federal drug agents on a rogue operation drove near it one night, determined to arrest Zartosa for the cartel's murders of their fellow officers.

Soon after, their car was found parked at a federal police station—their corpses in the trunk.

Zartosa's compound was a small village of buildings for his cars, his security team, their quarters and vehicles, their equipment, the servants and other compound staff. Zartosa's house was a three-story, ten-bedroom colonial hacienda overlooking a man-made pond, gardens, two swimming pools, a private zoo and a small amusement park.

The house had several offices. The largest was Zartosa's. Next to it was the office for his second-in-command, his Comandante, Garcia Deltrano.

Deltrano was on the phone, managing a shipment with a troublesome contact controlling Norte routes into New York City. A problem had arisen from a greedy distributor, an ex-Wall Street player whose voice dripped with arrogance toward Mexicans.

"Give me bigger numbers or nothing moves," he said. "That's the deal."

The cartel had taken steps in advance and Deltrano would resolve matters with a few sentences and a few mouse clicks.

"Is this not your nine-year-old daughter entering her private school?" Deltrano sent a photo, then another. "And is this not your wife, only thirty minutes ago, shopping for your daughter's birthday?" Deltrano sent one last photo. "And here are the overweight, overpaid security men you hired to protect them." Two white men, naked and bound, guns held to their heads stared in fearful humiliation at the camera. "Do you wish to accept our new number?"

Deltrano quoted a figure that halved that of the original shipment.

Stunned, the American said nothing.

Deltrano whispered a command into a second phone and the head of one of the naked men exploded from a gunshot. The man beside him, drenched with warm visceral matter, screamed for his life.

"This is the last time I ask. Do you accept our new figure?"

"I accept. Yes, God, yes."

Deltrano ended the call, went to the kitchen and got a

cold Canadian beer, a gift from a distributor in Toronto. Upon his return, one of his secure lines was ringing. He didn't recognize the number. Deltrano checked his state-of-the-art call tracking system. The call was coming from Las Vegas, Nevada. Deltrano answered.

"Sí?"

"My Spanish is not so good, so I'll say this in English, okay?"

The voice was coming through a voice changer, making it sound digitized, robotic. Deltrano listened.

"This is for Samson Zartosa and concerns the unsolved murder of his brother Eduardo twenty years ago in San Francisco. Fate, it seems, has delivered an answer. The mother in the Phoenix kidnapping, Cora, is responsible for Eduardo's murder. She was there.

"Tell Zartosa that no matter what he hears or sees, all of his attention should be focused on Cora. To prove the validity of my information, tell Zartosa that I know Eduardo died with God in his hand."

The line went dead.

Who was this caller? How did he get this number? Was this a police tactic? Deltrano's mind raced. He used the most current phone tracking program, obtained from a military intelligence source; he had linked it to credit card and financial databases obtained through several international banks controlled by the cartel.

The number came up for a cell phone owned by Harry Burgelmeyer, of Muncie, Indiana. A deeper check showed he owned a tow truck company in Muncie. Recent credit card use showed he was a guest at Caesars. Deltrano called the cell phone number. It rang through to the message: "You've got Harry. You know what to do and I'll get back to you. If you need service, call the shop's twenty-four-hour line."

Deltrano went with his instinct: Harry's phone was stolen for the call.

By who? Why? And was the information true?

After ruling out Harry Burgelmeyer, Deltrano continued using all of the cartel's resources to try to track down the person behind the call. He worked at it in vain for some forty-five minutes until he heard distant thunder, rising until it grew deafening.

Paintings rattled on the walls as the helicopter ferrying Samson Zartosa from his private airstrip landed on the compound's helipad. He was returning from a business meeting in Buenos Aires.

Deltrano's hair lifted in the prop wash as he greeted Zartosa, taking his bags as he walked with him into the house.

"I need to piss, then a little swim and eat, Garcia. Then we'll talk."

Twenty minutes later, servants brought them club sandwiches at the poolside. The two men sat alone, working, while armed guards patrolled the grounds.

Deltrano had two laptops showing Zartosa the latest shipments, updating him on issues and outstanding security matters.

"You've taken care of the asshole in New York, Garcia?"

"Yes."

"Good. I am growing tied of our situation in Arizona. On the plane I saw the latest news, all those pictures, all this attention on us. I don't like it, of course. We need to end it."

"Just before you landed, I got a call, a strange call. I'm sorry to speak of this, but I think you should be aware. It was about Eduardo's murder."

"Eduardo?"

As Deltrano recounted the call, he watched a dark curtain fall over Zartosa. It was Samson who had flown alone to California to bring the body of his little brother home.

"The caller said to tell you that he knew that Eduardo

had died with God in his hand. What does that mean, Sam?"

Zartosa's gaze bored into Deltrano, who then watched pain seep into Zartosa's eyes.

"It means the information is true. Only those who witnessed Eduardo die would know what was in his hand. Do we know who called?"

"We're working on finding out."

"And the caller said the mother in the Phoenix kidnapping case is behind Eduardo's murder?"

"Yes. What do you want me to do?"

"I need to be alone, to think."

Samson Zartosa looked to the mountains and back on his life, back to when he was a boy growing up with his brothers in the barrio in Juarez. For a few joyous years, they were so happy, never realizing how poor they were because everybody was poor.

Samson, Hector and Eduardo did everything together—played together, ate together, bathed together, slept in the same bed and dreamed together. Eduardo was always in the middle, safe between his two older brothers.

"I want to be a pilot and fly jets when I grow up," he said.

"I want to be a bullfighter," Hector said.

"I want to lead an army like Zapata," Samson said.

Then came the night of their father's murder, the night the Zartosa family's destiny was written in blood.

They were all gone now, his mother, father, Hector and Eduardo.

While Zartosa could do nothing about his mother's death, he had avenged his father's murder and his brother Hector's murder. He thought back to that long flight from California with Eduardo's coffin in the belly of the plane—*I want to be a pilot*—thought back to the cemetery where Eduardo was buried.

Who would have thought that in all the galaxies of

chance that this arrogance by the Americans—Salazar, Johnson, this Lyle Galviera—to plot a betrayal of the cartel, would actually lead him to Eduardo's killer?

Anger began to bubble in the pit of Zartosa's stomach.

At first Zartosa only wanted to use Galviera's girl-friend's daughter to draw him out, to retrieve their stolen millions and teach them all a lesson about the Norte Cartel.

He had even contemplated returning the girl—if they'd cooperated.

But now this happens.

Zartosa thought of Cora, thought of the piece of information the caller had given: *Eduardo died with God in his hand.*

This changes everything.

Zartosa picked up his house phone and pressed a button.

"Garcia?"

"Yes."

Garcia was like a brother to Zartosa. Garcia had grown up with him, with Hector, with Eduardo and was the first to join their little gang after they'd avenged their father's murder.

"Garcia—" Zartosa cleared his throat "—is everything still in play for Arizona?"

"Everything is in play."

"You know Eduardo was the best of us all."

"He was, Sam."

"You know when we lowered him into the ground I made him a promise."

"I was there beside you when you made it."

"It is time to honor my promise."

51

As Cora, her lawyer and her brother were led through the FBI offices, she remembered that distant night when she'd given birth to Tilly.

She recalled the antiseptic smells, the blinding lights, everyone masked, leaving her afraid and alone, until the moment she held her baby in her arms.

Now her fear that she would never hold Tilly again grew with each step she took. It carried her along a blue hazy stream of sounds and images that flowed to the truth buried in her past.

They'd arrived at a large meeting room.

Here again were Hackett; Larson; their boss, Bruller; and the two San Francisco inspectors, Paul Pruitt and Russ Moseley.

"We'll be observing," Pruitt said after the usual greetings. "We helped Agent Hackett with some questions. Then we'll talk to you afterward about your time in San Francisco."

Cora nodded before turning to Oren Krendler, the FBI's polygraph examiner. On the polished table beside him was a collection of files next to a hard-shell case.

"I will need some time alone to chat with you." Krendler offered Cora an officious smile.

After the others left, he acknowledged her anxiety.

"I've been doing this a long time and I know you're nervous—that's expected." He unscrewed a fountain pen and for the next twenty minutes, asked her about her medical history, about medication, if she felt rested, able and willing to help with the investigation by undergoing the examination.

Satisfied that Cora was a capable subject, Krendler then snapped open the latches of his case and showed her his polygraph machine. He tried to make her comfortable with it, telling her that it was an older standard five-pen analog that he swore by.

"These models are very efficient."

The machine worked by using instruments he would connect near Cora's heart and on her fingertips to electronically measure her breathing, perspiration, respiratory activity, galvanic skin reflex, blood and pulse rate, recording her responses on a moving chart as she answered questions.

Krendler said the questions would concern her original statements to the FBI about the kidnapping, her relation to it and her time in San Francisco. He would look at how her answers fit with the facts and known evidence, analyze her chart and determine one of three possible outcomes: She was truthful, untruthful, or the results were inconclusive.

Cora understood and was ready.

When the others returned, Hackett came to her and said, "Before we get started, I want to advise you of your rights."

She glanced at Baker-Brown, who nodded, and Hackett proceeded.

"You have the right to remain silent. Anything you say can and will be used against you…" *How did her life come to this?* "Do you understand each of these rights I have explained to you?" *No, I do not understand any of this.* "Having these rights in mind, do you wish to proceed?"

"Yes."

Hackett and the others took seats at one end of the room, behind Cora, who sat in a chair facing Krendler. As he connected her to the machine, she tried to remain calm.

This was her moment of reckoning.

Krendler began with establishing questions, reminding Cora to answer "yes" or "no."

"Is your name Cora Martin?"

"Yes."

"Did you change your name from Cora Gannon?"

"Yes."

"Were you born in Buffalo, New York?"

"Yes."

"Are your parents deceased?"

The needles scratched the graph paper.

"Yes."

"Do you have any sisters?"

"No."

"Do you have any brothers?"

"Yes."

"Is Jack Gannon your brother?"

"Yes."

"Do you have a daughter?"

"Yes."

"Are you married?"

"No."

"Do you have a boyfriend?"

Cora hesitated.

"Do you have a boyfriend?"

"I did."

"Answer yes or no, please."

"No."

"Are you employed at Quick Draw Courier?"

"Yes."

"Do you know Lyle Galviera?"

"Yes."

"Did you have a romantic relationship with Lyle Galviera?"

"Yes."

"Was your daughter kidnapped from your house?"

"Yes."

"Are you in any way responsible for her kidnapping?"

Cora hesitated for one moment, then another.

"Are you in any way responsible for her kidnapping?"

A tear rolled down her cheek.

"I feel that I am."

"Answer yes or no, please."

"I don't know."

Krendler made notations on the graph paper with his fountain pen.

"We'll move on. Prior to your daughter's kidnapping, were you aware of Lyle Galviera's involvement in any illegal activity?"

"No."

"Did you know he associated with people involved in criminal activity?"

"No."

"Do you presently know the whereabouts of Lyle Galviera?"

"No."

"Since the kidnapping, have you had any contact with Lyle Galviera?"

"No." –

"Do you presently know the whereabouts of your daughter?"

"No."

"Do you know who is responsible for your daughter's kidnapping?"

"No."

"Have you ever used illegal drugs?"

"Yes."

"Are you currently using illegal drugs?"

"No."

"Do you know Octavio Sergio Salazar?"

"No. Wait, yes. No. I mean I know that name from the news reports on the men murdered—"

"Answer yes or no, please. Do you know Octavio Sergio Salazar?"

"No."

"Do you know John Walker Johnson?"

"No."

"Do you know Ruiz Limon-Rocha?"

"No."

"Do you know Alfredo Hector Tecaza?"

"No."

"Do you know of Carlos Manolo Sanchez, or anyone using that alias?"

"No."

"Did you ever reside in San Francisco, California?"

"Yes."

"Were you residing in San Francisco in 1991?"

"Yes."

"Were you using illegal drugs at that time?"

"Yes."

"Did you commit any criminal acts at that time?"

Cora's chin crumpled.

"Did you commit any criminal acts at that time?"

"Yes."

"Were you ever arrested for your crimes?"

"No."

"Do you know Donald Montradori?"

"No."

"Do you know a man named Donnie Cargo?"

"Yes."

"Did you associate with Donnie Cargo in San Francisco?"

Cora hesitated and started breathing a little deeper.

"Yes."

"Did you and Donnie Cargo associate with a man named Vic?"

"Yes."

"Did you associate with Eduardo Zartosa?"

"No."

"Did you ever know a person named Eduardo Zartosa?"

"No. I don't know who that is."

"Yes or no, please."

"No."

"Were you, Vic and Donnie Cargo ever in the vicinity of Haight-Ashbury in 1991?"

Cora hesitated.

"Yes."

"Were you in the vicinity of Belvedere and Waller?"

"I think so. Yes."

"Was a fourth person present?"

"Yes."

"Was a gun present?"

"Yes."

Tears rolled down her face. It was raining so hard that night….

…Donnie wheels the car hard…there's a shadow standing under the building's overhang…taking shelter from the rain…. She's with Donnie and Vic. Vic's angry. Crazy mother is dealing on my territory…. Donnie and Vic leap out…don't leave me alone…she's so wired… wired to heaven she floats from the car…floating…everything turns blue…shouting…arguing…she's there…no, she's not anywhere… Vic's shouting, swearing…. What's happening…a gun…the muzzle flashes fire in the night… CRACK…groaning…

"Was someone shot?"

"Yes."

"Were you present when someone was shot?"

…screams…now there's a hot gun in her hand and someone's squirming on the ground…. Donnie…Vic,

what's happening...she's holding the gun...why...why is the gun in her hand...did she fire the gun...the car is leaving.... Donnie and Vic are leaving...leaving her behind... DONNIEEE... VIC...

"Were you present when someone was shot?"

...everything is blue...confusing in the rain...who'll stop the rain...trouble on the rise...a hand seizes her ankle...a voice gurgling...begging...pulling her down to her knees...to see that he's young like her...scared like her...eyes blazing...help me...he squeezes...God help!!... por favor...touching him...warm blood on her hands...so much blood...help me...he's been shot...somebody help... the rain glistening on his face...he's young like her... begging in Spanish...por favor...por favor...he's praying in Spanish...he's dying...I'm sorry...por favor...she supports his head...I'm so sorry...holds his hand...sirens approaching...por favor...sirens getting louder...she's alone with him...with the gun...blood on her hands... sirens...I'm sorry...they're coming...por favor...he's calling his mother...he's dying...she has to go...por favor... I'm sorry...she has to run...but she can't leave him to die like this...I'm so sorry...she removes her necklace...a crucifix...he receives it...crushes it hard in his hand... blood to blood...I'm so sorry...blood on her hands she runs away...por favor...his pleas echo...follow her, haunt her in the rain...rip into her...por favor...she throws the gun into the trash and runs...God please forgive me... and runs...leaving him to die...alone in the rain clutching the crucifix her mother and father gave her for her fourteenth birthday at the kitchen table in their home in Buffalo...she ached for home...sirens are screaming... she is screaming...and running...running for her life...

Krendler is asking her...

"Was someone shot?"

"Yes."

"Were you present when someone was shot?"

"Yes."

"Did you shoot someone?"

The needles of the polygraph swayed wildly as if scratching in desperation.

"Did you shoot anyone?"

She turned in her chair. Her eyes filled with pain, she found her brother.

"Cora, please face me and answer the question," Krendler said. "Did you shoot anyone?"

Cora did not turn back. She met the stares of Hackett, Pruitt and the other investigators.

"I can't do this anymore," she said.

Krendler disconnected Cora from the machine. Then, against Baker-Brown's advice, she began recounting all she could of that rainy night.

"I was so stoned. I nearly died later when Vic told me that I shot the guy, that I took the gun from them and shot him. I don't remember doing that. I really don't think I did that. I was so wired. Donnie disappeared. I never saw Donnie again. But Vic told me I did it." Cora sobbed. "Maybe I did. Vic said that the kid was connected to very bad drug people who would come after me, come after my family in Buffalo. So I could never go home again. Never contact my family. Vic said he would watch over me, that what happened would be our secret, that I had to hide and never breathe a word to anyone. I was terrified. He sent me to New York, then Miami. Then I went to L.A., where he had set things up."

Cora was anguished by what she'd done.

"I never should have left him to die alone. After the shooting I wondered about him. Who was the young man who died on the street in the rain? Did he have a family? I was going to check the San Francisco papers to see what they'd reported, but I didn't. It was too painful. I didn't want to know. I never knew anything about him."

While Cora was running, she had no one to turn to. Vic had sent her money, which she used for drugs. She was so messed up and so scared. She ached to go home but thought she would be followed and killed, along with her family. Vic had control over much of her life because he knew about that night in San Francisco.

Cora looked to her brother for understanding but his face betrayed nothing.

"For ten years I drifted," she said, "scraping along the bottom, believing I had taken a life and wasted my own. Then I was given a miracle. I had Tilly. She was my salvation, my chance to start over. I pulled myself together for her."

Still, for some twenty years Cora had been tormented by guilt. Struggling to build a good life, she never told a soul about her past.

"I know I was wrong not to tell you when you were trying to help me find Tilly. I kept this one secret to protect Tilly, to keep anyone, especially cartels, from knowing my connection to the San Francisco murder because that would guarantee her death. If no one knows, then there's hope they might let her go.

"I swear to you that I am not involved in Tilly's kidnapping. I've worked hard at making a good life for her. I know nothing about what Lyle was up to. Nothing. Yes, I did dream that maybe I could have a better life with him, for Tilly, but that dream died the night she was kidnapped. Over the years, I read legal stuff about murder, about participating in crimes that result in murder. Before you arrest me, I beg that if you find Tilly safe, you will let me hold her one last time."

A long moment of silence passed before Hackett shot Pruitt a glance.

"Cora," Pruitt said, "Donald Montradori, the man you knew as Donnie Cargo, died a short time ago in Canada."

"What?"

"Cancer. Before he died, he gave us a sworn statement about what happened that night. After seeing you pleading for your daughter on the news, he wanted to clear his conscience. All I can tell you is that he said that you did not fire the gun. After the shooting, the gun was placed in your hands. He and Vic knew that you were too high to remember anything. He said you had nothing to do with the murder and that Vic knew the truth."

"Is this true?" Cora asked the investigators.

Moseley nodded.

"Then why all this?" Cora indicated Krendler and the polygraph.

"We had to see if your account of that night fit with Donnie's and all the evidence."

"Evidence."

"The fingerprints you submitted for your daughter's case matched those on the murder weapon and this." Pruitt passed her a large color photograph of the cruci- fix. *Her crucifix.* "This was held back. Very few people knew what the victim held in his hand, or what he told paramedics before he died."

"He spoke before he died?"

"He said an angel put him in God's hands."

Cora covered her face with her hands.

"Cora," Pruitt said. "We're not going to arrest you or charge you. Not at this time. You were present at the com- mission of a crime and you fled the scene, but we'll talk to our D.A. There are plenty of complications and miti- gating factors. We need to talk to other parties. We'll be in touch."

"Hold on. With regards to the victim…" Hackett, who had not eased off on his suspicions entirely, folded his arms across his chest, turned to Cora and said, "The man who was murdered in San Francisco was Eduardo Zar- tosa, the youngest brother of Samson Zartosa, leader of the Norte Cartel. The men who have your daughter work for him."

All the color drained from Cora's face.

A soft knock sounded at the door and a man opened it.

"Sorry to interrupt but the task force at the house just received a call for Cora. The caller said he was Lyle Galviera."

52

Lyle Galviera was under siege.

A couple of boys were kicking the shit out of the soda machine outside his room at the Sleep City Motel because it had swallowed their money without giving up a drink.

Galviera had been striving to find a way out of his situation with the cartel but the assault outside on the machine was interfering. *"Come on, you stupid freaking—"* The earsplitting racket, the vibrating floor, as if forces were coming for him.

His chest was tightening; he couldn't think.

Since the kidnapping, his face had appeared in the news next to Tilly's, then Salazar and Johnson's. But he had cut his hair, had stopped shaving, wore a ball cap, dark glasses and managed to move around freely.

For how much longer? I don't know.

His entire room shook.

Christ, he wanted to go outside and slap those little assholes, but he couldn't afford to cause a scene, to give anyone reason to remember him. He turned back to the TV to face himself on the news again, then concentrated on his work on the desk.

He'd emptied all the contents from his wallet—not his fake wallet, but the real one that he'd kept hidden in the liner of his travel bag. The desk was layered with credit cards, membership cards, cash, business cards, worn tattered bits of paper with notes scrawled on them.

Where is it? It has *to be here.*

He inspected each item, looking for an elusive scrap of information he had seen before. He'd placed a mental flag on it. He reexamined each business card, searching for the one possibility, the tiny thread that could lead him out of this.

His attempt back at Apache Junction to contact the cartel by trying Salazar's secret number, using the phone he'd stolen in the restaurant, had failed.

The line just rang and rang.

He'd gotten nervous and given up. He'd left Apache Junction and driven aimlessly, trying to find a way out, until exhaustion stopped him here.

He wasn't sure where *here* was but it seemed fitting for the hell he was in. The room smelled bad, there were cigarette butts in the corner of the bathroom floor, the ceiling was scuffed and the sheets were frayed.

Is this it?

It was a card Johnson or Salazar had given him long ago for their hotel, one he'd overlooked because it had been compressed against another card. He turned it over to a faded notation. A telephone number and next to it *Thirty,* penned in ink and crossed out.

Was this his link to the Norte Cartel?

Galviera recognized the area code as Ciudad Juarez. He knew that major cartel operators used numbers for aliases. Studying the number, he came back to his dilemma. If he surrendered to police, it was over. He'd lose his business, go to jail and risk Tilly's life.

If he could reach the Norte Cartel, reason with them, put this all on Salazar and Johnson, give the cartel the money in exchange for Tilly, he might be able to make it work.

What do I do?

He returned to the all-news channel as once more it replayed the most recent development: the identities of Tilly's kidnappers, who were known to belong to the Norte Cartel. And there was a new suspect, a young one, who'd been on a Phoenix-bound bus before eluding arrest. Then he saw Tilly's face again.

Oh Jesus, should I go to police or try the cartel option?

Either way, I'm dead.

Time was running out.

Do something. Now.

Galviera gathered his wallet items, locked his room and drove through town until he found a bar that looked like it would do: The Cha Cha Club. Chicken wire covered the windows. The linoleum floor was warped. A few people were inside. A sign over the bar said Cash Only. There was a jukebox playing something painful, a pool table, two TVs mounted in the far corners, and there was a pay phone in a booth with a folding privacy door.

Galviera got change from the bartender, got into the booth, held his card up to the neon to read the number, checked with the operator, deposited coins and placed his call. The number clicked, followed by long-distance static, then it rang.

He licked his lips. He'd expected a recording, a disconnection, a wrong number, but it rang two, three, four times, then, *"Sí?"*

Galviera's heart skipped and he focused his thoughts. This was it, his shot. He spoke in Spanish.

"This is Lyle Galviera."

A long, cautious silence.

"Who gave you this number?"

"Salazar, before he was murdered in the desert." Another long silence passed before Galviera broke it. "It's very important that I speak to Thirty now."

"Speak."

"Your people are looking for me."

"My people are concerned about the theft of our property and are holding an asset for return of that property."

"I am an innocent third party in this dispute," Galviera said. "So are the others connected to the asset. But I have a solution."

"And what is it?"

"That we meet in the Phoenix area. I will return your property in exchange for the asset, undamaged. Then the matter will be closed."

"That is desirable. We wish to resolve the issue quickly, amicably. I assure you no damage has been done to the asset."

"I will give you an email address and propose the time and location."

"No. We will tell you the time and location, in the Phoenix area as you prefer. Your email?"

Galviera gave him an email address from an online account he used under another name.

"If this is a setup, the asset we're holding will be destroyed."

"I assure you, this is not a setup."

"Good, Mr. Galviera, we'll contact you. We'll finish this within the next forty-eight hours."

The call ended.

Did that happen?

Adrenaline pumped through Galviera, blood drummed in his ears. He sat at the bar, ordered a Coke and took a few minutes to let his pulse level off.

"You all right there, pal?" the bartender asked.

"I lost my cell phone and need to buy a new one. Is there a good place around here?"

"Six Feathers Mall, down the street. Can't miss it."

The clerk at the Six Feathers Mall cell phone store fixed him up quickly with a top-notch, good-to-go, pre-paid plan for a phone. Galviera paid cash for it and felt relatively safe with a new phone under an alias. He knew that you did not have to be making a cell phone call for the location of the caller to be tracked; something about triangulating the roaming signals. So to be safe while driving to Phoenix, he shut it off and removed the battery when he wasn't using it, to ensure he did not accidentally switch it on.

When Galviera got to the outskirts of the city, he went to JBD Mini-Storage and found the self-storage unit he'd rented. He collected the nylon gym bags containing the $1.1 million in cash. Then he drove across the metro area to another self-storage outlet and collected more bags until he had a total of $2.5 million in brick-sized bundles of unmarked tens and twenties.

He checked his email.

Nothing had come in.

Sweat beaded on his upper lip as he drove along the edges of Phoenix. From the news reports, seeing Cora begging for Tilly, urging him to go to police, he knew Cora was in agony. That Cora and Tilly were suffering because of him was tearing him up.

God, he was so sorry. He'd never, ever meant for any of this to happen.

He scanned the streets, thinking that whatever Cora thought of him now, she had to know that he was doing all he could. First, he needed gas. He spotted a service station.

One with a pay phone.

While filling up he decided he had to tell Cora, he had to risk the call being traced. He'd do it to give her some relief. After filling up, he went to the phone and called her number. A man answered, put him on hold, then—

"Lyle! Oh my God! Oh my God, Lyle!"

"Cora, I'm so—"

"Do you have Tilly?"

"I'm working on it…. I—"

"Where are you?"

"Cora, listen, I am so sorry…this is all so complicated. I know we had dreams—"

"Turn yourself in now! Tell the FBI where you are. We have to find Tilly! Where are you?"

"I'm going to see Tilly soon, Cora. I swear to you I am going to fix this!"

53

Soon it would be over.

Ruiz Limon-Rocha finished his call and switched off the stolen cell phone. After taking the precaution of removing the battery, he hurled the pieces into the river, looking at the silvery rush of water for relief from his apprehension.

Considering their recent narrow escape from the motel and their brush with the patrolmen at the gas station, Ruiz figured it was a race between completion of the job or their luck running out.

Ruiz would be glad to return to Mexico; for the first time he missed the low-paying job of a soldier in the military.

It was a much simpler life.

Now they were wanted, hunted men in America and the FBI was gaining on them, given that Ruiz and Alfredo's faces were as prominent in news stories about the kidnapping as the girl's.

Since fleeing the motel, they had lain low, awaiting orders here on an isolated back road east of Interstate 17. They'd found sanctuary among a stand of mesquite trees. Their twisting branches offered cool shade. Nothing and no one else in sight.

"Was that Thirty again?" Alfredo said from the car's reclined passenger seat.

"Yes. He said the *sicario* is coming, that he is close."

"That's what he said an hour ago. Does he have our coordinates?"

"Yes."

"We should abort the operation. There is too much heat."

"They don't care. The operation will be completed. It's a matter of honor for them. Remember, they want everyone to get the message."

Ruiz narrowed his eyes, keeping vigil on the long dirt road.

"I have never killed anyone, Ruiz, have you?"

"Yes."

"Who did you kill?"

"I don't wish to talk about it," Limon-Rocha said.

"If it comes down to us, I cannot kill a child. I have children."

"Alfredo, I told you we do not do this, the *sicario* does it. We follow his orders. That is how it is done. And he does it in the most stunning way. You saw the news. You saw what he did to the American cops."

"The Tarantula."

"Yes."

"He is a legend, there are *narcocorridos* written about him. Have you ever met him?"

"Yes, I helped him once before."

"What can you tell me about him?"

"He is a perfect assassin."

"Why do you say that?"

"He will kill anyone. He is hollow, nothing inside."

Ruiz nodded to the distance. Alfredo sat up and saw the rising dust clouds. After a long moment, a battered pickup truck emerged. As it drew closer they distinguished an old man in a straw hat behind the wheel.

The brakes creaked as it came to a halt with the engine running.

The young man in the passenger seat gave the driver cash and got out. He retrieved a backpack from the bed of the truck, tapped it with his palm, waving to the driver as the truck disappeared down the road, leaving his passenger standing before Ruiz and Alfredo.

Wearing sunglasses, a Lady Gaga T-shirt and torn, faded jeans, his pack slung over his shoulder, Angel Quinterra—the most feared cartel assassin—looked as if he'd just come from a high school class.

"Hola, Ruiz."

54

Tilly could hear the creeps.

Beyond the metal walls of the trunk, their voices were clear, but they were talking so fast in Spanish she couldn't understand everything they were saying.

Something about the legend of a dangerous spider, a tarantula.

Now she heard the crunch of wheels on dirt; a car was approaching, coming very close then creaking. It stopped but a motor was running.

A door opened then shut and the car drove away.

A new voice—it sounded younger.

Was this help? Or was this danger?

Fast talking in Spanish that Tilly could not understand before the voices faded and the talkers walked away, leaving her on the brink of tears.

Alone in this hot, dark, stupid coffin.

She wanted to scream at them.

Let me out! Let me go! I want my mom!

But she kept quiet. Noise made them angry.

Her eyes stung.

How long had it been? What day was this? She didn't know how much longer she could last.

Don't cry. Don't give in. Be strong. Be smart.

The creeps fed her by placing bags of hamburgers,

French fries, tacos, potato chips, chocolate bars and cans of soda in the trunk. Then they removed her gag and stood over her, watching for anyone approaching until she finished. Then they'd replace the gag. And she had no privacy. For a toilet, they'd take her to rest stops, one of them always entering with her, keeping the stall door open, making her hurry, making sure no one saw. It made her feel like an animal.

But she got used to it.

It was a little better now—now that they'd stopped cramming her into the suitcase. When they'd let her out, her hopes rose with the glowing interior trunk-release handle. Tilly pulled it but it didn't work because the creeps had cut the cable. They'd put thick blankets and pillows on the trunk's floor, letting her stretch out. They'd still kept her gagged with a bandanna and bound with duct tape. It was a bit cooler, too, but it was still stinky like rubber tires, exhaust and gasoline.

What's going to happen? What're they going to do to me?

A wave of sadness rolled over her.

Tilly missed her mom. She was the best mom in the world.

"Sweetheart, if you see me, I love you. We're doing everything to bring you home safely...." When Tilly saw her on the TV news, she knew her mom would never give up looking for her.

And Tilly knew her mom would tell her the same thing she'd always told her: *"You shouldn't think about what you don't have. Instead, you should thank God for what you do have—a mother who loves you and will always love you, no matter what."*

There were a few other things Tilly had learned from her mother.

Never ever give up on the important things, because they don't come easy.

Tilly's heart began to beat faster. Her pulse quickened.

Always fight back.

Like the day she showed Lenny Griffin how wrong he was to try to drown her in the pool.

Anger bubbled in the pit of Tilly's stomach, anger at Lenny Griffin, anger at these creeps who'd taken her. She began kicking and pounding the trunk, rage burning through her as she writhed and struggled with her bindings.

The fury she'd unleashed strained the tape around her wrists. Her sweat and the wear had transformed it to material akin to fabric that now gave her enough play to nearly work her hands out.

Oh! Almost free! Please! Oh, please!

Tilly froze.

Footsteps of people approaching, the trunk's lock being keyed. *Don't let them see my work on the tape.* She held her breath under an explosion of sunlight diffused through the trees.

She shut her eyes tight for a long moment before gradually relaxing them to squint at the silhouettes looking down on her.

There were three people now.

Who was the third person?

Her eyes adjusted to the new face, which belonged to a man who was younger than the creeps.

He stared at Tilly as if she were something more than an eleven-year-old girl who'd been kidnapped.

Much more.

55

Angel gazed upon the girl in the trunk.

So this was the famous face that had stared at him from newscasts. He took his time appraising her, the way a collector assesses art.

She exuded fear.

But he saw something more. A mixture of courage, defiance and, despite her ordeal, the polish of a privileged middle-class American life that was a universe away from the barrio he had known at her age.

Bound with silver tape, gagged with a blue bandanna, packaged in jeans and a pink embroidered T-shirt, this was the prize in his final job, his ticket out of narco world before someone put him in his grave.

He lowered the trunk with consideration, closing it gently with a snap.

"Let's go," he said to Limon-Rocha and Tecaza.

Angel sat in the rear seat of the car among their luggage and the equipment he required for finishing the job. Tecaza, behind the wheel, found him in the rearview mirror.

"Where are we going?"

"Head for Phoenix."

"What are the next steps for the operation?" Limon-Rocha asked.

Angel looked away, preferring not to talk about a job. Instead he reflected on the landscape and how he'd escaped capture; how he'd traveled by using his youth to persuade strangers to give him a ride.

"I beg you. My mother is dying. I have no money."

The incident on the bus had been a close one but Angel was confident in his training, proud of his survival skills. He didn't know about these two ex-soldiers, who'd had their own narrow escape from FBI, as he'd seen on a news report he'd watched on a TV in a diner at a small-town gas station.

Assassinations in the U.S. were always a problem.

Unlike jobs in Mexico, they had no guarantee of support from dirty cops on the payroll, and now, because this one was high-profile, they were more exposed. Everyone's picture was shown in the press.

Angel shrugged.

They still held the most vital piece: the girl.

He considered her again.

She did not come from the drug world like most of his targets. Yet in the moments he'd studied her, he'd found something about her he resented. As a top *sicario* for the cartel he had enjoyed the world in luxury, but looking upon the girl, this innocent from a wealthier class, took him back to what he had come from.

Angel could smell the dump, taste the despair of the tumbledown shack his family had lived in, feel the shame of other kids laughing at his drunken father picking through the trash.

No, Angel would have no trouble completing this job. It was just a matter of choosing a method, a thought that gave rise to a familiar worry.

Will she haunt me like the others haunt me?

Angel's cell phone rang and he fished it out of his backpack. The phone was a special design costing about $35,000 and stolen from the U.S. military. The cartel had obtained ten through a black market source. The phone's signals were scrambled, encrypted, then scrambled and encrypted repeatedly. For now, the calls were untrace-able.

The instant Angel answered, Thirty said, "Did you find them?"

"Yes."

"And did you inspect the asset?"

"Yes. It looks good."

"There's been a twist."

"What is it?"

"The man with our property has finally contacted us. He wants to make your job easier for you."

"How?"

"He wants to meet, to exchange our property for the seized asset. As we'd planned, he feels pressured to come to us. We will arrange it. One of the soldiers will know the locations. Are they present?"

Angel glanced at them in the front of the car.

"Yes."

"Put the older one on."

"Ruiz, for you."

Angel passed up his phone and watched several moments of nods punctuated with, "*Si, si.* I know it. We will." When Ruiz returned the phone, Angel asked a question of Thirty.

"How do we know our contact won't bring problems wearing badges with him. They are getting closer."

"We possess the asset—that's our strength. His weakness is his greed. We know that he needs the asset and our property. If he involves other parties, he will not achieve his goal."

"It's dangerous for us."

"There is no other way. We have arranged shipment of the special material for you to ensure that he will surrender all of our property. It is all in place, waiting for you."

"All right."

"We are not happy about the close calls we've had. This attention creates difficulties. But we must use it to our advantage. We must not back down. This is a time of intense interest. It is precisely the time to tell the world that if you fuck with us, you die. The arrogance of the dirty American cops and the sniveling messenger, to steal from the Norte Cartel, the cartel Zartosa built upon the graves of his family, is an insult. We are at war. Do you understand?"

"Yes."

"Zartosa's orders are to kill them all."

56

Lyle Galviera was still on his call to Cora when the FBI took action to arrest him.

Task Force members who were monitoring Cora's home line knew he was calling from the pay phone at the FirstRate Gas Station on Old Gatehouse Road, at the city's southern edge.

Before patching it to Cora at the FBI's divisional office, they'd alerted the Maricopa County 911 Center to send police units to the gas station, stressing that they not use lights or sirens. After dispatching cars, the emergency co-ordinator phoned the gas station directly to request staff make a visual of the person using the pay phone.

The coordinator's call was answered on the first ring. A male voice said: "I told you we are through, Darlene!"

The line clicked dead.

The dispatcher tried again but the line rang unanswered because Sheldon Cardick, the twenty-six-year-old clerk, was breaking up with his girlfriend. Actually, she'd dumped him and was now sorry. W*ell, tough titty.*

Let the phone ring.

To calm down, Sheldon went outside to sweep the front walk, waving to his last customer as he drove off in a beat-up Cherokee after using the pay phone. Not many people used that phone these days, since everyone had a cell phone. After cleaning up, Sheldon returned to the counter and his manager-trainee binders, still pissed at Darlene.

She was the loser. Despite what her mother said, Sheldon Cardick was not going be "just a clerk all of his sad little life." He was studying to be an executive with First-Rate. A lofty goal, Sheldon thought, just as a commotion outside pulled him from his binder.

What the—?

Four sheriff's cars had materialized.

Two large deputies entered, their shoulder radios squawking. They were pumped.

"Can you tell us if you saw anyone using the pay phone out front in the last few minutes?"

Sheldon craned his neck, seeing the other deputies unrolling police tape around the area by the phone. What's up with that? A knuckle knock on his counter got his attention.

"Hey, skip, eyes front! Did you see anybody on the phone?"

"Yeah, some guy, bought gas, driving a shit box Cherokee."

"What color and year?"

"White, 1990s I would guess."

"You'd guess?"

"What's going on?"

The second deputy was taking notes and talking in his radio as the first continued questioning Sheldon.

"Did the phone guy use a credit card?"

"Cash."

"Any chance you got a license plate?"

"No. Why? What's this about?"

The deputy pointed at the security cameras.

"Those work?"

"Yes."

"You going to volunteer your tapes, or do we need to get a warrant?"

"I, uh…well, I have to call my manager."

"Do it now."

Across the city in the FBI's Phoenix offices, Jack Gannon and Cora demanded to know what Hackett and the task force had learned in the wake of Galviera's call.

It was a major break.

They'd put the call through to this meeting room where Cora had taken her polygraph exam. Gannon checked his watch. Some twenty-five minutes had passed since Cora had spoken to Galviera.

It seemed like a lifetime.

They'd been here, waiting alone behind the room's glass walls while in the outer office agents worked with quiet intensity on the break. Hackett returned head down, concentrating on his BlackBerry.

"What do you have?" Gannon asked.

"We know he called from a pay phone at a gas station."

"You must know where."

"We do but we're not disclosing that now. We've got people on-site investigating."

"Are you going to tell us?"

"You're media, Jack."

"Come on. This is the closest we've ever been."

"No. We want it off the airwaves because we think these guys monitor police chatter on radio scanners. Everything's still hot right now." Hackett's phone rang. "Excuse me."

When they were alone again, Cora, overwhelmed by the polygraph and Galviera's call, contended with her emotions. Gannon put his arm around her. For twenty

years she'd lived with the burden of believing she'd murdered a man and destroyed so many lives.

"I'm so sorry for everything, Jack."

"Now you know the truth—you never killed anyone.
You did the opposite, Cora. You gave comfort to a dying
man. The San Francisco guys didn't charge you, or arrest
you. That's a good sign. You can't rewrite all the mistakes
you made in your life—no one can."

She nodded.

"All this time, I believed I was being punished for my
sins, and maybe I was. But it's strange how once I told
everyone what I'd done, Lyle's call came, like a karmic
connection. Maybe now I'm closer to getting Tilly back
than we've ever been."

"Let's hope so."

"I feel it, Jack. It's what Lyle said to me on the phone.
His exact words were, 'I'm going to see Tilly soon.' I
think it means he knows where she is."

"Maybe not." Hackett had returned and had been listening.

"Why not?" Cora asked.

"It could mean the cartel is luring Galviera with the
promise of seeing Tilly. And there's another key consideration."

"What's that?" Gannon asked.

"The cartel may also know that you were present when
Eduardo Zartosa was murdered in San Francisco. If so,
they may be planning to exact revenge. It's what they
do."

Cora swallowed hard.

The security cameras at the FirstRate Gas Station had
recorded Lyle Galviera in a ball cap and dark glasses,
buying gas. They'd also captured clear pictures of the
Arizona license plate on his Cherokee.

Within an hour those pictures were circulated in

citywide and statewide alerts to all police and media. Within two hours, the FBI held another news briefing. They asked the public to help locate Galviera, or his vehicle, or the other suspects, to aid in the investigation of Tilly Martin's kidnapping.

The appeal yielded few solid tips.

As the day gave in to the evening, Cora and Gannon returned to her home in Mesa Mirage, where she made a short statement to the news crews waiting in her driveway.

"I'm praying we'll bring Tilly home and I beg anyone with any information to call police. Please."

Exhausted, Cora went to Tilly's room. She held a stuffed polar bear in her arms, looked out the window to the stars and asked God for mercy.

Tilly, I love you. Wherever you are, Mommy loves you.

57

Somewhere in Metropolitan Phoenix, Arizona

Pit-a-pat pit-a-pat pit-a-pat.

Stones tapped and popped against the car's undercarriage.

Where are they taking me? We've been driving for hours.

Tilly had a bad feeling with the new kidnapper, the younger guy. The way he stared at her had creeped her out. All the more reason for her to keep trying everything she could to get away from her monsters.

With a few deep breaths, she'd gathered the strength to resume working on her bindings. Her captors had paid no attention to them. The tape was still secure but she had been loosening it.

Again Tilly twisted her aching wrists against the tape until they were numb.

The car slowed, then stopped.

Weight shifted and doors opened, followed by low talking. Then she heard the rattle, clank and shuffle as they began unloading the car and carrying items away. Tilly was overwhelmed with a sense of finality.

What's going to happen? What're they going to do to me?

Footsteps approached. A key was inserted in the trunk and it opened to the night and something moved swiftly toward her, leaving her no time to react as her head was swallowed by a sack.

Hands lifted her from the trunk, her feet found the ground. Dirt, sand and small stones bumped under her sneakers. She sensed the still air of a vast, remote place before she was escorted like a blind person to another location.

They had not gone far when they stopped.

"Step up," one of the creeps said.

Tilly raised her foot, feeling a step, then she found a smooth floor as they entered a structure. She was overwhelmed by the smell. It took her back to a school trip to ghost towns near Casa Grande. The decaying buildings were filled with birds' nests. The walls were layered with "sun-cooked bird shit," as Dylan Fuller had called it.

Now as they moved along, Tilly listened for anyone else who might be inside, anyone who could help her.

She heard nothing but creaking, dripping and the echoes of her own shuffling as they entered another area. Here Tilly sensed a dim light through the bottom of her hood as it was pulled from her head.

Standing there, she took stock of the room. It was as large as her classroom but illuminated by a naked bulb hanging like a noose from a pipe and wired to a car battery. The light created ominous shadows, for the room was abandoned, neglected. Paint peeled in sheets as if the walls were diseased. Tiles had fallen from the ceiling. At one end she saw a series of huge pipes horseshoed from the floor for about three feet before bending back into the floor like upside-down U's as high as Tilly's waist.

A mattress was pushed near one of the big upside-down U's.

Tilly saw a chain.

Handcuffs.

The creep Alfredo nudged her closer. He wrapped the chain around one of the pipes, looped one handcuff around the chain, clamped the other on Tilly's wrist, then snapped it shut on her.

The steel click destroyed the speck of hope she'd nurtured by loosening the tape.

Alfredo said nothing and removed her gag.

Before he left, he nudged the toe of his boot against a plastic bag. Tilly saw bottled water, potato chips, pastries, an apple and what looked like a sandwich.

Standing there, awaiting her fate, she felt the onset of tears but forced herself not to cry.

She could hear her captors in the next area, their low voices echoing as they talked quickly in Spanish with each other. She heard the digital chirp of a keypad and guessed one was making a call on a cell phone.

This was it.

Tilly sensed that whatever they were going to do to her, they would do it here.

She was so scared.

As she prayed, she looked to her left through the room's only window well. It had no glass or frame. It was a low-set, large square opening to the vast night. On the horizon, Tilly saw a few small lights, twinkling like a distant shore, and wondered what they were connected to.

A house? With people living a normal life and children happy and safe in their beds, while she was imprisoned here waiting for whatever was to come.

Did anyone know she was here?

Was anyone rushing to save her?

Why was this happening?

Why?

Furious, she yanked against her handcuff, rattling her chain against the pipe, causing a loud clanking of metal rings against metal.

Tilly looked at the pipe, at its upside-down U shape. It was about as big in circumference as a soda can, with a bigger circular collar at each end. In the middle it had several rings, each about three inches wide, that slid along the main pipe like bracelets.

Tilly focused on them.

One bracelet was out of alignment.

It seemed slanted.

Did she do that by jerking the chain?

Tilly slid the bracelets away from the slanted one. Then she slid the slanted one to reveal a clear two-inch gap in the pipe. A section had been removed, but the bracelet ring had covered the gap.

Alfredo never checked! The stupid creeps missed this!

Tilly's heart raced.

Would the chain fit? She looked around—no one was near. Quietly and carefully she slid the chain through the gap.

Yes! Oh my God! Oh my God!

Then with the utmost care she threaded the chain from her handcuff. She let out her breath slowly. All that was fastened to her now was the one handcuff on her wrist. Its open mate dangled from it and she held it to keep it from clinking.

She walked softly to the edge of the room, peered around the entrance carefully and saw a large warehouse area where her captors were at a table eating, surrounded by their luggage and equipment.

In the opposite direction, she saw a darkened hall-way.

She moved slowly down the hallway until she came to another open doorway and night air.

And just like that she was outside under the stars.

Free.

In an instant she searched for her bearings, for any sign of civilization or help in the vast darkness surrounding her. She scanned every direction until she found the small lights blinking in the distance.

There!

Tilly ran toward them as fast as she could.

Blood pounding in her ears, her heart nearly bursting, she wanted to cry and scream at the same time as she ran for her life.

58

Lago de Rosas, Mexico

The phone in the priest's rectory was an old wall-mounted touch-tone.

Father Francisco Ortero was folding his laundered shirts when it rang. He went to the kitchen and answered it.

"Is this Ortero, the priest who hears confessions in Lago de Rosas?"

The young male voice was familiar.

"Sí," Ortero said.

"This is the *sicario* you promised to help."

Several icy seconds of silence passed.

"I told you I would be calling, Father. You remember our discussion?"

"Yes." Ortero adjusted his grip on the handset.

"And my proposal?"

"Yes."

"I am about to finish my last job."

"Don't go through with it. Surrender, I beg you."

"Listen to me. You made a promise in the confessional to help me."

"You must stop."

"Have you arranged for a journalist you trust to tell my story?"

Ortero thought of all the funerals of the innocents

murdered by *narcotraficantes* that he had officiated; how the bloodshed had challenged his faith.

How much suffering does God allow?

"Father? Have you arranged for a journalist you trust to tell my story?"

"Yes."

"Good. Take note of this information."

The *sicario* gave the priest the time and the location near Phoenix, Arizona, where the journalist was to meet him tomorrow, confirming what the priest had suspected.

"Please, surrender. Police everywhere are looking for you and the others. Your faces are on all the news channels. Surrender!"

"It does not matter now. I am nearly finished."

"Please, I beg you, no more killing. Surrender now and atone."

"This is how it must happen. This is how it will happen."

The priest was disgusted with himself. He was aiding a *sicario*. He squeezed the handset as revulsion and fear coiled within him. What he was doing was akin to the devil's bidding.

"I am considering sending police," Ortero said.

"You would break the seal of the confessional?"

"What if it did not matter? What if I stopped being a priest to stop the killing?"

"If you send police, I will kill the girl before their eyes in the most memorable way you could ever imagine."

"I beg you to surrender."

"The girl's life is in your hands, priest. Your betrayal would result in her death. I have killed nearly two hundred people. Do you think I would hesitate to kill her? Do you want to gamble her life with an executioner of my stature?"

"Do you want to gamble with eternal damnation?"

"That is exactly what I'm doing," the *sicario* said. "I

know my days are numbered. Either way I am damned. This is my last chance at a new life. Send the reporter, or the girl will die. Wait. You anger me, Father. Maybe she will die anyway. Consider this your only hope to save her."

The line went dead.

Shaking, Ortero fell back to the wall, sliding down to the floor.

What have I set in motion?

59

Near Phoenix, Arizona

Angel dragged the back of his hand across his mouth to contend with his mounting tension.

Could he trust the priest?

It didn't matter. Angel knew that the cartel was going to kill him when this job was finished.

That he had enacted his survival plan gave him a measure of relief as he walked across the abandoned hangar, focusing on Limon-Rocha and Tecaza ready at the small table. They'd changed into their police uniforms and looked like real cops sitting there, listening to emergency scanners, checking their weapons, waiting for a green light.

"They've got an alert out for a license plate belonging to Galviera." Limon-Rocha tilted his head to the scanners. "Nobody can find him. Maybe he did the smart thing and changed the plate, or his vehicle."

"So, do we go now?" Tecaza asked.

"Did you secure the girl?" Angel asked him.

"Yes."

Angel's cell phone rang. It was Thirty.

"Are you set?"

"We're ready."

"I've just contacted him and set up the meeting. Do you have a detailed map?"

Angel snapped open the new fanfold map. With one hand, he spread it over one end of the table and pinpointed where Thirty directed them to go.

"He will be at that location in two hours."

"We'll leave now."

"And bring the girl. Let him see she is alive. He'll be cooperative if he thinks he is returning with her. Then you do your job and come home. Twenty-five will want to thank you personally."

"Personally?"

"You know he thinks you are the best."

Angel swallowed the lie, tapping the phone against his leg as he studied the map before making precise folds.

"It's time," he said to Tecaza. "Get the girl."

Tecaza, keen to get back to Mexico, strode to the room where he'd chained Tilly to the pipe. A moment later, a stream of cursing filled the empty building as he ran back to the table and riffled through the equipment bag.

"She got away."

Incredulous, Limon-Rocha and Angel ran to the room. After confirming what they'd been told, they'd returned to see Tecaza climbing the stairs to the roof, a small case slung over his shoulder.

"She could not have gone far," Tecaza said. "Ruiz, get your night-vision goggles! Help me look for her!"

Both men had military-issue binoculars that enabled them to see human images in the dark by perceiving thermal radiation or body heat. On the roof, goggles pressing over their eyes, they scanned the empty, flat land surrounding the abandoned airfield. Limon-Rocha searched clockwise, while Tecaza, cursing the whole time, searched counterclockwise, finding nothing but a sea of black, the edges occasionally dotted by distant lights.

A tiny flicker of brilliant white shot by the rim of Tecaza's lens.

He froze.

He moved back slowly until he found it again.

Then another tiny white light shot across his lens, then another.

Like minuscule white orbs rising and falling.

Then a larger one between them.

They were hands. The middle glowing orb was a face.

All several hundred yards away.

"That's her!"

60

Tilly's heart was bursting.

She was running on pure adrenaline. Each time she stumbled in the desert, her skin peeled and blood seeped from her cuts.

Don't stop. You can't stop. They'll find you.

Her pulse pounding in her ears, she wanted to cry out—*Please! Somebody help me! Please!*—but she didn't want to alert the creeps. Her hard breathing and soft whimpering pierced the night air.

In the distance behind her a motor revved. She looked back. Doors slammed, headlights swept and began undulating, acccelerating in her direction. At the edge of the lights' reach, Tilly saw a cluster of buildings and ran toward them. They looked like run-down wooden garages with steel drums and crates of junk inside.

The car lights shot through the gaps between the boards of the buildings, making the ground glow as shadows rose.

Hide! Run! Hide!

The car churned dirt into dust that swirled in the headlights as Tecaza braked near the buildings.

"She's here. Spread out."

Limon-Rocha and Tecaza used their night-vision

goggles to probe the buildings. Angel had a flashlight and searched the perimeter.

Tilly had found a gully surrounded by tall grass and shrubs and scrambled into it, laying flat on her stomach. She could hear them talking, glimpsed them searching the buildings. A flashlight beam raked the ground near her as a silhouette approached.

She held her breath.

No, please! No!

A cell phone rang and someone answered in Spanish but ended the call abruptly. The silhouette suddenly veered. At the same time one of the creeps near the buildings called out, "I see her!"

Oh no! Please, no!

It sounded like Alfredo, but his voice was lower, as if he'd turned from her. The others were with him. Tilly risked lifting her head and discerned three silhouettes near the idling car. By their posture, it appeared two of them were using binoculars.

"Where?" one of them asked.

"There, to the left."

"That's a coyote."

"No, that's her. She got away behind the buildings, let's go."

Doors slammed. The car roared off.

Tilly waited, got to her feet and ran toward the lights in the distance. She kept her eye on the car, way off to her left bounding over the vast field.

Keep running. Keep running.

Her side began aching, burning.

Tears blurred her vision but she saw a house ahead.

Please, somebody help me!

Far off to her left, the car changed direction, headlights turned toward her, the engine growling.

Virginia Dortman gripped her knife and cut potatoes into chunks. She was making a salad and desserts for the hospital fundraiser potluck tomorrow.

Judging from the aroma filling the kitchen of her small double-wide, the pies baking in her oven should almost be ready. Give them a few more minutes, she thought, gazing out her window at the flat land stretching toward the abandoned airfield.

Look at those lights bouncing and waving around out there. It must be teenagers again. All that tomfoolery can get dangerous. One time, they started a fire. Virginia had a good mind to call the sheriff's office.

She'd let it go for now. She had too much to do.

For the past year, since her husband died of a heart attack at fifty-two years of age, Virginia busied herself baking, volunteering and working at the library. But most of the time she feared for her son, Clay.

He looked at her from his framed photo atop the TV he'd bought her. Handsome in his dress blues, eyes intense under his white cap. He was a proud Marine, like his dad.

Clay had been posted to South Korea three months ago.

He was twenty-four.

Virginia whispered a prayer for him each day.

What was that?

Her attention shifted to her window.

Something outside was moving, approaching her house. She searched the night beyond the floodlights illuminating her property.

A coyote? No. That's a—

Virginia's eyes widened.

"Please, help me!"

Tilly ran up the wooden stairs to Virginia Dortman's front porch.

"Help me!"

Stunned at the site of a sobbing little girl at her door, Virginia's immediate thought was that this was a joke, set up by teenagers.

She opened her door, her disbelief turning to shock at Tilly's dirty T-shirt, torn jeans, frazzled hair and bloodied arms. When the kitchen light glinted off the steel handcuff dangling from Tilly's wrist, Virginia gasped.

"Oh my Lord, sweetheart, what happened to you?"

Tilly fused herself to Virginia, inhaling the smells of her kitchen, her apron, shaking so badly, her words spilled through a torrent of tears.

"P-p-please…h-h-help…"

Virginia's next thought was calling 911, and she glanced toward her cordless phone on the sofa of her living room.

But before she moved to get it, her kitchen was awash in blood-red pulsating light.

A police car?

An unmarked patrol car halted at her doorstep, a red emergency light revolving on the interior dash. Two uniformed officers rushed toward Virginia. Confusion then recognition dawned, memory swirling with TV news images of a kidnapped child, drug gangs, fake police officers— *Oh, dear Lord.*

"Release the child, ma'am!"

Both officers put their hands on their holstered guns.

"No!" Tilly screamed. "They're not police!"

"Ma'am, release the child! We have reports that a missing girl was sighted here. Now, release the child and step forward with your hands above your head palms out. Now!"

"No! Don't listen to them!" Tilly screamed.

A third figure left the rear of the car, disappearing in the night.

Paralyzed with fear, Virginia glanced to her counter for her knife.

"Freeze! Release her, now!"

One of the officers drew his weapon and pointed it at Virginia while his partner charged at Tilly. She broke free, bolting to the living room for the phone just as Angel smashed through the rear door and seized it from Tilly.

The two men held her down, clamped the loose hand-cuff around her free wrist. One of the creeps, Alfredo, dragged her wailing to the car and locked her in the trunk.

Inside the house, Limon-Rocha held Virginia at gun-point in a chair in her kitchen.

Angel entered, glanced at her, then picked up the knife she had been using a moment ago.

Angel took stock of Virginia's double-wide trailer, the photograph of her Marine son. Running his finger along the serrated edges of the blade, he looked into her eyes. They glistened with terror.

"I am very sorry," he said.

61

Phoenix, Arizona

Lyle Galviera kept the Cherokee a few miles under the speed limit, moving south along the freeway.

The AC had quit. His hands were sweating on the wheel. He opened the windows and concentrated.

This was it, his only shot.

The cartel had given him the location for the meeting. He knew the area but still had a long way to go. Amid the multilane streams of headlights and taillights, he checked his mirrors again, glad the guy in California who'd provided him with the Cherokee and new ID had put several different plates in the storage bin.

"Never know when you might need 'em."

Galviera had switched to a Colorado plate a few hours ago. There was no margin for error here. As the road rushed under him, he looked out at the ocean of city lights and floated with memories of his father.

His old man had driven a bus all day, taking every overtime shift. At home, his mother kneaded the cords of stress from his neck. His old man worked extra hours because he wanted Lyle to be the first in the family line to go to college.

Make something of yourself. Make me proud.

It had happened; Lyle was accepted at Arizona State and, man, it brought tears to his father's eyes. Then came the day Lyle was called to the faculty office. A phone was passed to him and he heard his mother's voice: *"Come to the hospital!"*

After they buried his dad, Galviera dropped out and worked like a dog as a bicycle courier and delivering pizzas before finally carving his own business out of nothing.

Nothing.

He nearly lost it all when his first marriage ended but he triumphed, battered but wiser. Then he met Cora, admired how she'd survived her own problems. They were alike; they were good together. They had dreams but he'd put them on hold because his company was in trouble.

He refused to lose it.

He pounded the wheel with both fists and cursed.

Tilly kidnapped, Salazar and Johnson murdered, leaving me a wanted man, a marked man. Half of the money is mine. I earned it. I need it. Without it, I lose everything. I can't lose.

He could fix this.

The solution lay behind him under the tarp in the sports bags filled with cash—cash from high school potheads hustling fast food to suburban soccer moms, university dope smokers, music types, movie types, bottom feeders, high flyers, pimps, hos, street trash, tripped-out execs and all-round losers; drug users from every scene of the American dream. Three million dollars in unmarked bills for Tilly's life.

No one knew about the two million he was hiding for his own use.

This was it.

He came to an industrial wasteland at the city's edge, a railcar repair depot that had closed down after an explosion some thirty years ago.

In the darkness, the Cherokee crawled by the crumbling brick buildings rising like headstones from the yard.

Galviera's instructions were to go to the tallest building, park at the base and wait in the car with his lights off.

He turned down a road that ran between two long tracks, both lined with weatherworn box and hopper cars. He followed the dark road to the metal tower that supported a deteriorated storage tank, the tallest structure in the site.

He parked near the base.

He waited, watching the strobe lights of jetliners sailing by overhead. After nearly an hour, his rearview mirror glowed with the headlights of an approaching vehicle.

It stopped behind him.

Two figures got out, carrying flashlights, and came to his passenger and driver doors, where one directed a blinding beam into his eyes.

"Mr. Galviera?"

He glimpsed a shoulder patch—a uniform—and his heart sank.

"Yes."

"Step out of the car, please, with your hands above your head, palms out."

Galviera complied, grappling with the fact it was over as they patted him for weapons. The men kept the light burning in his eyes before taking him to the rear of their vehicle, where another figure stood in the dark.

The trunk opened and Galviera's heart lifted.

Light washed over Tilly—bound, haggard, scared, but alive.

"You brought our property, Mr. Galviera?"

"Yes, in the back, under the tarp. In the bags."

One of the men opened the rear door of the Cherokee, dropped two laden sports bags on the ground in front of the car and unzipped them to display thick bundles of cash. He took one and fanned the edges.

"Did you bring all of it?"

"It's all there in all the bags. Let me take Tilly and go. Our business is done."

"No."

"We each fulfilled our obligations. You can count it."

"We're not going to count it here."

"Why not?"

"We're not done, not yet."

"I don't under—"

Stars exploded across Galviera's eyes.

DAY 5

62

At dawn, climbing out of a short, troubled sleep on Cora's sofa, Jack noticed the task force agents huddled around the laptops on the kitchen table.

One of them—*was that Detective Coulter?*—was whispering on a cell phone with a heightened degree of intensity.

Something's going on. They've got something.

Hair tousled, Gannon wrapped a blanket around himself, smelling fresh coffee as he went to them.

"What do you have?"

All eyes turned to him before Coulter, who was with Phoenix PD's Home Invasion and Kidnapping Enforcement Task Force, shook his head.

"Nothing, Jack."

"Bullshit."

"Nothing that's confirmed," Coulter said.

"Well, what is it you *think* you have?"

"Jack, we can't tell you anything right now. Agent Hackett—"

Gannon looked around quickly.

"Where is he? He's usually here before the sun rises."

"He's out in the field."

"Out in the field, where? Doing what?"

No one responded. Tension mounted until Gannon's cell phone rang.

"Jack, it's Henrietta. Can you talk?"

He turned away from the investigators, pulling up his bitterness at her for ambushing him outside FBI offices before Cora's polygraph exam.

"I'm not giving you an interview."

"No, that's not it. And I'm sorry about the FBI thing, but I had to do it. You'd do the same thing if the tables were turned."

It took a second for him to agree. He'd only himself to blame, anyway, for calling her and asking about defense lawyers.

"My sister's not a suspect."

"Our story never said she was. We reported that she hired a lawyer and the FBI said she was cooperating on the case."

"Is that what you called to tell me?"

"I got a call from one of our stringers who sleeps with his police scanners on. Seems there's a lot of chatter about something in the south. We don't know for sure, but one cop apparently blurted something on the air that 'this is related to the kidnapped girl' before a supervisor shut him up. We're doing all we can to get a location. I'm rolling south now."

"Call me when you get it."

Gannon took a quick shower and woke Cora, telling her, "Get dressed quick. Something's going on." Then he ate a bagel and gulped some coffee, all within twenty minutes, and confronted Coulter again. "Are you guys going to tell me what's going on?"

"Jack, we can't."

Gannon strode out the front door to the driveway. The few news crews who'd arrived already were gossiping over take-out coffee and high-fiber muffins. When they saw him, camera operators reflexively hoisted their cameras to their shoulders and someone shouted a question.

"Hey, why does your sister need an attorney?"

Reporters scrambled to ready microphones, incredulous that he was coming to them, until he held up his palms.

"No interviews. I need your help."

"Come on, Gannon."

"Have any of your desks heard any chatter about something going on at the south end related to the case?"

Most people shook their heads. Gannon studied the pack, looking for telltale signs. He saw one reporter on his cell phone and trying to take notes, ignoring Gannon. *The only time you can afford to ignore a primary source on a major story is when you know something bigger.* The reporter met Gannon's stare. "Who are you?"

"Sonny Watson, AZ Instant News Agency."

"What?"

"New online news service." Watson glanced around.

"Sonny, has your desk heard anything going on this morning in the south end, related to the case?"

Again, Watson looked around, reluctant to answer. Gannon figured he was adhering to the code of keeping exclusive information from a competitor.

"Kid, we're all going to find out," Dave Davis, a seasoned TV reporter with the FOX affiliate, boomed. "Half of us likely know already anyway."

"They think they have a major crime scene at the NewIron Rail yards. We've got somebody there already. That's all I know."

Reporters called their desks while hurrying to their cars.

Gannon returned to the house for Cora. They rushed to her Pontiac Vibe and used the GPS system to direct them to NewIron.

"Please, please don't let this be Tilly!"

"Take it easy, Cora. We don't have many facts yet."

Gannon's gut twisted as they threaded through traffic

while Cora prayed out loud. He got her to call Henrietta Chong, who'd just arrived at the scene.

"They're so tight-lipped. No one knows anything," said Chong. "I think I see a good source. I'll call you back."

"I think it's bad, Jack," Cora said. "It has to be bad if they won't tell us anything."

It took another fifteen minutes before Gannon and Cora reached the location. The area was an immense industrial graveyard of old factories and warehouses. As they neared the NewIron Rail yards they came upon scores of emergency vehicles lined up and blocking the entrance. News trucks dotted the road. Reporters were gathering around a cluster of police-types near a gate cordoned with crime scene tape. A breeze jiggled the brilliant yellow in festive juxtaposition to the hopelessness of the drab depot.

Gannon searched in vain for Hackett, Larson—anyone who could tell him what they'd discovered.

Reporters had encircled someone who was with the County Sheriff's Office.

"We have nothing to say," he told them. "We're supporting the FBI."

"Jack!"

Henrietta Chong tugged on his arm, pulling him and Cora away behind a satellite truck out of sight of the pack.

"What's going on?" Cora asked her.

"Listen, I just got this from a deputy I know. This is way off the record, but late last night two homeless guys who were sleeping in a boxcar flagged down a patrol car. Turns out they think they witnessed a murder in the yards, some kind of confrontation. They saw a body being hefted into the trunk of a car that drove off."

Protective of Cora, Gannon challenged the information.

"That's pretty vague. How do they link this to Tilly?"

"There's an abandoned Cherokee in there that matches the one they linked to Galviera."

"Oh God, no!" Cora whispered. "If they've killed Lyle…oh Jack, what about Tilly? Oh please, God, no!"

The sky above them split as a TV news helicopter hammered overhead, transmitting live footage that interrupted morning shows across Arizona. Soon the story would go national with Breaking News on a major development in the local story.

"…on what police sources say is a major crime scene linked to the case of Tilly Martin, an eleven-year-old Phoenix girl who was the victim of a brazen kidnapping from her home by a drug cartel to settle a debt with her mother's boyfriend, missing Phoenix businessman Lyle Galviera…"

63

Phoenix, Arizona

Lyle Galviera's head throbbed.

He tried to move but couldn't. He was tied to a chair.

He tried to see but he was blindfolded.

He heard only the echoed drips and creaks of an infinite space, like an enormous warehouse, punctuated with bursts of sporadic chatter from emergency scanners, like police dispatches.

Push the fear aside. Concentrate.

Footsteps approached behind him and someone removed his blindfold.

Galviera's eyes opened wide.

Taking in his surroundings, the airy vastness, the high ceiling, he recognized that he was in an abandoned hangar. Sitting a yard or two from him on a worktable, legs dangling playfully, was a young man wearing a shoulder holster, showing the grip of a handgun. He stared at Galviera while he ate potato chips from a bag and sipped from a can of soda.

"You know why you're here, Mr. Galviera?" Angel asked in Spanish.

Is that the sicario? *Think.*

Galviera did not respond as his eyes swept over the array of his sports bags, lined up on the floor between them. All were open displaying bundles of cash.

"It seems," the young man said between chips, "that

we have a discrepancy on the amount of our stolen property. You've provided us with three million, when our calculation shows the amount owing to be five."

I need the two million. I can't give it up.

"That's all there is."

"Don't lie. That's not all there is."

"Where's Tilly?"

"Our agreement was a simple one. You return our stolen property, all five million, and we return the girl. We've shown you the girl. We've kept our side of the agreement."

"Where is she? I need to see her."

Ignoring the question to sip his soda, the young man said, "You have failed to keep your part of the agreement. You've misled us and that is a mistake."

I've got nothing left to bargain with. No leverage.

"No. It's all there."

"Your first mistake, Mr. Galviera, was to conspire to steal from us."

"No, I never did that. What have you done with Tilly?"

"I will give you the opportunity right now to tell us where the rest of our property is so we can retrieve it and conclude our dealings."

Either way, I am dead. If I get out of this, I'll have Tilly and two million.

"But that is all there is. I swear."

"You swear?"

"Salazar and Johnson controlled everything," Galviera said. "They used my company for distribution for a limited term. All fees collected were stored until each collection period, then everything went to them to process to you."

"So, Salazar and Johnson are responsible for any discrepancies?"

"Yes. It was them."

Someone other than the young man cleared his throat.

Galviera saw two other men, older men, watching from the periphery.

"This complicates the situation," Angel said. "Let's simplify it. Salazar and Johnson were stealing from us. They'd planned to set up their own cartel, the Diablo Cartel, to compete with us. With your help, they stole five million dollars from our organization for that very purpose."

That's what happened and they know it.

"I had no part in that."

Something coiled; something out of sight was being prepared.

"I am afraid you are not being truthful, Mr. Galviera. I don't think you appreciate the gravity of your situation."

"I do. With the utmost respect, please, I've brought you the money. Give me Tilly and we'll close the matter. I'm telling you the truth. That is all the money there is."

Angel signaled to Limon-Rocha and Tecaza.

In an instant they left, then returned, carrying Tilly. She was bound to a chair by rope and chains. No hope of escaping this time. They set her down opposite Galviera. Her mouth was taped.

Angel hopped from the table, tugged on white latex surgical gloves, then picked up a sports bag that had been behind him and out of sight.

"I think you need an illustration to understand."

Angel opened the big bag, reached into it and retrieved a round object that was slightly smaller than a ten-pin bowling ball. Then he reached into the bag for a second similar object, placing both on the ground before Galviera.

"You see, this is what happens when you lie to me."

Amid the mass of hair, decomposing flesh and open eyes, Galviera met the faces of Octavio Sergio Salazar and John Walker Johnson.

64

Greater Phoenix, Arizona

"Goodness, girl, slow down!"

Olive McKay scolded herself as her old Silverado SUV bumped along the dirt road leading to her friend Virginia's house.

Olive was running a titch late this morning but that was no reason to spill all the food she'd made the night before for the charity potluck—pecan tarts, a pineapple upside-down cake and pasta salad. Thank goodness she'd put it all in the cooler and belted it to the rear passenger seat.

Virginia's double-wide emerged into view. Olive tooted the horn as she wheeled up, noticing that Virginia had left her front porch light on. *Odd.* Being a penny-pincher on a tight budget, Virginia just never did that.

She's probably a bit preoccupied this morning.

Olive got out of her SUV, intent on helping load it with Virginia's food as quickly as possible. Raising her hand to ring the doorbell, she paused.

The door was ajar.

Did she leave it open for me? That's strange. She always keeps it locked, on account of the teenagers who sometimes get out of hand, out at the old airfield.

"Virginia?"

What's that clicking?

"Hello! Virginia, it's me, Olive! We have to get going. Flo said we should be there by now!"

She listened harder to the soft vibrations. What is that?

"Virginia?"

Olive's smile melted as the first icy thread of concern slithered up her back. *What's that rapid clicking?* The door creaked as she slowly pushed it open, seeing tomato juice all over the kitchen floor and thinking, what a mess. Then...*that can't be tomato juice...the consistency and the color's not right.* As the door swung wider. Olive saw a foot, then a leg, both legs, and Virginia lying on her back with a knife handle rising from her chest, her hand twitching in the puddle of blood.

Olive's scalp tingled. Her skin prickled with goose-flesh.

She called 911 and screamed for an ambulance, for police, for God to come right away because Virginia had been stabbed.

So much blood. Too much blood.

Olive took her friend's hand. It was still warm.

"You stay with me, Virginia."

Red foam bubbled at Virginia's mouth as she moaned, crying out to her dead husband, to Clay, to Olive, trying to tell her.

"...the girl...please... "

"Don't try to talk."

"...missing girl...news...bad please..."

But Olive couldn't understand.

She didn't remember the sirens, the paramedics, the deputies pulling her away, working on Virginia, starting an IV, slipping an oxygen mask over her mouth, lifting her to a board, the gurney and loading her into the ambulance.

The deputy had to catch Olive before she collapsed, watching the ambulance wail down the same bumpy road she'd taken moments ago in her Silverado.

Virginia died en route to the hospital.

The same hospital where her husband had died, the same hospital she was helping with her potato salad and apple pies for the charity potluck.

65

As TV helicopters circled overhead Cora stared blankly into the press and police chaos at the NewIron Rail yards.

"Tilly's dead. That's it, isn't it?" she said, waiting in her car with Gannon while he left another cell phone message in his attempt to reach Hackett.

"I know this is hard, Cora." Gannon tried to console her. "But until we know everything, we know nothing."

"Henrietta Chong said that they'd found Lyle's car, that witnesses saw a body. I can't take it anymore, Jack, I just can't."

She covered her face with her hands.

"You've got to hang on to hope while we still have it."

Someone tapped on Gannon's window. He turned to the clean-cut face of a uniformed deputy, who'd approached from behind.

"Jack Gannon and Cora Martin?"

"Yes."

"Deputy Wadden. Agent Hackett is in there at the scene." Wadden nodded to the storage tank tower and the lines of railcars. "He got your message and requested we get word to you." Wadden's shoulder microphone bleated with a coded transmission. "One moment, please."

Wadden leaned into it, responding with a numeric code before resuming matters with Gannon and Cora.

"I'm parked behind you. Please follow me in your vehicle."

"What's going on?" Gannon asked.

"I'm going to lead you to a location a few blocks from here. Agent Hackett said he'd meet you there in fifteen minutes."

The sign in the window of The Bluebird Diner said, Today's Special $1.99 Fish N' Chips. Two men in their fifties were hunched over the counter, wearing faded T-shirts and jeans. The talk wafting from under their worn ball caps concerned pensions and a major league pitcher.

Gannon and Cora waited alone in a booth for Hackett.

From his days on the police beat at the *Buffalo Sentinel,* Gannon knew that investigators often took people away from the scene and the cameras in order to tell them the worst news. He steadied himself by staring at the milk clouds swirling in his coffee while Cora took deep breaths, her fear tightening around her.

Sitting there with his sister in the ominous air pulled Gannon back to Buffalo.

He is eight; Cora is thirteen. They are terrified waiting at their kitchen table. They'd been in the yard, Cora lobbing a baseball to him when he popped one that went up, up, so far up that it landed with enough velocity on their father's new Ford to leave a fracture that spiderwebbed across the windshield. Mom's aghast. "Holy cow, Jack, Dad's new car. He's going to be sick about this, just sick!" Cora telling her, "Don't blame Jack. It was my fault, Mom. I should have caught it. It was an accident, I swear." At that moment Cora is his hero. Dad says nothing, works overtime and fixes the problem. That's the way he did things. Jack felt horrible but loved Cora for being the big sister protector.

Despite all the pain-soaked years between them, despite her mistakes, his misgivings and the wounds, she was still his sister.

And she needed him.

He clasped his hand over hers. "Hang in there, okay? It's going to be all right. Just hang on."

Cora took his hand, squeezing it, until they saw Hackett's sedan arrive out front. He was alone and sober-faced when he entered, pulling a chair to the end of the table.

Cora steeled herself and hit him with her question.

"Is my daughter dead? If it's true, I want you to tell me right now?"

The two men at the counter turned.

Hackett kept his voice low, choosing his words carefully.

"We found no evidence at this scene to confirm that."

"Please stop talking that way," Cora said. "I took a polygraph, like you wanted. I told you everything, like you wanted. I may not have lived a perfect life, but please, can't you show me a scrap of respect. She's my child and I think I deserve to know the truth."

Hackett loosened his collar.

"Two homeless men who'd been drinking in a boxcar claim they witnessed a possible drug deal go sideways. They say they saw two figures deposit a body into the trunk of a car. Then the car drove off. The men were frightened and stopped a patrol car. They led the deputy to the location, where he found an abandoned Cherokee SUV matching the vehicle we've linked to Galviera," Hackett said.

"Our people have been working the scene since 3:00 a.m., going full bore. Fingerprints in the SUV match Galviera's and we found blood traces consistent with his type."

"What do you think happened here?" Gannon asked.

"In his call to Cora," Hackett said, "Galviera indicated

he was going to fix things. He said that he was going to see Tilly. We suspect the cartel lured him here with the intention of torturing him into giving them their money."

"Oh Jesus, what about Tilly?" Cora asked.

"They may have used her as the bait. The cartel may have lured him with the promise of seeing Tilly."

Cora moaned.

"We can't rule it out," Hackett said.

"They're just theories, Cora." Gannon tried to comfort her.

"He's right," Hackett said. "Just theories, but we can't discount another concern—that Cora was present when Eduardo Zartosa, the youngest brother of Samson Zartosa, leader of the Norte Cartel, was murdered."

"But I never knew who that boy in San Francisco was until now."

"It doesn't matter. We have to assume that Samson Zartosa knows now and take that into account. Think about it. Through circumstance, he is now holding the child of the woman involved in his little brother's murder, the woman whose boyfriend has stolen from his operation. That's about as bad as things can get. You wanted the truth. Well, that's it."

Cora tried to keep herself from coming apart, staring off at the helicopters in the distance, circling the rail yards like giant vultures.

Please, God, help me find her.

Hackett's cell phone rang. He turned away slightly to take the call. It was short and he finished by saying, "I'll head that way now and meet you there."

Cora saw something troubling in his expression.

"What is it? What's happening?"

"I can't tell you right now, I have to go."

"Please!"

"I'm sorry, I'll keep in touch."

When Hackett got to his car, Gannon stood, tossed some bills on the table. "Let's go. I could hear part of the call, something about a homicide. We'll follow him."

66

Phoenix, Arizona

"Oh, Jesus."

Salazar's and Johnson's severed heads stared up at Galviera. Across from him, Tilly's screams were muffled by the tape over her mouth.

"You have thirty seconds to tell us where you've put our two million dollars," Angel said. "Or I will add a new one to the collection."

Galviera turned white and was breathing hard.

"There's more money. Please take them away. I'll tell you where it is."

"They will remain to inspire you to tell the truth."

"I rented several storage lockers under the name of Pilsner at JBD Mini-Storage in Phoenix. The two million is in locker 787A, northwest sector of the yard. You need the gate code and the key for the steel lock on the unit. The money is in two sports bags. The code and key are in the hollowed section of the heel of my right boot."

Angel nodded to Tecaza, who yanked off Galviera's right boot and twisted the heel, extracting a metal key and a folded business card with numbers jotted in pen on the back.

He held them up for Angel.

Tecaza and Limon-Rocha entered JBD's address into

a GPS, preparing to go retrieve their cash now as Angel stood before Galviera.

"To ensure you are not working with police, I'll call my associates every twenty minutes. If they do not answer me, I will remove the girl's head."

In the time that Limon-Rocha and Tecaza were gone, Galviera tried to soothe Tilly.

"It'll be okay, I promise. Soon they'll have what they want and they'll let us go. I am so sorry for this, Tilly. It'll be okay now. Soon you'll see your mom and everything's going to be fine. I promise."

Tilly could not stop shaking. Her widened eyes seemed even larger as she kept them on Angel. Her stomach knotted each time he made a phone call. She thanked God each time his call was answered.

Angel occupied himself by eating potato chips and chocolate cupcakes, drinking Coke and playing a handheld computer game, the soft beeping and ponging sound a cruel juxtaposition to the horror he'd put on hold.

An hour after they'd left, Limon-Rocha and Tecaza had returned. They placed two sports bags on the table and started counting the bundled cash, counting twice to verify the amount.

The total: $2,176,000.

"Back the car into the hangar close to the table—" Angel nodded to Galviera "—and load all the money in the trunk, with the shovel and the pick."

"Wait." Galviera struggled. "Aren't you going to let us go?"

No one responded. As Limon-Rocha and Tecaza loaded the car, Angel checked Galviera's bindings and the handcuffs on his wrists and ankles.

"What are you doing?" Galviera winced when Angel tightened the cuffs.

"Get him ready," Angel said.

"Please," Galviera said. "I'm begging you, please!"

"Mr. Galviera, did you believe for one moment that after stealing from us you would come out of this alive?"

No more pleading or begging. This was how it was done.

Angel pulled on a large rubber apron and a surgeon's clear face shield, then set a gas-powered chain saw on the floor next to Tilly.

Galviera bucked wildly against his restraints. Tilly screamed under her tape. Angel kept the saw on the ground, expertly threw the *on* switch, the throttle, and adjusted the choke. He jerked the engine's crank cord. It popped to life, filling the hangar with a deafening roar.

Gently squeezing the throttle trigger, Angel lifted the saw and very carefully leveled it at Tilly's neck. The engine was turning at nearly thirteen-thousand rpm, powering the teeth in the semichisel chain. Tilly could feel the air rippling as Angel brought it closer. Her eyes bulged as she thrashed in vain away from the eighteen-inch blade.

As the saw's raging teeth came within half an inch of Tilly's skin she prayed and thought of her mother.

Angel was practiced.

A quick touch was all it took.

67

Phoenix, Arizona

A Maricopa County patrol car blocked the entrance to Virginia Dortman's property. Cued by an approaching vehicle, the sheriff's deputy got out, adjusted his hat and went to the driver.

Hackett extended his FBI credentials. The deputy studied them and waved him on. Hackett drove nearly a quarter mile down the lane leading to Virginia's double-wide trailer, where he counted ten emergency vehicles lining the road. Yellow crime scene tape zigzagged among the trees surrounding Virginia's house. He heard a yelp and saw a K-9 unit scouring the property. Another deputy stood at the tape.

"Sir, Agent Larson is by the ambulance." The deputy nodded to a far corner.

Larson was with two county investigators standing at the open rear doors of an ambulance, where a distraught woman in her sixties was being tended to by paramedics. Upon seeing Hackett, Larson stepped away, paged through her notebook and updated him.

"The deceased is Virginia Dortman, the apparent victim of a home invasion. She was discovered by her friend, Olive McKay, the woman in the ambulance."

"And the link to our kidnapping?"

"When Olive found Virginia, she was alive and talking. Olive is trying to remember her friend's last words. She insists it was about our case."

Hackett and Larson joined the other investigators respectfully listening while Olive, contending with her shock, did all she could to decipher Virginia's last words.

"I'm sorry," Olive said, "but this is so hard."

"We understand, ma'am," Sheriff's detective Hal Atcher said. "If you could just try for us again, it's very important."

"It was something like, the missing girl on TV, and bad please."

"'Bad please?'" Atcher repeated.

"That's what it sounded like."

"Could it be bad *police?*" Hackett offered.

"It could be, but I'm not sure. This is awful, awful, awful!" Olive sobbed.

"Thank you, Olive. Thank you," Atcher said. "We'll give you a little break while you wait for your husband to get here."

Atcher and his partner, Brad Gerard, introduced themselves after stepping aside to give Olive a respite with the paramedics.

"What do you make of this, Earl?" Atcher asked.

"I don't know. I just got here. Did you find anything that places our people at this scene?"

"Nothing yet. It's all fresh, like the thing you got going at the rail yards."

"Right." Hackett took stock of the area's isolation and the cluster of buildings dotting the horizon. "What's that way over there?"

"That is the old Spangler Airfield. Used to service crop dusters until it closed in the 1950s and was abandoned. I believe the family estate is hoping for a mall development but over the years parceled off some of the border property, like this lot that Virginia and her husband bought."

"What's the Dortman family situation?"

"No records. Lem is former military. He was a trucker until he died a year ago. Virginia was a librarian. Their son, Clay, is a U.S. Marine posted overseas. We've sent word to him. We're going to start a canvass, but the neighbors are about an eighth of a mile apart on property surrounding the airfield."

"Excuse me, Agent Hackett?" A deputy nodded to the police tape. "That gentleman there talked his way to the line. He says he needs to speak to you."

Hackett winced, recognizing Gannon and Cora at the tape. They'd followed him. He signaled that he would speak to them later and returned to the detectives.

"Okay, what I would do—" Hackett nodded toward the abandoned airfield "—is send a few units over there right away because—"

"Hal, we got something!" The radio in Gerard's hand blurted and they heard a bark. The group turned to a county crime scene tech approaching, gripping a large digital camera in her gloved hands. "Clarkson and Sheba found it. It's a shoe, child-sized. I flagged it. It's in the yard out back. Alone. No other items. Have a look."

The investigators crowded around the screen and examined the photo of a small sneaker. Larson thumbed through her notebook to Tilly's clothing description, then went back to the photo.

"Earl, that pretty much fits… Earl?"

Hackett waved to the deputy to admit Gannon and Cora to the scene and the group.

"We'll get an identification from the mother."

Gannon and Cora, questions written on their faces, hurried to the group and looked at the photo.

"Is that Tilly's shoe?" Hackett asked.

Two seconds of intense concentration was all Cora needed before her eyes brimmed with tears and she nodded.

A dog yelped and the group's attention turned to the expanse of shrub and grass stretching beyond them to the airstrip. Sheba, the police dog, was tugging Sheriff's Deputy Clarkson toward it.

68

Three Sheriffs' SUVs cut a fast-moving line over the scrub, stretching toward the abandoned buildings of the airfield.

A hot wind lifted desert detritus with the dust clouds churning in their wake. Their wigwagging emergency lights underscored urgency. Deputy Pate was driving the lead car. FBI Agent Bonnie Larson was his passenger. As they arrived, Larson scanned the structures. No vehicles, people or indications of activity.

"Let's start with the hangar. The doors are open," Pate said into his shoulder microphone. "Chet and Marty, take the east entrance. We'll take the west. Somers, Briscoe, take the back side."

"Ten-four."

Pate got his shotgun, Larson unholstered her Glock-27 and they positioned themselves on either side of the hangar's west doors, which were open to a gap of some fifteen feet. Larson's heart rate picked up and she started processing the situation.

One thing for sure: It was quiet.

Deathly quiet.

Before Hackett pulled away from Virginia Dortman's property, he made a judgment call.

He had no grounds to detain Gannon and Cora, but he knew that after he'd invited them to identify Tilly's shoe—evidence that she'd been present—they'd get to the airport, one way or another.

"I'll lead you in. You follow me in your car. But you do as I say," Hackett instructed Gannon before they set out across the expanse to catch up to Larson and the deputies.

Hackett knew it ran up against the rules, but it was a matter of control. They were closing in on Tilly's kidnappers and he couldn't risk Gannon rushing off on his own and jeopardizing the work of the task force.

Not at this stage.

Hackett would keep an eye on him.

As they neared the buildings, Hackett saw the SUVs and the deputies holding their positions. In his rearview mirror, he found Gannon and Cora's small Pontiac. He lowered his window, stuck out his arm, signaling for them to stop and keep back, way back, behind him.

At that moment the radio on Hackett's passenger seat crackled with a dispatch from Larson.

"We're going in, Earl."

Waiting for their eyes to adjust to the light, Larson and Pate inched around the big doors and assessed the hangar's interior.

Soaking wet trash and rags were strewn everywhere. *Disgusting.*

No sounds, until Pate's command boomed. "Maricopa County Sheriff! Come out with your hands open and held up above your head!"

No response.

After a full minute and a few soft dispatches on the radio, they moved in. Larson was suddenly reminded of her grandfather's cabin in northern New York; the gas smell of his small outboard motor. Before she became an agent, Larson worked as a state trooper. In that time, she had seen people who'd been shot, drowned, burned, frozen, stabbed and buried alive but she'd never seen anything like... *Oh Jesus...* She was overcome as she and the deputies realized what the garbage was....

"Oh Jesus Christ...oh Christ!"

Staring at the drenched rags, Larson soon picked out arms, legs, a head, then another, all severed.

The floor was slick with blood.

Larson saw the blood-splattered chain saw.

"Oh Jesus!"

Struggling to make sense of the scene, she stepped back and held the back of her hand to her mouth as some of the deputies shouted and pivoted with their weapons extended, wary of suspects at the scene.

Someone got on their radio and called for an ambulance.

It didn't matter. Everyone was dead.

Larson's radio crackled.

"Bonnie, I heard shouting. What do you have?" Hackett asked.

Outside, the wind had carried the chaos beyond the hangar and over the desert to Hackett's car, where his radio blurted Larson's response.

"Homicides, at least three, possibly more. They look fresh."

"Any indication on the victims?"

"Three adult males, two appear to be in police uniforms. They could be our kidnappers with the Norte Cartel. It looks like we have additional body parts, two severed male heads. It's really bad, Earl— I've never—"

Upon hearing the distant voices of alarmed cops, Gannon and Cora rushed from their car to Hackett's.

"What is it?" Gannon leaned into the open passenger window.

"What did they find?" Cora's eyes were rimmed with tears.

At that moment Hackett's radio crackled with another dispatch from Larson as she fought to keep control of her emotions.

"I've never seen anything like this, Earl. Do not come in here. You do not want to see this!"

That transmission stole Cora's breath. Hackett fumbled to turn down the volume but he had the radio with the loose swivel knob.

"What is it?" Cora's eyes bulged. "What's happened?"

Hackett shot a look to Gannon that demanded his help.

"We don't know for certain," Hackett said. "They're assessing the scene."

"Is my daughter in there?"

Gannon tried to pull Cora back to the car but she broke away, ran toward the hangar before he caught her. She fought him, battled furiously, refusing to surrender to the horror that awaited her while Gannon and Hackett got her back to her Pontiac Vibe.

Hackett radioed for an ambulance.

They opened the front passenger door, Cora sat sideways, her feet on the ground, staring inside her car, the car she drove Tilly to school in, the car they drove to church in, to the mall.

Then Cora stared at the hangar, shaking her head.

"It's not true. She's not dead. Because if she's dead, it's my fault," Cora said. "She can't be dead. Tell me it's not true, Jack. You tell me my daughter's not in there!"

"We don't know, Cora."

"Oh God."

Her shoulders shook as she sobbed. She slid from the passenger seat to the ground, pounding the sand. Gannon slid to the earth with her, holding her as the dust swirled around them, as sirens wailed and helicopters hammered the sky. They stayed that way while investigators processed the scene.

Two scared kids in a Buffalo kitchen, waiting for Dad to get home.

There are times in your life when you think, this is it. Everything important ends here. Gannon thought it was all over, that day in the kitchen when he was eight. He'd never forget that look in his father's eyes like something was lost. They'd wrecked his new car. All those overtime shifts he'd worked.

They'd taken something from him.

And Gannon thought it again when he was twelve and Cora, Mom and Dad were screaming at each other before she left. At first, all he felt was disbelief. Cora had to be kidding, she wasn't really running away. But time passed, tightening on him like a vice, crushing him with the truth: Cora was gone for real. Gone for good.

He'd lost his big sister.

How would he overcome the blow?

He'd reached another ending when his parents died in the car crash and he watched their caskets lower into the ground.

He'd lost his family.

Then days ago, out of the blue, he received a miracle in the form of Cora's call. Across a chasm filled with pain, he found the sister he thought he'd lost forever. He learned he had a niece.

But the miracle came with a tragedy.

His niece's face in the FBI's gallery of kidnapped and missing persons.

He sees the family resemblance and wants to reach out and hug her.

It can't end here.

It just can't.

Gannon was numb, oblivious to how long he and Cora had kept a vigil in the desert until Hackett tapped his shoulder.

"We've conducted searches of every building, Jack, and we have not located Tilly."

Cora blinked as if staring into a pinpoint light of hope.

"That means she's still alive?"

"There's reason to hope so."

At that moment, Gannon's cell phone rang and he climbed to his feet and walked away to answer it.

"Jack, this is Isabel Luna. We need to meet immediately. I have information."

"Isabel, this is a bad time. I can't come to Mexico."

"I'm not in Mexico. I am in Phoenix."

"What?"

"I have information that is critical to your case. Tell no one about this call and come alone to meet me at this location. Do you have something to write with?"

"Isabel, you'd better tell me."

"Jack, this is absolutely critical to your case. Do you understand?"

Gannon glanced around to confirm he was out of earshot.

"Okay, go ahead."

69

Somewhere South of Phoenix, Arizona

Isabel Luna leaned against the airport rental she'd parked under the shady canopy of a pine grove near an abandoned mission that had been built by Franciscans in the 1800s.

She was about to check her watch again but saw chrome glint from an oncoming car. As it slowed to a stop, she saw Jack Gannon behind the wheel. She recognized his sister, Cora, from news pictures, in the passenger seat.

Gannon got out, uneasy as he scanned the isolated surroundings.

"Why are you here? What's going on?" he asked her.

"Do you know where my daughter is?" Cora was desperate.

"This is my sister, Cora. Tilly's mother."

Luna nodded to her, but she was slightly annoyed at Gannon. She'd told him to come alone.

"Cora, this is Isabel Luna, the journalist I met in Juarez who's been helping us." Gannon's attention went to Luna. "What's the important information you have on Tilly?"

"A meeting has been arranged."

"A meeting? About what? With who? Where?" Gannon looked to the few empty buildings next to the old church, now fearing that they'd made a mistake leaving Hackett at the airstrip.

"Please, if you know, tell me where my daughter is," Cora pleaded.

Luna glanced around without answering.

"Isabel—" Gannon's frustration was mounting "—we've just come from some very bad scenes to this godforsaken place. We don't know where Tilly is or if she's been hurt. Your call offered us hope." Gannon again surveyed the buildings, bereft of life. "Why did you come here from Juarez? What's going on? What do you know? If you don't give us some answers, I'll call the FBI, I swear, Isabel."

Luna glanced at her watch.

"I'm sorry I have to be cryptic," she said. "Please, come with me."

They walked to the old church. Gannon saw fresh tire tracks in the sand near the front and sides, evidence of some sort of recent activity.

Are there other people here?

The old white building was constructed of clay brick, pocked and weatherworn by time. Its shutters dangled in surrender, the doors to the entrance had fallen off.

Upon entering they were met in silence by statues, heads bowed as if to hide the leprous disfigurement from the plaster that had blistered on their faces, hands and bodies. The roof had holes. Water had seeped into the walls and bled around the shattered stained-glass window. The wooden floors creaked as they moved forward, gazing at the rotting wooden pews leading to the altar.

The church was empty except…

Cora gasped.

A young man was perched on the prayer rail of a pew with his back to the altar and his feet on the bench. Facing the arrivals, he waited calmly. He was wearing a T-shirt and jeans. A massive cross bearing the crucified Christ looked down on him and the world below.

"Are you Angel?" Luna asked.

The young man nodded but held up his hand, stopping them cold a distance away at the back of the church.

"Father Ortero sent me. I am Isabel Luna, a reporter with *El Heraldo*."

Recognition twigged briefly and died in Angel's eyes.

"And the others?" he asked. "You were instructed to come alone."

"They are associates, here to bear witness to your legend and verify your account so police cannot lie. This is Jack Gannon. He is a correspondent with the World Press Alliance, one of the largest newswires in the world. Beside him is his assistant." As Angel considered the situation, Luna reached into her shoulder bag. "Before we start, may I take your photo?"

Gannon stared in confusion at Luna. Cora was going to burst. She refused to believe Tilly was dead. She would never accept it, not while she could still fight to find her.

"Please," Cora whispered, "let's get out of here and go back."

Luna ignored her. Gannon noticed Luna was trembling as if she were standing before a rattlesnake.

"A photo, Angel?" Luna pressed. "To verify this moment in history?"

Wary and exhausted, he nearly smiled before he turned slightly to indicate two large sports bags on the altar. Gannon saw Luna's attention dart to the windows at the side of the church, then back to Angel.

"My donation to Ortero's church is in the bags," Angel said. "Two million dollars. I have made my confessions to him. You will tell my story, then go to police with my offer to exchange information for a deal."

Light flashed as Luna took Angel's picture without his objection. She stepped forward and took several more, licking her lips in nervous tension.

"Enough," Angel said. "Let's get started."

"Certainly." Luna opened her notebook, nodding to Gannon, who, not quite understanding, pulled his out as well. "First," Luna said, "as the Norte Cartel's number one *sicario,* how many people have you killed?"

"As of today, one hundred and ninety-five."

Cora stifled a low cry.

"And you will confirm that you work under orders from the leader of the Norte Cartel, Samson Zartosa."

"Yes, that is true."

"And did he instruct you to murder the editor of my newspaper, *El Heraldo?*"

Luna's question exhumed a memory. His face confirmed what she knew: She'd found her father's killer. The realization caught up to Angel, but he shrugged.

"Perhaps. I just told you, I had nearly two hundred jobs—"

Near and unseen a soft muffle echoed. Instinctively, Cora started toward Angel.

"Tell me where my daughter is. Where's Tilly?"

In one motion, Angel reached down for the AK-47 assault rifle he'd kept out of sight and pointed it at Cora.

Gannon pulled her to him.

"You look familiar to me," Angel said to Cora.

"I am the mother of the child your people stole and I want her back!"

"What is this?" Angel face contorted with rage. "I trusted the priest!"

Gannon noticed a shadow, a tremor of light outside.

In an instant, Angel yanked Tilly up from under the pew and locked his arm around her neck. Her eyes were filled with fear.

"Mommy!!!"

"Tilly!" Cora struggled against Gannon.

"Nobody move or I will kill her!" Angel said.

"Let her go!" Cora said. "I did not kill Eduardo Zartosa."

"What?" Angel was confused. "What are you talking about?"

"Look at you!" Luna shouted. "Using a child as your shield in a church. You are a coward who will never see heaven!"

"Neither will you!"

As Angel steadied his gun to shoot Luna, Gannon saw a piercing sunray reflected from a window on the scope of a sharpshooter's rifle as the muzzle flashed.

The sniper's bullet smashed into Angel's temple, tore through his skull and removed the back of his head. This was how Angel Quinterra—the *sicario,* the son of an alcoholic garbage picker from the shantytown near the Juarez dump—died. With his cranial matter splattered on the feet of the crucified Christ.

Tilly ran into Cora's arms.

Luna and Gannon turned to the window where Esteban Cruz, Isabel's stepbrother, lowered his rifle.

Numbed, the five of them moved to the front steps of the old mission.

They waited in the sunlight as Cora freed Tilly from her bindings and held her as she trembled.

"Mommy, he killed Lyle…he killed them all…. I thought I was going to die!"

Cora hushed and soothed her as both of them sobbed softly.

Gannon called Hackett and told him what had happened. Hackett said they were already on their way.

"A priest in Mexico had called the task force. He was concerned about the safety of a reporter from Juarez, who he believed had key information on the case. Then we got a call from a Mexican cop on the case."

Afterward, Gannon called Melody Lyon in New York.

"It's over, Mel. We found Tilly. She's traumatized but alive."

"Thank God."

"You can put out a story alert. I'll file something over the phone later."

"Thanks, but wait. Jack, how's your sister doing?"

"She's going to be okay."

"And you?"

"It doesn't matter about me."

After hanging up, Gannon and Cora thanked Luna and Esteban and they looked to the horizon, saying little until they heard the sirens.

70

Arizona

It rained the day they buried Lyle Galviera.

The funeral was held about a week after the FBI and the County had processed the scene and the medical examiner released the remains to his family.

Cora and Gannon attended the service.

Mourners offered condolences and kind words to his mother. Later, at the funeral reception, they huddled in quiet groups and grappled with the tragedy, asking questions no one could answer.

"How the hell did he think he would come out ahead, doing business with a freakin' drug cartel?"

Ed Kilpatrick, the operations manager, was among the last people to talk with Cora and Gannon at the gathering.

"How are you holding up, Cora?"

"Minute by minute, Ed. Thanks."

"And Tilly?"

"She has nightmares and sleeps in my room. She wasn't physically hurt, but the counselor said to expect stages of post-traumatic stress. He said that she might be able to progress through it all. Tilly told me she shut her eyes through the worst of it with the chain saw, but that she'd heard everything."

Ed shook his head.

"Thank God you got her back."

Cora nodded and touched a tissue to her eyes.

"Jack—" Ed turned to Gannon "—looks like the press had a big part in stopping the cartel. I see the police arrested quite a few people on both sides of the border. It's a hell of a thing."

"A lot of people, cops *and* reporters, worked on this and a lot of people got lucky when they needed to get lucky," Gannon said.

"Forgive me, Cora—" Ed went back to her "—I know this may not be the proper time, but there's a company out of Albuquerque that's looking to take over Quick Draw, clear the debt, restructure but keep all the staff. In fact, they plan to expand. Looks like we'll be okay."

Cora patted his hand.

"Thank you, Ed."

"Just don't want you to worry about that."

Cora and Gannon turned, surprised to find FBI Agents Hackett and Larson waiting to talk with them after Ed left.

"Our condolences," Hackett said.

"And our prayers for Tilly, and you, to heal," Larson said.

Cora nodded with a smile.

"Listen—" Hackett cleared his throat "—we're sorry things got intense and we went hard at both of you. These things get complex, and no one ever tells us everything at the outset."

"I didn't help much at the start," Cora said.

"What's the latest on the San Francisco homicide?" Gannon asked.

"SFPD and our people in Las Vegas have issued warrants for Vic Lomax. So far no one's located him."

"Is he facing charges on Eduardo Zartosa's death?"

"Yes, based on Donnie Cargo's statements. Also SFPD processed the gun again. This time they were able to find a print that belonged to Lomax," Hackett said. "By the way, if you need anything more for that story you're working on, let me know. How's that going?"

"Can we get the full deathbed statement from Cargo?"

"I'll see what we can do."

"Thanks. The WPA is writing a series on Tilly, cartels, everything. I'm working with Henrietta Chong, our bureaus and Isabel Luna. Isabel told me the priest, Father Ortero, was our link to Angel and that the Vatican has posted him to Spain."

"That's right. He's retired."

"What about Esteban Cruz? What kind of trouble is he facing?"

"The ex-SWAT team sniper. Yeah, he broke a few rules. But we heard that our State and Justice departments and the Mexican government have agreed to regard him as a zealous cop investigating a homicide who followed a complex lead here in hot pursuit. He ultimately saved lives."

"No reprimand?"

"I doubt it," Hackett said. "But there's a lot of heat out of Washington about this kind of crime spilling from Mexico into the U.S. and that laws are being flouted."

"Not all of them," Gannon said. "The law of supply and demand is certainly being respected. We demand dope and cartels supply it."

Several days after the WPA released its series, before Gannon was scheduled to fly back to New York, Jack, Cora and Tilly went to the Grand Canyon.

On their way, Gannon got a call from Hackett.

"That was a good feature."

"Thanks."

"Pruitt said San Francisco Homicide particularly liked your story on Eduardo Zartosa's murder. It appears Samson Zartosa liked it, too, given that you spelled out exactly who killed Eduardo. Here's a tip. This morning,

Las Vegas Metro found Lomax's corpse in the desert. They found his head on a stick next to it."

"So Cora's cleared?"

"Our intel indicates the Norte Cartel is satisfied that it exacted vengeance for the rip-off, but more importantly, for Eduardo's murder."

"What about things with Cora and San Francisco?"

"Clear. The D.A. will send her a letter, thanking her for her cooperation."

"Thanks, Earl. I'll alert our Las Vegas bureau about Lomax."

Gannon told Cora the old San Francisco murder case was closed.

She turned to the horizon.

In their short time at the Canyon, he tried to get to know Tilly.

"I think it's awesome that I have an uncle who's a reporter in New York City," she said.

"I think it's cool that I have a niece who can text faster than I can write when I'm on deadline."

Gannon stole glances at Tilly whenever he could, amazed at how she resembled Cora at that age. It warmed him, because something he thought he'd lost had come back to him. When he wasn't looking at Tilly, he gazed across the great gorge. In their private moments, he and Cora had reconciled the gulf of time that had passed between them.

"I'm sorry for being a bad sister. I should've come home."

"I was a terrible brother. I should have looked for you, but I was angry."

"We lost so much."

"Other people have it worse, Cora." He shrugged. "Next to Mom and Dad, you were the most important person in my life. You changed my life, gave me direction. My bond with you never ended."

"I was just so guilty and ashamed of the mistakes I'd

made. I believed I had put my family in danger. I wanted to bury that, keep it hidden. I could never bear to face you, Mom and Dad again."

"That was the biggest mistake of all."

"I know and I was coming 'round to dealing with it. The fact I had Tilly and was getting my life on track was all part of it. Can you ever forgive me?"

"I did, the moment you called for help."

Cora hugged her brother.

"Want to join us for Thanksgiving in Phoenix?"

"Sure. What about Christmas in New York?"

* * * * *

Acknowledgments

My heartfelt thanks to Amy Moore-Benson, Marianne Moore, Valerie Gray, Dianne Moggy, Miranda Indrigo and the scores of editorial, marketing, sales and PR teams at Harlequin and MIRA Books in Toronto, New York and around the world.

I am grateful to Eddie J. Erdelatz, San Francisco Homicide Detail (Ret.) and Wendy Dudley. A special thanks to Rob Galbraith for his expertise and guidance on digital photography that came into play in *THE PANIC ZONE*, the prequel to *IN DESPERATION*.

I would like to thank all of my journalist friends in and out of the news business for their help and support, in particular, John Kryk, Eric Dawson, Glen Miller, friends at *Associated Press, Reuters, Canadian Press, Canwest News, Chicago Tribune, Wall Street Journal, Sun Media, Calgary Herald, Ottawa Citizen, Edmonton Journal, The Toronto Star, The Globe and Mail, Los Angeles Times* and so many others. You know who you are.

Very special thanks to Barbara, Laura and Michael.

I would also like to thank Milly Marmur in New York, Lorella Belli in London and Ib Lauritzen in Denmark.

There are scores of others who each played a small part in making this book a reality; their number precludes my thanking them all here. I am indebted to sales representatives, booksellers and librarians for putting my work in your hands. Which brings me to you, the reader; the most critical part of the entire enterprise.

Thank you very much for your time, for without you, a book remains an untold tale. I deeply appreciate my growing audience and those who've been with me since the beginning and keep in touch. Thank you for your very kind words. And to you, the new reader: Welcome. I hope you enjoyed the ride and will check out my earlier books while watching for my next one. I welcome your feedback. Drop by at www.rickmofina.com to subscribe to my newsletter and send me a note.

*Here's a sneak peek of Rick Mofina's next
Jack Gannon thriller, THE BURNING EDGE
coming in early 2011!*

...Please God, someone call the police, Lisa Palmer
thought.

The man on the floor next to Lisa turned his face to her.
He looked about thirty, was clean shaven with quick, intelligent eyes. He was wearing jeans, a jacket and T-shirt.

"I'm a cop," he whispered, keeping his hands out-
stretched over his head. "My gun's on my right hip under
my shirt."

She nodded.

"You slide closer, lift it out," he said. "Tuck it under
me. They're wearing vests but I can get off head shots."

Lisa could not breathe.

She was motionless until the man's urgent gaze com-
pelled her to move. She worked her way closer to him,
carefully extending her left hand, pulling away his jacket,
feeling the hardness of his gun. Lisa got it loose. Her
sweating face was about two feet from his.

He nodded encouragement.

As Lisa pulled, the weapon slipped from her fingers
and rattled on the floor. The gunman flew to them, grabbing the gun before the cop could. He patted the man,
taking his second gun from his ankle holster. He jerked
at the man's jacket, extracting a folding police wallet
and examined it.

Lisa looked into the cop's eyes.

The gunman placed the muzzle against the cop's head.

Lisa's breathing quickened, the cop blinked and
called out, "Jennifer, I love you," before his skull exploded, propelling brain matter onto Lisa's face.

The killer moved and pressed his gun to Lisa's head.

RICK MOFINA

MIRA®

www.MIRABooks.com

MRM0411BLTALL